MORE THAN YOU MIGHT IMAGINE

A Courtesan's Journey into the Heart of Desire

ISABELLE M.

Copyright © 2025 Isabelle M.
All rights reserved

The characters and events portrayed in this book are fictitious. Any similarity to real persons, living or dead, is coincidental and not intended by the author.

Isabelle M. is a pseudonym.

No part of this book may be reproduced, or stored in a retrieval system, or transmitted in any form or by any means, electronic, mechanical, photocopying, recording, or otherwise, without express written permission of the publisher.

ISBN-13: 979-8-218-67235-5

Cover design by: Karl Backus
Photo: Don Mirra

For S.B., who reminds me that vulnerability requires more courage than strength.

For R.B., whose conviction that beauty lies in truth transforms how I witness others.

For A.X.A., who taught me that the most profound connections transcend words and flesh alike.

For E. S., my first lover, who guided me to understand the essential distinction between love and mere physical congress, a lesson that became the foundation of my life's work.

And for all those navigating the exquisite wilderness of human connection, may you discover that loving another well begins with the courage to be fully known yourself.

—Isabelle M.
   Monaco, 2025

Table of Contents

Introduction 1
A Brief History 5
Two Decades. 15
Introduction to The Intimate Archives 27

Part 1: Foundations 31
    The Map of Pleasure 33
    The Foundation of Attraction 43
    The Power of Scent 55
    The Power of the Pause 67
    The Language of Touch 77

Part 2: Psychology & Connection 91
    The Connection Beyond the Physical 93
    The Power of Presence 105
    The Exploration of Boundaries 117
    The Gift of Vulnerability 129

Part 3: Female Pleasure & Empowerment 147
    The Elusive Pearl 149
    The Inner Landscape 163
    The Empowering Ride 175
    The Multi-Orgasmic Path 185

Part 4: Rhythm & Technique 197
    The Rhythm of Connection 199
    The Lingering Caress 215
    The Art of Arousal 225
    The Taste of Skin 237

Part 5: Deeper Dimensions 247
    The Body Electric 249
    The Language of Desire 263
    The Breathless Embrace 275
    The Art of Teasing 287
    The Proper Preparation 303

Part 6: Integration & Closure 319
    The Power of Sound 321
    The Art of Surrender 331
    The Enduring Connection 347

Epilogue: The Continuing Education 361

The Shadow Aspects: Acknowledging Reality 369

Introduction

Last Tuesday, a client, a finance minister from a country I won't name, lay beside me in post-coital reflection and asked why I never married. Before I could formulate a response, he answered for me: "Of course, you wouldn't want to. You've seen too much of what happens behind closed doors." He wasn't entirely wrong, though his conclusion revealed more about his own circumstances than mine.

The light in Monaco has a particular quality, sharp and pristine in the mornings, then softening to a golden glow as afternoon turns to evening. From my apartment balcony overlooking the Mediterranean, I've watched this daily transformation for over two decades now. The salt-tinged breeze carries the distant purr of luxury engines and the faint clink of champagne glasses. The yachts in the harbor below, their polished surfaces gleaming like wet marble, the precisely manicured gardens with their mathematically perfect arrangements, the immaculate buildings climbing the hillside, all exist in a world apart from ordinary life. Monaco cultivates this sense of exception, this bubble of privilege and discretion. It's precisely why I chose it all those years ago, and why I've remained.

I turned forty-six last month. The milestone wasn't particularly significant in itself, but it prompted an evening of reflection as I sat with a glass of Bordeaux, reviewing the leather-bound journals stacked neatly in my study. Presence of meticulous documentation. Twenty-four years of encounters, observations, and insights into the most intimate aspects of human desire. The weight of this accumulated knowledge suddenly felt too substantial to keep to myself.

Let me be direct: I am what society euphemistically calls an "escort," though I prefer "companion." I provide intimate services to a select clientele in one of the world's wealthiest enclaves. I've watched banking titans tremble at a touch. I've heard corporate strategists stammer like schoolboys when asking for what they truly desire. I've held government ministers as they wept from simple tenderness, perhaps for the first time since childhood. This admission about my profession will undoubtedly color how some readers approach this book. I understand that reaction, the assumptions, the judgments, perhaps even the titillation. I ask only that you set these aside temporarily and consider what two decades of privileged access to human beings at their most vulnerable might reveal about the nature of desire, connection, and what we all ultimately seek behind our carefully constructed facades.

My background in psychology and anthropology from the Université Nice Sophia Antipolis wasn't intended as preparation for this career, but it has provided an invaluable framework for my insights. From the beginning, I approached each encounter with a researcher's eye and a clinician's empathy. What began as personal notes evolved into a comprehensive study of human intimacy, desire, and connection.

Why share these insights now? The simplest answer is that knowledge unshared feels incomplete. These journals contain practical wisdom about pleasure, communication, and connection that transcends the commercial context in which they were gathered. There's a universality to desire, to vulnerability, to the need for touch and understanding that cuts across all boundaries.

Perhaps there's also a selfish motivation, a desire to be seen, truly seen, beyond the fantasy I've carefully constructed for others. Or maybe it's the recognition that as the years pass, I need to consider what legacy I might leave. Not children, not property, but perhaps this: a clear-eyed exploration of intimacy from someone who has made it her life's work.

I also write with the hope of challenging perceptions about sex work and those who engage in it. The reality I've lived is neither the sordid exploitation nor the glamorized fantasy that dominates popular imagination. It has been, quite simply, a profession pursued with intelligence, boundaries, and a genuine interest in human nature.

What will you gain from these pages? First, practical insights into physical pleasure, techniques, approaches, and understandings that can enhance intimate experiences. You'll learn why the most technically skilled lover might leave you cold while an awkward but attentive partner ignites unexpected passion. You'll understand why what worked magnificently with one person falls flat with another. Beyond these mechanics, you'll develop a deeper appreciation for the psychology of desire, the nuances of communication, and the complexity of human needs. You'll recognize the patterns that repeat across seemingly different relationships and the subtle signals that reveal more than words ever could. Perhaps most importantly, you'll find permission to approach your own sexuality with curiosity rather than judgment, with playfulness rather than performance anxiety, the same permission I've granted countless clients who discovered, often to their shock, what pleasure truly feels like when unburdened by expectation.

This book distills 24 encounters from thousands, selected not for their sensationalism but for the clarity of their lessons. Each client described here is a composite, with identifying details altered or obscured. My focus is not on exposing individuals but on illuminating patterns, techniques, and insights that might benefit others.

I approach this work with a deep awareness of the ethical complexities involved. Some might question whether intimate encounters that begin as commercial transactions can offer authentic insights into human connection. Others might wonder about the power dynamics at play, or whether my observations exploit vulnerabilities shared in private moments. These are valid concerns that I've wrestled with throughout my career and in deciding to write this book.

What I've come to understand is that ethical intimacy, whether paid or not, rests on foundations of consent, respect, and honesty about the parameters of the exchange. In many ways, the explicit boundaries of my professional arrangements create a clarity often missing in conventional relationships, where expectations frequently remain unspoken until violated. This clarity doesn't diminish the authenticity of the human connection that occurs within these boundaries; sometimes, paradoxically, it enhances it by removing pretense.

The encounters I've chosen span the spectrum of human experience, from awkward to transcendent, from purely physical to unexpectedly emotional. What unites them is their authenticity and the genuine lessons they contain. My hope is that by sharing these experiences, I can contribute something meaningful to our understanding of intimacy, desire, and connection, territories often shrouded in myth, shame, or simplistic cultural narratives.

I offer these pages not as an apology nor as a provocation, but simply as what they are: one woman's accumulated wisdom from a life spent studying desire in its most direct expression.

—*Isabelle M.*
Monaco, Spring 2025

My Journey to the Principality: A Brief History

Early Life in La Trinité

La Trinité sits in the hills above Nice, neither wealthy nor impoverished, a working-class community where people minded their business and occasionally each other's. The village clings to the hillside like a hesitant climber, neither committed to the heights nor comfortable with descent. The air there carries the contradictory scents of the Mediterranean: lavender and gasoline, fresh bread and cigarette smoke. My father worked as a mechanic in a garage that serviced the luxury cars that would pass through on their way to Monaco or Cannes. He would return home with hands perpetually stained with grease, no matter how vigorously he scrubbed them, the dark lines in his knuckles and nail beds like a permanent shadow. My mother taught at the local primary school, her voice always slightly hoarse from a day of projecting over the chaos of young children. Ours was a home of reasonable comfort and unremarkable stability, punctuated by occasional tensions about money that children are not meant to notice but invariably do, hushed conversations behind doors not quite thick enough, the abrupt end to discussions when I entered a room.

What shaped me most profoundly were not dramatic events but subtle patterns of perceptions. From my bedroom window, I could see into the apartments across the street, glimpses of lives unfolding in casual intimacy. A couple arguing with theatrical gestures but inaudible words. An elderly woman brushing her hair with ritualistic precision each evening. A middle-aged man sitting alone at his table, eating dinner while reading a book.

These fragments of private existence fascinated me far more than the dolls my cousins played with. While other children created elaborate fantasy lives for their toys, I was busy constructing elaborate psychological profiles for the neighbors. In retrospect, I was a rather peculiar child: less Madeline and more miniature Freud with a better fashion sense.

My mother often said I was born with "des yeux qui percent les murs", eyes that pierce walls. It wasn't meant as a compliment, not entirely. My tendency to notice things others missed: the way Monsieur Blanc from the bakery looked at my mother when she wore her blue dress, the hidden tension in my teacher's smile when certain parents visited, the careful way my father counted coins when he thought no one was watching, made adults uneasy. Children are supposed to be oblivious, not observant. "Isabelle sees too much," they would whisper when they thought I couldn't hear, which was ironic given my apparent talent for insight. Had they been more observant themselves, they might have whispered more quietly or, revolutionary thought, perhaps not discussed me as if I were a mildly concerning medical condition while I sat reading in the same room.

Perhaps most formative was witnessing my aunt Claire's gradual transformation after her divorce. She moved into our spare room temporarily when I was twelve, arriving hollow-eyed and diminished, her possessions in cardboard boxes that smelled of a failed marriage. I remember her that first night, sitting at our kitchen table in my mother's borrowed robe, her hands trembling slightly as she brought a cigarette to her lips.

"He left me with nothing," she told my mother, unaware or uncaring that I sat reading in the corner. "Twenty years, and he left me with nothing."

Over the months, I watched her reconstruct herself. First through careful attention to appearance, then through a newfound assertiveness, and finally through the quiet power she discovered in her relationships with men. The mechanics of this transformation fascinated me. I observed how she would adjust her posture when attractive men entered the café where she eventually found work. I noticed how her voice would shift in tone, becoming slightly lower, more melodic. Most intriguingly, I watched how men responded, how they leaned toward her, how their eyes dilated, how they would find reasons to return to the café.

One evening, I found her preparing for a date, applying perfume to her wrists and behind her ears.

"Isabelle," she said, catching me watching from the doorway, "remember this: a woman alone is vulnerable in this world, but a woman who understands desire has power." She never elaborated, never spoke to me about these things directly again, but I absorbed the unspoken lesson: intimacy was currency, and one could choose how to spend it. Years later, when I told her about my career choice, the only family member I've ever confided in, she wasn't shocked or dismayed as I had feared. She simply nodded and said, "You were always watching, weren't you? Always understanding more than a child should." Then she took my hand and added something that has stayed with me: "Just remember that power comes with responsibility. Don't become like the men who use others thoughtlessly." I've carried that warning through my career, a quiet ethical touchstone when navigating the complex terrain between transaction and exploitation.

Within a year of coming to live with us, my aunt had her own apartment, a new car, and a confidence that made her almost unrecognizable from the broken woman who had arrived at our door. What lingered with me wasn't just the lesson about intimacy as currency, but the realization that transformation was possible: that one could reimagine oneself, that vulnerability could be followed by strength, that perceived powerlessness could evolve into agency. Perhaps this early impression planted the seed for my later professional choices, though it would take years and considerable academic framework before I could articulate why.

The University Years

The Université Nice Sophia Antipolis offered me escape and focus simultaneously. Psychology seemed the natural choice for someone who had spent her life studying human behavior informally. The addition of Anthropology came later, when I discovered its potential to contextualize what psychology often individualized.

University expanded my understanding beyond discernment to explanation. Where before I had noted behaviors and reactions, now I learned the theories behind them: Maslow's hierarchy illuminating the baker's longing glances, attachment theory explaining my teacher's strained smile, economic anxiety clarifying my father's relationship with money.

Dr. Moreau became my mentor in my third year. A formidable woman in her fifties with silver-streaked hair perpetually escaping its pins, she was infamous among undergraduates for her uncompromising standards and among faculty for her controversial research on desire and power.

"Most researchers," she told me during our first meeting, her office cluttered with books and the air heavy with the scent of strong coffee, "study sex as if they're examining bacteria through a microscope, with clinical detachment and an underlying disgust. I prefer to study it as a natural phenomenon, like weather or migration patterns."

Her research on intimacy and social bonds introduced me to concepts that would later become central to my understanding: how vulnerability creates connection, how power dynamics influence desire, how cultural scripts shape our expressions of need and want. She challenged me in ways other professors didn't dare. When I presented a conventional analysis of attachment styles in my first paper for her, she returned it with a single comment: "You're capable of more original thought than this. Try again."

Under her guidance, I conducted a small study on non-verbal communication between couples in public spaces, spending hours in cafés noting the micro-expressions and body language that revealed the true nature of relationships regardless of what was being said. I still recall one couple in particular, outwardly affectionate with constant touches and terms of endearment, yet his eyes constantly scanned the room while speaking to her, and she would briefly close her eyes each time he interrupted her. Their bodies told a story of disconnect entirely at odds with their verbal performance of devotion.

"Isabelle," Dr. Moreau said to me during one of our last meetings before graduation, her eyes sharp and evaluating, "you have a rare gift for seeing beneath surfaces, but this gift comes with an ethical burden. When you perceive what others don't, or won't, acknowledge about themselves, you must decide whether to illuminate or respect the darkness. This choice will define your work, whatever path you take." She paused then, seeming to weigh her words. "And remember that awareness, however astute, is not the same as understanding. True insight requires empathy. The willingness to not just see but to feel alongside another person. Without this, knowledge becomes merely an intellectual exercise, or worse, a tool for manipulation."

That advice has echoed throughout my career, a compass when navigating the complex ethics of intimacy for hire. The line between illumination and exploitation is not always clear, and I've learned that respecting someone's protective darkness can sometimes be a greater kindness than forcing them into self-awareness they aren't ready to bear.

Equally important has been the recognition that my observational skills, however precise, require the complement of genuine emotional presence: that understanding another's desires is not merely academic but profoundly human.

It was during this period that I began to understand sex not merely as a physical act but as a complex communication system, a language with dialects and accents, spoken more or less fluently by different people. My personal experiences during these years were remarkable and extremely educational. Like many students, I had relationships of varying seriousness and casual encounters of varying satisfaction. Unlike my peers, I approached each with analytical curiosity alongside the usual emotional and physical involvement.

For my thesis, I explored the ways people constructed narratives about their sexual experiences, focusing on the gap between what they claimed to want and what their stories revealed they truly sought. Dr. Moreau warned me that such research would earn me few friends in the more conservative corners of academia, but it earned me a distinction and solidified my interest in human intimate behavior as worthy of serious study.

I graduated with my psychology degree and anthropology minor in the spring, my academic achievements providing a foundation that would prove invaluable in my later work, though in ways the university administration likely never imagined.

"You've chosen a path that ensures fascinating dinner conversations and uncomfortable family reunions," Dr. Moreau told me at my graduation. She wasn't wrong. My mother still tells acquaintances that I work in "psychological consulting," which isn't entirely false. The fact that my consultations often occur in five-star hotel rooms rather than offices with leather couches is merely a detail, albeit one that would give my poor father heart palpitations if he knew.

The Unexpected Path

The transition from academic study to professional participation was neither abrupt nor predetermined. After graduation, I worked briefly at a counseling center in Nice, but found the bureaucracy stifling and the pace of insight glacial. In the evenings, I would sit in upscale hotel bars, observing the dance of attraction and transaction among the wealthy visitors and the beautiful locals who gravitated to their orbit.

It was in such a setting that I met Dominique, a woman in her forties with an elegant pragmatism about her. When she explained what she did, "I provide companionship to successful men who desire discretion and sophistication", it was without shame or euphemism. We spoke for hours about psychology, about human nature, about the strange arbitrariness of which forms of emotional and physical labor society deemed acceptable or unacceptable.

"You have the mind for this work," she told me as she paid for her Kir Royale. "You understand people, you're naturally discreet, and you're not burdened by conventional morality, merely curious about it."

Her assessment was accurate, though I took several months to consider it properly. My decision ultimately came from multiple convergent realizations: that I possessed a genuine curiosity about human sexuality in its lived expression; that I had both the emotional intelligence and psychological training to navigate intimate encounters skillfully; that I derived satisfaction from providing experiences of pleasure and connection; and yes, that the financial compensation would grant me independence unavailable through conventional paths.

It wasn't a decision made from desperation or lack of options, but from a clear-eyed assessment of what I valued: autonomy, insight, and meaningful human connection, even if temporary. If I'm entirely honest, there was also an element of rebellion against the academic establishment that studied human sexuality from a safe theoretical distance while often judging those who experienced it directly.

Arrival in Monaco

Monaco represents the apotheosis of discretion as virtue. The principality exists as a haven for wealth and the activities wealth enables, all conducted behind an impeccable façade of propriety. I arrived in the spring of 1999, having spent six months in Nice under Dominique's mentorship, learning the practical aspects of the profession she had introduced me to theoretically.

My first apartment was small but well-situated in Larvotto, with a sliver of sea view if one stood at the precise right angle on the balcony, performed a subtle leftward lean, and possessed the optimistic imagination of a romantic poet. I called it my "theoretical sea view apartment" and charged only slightly more than was reasonable because of it. Through Dominique's connections, I was introduced to a select clientele, primarily businessmen and occasional nobility, men for whom discretion was paramount and for whom the exchange of money for companionship was merely an efficiency, not a moral consideration. The irony wasn't lost on me that I'd spent years studying the complexities of human connection only to end up in a profession where clarity of transaction was the foundation. Sometimes the most straightforward relationships are the most honest ones, a lesson that cost me considerably less than my university education yet proved infinitely more practical.

The early years were a period of careful attention and adaptation. I learned the unspoken protocols of Monaco's stratified society: which hotels welcomed arrangements like mine, which did not; which concierges could be trusted as intermediaries; which events one could attend as an unaccompanied woman without raising eyebrows. I studied the cultural differences in expectations and desires, the emotional expressiveness of Italian clients, the formal reserve of certain British visitors, the straightforward approach of Americans, the elaborate courtesies preferred by older French gentlemen.

I recall one of my first clients, a British shipping magnate in his fifties. When I arrived at his hotel suite, he offered me a drink with precise formality, maintaining a carefully calibrated distance between us. Our conversation was impeccably polite, touching on art and current events, as if we were at a diplomatic reception rather than the prelude to an intimate encounter. Only after nearly an hour of this verbal minuet did he finally reach for my hand, the touch almost startling after such verbal restraint.

The next evening, I met with an Italian businessman who embraced me immediately upon my arrival, kissing both cheeks and complimenting my appearance with operatic enthusiasm. He poured wine, insisted I try the chocolates he'd ordered, and spoke openly about his desire from the first moment, yet when the time came for physical intimacy, he revealed a surprising gentleness and attentiveness that belied his exuberant approach.

These cultural contrasts fascinated me, revealing how deeply our expressions of desire are shaped by social context. The British client's formality wasn't coldness but a culturally specific approach to respect and anticipation. The Italian's immediacy wasn't mere impulsiveness but a different language of appreciation and connection. Learning to read these cultural codes, to translate between them, became as important a skill as any physical technique.

What surprised me most was the consistency beneath these surface variations. Men who commanded corporate empires or governmental departments shared the same fundamental vulnerabilities and needs as everyone else, perhaps even more acutely due to positions that often isolated them from authentic connection. Behind closed doors, titles and wealth fell away, revealing simply human beings seeking pleasure, validation, understanding, or momentary escape.

The Genesis of the Logs

The documentation began as professional prudence. In those early years, I kept brief notes on clients' preferences and boundaries to ensure I provided consistent experiences, who preferred conversation before intimacy, who enjoyed particular activities, who needed extra reassurance or specific forms of attention. These notes were utilitarian and sparse:

> M.D. - American banker. Likes neck kissed. No marks. Talks about sailing. Prefers lights dimmed.

> J.B. - British executive. Needs 30+ minutes conversation first. Brandy, not whisky. Self-conscious about body. Responds well to praise.

The transition to more detailed analysis came after an encounter with a professor of literature visiting for a conference. He was in his sixties, with thoughtful eyes and hands that moved expressively when he spoke. Unlike many clients who treated our time as an escape from their intellectual lives, he seemed to want integration, connection between mind and body.

During our evening together, he sat on the edge of the bed in his underwear, unexpectedly vulnerable yet completely at ease, and spoke about his journal practice, how the act of writing about experience transformed it from fleeting sensation to acquired wisdom. "We don't learn from experience," he said, paraphrasing someone he didn't name, "we learn from reflecting on experience."

"And what will you write about this evening?" I asked, genuinely curious.

He smiled. "Not the details you might imagine. Rather, how strange it is that I can feel more authentic with a stranger I'm paying than with colleagues I've known for decades. I'll explore why the transactional nature of this encounter creates a freedom that supposed intimacy often doesn't." He regarded me thoughtfully. "And you? Do you reflect on these encounters, or are they simply work to you?"

That night, after he left, I began my first true entry, not just practical notes but a detailed reflection on the encounter, the dynamics at play, the motivations I perceived, and what insights I could extract. The process was immediately clarifying, revealing patterns and understandings that had been present but unarticulated in my mind.

The encounter with Prof. J revealed something I've sensed but never articulated: the paradoxical intimacy that can exist within clear boundaries. There is a freedom in the temporary, in the clearly defined nature of our arrangement, that allows for a kind of honesty rarely found in conventional relationships. Without the fear of future judgment or the weight of accumulated history, we can be present in ways that feel almost transcendent.

What began as a commercial exchange evolved into something more complex, not a romantic connection, but a genuine human meeting. The transaction created the container, but what happened within that container transcended its origins. This challenges my previous understanding of intimacy as something that either exists authentically or is merely performed.

Question to explore: Is the clarity of the exchange, the absence of unstated expectations or hidden agendas, what creates this space for authentic connection? And if so, what does this suggest about more conventional intimacies with their often unacknowledged transactional elements?

This first reflective entry marked a transformation in how I understood my work: not merely as a service provided but as a unique vantage point from which to observe and understand human connection in its most vulnerable expression. The professor had unknowingly given me permission to approach my experiences as legitimate subjects for intellectual and emotional exploration, worthy of documentation and analysis.

The logs evolved in structure and depth over the years. Early entries were primarily descriptive with basic analysis. As my understanding and experience grew, so did the sophistication of my discernments. I developed categories and frameworks, analyzing encounters through lenses of power dynamics, attachment styles, love languages, cultural contexts, and psychological needs.

What began as professional documentation became an intellectual passion and eventually the most comprehensive longitudinal study of human intimate behavior ever conducted, albeit one never intended for academic publication. Twenty-four years of detailed examinations, thousands of encounters with hundreds of individuals, all meticulously recorded and analyzed through both experiential wisdom and theoretical understanding.

These logs became my private education, more valuable than any university degree. They traced not only the particulars of human desire but also my own evolution as an observer and participant in these most vulnerable of human exchanges. They are the foundation of everything I share in the pages that follow, selected and distilled into entries that represent a fraction of the wisdom gathered in nearly a quarter century of intimate study.

Two Decades: What I've Learned and How It Changed Me

Shifting Perspectives on Sex

When I began this journey, I carried what I believed was an enlightened view of sexuality. How wonderfully naïve I was, wrapped in the comfortable cocoon of academic theories and limited personal exploration. The universe has a particular talent for humbling those who believe themselves already humble. Nothing quite punctures intellectual certainty like having a sixty-year-old investment banker teach you something about female pleasure that wasn't in any textbook, a moment that left me reconsidering not just my academic overconfidence, but the narrow scope of my personal experiences.

The chasm between intellectual comprehension and experiential wisdom yawned before me like Monaco's harbor at midnight: vast, deep, and impossible to cross without actually diving in. I had read Kinsey, Masters and Johnson, and dozens of scholarly papers, but these were merely maps of territories I had barely begun to explore. My psychology professors would likely be horrified at my research methodology, though I suspect their horror might be tinged with a certain envy. After all, I've gathered more authentic data on human sexuality in a month than most researchers collect in a decade, without the questionable accuracy of self-reported surveys or the clinical sterility of laboratory observations.

I entered this profession carrying assumptions that experience methodically dismantled, one encounter at a time. I believed sex was primarily physical for men and emotional for women, that tired dichotomy reinforced by popular psychology and women's magazines. Reality proved infinitely more complex, like intricate lace compared to rough burlap. I encountered men whose need for emotional connection transcended physical release, who sought the gentle sanctuary of arms holding them more than climactic relief. And I met women whose desires were straightforwardly carnal, who approached pleasure with a directness that would make a sailor blush.

I remember the first encounter that shattered my preconceptions as clearly as I recall the view from my childhood bedroom. A female client, a rarity in my practice, sought me at the recommendation of a male client who knew of her interest in women. She was in her forties, a CFO of a multinational corporation with an office in Port Hercules, impeccably groomed and fiercely intelligent. Based on everything I'd been taught, I anticipated an encounter focused on emotional connection and gentle exploration.

Instead, she approached her desires with startling directness that made me, briefly, the student rather than the teacher. She wanted specific acts, intense sensations, and minimal emotional engagement. Her approach was methodical, almost clinical in its precision.

"I spend my days managing other people's emotions and needs," she explained afterward, curled against my pillows with a glass of Sancerre, her body still flushed from exertion. "This is purely for me, purely physical, with clear boundaries and no emotional expectations. That's the one luxury my position rarely affords me."

Conversely, one of my most consistently physical-seeming male clients, a renowned architect known for his masculine public persona, eventually revealed that what he truly craved was to be held, to experience gentle caresses and whispered affirmations. The sex was secondary to this emotional nourishment he couldn't request anywhere else in his life.

"In my world," he confessed, his head resting on my bare stomach as my fingers traced lazy patterns through his silver-streaked hair, "vulnerability is a design flaw, not a feature. Here, in this room with you, is the only place I don't have to be the unshakeable pillar everyone leans on."

These experiences taught me to approach each person as a unique landscape waiting to be mapped, rather than a representative of their gender following predictable topographies. I learned to suspend assumptions about desire until they revealed themselves through interaction rather than projecting them through the distorted lens of societal expectations. It was a humbling lesson in how theory without direct experience can reinforce limiting stereotypes rather than illuminate complex realities.

Perhaps most significantly, I had unconsciously absorbed the cultural narrative that commodified sex was inherently lesser, that genuine connection could not possibly exist within a commercial interaction. This proved to be perhaps the most limiting assumption of all. While transactional encounters certainly can be mechanical and disconnected, they are not inherently so. I experienced moments of genuine human connection, mutual vulnerability, and authentic pleasure that challenged any simplistic dichotomy between "real" and "purchased" intimacy.

Over time, I came to understand sex not as a single terrain but as a spectrum of experiences ranging from purely physical release to profound communion, with all gradations between possible in any context, whether commercial, casual, or committed. The determining factors had less to do with the relationship's official categorization and more to do with the awareness, intention, and emotional presence of the participants.

Decoding Desire

After thousands of intimate encounters with hundreds of individuals, patterns emerge like constellations from seemingly random stars. Beneath the infinite variety of human sexual expression lie recognizable currents of desire that transcend the particular acts or scenarios through which they manifest.

At its most fundamental, desire operates simultaneously on multiple levels: physical, emotional, psychological, and even spiritual. Few people access or acknowledge all these dimensions, instead focusing on whichever aspect feels most accessible or acceptable to them. The businessman who claims to want "just physical release" may actually be seeking momentary freedom from decision-making responsibility. The client requesting submission scenarios may be seeking not domination but the liberation of surrendering control in a contained environment.

I've observed three primary inhibitors of authentic desire: shame, which prevents acknowledgment of what one truly wants; fear, which prevents pursuit of acknowledged desires; and script adherence, which prevents exploration beyond familiar patterns. The clients who achieved the most profound satisfaction were inevitably those who had moved beyond at least two of these inhibitors, while those most chronically dissatisfied remained constrained by all three.

A particularly revealing pattern emerged around the timing of desire disclosure. Those who announced specific sexual requirements immediately, before any connection was established, were often using these acts as substitutes for deeper needs they couldn't articulate. They reminded me of tourists arriving in Monaco with a checklist of sights, so focused on documenting their visit to the Casino that they miss the breathtaking beauty of the coast itself.

Conversely, those who allowed connection to develop before expressing specific desires were typically seeking the act itself rather than using it as proxy for something else. Their approach resembled locals who know that Monaco's true treasures reveal themselves gradually, through unhurried exploration rather than guidebook insistence.

Power dynamics infuse nearly all sexual encounters, though they manifest in countless variations. What became clear through my observations was that official power positions (who was paying whom, who was physically stronger, who held higher social status) often bore little relationship to the actual flow of power within intimate exchanges. A physically imposing CEO might crave submission; a young woman of modest means might naturally assume psychological dominance. Understanding this distinction between apparent and actual power dynamics was crucial to facilitating satisfying encounters.

Perhaps the most consistent finding across my years of interpretation was this: desire flourishes with permission and withers under pressure. The simple act of creating a non-judgmental space where desires could be expressed without fear of ridicule or rejection was often more arousing than any specific technique or activity. My bedroom became a temporary embassy, neutral territory where the usual rules of engagement were suspended, allowing authentic desires to emerge from hiding.

I recall a particular client, a renowned surgeon whose hands could perform microscopic repairs on the human heart yet trembled when he attempted to express what he truly wanted in bed. During our third meeting, after establishing trust through less vulnerable exchanges, I created an exercise where he could only communicate his desires in writing, passing notes to me without having to vocalize his requests.

The transformation was immediate and profound. Free from the fear of hearing himself ask for what he wanted, gentle, nurturing touch and soft reassurance, desires that conflicted with his professional identity as a decisive authority figure, his entire body relaxed. His breathing deepened, his eyes softened, and for the first time, he became fully present in the experience rather than hovering outside it in anxious self-examination.

"No one has ever seen me like this," he whispered afterward, his voice containing equal measures of terror and relief, his body curled against mine like a question mark seeking its answer.

"And how does it feel to be seen?" I asked, my fingers tracing the knobs of his spine.

"Like finally existing," he replied.

The Psychology of Pleasure

Pleasure, I've found, is less about what is done and more about how it is experienced. The same physical acts that create transcendent ecstasy for one person may leave another unmoved or even uncomfortable. This is not merely a matter of different erogenous zones or technical preferences, but of different psychological relationships to pleasure itself.

I've identified several distinct psychological barriers to pleasure that repeatedly manifest in my practice, as recognizable to me now as the silhouette of La Tête de Chien against Monaco's skyline:

The Performance Orientation transforms potential pleasure into anxious work. Clients with this orientation approach sex as a test they might fail, focusing on demonstration of skill or stamina rather than sensation. These are the men who appear to be mentally calculating their thrusting rhythm while silently reciting baseball statistics to delay orgasm, a multitasking feat that would be impressive if it weren't so antithetical to actual enjoyment.

A tech entrepreneur in his thirties embodied this orientation perfectly. During our first encounter, he narrated his own performance with running commentary that sounded like a sports announcer mixed with a self-help guru: "You like that? I can go deeper. I know exactly how to make you feel good. I'm going to make sure you finish at least twice before I do."

His focus was so completely on demonstrating prowess that he missed every subtle cue from my body. He wasn't making love to me but to an imaginary audience evaluating his sexual performance. His eyes constantly searched my face for confirmation of his skill, desperately seeking the validation that would prove his worth.

For these individuals, creating experiences where they had no responsibilities except to feel often resulted in breakthrough moments of genuine pleasure. With this particular client, I eventually blindfolded him and bound his hands loosely, not as a dominance exercise but to remove his ability to "perform." Without visual feedback and with limited physical agency, he had no choice but to surrender to sensation.

"I feel like I'm experiencing sex for the first time," he said afterward, a note of wonder in his voice. "I never realized how much mental energy I was using to monitor myself."

The Pleasure Guilt manifests in those who believe they don't deserve enjoyment or must earn it through suffering or achievement. Such individuals often sabotage approaching pleasure or diminish it when it occurs. The temporary nature of our arrangement sometimes provided a unique opportunity to suspend this pattern, framing pleasure as a legitimate service being purchased rather than an unearned indulgence.

The Spectator Mind creates a meta-awareness that observes rather than experiences, analyzing and judging rather than feeling. These clients are perpetually slightly detached from their own experiences, watching themselves have sex rather than being fully embodied. Sensory-focused practices that anchor attention in physical sensation sometimes helped overcome this division.

The Control Imperative manifests in people unable to surrender to pleasure because it requires momentarily relinquishing control. For such individuals, pleasure exists in constant tension with security, with the latter usually winning. Establishing profound trust or creating scenarios where surrender was explicitly contained often helped resolve this tension.

What consistently produces the deepest pleasure, regardless of specific acts, is the alignment of physical sensation, emotional presence, and psychological permission. When body, heart, and mind are unified in the experience rather than working at cross-purposes, pleasure amplifies exponentially, like sunlight through a perfectly focused lens.

Beyond the Physical

When I began this work, I expected the physical dimension to dominate both the experience and its significance. What surprised me was how frequently the emotional and psychological aspects took precedence, even in arrangements explicitly framed as physical in nature.

The power of being truly seen cannot be overstated. Many clients, particularly those of high social status, moved through worlds where they were related to primarily through their function, title, or wealth. The experience of being perceived and accepted as a complete human being, with desires, insecurities, playfulness, and complexity, was often more meaningful than any physical pleasure provided.

I remember a finance minister whose name regularly appeared in international newspapers, a man who could shift markets with a single statement. In our third session, after skillful physical intimacy that left us both satisfied, he began to weep. Not dramatically, but with the quiet dignity of someone accustomed to containing emotions in public settings. When I asked what had moved him, he replied simply: "You looked at me the entire time. Not at what I represent, not at what I can provide, but at me."

Temporary intimacy creates a fascinating paradox. The time-bounded and clearly defined nature of our encounters often enabled a depth of vulnerability that many clients rarely achieved in their permanent relationships. Precisely because there were no future expectations or ongoing entanglements, many felt free to reveal aspects of themselves, from benign fantasies to profound emotional needs, that they had never expressed to long-term partners.

Trust in these contexts operated differently than in conventional relationships. Rather than building slowly over time through consistent reliability, it was often established rapidly through demonstrating absolute presence, non-judgment, and appropriate boundaries. Once established, this trust created a container for experiences that would have felt too vulnerable in other settings.

What many sought, though few would articulate it directly, was permission to desire, to receive, to be exactly as they were without performance or pretense. In a world of constant evaluation and judgment, the experience of unconditional acceptance, even temporarily purchased, fulfilled a profound human need.

Humanity in All Its Forms

When people imagine the clientele for high-end companionship in Monaco, they typically envision a homogeneous parade of wealthy, powerful men. While there is some truth to this demographic profile, what consistently struck me was not the similarities but the profound diversity beneath the surface uniformity of tailored suits and luxury watches. Yes, from a distance they might appear interchangeable, like emperor penguins that only their mates can distinguish, but beneath the Tom Ford suits and Patek Philippe watches exists a startling variety of human beings.

I've spent evenings with technological visionaries whose brilliance and social awkwardness were equally pronounced; with inherited wealth aristocrats carrying the weight of family legacies they never chose; with self-made entrepreneurs driven by childhood wounds transformed into relentless ambition; with aging celebrities navigating the complexities of diminished relevance; with married men in both fulfilling and empty relationships; with widowers seeking comfort without commitment; with the occasionally discreet woman exploring desires she couldn't acknowledge elsewhere.

What united them was not their external circumstances but their humanity, their universal need for connection, understanding, pleasure, and momentary freedom from the constraints of their daily identities. The banker worried about his performance. The diplomat feared rejection of his particular desires. The real estate magnate craved simple affection without agenda. In my dimly lit bedroom, with Monaco's lights glittering beyond the windows like fallen stars, the trappings of status fell away, revealing the vulnerable humans beneath.

The most profound pattern I observed was the universality of vulnerability. Regardless of status, wealth, or power, each person carried private insecurities, unfulfilled longings, and wounds seeking healing. The corporate titan who commanded thousands professionally might harbor deep uncertainty about his desirability. The ruthless negotiator famous for his aggression might secretly crave gentle nurturing.

I remember a particular client, a man whose name appears on buildings across three continents, whose fortune would make small nations envious. During our first encounter, as I began to undress him, he stopped my hands, his eyes suddenly uncertain.

"I should warn you," he said, his voice lower than in our previous conversation, "I have significant scarring on my torso from childhood burns. I can keep my shirt on if you prefer."

The vulnerability in this moment, this fear of rejection from a man who could purchase small islands without blinking, moved me deeply. When I finally removed his shirt to reveal the rippled landscape of old burn scars, I touched them with the same appreciation I showed the rest of his body, neither focusing on nor avoiding them. His relief was palpable, his shoulders dropping inches as decades of tension momentarily released.

"Most women ask what happened," he said, wonder coloring his voice. "Or they pretend not to notice while carefully avoiding touching me there."

"Your scars are part of your story," I replied, allowing my palms to rest against the textured skin. "Neither more nor less worthy of touch than any other part of you."

What also became clear was how frequently sexual desires served as metaphors or proxies for deeper emotional and psychological needs. The client requesting dominance scenarios was often seeking respite from crushing responsibility rather than control for its own sake. Those requesting elaborate role-plays were typically seeking permission to express aspects of themselves that had no outlet in their daily lives.

Personal Transformation

No one engages in such intimate work for decades without being profoundly changed by it. While I entered this profession with certain strengths, discernment skills, psychological understanding, emotional intelligence, the experiences of these years have shaped me in ways both expected and surprising.

The most significant development has been a deepening capacity for presence. When your profession involves being fully attentive to another human being in their most vulnerable state, you develop an ability to suspend judgment, projection, and distraction that carries beyond professional contexts. I find I can be more fully present with all people in my life, attending to what is actually occurring rather than my interpretations or expectations. This quality makes me surprisingly popular at dinner parties. It turns out that genuine attention is rarer than Monegasque real estate. Though I suspect my friends might be less enthusiastic if they realized that the same focused attentiveness I bring to their stories about vacation homes and children's accomplishments was honed in considerably more intimate settings.

My understanding of boundaries has been refined through thousands of interactions requiring clear but flexible delineation between acceptable and unacceptable. I've learned that true boundaries are not rigid walls but permeable membranes, requiring constant intuitive attention rather than fixed rules. This understanding has enhanced all my relationships, allowing intimacy without merger, connection without loss of self.

Perhaps counterintuitively, this work has deepened my capacity for genuine emotional connection. When you regularly witness the profound human need for understanding and acceptance, when you see how rarely this need is met in conventional relationships, you develop both greater appreciation for authentic connection and greater skill in facilitating it. I find myself more moved by simple human exchanges, the genuine smile of a barista, the unconscious kindness of a stranger helping an elderly person across the street, than by grand romantic gestures portrayed in films.

The profession has also transformed my relationship with my own body and desires. Observing the infinite variety of human sexual expression and response has freed me from normative expectations about how pleasure "should" look or feel. I've become more attuned to my own authentic desires rather than scripted performances of sexuality, more interested in what genuinely brings me pleasure than what might appear impressive or sophisticated.

There have been costs as well. Maintaining a divided life between professional and private personas creates a particular kind of loneliness that aches in unexpected moments. Last year, I attended a friend's dinner party, a sophisticated affair with cultured conversation about art, politics, and travel. The host, a gallery owner who knows me only as an independently wealthy former psychology consultant, introduced me to another guest, a Swiss banker I had seen professionally for nearly three years.

We performed the elaborate social dance required, pretending to meet for the first time, manufacturing appropriate small talk, carefully avoiding any hint of recognition. As he discussed his recent divorce (which I had helped him through in hotel rooms, not with words but with touch and presence), I experienced a fractured sense of self that was almost dizzying. Here was someone who had wept in my arms, revealed his deepest insecurities, and shared profound physical intimacy with me, now discussing the weather and the recent Picasso exhibition as if we were strangers.

This compartmentalization exacts an emotional toll I hadn't anticipated when entering this profession. There are moments when I crave integration, when I long to be fully known by someone who accepts all dimensions of my experience without judgment or prurient curiosity. It's a particular form of invisibility, to be so intimately known by so many, yet truly seen by so few.

Perhaps the most profound personal transformation has been a deepening compassion, not the sentimental pity often mistaken for compassion, but the clear-eyed recognition of shared humanity across all differences of circumstance, behavior, or belief. When you have been intimate with humans across the spectrum of age, nationality, personality, and desire, the artificial boundaries between self and other begin to dissolve, revealing the universal experiences that unite us: the need for connection, the fear of rejection, the longing for understanding, and the simple human hunger to be valued exactly as we are.

In my most honest moments, I recognize that while my clients have paid me for physical services, I have received something equally valuable: an education in human nature so comprehensive that no university could possibly offer it. Each encounter added another piece to a mosaic that gradually revealed the full picture of our shared humanity, beautiful and flawed, courageous and frightened, selfish and generous, all seeking connection in the ways available to us, all hoping to be seen, if only briefly, in our unguarded authenticity.

Introduction to
The Intimate Archives

On the Nature of Memory, Documentation, and Discretion

As you prepare to enter these archives of intimate experience, I feel I should offer a note on their creation. What you are about to read is not, strictly speaking, a direct transcription of my professional log books. Those volumes, stacked in a locked cabinet in my study, contain something far more utilitarian: brief observations captured in the immediate aftermath of encounters, often in a hastily rendered shorthand comprehensible only to myself.

My actual documentation process has always been functional rather than literary. Each entry in my logs follows a simple structure: The Encounter, my Professional Analysis and Reflections, and the Lesson. These are not elaborate narratives but rather collections of impressions, observations, and insights, sometimes merely fragments of thought or sensation that seemed significant in the moment. A client's unusual tension in the shoulders. The way light fell across skin. A theoretical connection that suddenly crystallized during our time together.

What fascinates me about this documentation process is how even the sparest notation serves as a key that unlocks the full sensory memory of an encounter. A single line about the scent of oud oil can suddenly resurrect an entire afternoon years distant, complete with the quality of Mediterranean light, the texture of sheets, the particular cadence of a voice. Memory, I've discovered, operates not linearly but associatively, a fragment invokes the whole, a detail summons the complete experience with remarkable fidelity.

In creating these expanded narratives, I've allowed myself to inhabit these memories fully, to observe them as though they were unfolding anew before me. The psychological term for this is "episodic memory retrieval", the ability to mentally time-travel to specific autobiographical events and re-experience them in rich detail. This capacity serves both my profession and this project; intimate knowledge, after all, accumulates through attentive presence as much as intellectual understanding.

I must, of course, acknowledge certain necessary adaptations I've made for publication. The identities of all clients have been meticulously obscured, details altered, and in some cases, experiences combined to further protect privacy. This is not merely professional courtesy but ethical imperative. The trust placed in me by those who have shared their most vulnerable selves deserves nothing less than absolute discretion.

Some readers may wonder about the ethics of sharing these experiences at all, even anonymized. I've contemplated this question extensively over the years it took to refine these entries. What ultimately guided my decision was the recognition that the insights gained through these encounters extend far beyond the specific circumstances of their acquisition. The lessons about connection, embodiment, pleasure, and presence transcend the particular and touch upon the universal. They belong not to me alone, nor solely to those with whom I've shared physical intimacy, but to the broader human experience of seeking meaningful connection.

My profession has granted me a unique vantage point from which to observe human intimacy across an unusually broad spectrum of age, background, and expectation. The patterns that emerge from this privileged perspective offer insights too valuable to remain confined to my private archives. In sharing them, I hope to contribute to a more nuanced, compassionate, and joyful understanding of physical connection.

As you read these entries, I invite you to approach them not merely as chronicles of sexual encounters but as case studies in human connection. The techniques, observations, and insights presented here aim to help you achieve not just more satisfying sexual experiences but a more embodied existence, one in which pleasure becomes not an isolated event but an integrated aspect of living fully in your physical form.

It is my sincere hope that these entries, born from brief notations but expanded through memory and reflection, will guide you toward greater intimacy both with others and with yourself. May they help you revel in the profound pleasure of truly knowing and being known by another. Of dissolving the boundaries between separate selves, if only temporarily, to experience that rare communion of body and spirit that makes us most acutely alive.

Part 1: Foundations

I still remember the first time a man's fingertips traced the curve of my spine. How that simple contact awakened nerve endings I hadn't known existed, how my body responded before my mind could form a single coherent thought. That moment taught me what years of observation would later confirm: pleasure begins long before clothes are shed, before bodies intertwine, before we reach those territories conventional wisdom marks as erogenous.

We imagine ourselves sophisticated, yet most of us approach desire with maps drawn by strangers, navigating by landmarks others have established rather than discovering our own. I invite you to set aside these inherited charts. The true foundation of connection exists in elements so fundamental we typically overlook them: the silent language of scent that speaks directly to our primitive brain, the eloquent tension of a well-timed pause, the electricity that flows through skin barely touched.

In my apartment overlooking Monaco's harbor, I've witnessed countless powerful men and accomplished women suddenly rendered speechless by the simplest sensations, a breath against the nape of the neck, a deliberate withholding of expected touch, the sudden recognition of their own capacity for feeling. These moments reveal a truth many spend lifetimes avoiding: our bodies know pathways to pleasure our minds have never mapped.

The chapters that follow might seem deceptively simple, foundation stones rather than elaborate architecture. Yet like the seemingly placid surface of the Mediterranean that conceals entire ecosystems beneath, these elemental aspects of intimacy contain worlds within worlds. Approach them not as preliminary steps toward "real" pleasure but as the very essence of it, territory worth lingering within rather than merely passing through.

The Map of Pleasure

The Earth's roundness haunts me. This simple truth that once shattered worlds now whispers secrets of nature's hidden desires. I see it everywhere, this cosmic preference for curves: in celestial bodies hanging like ripe fruit in the night sky, in the tender slope where neck becomes shoulder, in the trembling arc of hip against palm. We are born of these curves, die into them, and between these symmetries we discover the cartography of pleasure, never a direct path but a spiral dance that returns us to origin, transformed.

The cartographer arrived at my Monaco apartment precisely at the appointed hour, when Mediterranean light was performing its evening alchemy, transforming the air to liquid gold. His posture was rigid, shoulders slightly hunched from long hours bent over maps, fingers unconsciously measuring invisible distances even in the simple act of greeting.

"I create detailed renderings of locations I've often never visited," he explained, accepting the Provençal rosé I offered. His voice carried the precise diction of a man who speaks primarily to himself. "My work is predominantly theoretical. I rely on data and secondhand accounts."

How strange the parallels that form between strangers. I watched him speak of distant lands he had never touched, and I saw myself as in a distorting mirror. We were both cartographers of sorts, collectors of knowledge that can never truly be possessed through measurement alone. His algorithms and sensing techniques reminded me of men who approach the body as territory to be conquered rather than landscape to be inhabited.

"And in your personal explorations?" I inquired, my voice dropping to the register where confidences are exchanged. His flush spread like watercolor across pale skin, neck to cheeks, the most honest response his body had offered since arriving.

"I've read extensively on the subject," he replied, eyes fixed on some invisible coordinate beyond my shoulder. "The theoretical aspects are quite fascinating."

As twilight transformed Monaco's harbor into a constellation of yacht lights, I sensed his readiness to begin a different kind of exploration. One that would require him to surrender his customary role as cartographer and instead become the territory itself.

"Perhaps," I suggested, moving to sit beside him, the space between us charged like the narrowing gap between storm clouds, "we might begin by establishing the principle coordinates."

His body tensed at my proximity. When I reached for his hand, his fingers were cool and stiff, like instruments crafted for precision but rarely used for connection. The contradiction moved me. This man whose life was dedicated to mapping space yet who seemed so uncomfortable occupying his own.

"The body's landscape contains many well-known features," I said, guiding his reluctant touch to my neck, just below my ear, where pulse speaks its secret morse code beneath delicate skin. His hand trembled slightly, hovering a millimeter above me. "You can actually touch me," I whispered with gentle humor. "Maps require ground-truthing, do they not?"

He swallowed visibly, his Adam's apple rising and falling above his buttoned collar. "I'm more accustomed to working with LiDAR data and satellite imagery," he admitted, voice tightened by the tension between desire and fear. When his fingertips finally made contact with my skin, the touch was so light as to be almost theoretical, more hypothesis than certainty.

"In cartography," he said, retreating to professional knowledge, "we establish control points before detailed mapping can begin."

"Precisely," I whispered, leaning closer until my breath warmed his ear. "And the most valuable lovers are those who understand that pleasure isn't merely concentrated in the places we've been conditioned to expect it."

I unbuttoned the top of my silk blouse, revealing not the obvious landscape he anticipated but the delicate hollow between my collarbones, that subtle depression where shadow and light perform their eternal dance. Taking his index finger, I placed it there, in that subtle valley where pulse and breath create their own rhythm beneath the skin, a place overlooked in traditional atlases of desire.

"This is territory rarely claimed," I told him. "Yet notice how the skin here is nearly translucent, how it registers even the lightest touch."

His finger followed the contour with unexpected tenderness, a natural cartographer's instinct for topographical nuance emerging despite his nervousness. I allowed my eyes to close briefly, surrendering to the circuit completed between his fingertip and this neglected landscape of my body. When I opened my eyes again, his expression had shifted from intellectual curiosity to something more primal, the analytical mind momentarily silenced by the body's wisdom.

"There are maps," I continued, my voice dropping to match the growing intimacy between us, "and then there are explorations. One documents what is already known; the other discovers what has yet to be charted."

Taking his hand again, I guided it to the inside of my elbow, that tender crease where skin remains sheltered from sun and wind, where nerves gather close to the surface. His touch there kindled a current of sensation that traveled unexpected pathways through my body, connecting regions seemingly unrelated in conventional anatomies of pleasure.

"The body doesn't experience pleasure in isolation," I explained, my breath catching slightly as his fingers discovered their own initiative. "It flows between points, creates connections and currents. The skilled lover understands these networks."

He leaned forward then, his scientific observation giving way to participation as his lips replaced his fingers at the crook of my arm, his tongue following the blue tributary of vein visible beneath my skin. The unexpectedness of this gesture sent a delicious shiver through me. Here was a student already synthesizing the lesson, applying theory to practice with impressive intuition.

"I've always been fascinated by rivers," he murmured against my skin. "How they connect disparate regions, how their patterns reveal the hidden nature of the land."

This observation signaled his readiness to progress beyond preliminary instruction. I rose from the sofa and offered my hand, leading him toward my bedroom where the evening light cast everything in amber and shadow, transforming ordinary space into the dreamscape where true discovery becomes possible.

Standing before him in that honeyed illumination, I slowly removed my blouse, then my skirt, revealing not just my body but an opportunity for education. Rather than allowing his gaze to settle immediately on the expected destinations, I took his hands and placed them on my shoulders, guiding his attention to where our journey should begin.

"Begin at the periphery," I instructed softly. "The known world of pleasure is smaller than you think. Beyond its borders lie territories worth claiming."

He needed no further encouragement, his hands moving across my shoulders with deliberate pressure, his thumbs finding the slight hollows above my shoulder blades where tension accumulates like sediment. I was struck by how carefully he watched my responses, the slight parting of my lips, the almost imperceptible arch of my spine, cataloging these reactions like landmarks on a developing chart.

"The nape of the neck," I whispered, turning to present this often-neglected expanse, "contains a gathering of nerves that respond to the lightest stimulation."

His breath warmed my skin a moment before his lips made contact, his hands gathering my hair with unexpected confidence, lifting its weight to expose the vulnerable curve where neck becomes shoulder. The gentle pressure of his mouth there awakened receptors that sent pleasure spiraling downward through my body, connecting points that existed on no anatomical diagram.

I heard myself make a sound that belonged to no language but was understood in all of them. That primal vocabulary that precedes and survives all constructed systems of communication.

"The body," I managed to explain as his explorations continued, "contains entire networks of sensation that traditional education ignores. We're taught to proceed directly to obvious destinations, bypassing landscapes worth lingering within."

He seemed to grasp this principle intuitively, his hands discovering the subtle topography of my back, the gentle valley of my spine, the rising plateau of my shoulder blades, the delicate slope where waist becomes hip. There was something exquisite about being explored with such thorough attention, about being discovered rather than merely possessed.

When I turned to face him again, I witnessed transformation etched across his features. His glasses had clouded with the heat of his awakening, those scientific lenses that had kept the world at objective distance now betraying his descent into subjective reality. The rigid cartographer was dissolving before me, his carefully constructed borders becoming permeable.

"Your turn to be mapped," I said, reaching for the buttons of his shirt. He froze momentarily, his hands moving instinctively to stop me before falling away in surrender.

"I'm not..." he began, then stopped, words inadequate to express the complex anxiety his body communicated so eloquently. "My physical form isn't particularly..."

"Men's bodies," I interrupted gently, continuing to undo his buttons, "contain similar uncharted territories. Your skin hungers for touch beyond the parameters you've been taught to expect."

As I exposed his pale chest, I noted how he resisted the urge to cover himself. The body that emerged from beneath his clothing was that of a man who spent his life at desks, slightly soft around the middle, shoulders hunched from years of bending over maps, skin rarely exposed to sunlight or touch. Yet there was a beauty in this authenticity, in this unmanufactured form that spoke of priorities beyond physical display.

To demonstrate my point, I ran my fingernails lightly along his sides, just beneath his ribs, where nerve endings gather unexpectedly dense beneath sensitive skin. His reaction was explosive. A gasping, almost startled response as though he'd received an electrical shock rather than a caress.

"Good lord!" he exclaimed, then immediately looked embarrassed by his outburst. "I had no idea that would—" He stopped, blinking rapidly behind his glasses. "The sensitivity differential is remarkable."

"The inner thigh," I continued, my hands moving lower to follow the seam of his trousers, "contains nerve endings that connect directly to arousal centers, yet remains largely unexplored in hasty encounters."

When his clothing finally joined mine on the floor, I guided him to lie on my bed, the crisp sheets a blank canvas for our developing map. Rather than immediately focusing on his evident arousal, I knelt beside him and touched the inside of his thigh with feather-light strokes, watching fascination and pleasure mingle in his expression.

"Close your eyes," I suggested. "When one sense is diminished, others become more acute."

As his lids lowered, I bent to press my lips to the hollow beneath his ankle bone, an area so rarely included in the geography of pleasure that his eyes flew open again in surprise before closing in surrender to the unexpected sensation. I continued my journey upward, mapping his body with lips and fingertips, claiming territories he had never considered worthy of exploration, the back of his knee, the curve of his hip bone, the sensitive skin beneath his arms.

His breathing changed, becoming deeper, less controlled. The disciplined cartographer was dissolving into something more elemental, his professional precision giving way to instinctive response. When my exploration finally included his obvious arousal, the context had been transformed. It existed now as part of a comprehensive landscape rather than the sole destination of our journey.

I took him into my mouth, not with the mechanical efficiency that characterizes so many encounters, but with the deliberate appreciation of a connoisseur sampling a complex vintage. The sound that escaped him, half surprise, half surrender, revealed how thoroughly his scholarly detachment had dissolved. My tongue circled the sensitive ridge, applying varying pressure that transformed his contained gasps into throaty moans.

"Every body," I whispered against his heated skin, "contains its own unique typography. What brings one person pleasure may leave another unmoved."

To illustrate this principle, I guided his hands to my body once again, encouraging him to discover rather than assume, to ask rather than presume. The revelation in his expression when he found how I responded to pressure along my hip bone, to the whisper of breath across my eyelids, to the gentle suction at the pulse point of my wrist: these discoveries clearly reshaped his understanding of female pleasure.

His confidence grew with each response he elicited, his hands and mouth becoming bolder in their explorations. When his lips closed around my nipple, the gentle suction sent fire racing through my veins. His tongue swirled and flicked with exquisite precision, as though he'd already mapped the exact pattern that would make my back arch and my breath catch.

"The clitoris is not merely a point on a map," I explained as his exploration eventually reached this familiar landmark. "It's an extensive network, with branches extending far beneath the surface, surrounding the vaginal entrance like roots around a wellspring."

Taking his hand, I guided his fingers in circular motions that acknowledged this broader geography, teaching through guided discovery rather than abstract instruction. His technique, tentative at first, then increasingly confident as he registered my response, suggested a genuine desire to integrate this new knowledge, to replace outdated maps with more accurate representations.

He proved an exceptionally attentive student, adjusting pressure and rhythm as my breathing quickened, as moisture gathered beneath his touch, reading my body's signals with increasing fluency. Where many men apply uniform pressure in mechanical repetition, he experimented with variations: firm circles that spiraled inward, feather-light flutters that barely made contact, long strokes that encompassed the entire vulva before returning to more concentrated attention.

This sensitivity to response rather than adherence to technique soon had me gasping, my hips rising involuntarily to meet his touch. When he slid a finger inside me while continuing his external exploration, the combination of sensations pushed me toward an explosive edge I hadn't anticipated reaching so quickly. The orgasm that followed wasn't the familiar wave I'd experienced countless times, but something more complex: a series of concentric circles rippling outward from a central point of pleasure, as if my body had become a stone-struck pond extending endlessly outward.

While I was still quivering in the aftermath, he moved between my legs with an urgency that transformed his scholarly appearance into something primal and compelling. He poised himself at my entrance, his eyes questioning despite his evident desire.

"Please," I whispered, reaching for him, completing the circuit between invitation and acceptance.

When our bodies finally joined, I could feel the transformation complete, the theoretical cartographer giving way entirely to the embodied explorer. The sensation of fullness was exquisite, heightened by the extended foreplay that had awakened every nerve ending. I showed how slight adjustments in angle transformed experience entirely, how lifting my pelvis directed his hardness against anterior wall where sensation concentrated, how pressure of pubic bone against external nerve center created complementary pleasure.

With each deliberate thrust, he angled his body differently, experimenting with depth and direction. Sometimes he withdrew almost completely before returning with agonizing slowness, the gradual stretching and filling creating a delicious anticipation that made me whimper. Other times he remained deep within me, barely moving except for subtle rotations of his hips that pressed against internal pleasure centers I'd rarely had partners discover.

"Oh," he gasped, his eyes widening behind askew glasses as he registered the difference. "I had no idea it could feel like this."

The most remarkable aspect wasn't just his willingness to learn but how quickly he synthesized information into intuitive action. He began to read my body's responses with uncanny precision, adjusting his movements to heighten the tremors that signaled approaching climax. When he felt me beginning to tighten around him, he maintained perfect consistency in his rhythm and angle, neither accelerating nor changing what was clearly working, a restraint many experienced lovers never master.

When release finally claimed me, it arrived not as the familiar tide but as cataclysm: a seismic dissolution that began everywhere at once. I felt myself scattered, unmade, the carefully drawn boundaries of selfhood suddenly meaningless as pleasure erased the lines between internal and external, between his body and mine, between knowing and being known. My consciousness shattered into prismatic fragments, each one containing a different sensation. Words escaped me that belonged to no language I recognized, sounds torn from some ancestral memory of pleasure before it was civilized into silence.

His own culmination followed immediately, his body arching against mine as if attempting to claim every territory simultaneously. His face in that instant of release was a revelation, all academic reserve dissolved, all self-consciousness obliterated in the pure animal joy of connection. He called my name like a man discovering language for the first time, the syllables fractured by the intensity of his pleasure.

Afterward, as we lay in the deepening twilight, I drew lazy patterns across his chest, feeling the gradual slowing of his heartbeat beneath my fingertips. His body had undergone a remarkable transformation, the rigid posture now melted into the mattress, his breathing deep and unrestricted.

He'd removed his glasses, and without them, his face appeared younger, more vulnerable. "I've been studying cartography for twenty-three years," he murmured eventually, his voice carrying none of the clipped precision from earlier. "Creating detailed maps of places I've never visited." He turned to face me, his expression holding wonder and a touch of regret. "And all this time, I've been living in a body I've never properly explored."

"Most people haven't," I replied, resting my head against his shoulder, which no longer hunched forward but lay relaxed against the sheets. "We're given inadequate diagrams and told they're complete. We learn to identify landmarks without understanding the territory they exist within."

He was silent for a moment, his fingers following the gentle depression along my spine. "In cartography," he said finally, "the most valuable maps are those that reveal resources previously undiscovered, routes previously unconsidered."

"Precisely," I agreed, pleased by his intuitive grasp of the parallel. "And in intimacy, the most valuable experiences are those that expand our understanding of what's possible, that reveal aspects of pleasure we didn't know existed."

Night descended over Monaco like a final curtain, transforming my windows into mirrors that reflected both the constellation of harbor lights and our intertwined forms. His willingness to surrender the false security of expertise moved me in ways I had not anticipated. It was a humble recognition that all maps contain fictional elements, these territories designated terra incognita that can never be charted except through direct exploration. Perhaps this is the only wisdom worth pursuing: this brave acknowledgment of our inevitable incompleteness, this perpetual openness to revision.

•

One holiday, I found myself in the American Midwest, traveling along highways that stretched before me in perfect straight lines, vanishing into distant horizons without a single curve to interrupt their relentless geometry. These roads, engineered to connect points with maximum efficiency, cutting through the natural landscape rather than flowing with it, struck me as the perfect metaphor for conventional approaches to sexuality.

We are taught to view pleasure as a direct route between points A and B: a straight line from arousal to climax with minimal deviation. Yet the most profound experiences of intimacy rarely follow such linear paths. Like rivers carving their way through varied terrain, like the ancient roads of Europe that follow the contours of mountains and valleys, pleasure finds its most rewarding expression when it responds to the natural landscape rather than imposing rigid structure upon it.

The cartographer taught me as much as I taught him. How easily we can become trapped in theoretical knowledge that never touches the earth, how transformative it can be to abandon our carefully plotted routes in favor of genuine exploration. Perhaps true wisdom lies not in knowing the most efficient path but in understanding when efficiency itself becomes an obstacle to discovery.

Even now, when I encounter someone too focused on reaching a destination to notice the territories they're passing through, I think of those American highways, impressive in their ambition but missing the rich experience of meandering through unexpected terrain, of discovering vistas that exist nowhere on the existing map. The body, like the earth itself, reveals its most profound secrets not to those who travel fastest but to those who journey with presence and wonder.

The Lesson:

The most profound sexual pleasure often exists beyond the obvious landmarks of erogenous zones. The body contains entire networks of sensation waiting to be discovered, territories that remain unexplored due to cultural conditioning rather than lack of potential.

Begin your explorations at the periphery rather than proceeding directly to familiar destinations. Notice how touch along seemingly neutral areas, the inside of elbows, the nape of the neck, the hollow of ankles, creates unexpected currents of sensation. Pay particular attention to threshold areas, where one type of skin meets another, where protection meets vulnerability.

Communication becomes your compass in this exploration. Ask your partner to indicate when a touch resonates, when pressure should increase or decrease, when a discovered territory deserves more thorough investigation. Remember that every body contains its own unique topography. What brings one person pleasure may leave another unmoved.

For women, recognize that the clitoris extends far beyond its visible portion, creating a complex network that surrounds the vaginal entrance. For men, understand that pleasure exists throughout the body, not merely in the obvious centers of arousal. When we expand our understanding of where pleasure can be experienced, we transform not just individual encounters but our entire relationship with physical intimacy.

The Foundation of Attraction

There exists between every two bodies a secret alphabet of connection, a language written in nerve endings and translated by skin. In the labyrinth of my profession, I have become fluent in this soundless discourse, able to read the hieroglyphics of desire etched into the most casual gesture, the most fleeting glance. Yet I remain eternally astonished by how many seek intimacy while wearing invisible armor, constructing elaborate fortresses against the very vulnerability they profess to desire. It is this paradox, this simultaneous reaching toward and withdrawal from authentic presence, that reveals the most profound truths about our nature.

The architect entered my life on an afternoon when Monaco's light possessed that particular crystalline quality unique to Mediterranean autumn: a clarity that strips pretense from all it touches. I knew of him before our meeting; his reputation for creating spaces that transformed human movement through invisible geometries had intrigued me. It is a habit of mine, part professional thoroughness, part dream-collector's instinct, to gather fragments of those who seek my company before we meet. Not from investigative impulse, but because I have discovered that the persona a man carefully constructs for public consumption often reveals, through its deliberate architecture, precisely what trembles beneath this conscious design.

I prepared my apartment with this awareness, arranging art books that spoke of structure and form on my coffee table, selecting a Bordeaux that suggested sophistication without pretension, adorning myself in a dress whose lines would appeal to one who appreciates both architectural precision and organic curve. The Mediterranean light streamed through my windows, creating pools of golden illumination across the parquet floors, nature's own contribution to the carefully curated stage.

As I applied a touch of bergamot perfume to my pulse points, I wondered what invisible geometries might emerge between us. Would he approach our encounter as he did his buildings, with precision, with vision, with clear understanding of how structure shapes experience? Or would there be, as I so often observed in my profession, a curious disconnect between his professional expertise and his intimate presence?

The doorbell chimed right on schedule, a subtle gesture that marked the beginning of our unspoken negotiation of trust.

He stood in my doorway, a vision of tailored elegance, as if designed rather than born. His bespoke suit whispered wealth; silver cufflinks caught the afternoon light as he extended his hand. His smile reached his eyes—a promising sign. But as I welcomed him into the amber glow of my apartment, I sensed a dissonance between what I saw and what my other senses perceived.

"Your home is exquisite," he remarked, his gaze taking in the careful arrangement of light and shadow I had cultivated over years. "The way you've maximized natural light while maintaining privacy. It's masterful."

I accepted the compliment with a smile, pouring us each a glass of the Bordeaux. "I believe that spaces, like bodies, speak their own language. They tell us secrets about those who inhabit them."

As we settled into conversation, the source of my unease crystallized. While he spoke eloquently about the poetry of space and the psychology of structures, how buildings shape human experience through invisible geometries, there lingered in the narrow space between us an unmistakable scent. A distinctly human odor, not overwhelming but persistent, that betrayed a day spent in Monaco's summer heat without proper attention to personal freshness.

How curious, I thought, that this man who understood the importance of environmental harmony had overlooked his own personal ecology. The contrast between his immaculate suit and the subtle but unmistakable body odor created a dissonance that distracted from his otherwise compelling presence. Each time he moved, the aroma of stale sweat emerged from beneath expensive cologne, a base note no perfumer would intentionally include.

I watched his hands as he spoke: elegant, expressive hands that sketched invisible buildings in the air between us. Hands that would soon touch my skin, but that now betrayed a tension his polished words concealed. When he reached for his wine glass, I caught the faint but unmistakable staleness that clung to his skin, the accumulated evidence of a body moving through a day without renewal.

Wine glasses emptied, conversation having traced its inevitable arc toward the purpose of our meeting, I rose from my armchair and approached him with deliberate slowness. The moment of transition, from social performance to intimate encounter, reveals so much about a person's relationship to desire. His eyes darkened as I moved toward him, his breath quickening slightly as I entered his personal space.

"Perhaps," I suggested, my fingers finding the precise Windsor knot of his silk tie while I carefully maintained a pleasant expression despite the subtle aroma now unmistakably registering in my consciousness, "we might begin by washing away the city from your skin. A refreshing shower before we proceed further."

The slight widening of his eyes suggested surprise, followed quickly by comprehension. A flicker of vulnerability crossed his features, that brief, unguarded moment when one realizes they have been seen more clearly than they had intended. I've learned to recognize this moment of exposure; it often contains the seed of genuine connection.

"My shower is rather exceptional," I added softly. "Another space designed for human pleasure."

He nodded, gratitude mingling with relief in his expression. In the steam-filled expanse of my marble bathroom, an indulgence I've never regretted, I suppressed a smile at the unspoken truth hovering between us. We all have our blind spots; I certainly possess mine. I've spent decades analyzing human intimacy while occasionally forgetting to call my mother on her birthday.

The ritual of undressing contains its own silent language. As I unbuttoned his shirt with practiced ease, I observed how his posture remained slightly rigid, the tension in his shoulders betraying his discomfort with being truly witnessed. This, too, is something I've noted over years of professional intimacy: how many prefer the performance of desire to its authentic experience, how challenging it is for most to be fully present in their unadorned humanity.

I allowed my fingertips to linger at each newly revealed expanse of skin, the hollow at the base of his throat, the slight prominence of his collarbone, the unexpected warmth radiating from his chest. His breath caught when my hands moved to his belt, that most obvious symbol of the boundary between public and private self.

The leather yielded to my practiced touch, followed by the metallic whisper of his zipper descending. His trousers joined his shirt on the marble floor, revealing boxer briefs that outlined his semi-arousal. I knelt before him, my fingers tracing the elastic waistband with deliberate slowness before finally drawing this last barrier downward. His erection emerged, not yet fully awakened but already suggesting the promise of complete hardness. I helped him step free of the fabric pooled at his ankles, his nakedness now complete, vulnerable, and unexpectedly beautiful in its masculine architecture.

Rising to meet his gaze, I unfastened my own dress with unhurried precision, allowing the silk to slide from my shoulders and cascade to the floor in a whisper of expensive fabric. His eyes darkened as he took in my revealed form, my breasts still contained in black lace, the shadow between my thighs veiled in matching silk. I reached behind to unhook my bra, feeling his gaze like a physical touch as I freed myself from its confines. When I finally removed my underwear, sliding it down my legs with a dancer's deliberation, we stood as equals in our nakedness, all social markers dissolved, leaving only the elemental truth of bare skin and awakening desire.

I guided him into the shower, turning the taps to release a warm cascade that revealed what his tailoring had both concealed and suggested, a body surprisingly well-formed beneath the armor of his suit. Water traced the contours of his chest, his shoulders, the subtle definition of his abdomen. Something in him seemed to surrender as the shower enveloped us both, as if the water dissolved not just the day's accumulation but also the performance he had maintained since arriving at my door.

Steam rose between us, veiling and unveiling our bodies in a dance of revelation. I reached for the soap, not the commercial products most use, but a handcrafted blend of sandalwood and cedar that complements rather than masks the natural human scent. The alchemy of water and skin and soap created an intoxicating fragrance unique to this moment, this man, this interplay of elements.

"You've been hiding assets that would appreciate with proper investment," I observed, enjoying his startled laugh as my soapy hands traced the architecture of his torso.

His shoulders lowered a fraction, his breath deepened. "I spend so much time thinking about how buildings make people feel," he confessed, eyes closing as I massaged his scalp with sandalwood-scented shampoo, "that I sometimes forget to notice how I feel in them."

This admission, this small surrender to truth, shifted something between us. I've observed this pattern countless times: authentic connection often begins not with attraction or desire but with the simple acknowledgment of our human imperfections. We are never more accessible to one another than in the moments when we set aside pretense.

I took my time with him, demonstrating through action rather than instruction how the ritual of cleansing can become an act of sensual awareness. Many rush through bathing as a perfunctory necessity, missing entirely the pleasure inherent in this daily sacrament. I showed him how water temperature creates its own language of sensation. How a slight cooling can heighten nerve receptivity. How the contrast between cool rivulets and warm palms can create delicious tension.

His hands, initially hesitant, grew bolder as they discovered the slick pathways of my body. Water rendered us new to each other, our skin gleaming, hypersensitive, alive with sensation. The shower's confined space created an intimacy beyond naked proximity; we breathed the same steamed air, inhaling each other's essence with each breath.

Guiding his hands over my soap-slicked skin, I invited him to explore the vocabulary of pressure: firm strokes following the muscles flanking my spine, feather-light touches tracing the curve where waist becomes hip, gentle circular motions at the nape of my neck. I was teaching him a grammar of touch that transcended our encounter, a sensory education he could translate to any future intimacy.

When I turned to face him, pressing him gently against the cool tile wall, his breathing had deepened, his gaze no longer darting away from mine. I reached for the handheld shower head, one of my favorite instruments for sensory play, and demonstrated how directed water pressure creates exquisite sensation when guided with intention. His sharp intake of breath when I directed the warm stream between his legs confirmed the lesson had been received.

"I had no idea," he murmured, his hands finding my waist with newfound purpose, "that getting clean could be so…"

"Revelatory?" I suggested, enjoying his quiet laughter against my neck.

Water cascaded between our pressed bodies, creating a liquid barrier that paradoxically dissolved the boundaries between us. I guided his hand between my thighs, showing him how the combination of his touch and the pulsing water could create sensations that made my breath catch and my eyes flutter closed. His ministrations, initially cautious, grew more confident as he witnessed my response, the arch of my back, the unconscious parting of my lips.

The architect in him awakened to this new form of design, the architecture of pleasure, the mapping of desire across responsive skin. He discovered how the slightest adjustment in angle or pressure could transform pleasant sensation into exquisite tension, how sustained rhythm could build structures of anticipation that defied gravity.

My sex throbbed under his careful attention, my clitoris swelling beneath the dual stimulation of his fingers and the water's pulsation. Each circle of his thumb sent electric currents radiating through my pelvis, my inner muscles clenching around emptiness that ached to be filled. I could feel my wetness mingling with the shower's flow, my body's own evidence of arousal indistinguishable from the water that enveloped us both.

By the time we stepped from the shower, the transformation was remarkable. Gone was the slightly stiff, self-conscious man who had appeared at my door. In his place stood someone present, awake to sensation, his body language open and responsive. I took my time drying him, demonstrating how even this mundane act can express care and attention, the plush towel creating friction and warmth, building anticipation rather than merely achieving utilitarian dryness.

"Touch," I told him as I led him toward my bedroom, where afternoon light filtered through gauzy curtains, "begins long before skin meets skin. It begins with attention."

In that golden-hour illumination, his confidence had visibly transformed. His movements now possessed fluidity, his gaze maintained connection rather than retreating into private calculation. When he reached for me, there was intention behind his touch, a quality often absent in those who approach intimacy as achievement rather than exploration.

I guided him to sit at the edge of my bed where afternoon light transformed ordinary cotton to spun gold. I stood before him, poised between his parted knees, our bodies creating negative space charged with anticipation. This deliberate inversion of expected positions, him below, me above, created a subtle realignment of conventional dynamics. In this new geography, he found himself looking up rather than down, receiving rather than pursuing. I've discovered that these unanticipated alterations in physical poetry often fracture habitual patterns, dissolving the script most carry within them and awakening them to the uncharted territories of actual encounter.

A universe exists in the narrow space between almost-touching lips. I leaned down to demonstrate this truth, my hands cradling his face as one might hold something simultaneously strong and fragile. Instead of rushing toward conventional satisfaction, I initiated him into the forgotten art of the lingering kiss, that exquisite suspension between intention and fulfillment. My lips barely grazed his, retreating when he pressed forward, returning when he remained still, teaching his body a new language of approach and withdrawal. The fluttering of his eyelids, the subtle tension in his shoulders, revealed how this deliberate restraint awakened nerve endings dulled by habitual consumption.

His hands moved instinctively to my hips, seeking to anchor this floating sensation, to direct our encounter along familiar channels. I captured his wrists with gentle pressure, guiding them to rest on the bed beside him.

"Not yet," I whispered, my breath becoming part of his inhalation, our lungs sharing invisible intimacies. "First, we must learn patience."

His quiet groan vibrated from his chest into mine. A sound more honest than any words he had spoken since arriving at my door. In this small surrender, I glimpsed the imprisoned being that lived beneath his architectural precision, the creature of sensation concealed within his professional carapace. I continued his education in pleasure's true geography, revealing how anticipation itself generates currents of sensation more exquisite than the blunt force of immediate gratification, how the pathway toward union contains treasures more varied than the destination itself.

The scent of clean skin now mingled with more ancient aromas rising between us, an alchemical transformation more potent than any perfumer's creation. This fragrant dialogue between our bodies, unmediated by artificial notes or social pretense, awakened something primordial within me, a responsive hunger beyond professional performance. I lowered my mouth to his chest, the tip of my tongue tracing invisible paths across territories now vibrating with heightened awareness. I discovered how his newly sensitized skin created its own topography of pleasure: the plateau of his sternum responding differently than the sensitive valley between his ribs, the slight saltiness near his collarbone contrasting with the sweeter taste of his throat.

His hands twisted in the sheets, knuckles whitening with the effort of remaining where I had placed them. This voluntary restraint, this chosen submission to pleasure on terms other than his habitual patterns, created visible tension that transformed his body into a instrument strung to exquisite tightness. I watched fascinated as conflicting desires wrote themselves across his features: the impulse to grasp warring with the novel pleasure of pure receptivity, the architect's need for control surrendering to the deeper hunger to be thoroughly known.

When I finally took his hands and guided them to my waiting flesh, the contact unleashed something transformed in him. He touched me with the reverence of an archaeologist discovering an ancient civilization: attentively, curiously, his fingers both questioning and declaring as they traveled across my landscape. This newly awakened presence manifested in his exquisite responsiveness to my body's subtle communications, the catch in my breath when he found a particularly sensitive hollow, the involuntary arch when pressure deepened, the flutter of eyelids signaling surrender. This sacred feedback loop, this wordless conversation between giving and receiving bodies, forms the essential foundation of profound connection. Yet how rarely do we encounter another willing to listen through their fingertips, to speak through pressure and release, to participate fully in sensation's unfolding symphony.

I straddled him then, our bodies still slightly damp, creating a delicious friction as skin met skin. The position allowed me to control our joining, to set a pace that built desire in measured increments rather than rushing toward culmination. I showed him how slight shifts in angle created entirely different sensations, how moments of absolute stillness intensified the awareness of fullness and connection.

My slick entrance hovered just above his erection, which strained upward to meet me, hot and hard and insistent against my inner thigh. I lowered myself with excruciating deliberation, taking him inside me millimeter by millimeter, both of us breathing in shallow gasps as our bodies joined. The slow penetration allowed me to feel every ridge, every vein of him stretching me open, filling the emptiness with exquisite pressure.

"Feel how different this is," I murmured, making the slightest adjustment in my position that changed everything, suddenly stimulating nerves that had been merely adjacent before. His eyes widened, his hands tightening on my hips as pleasure registered on his features.

As our bodies joined on silk sheets warmed by late-afternoon sun, I demonstrated how slight adjustments create entirely different sensations: how the tilt of a hip, the arch of a spine, the placement of a supporting hand can transform pleasant friction into extraordinary pleasure. His newly clean scent mingled with the subtle notes of arousal, creating an olfactory complement to physical sensation.

What might have been mere transaction became genuine exchange. I found myself responding to his growing presence, to the way he now moved with attention and intention. This is the hidden joy of my profession that few would comprehend, those moments when teaching transforms into mutual discovery, when professional engagement flowers into authentic pleasure.

The room filled with the sound of quickening breath, of skin meeting skin, of occasional words that emerged from some place beyond thought. Light played across our entangled bodies, turning sweat-sheened skin to gold, casting shadows that emphasized the negative spaces between us. Spaces that appeared and disappeared with our movements, creating a visual rhythm that complemented the physical one.

My inner muscles gripped him tightly as I rode him, the slick walls of my sex creating a wet velvet sheath around his hardness. Each time I raised my hips, I felt the delicious drag of him against my most sensitive inner spots, sending currents of pleasure spiraling outward from our point of connection. His cock pulsed inside me, growing impossibly harder as his own release approached.

When climax finally approached, it was not the frantic rush so many pursue, but a gradual building toward inevitable release, a wave that had been gathering force through every moment of attentive touch, every breath exchanged, every barrier dissolved. The architect's body tensed beneath mine, his focus completely present rather than lost in private fantasy. This, too, is rare, this capacity to remain connected even at the moment when most retreat into solitary sensation.

"Look at me," I instructed softly as the wave crested, wanting him to experience how intimacy transforms even this most primal of moments. His eyes met mine, vulnerable and trusting, as pleasure overtook us both, a synchronicity that cannot be manufactured, only discovered through mutual presence.

The orgasm radiated from my core in pulsing waves, my inner walls contracting rhythmically around his shaft as pleasure coursed through every nerve ending. My thighs trembled against his hips, my back arching as the sensation peaked, transforming my carefully maintained composure into something raw and uninhibited. His own release followed immediately, his hands grasping my waist with sudden urgency as he drove upward, emptying himself deep inside me with a groan that seemed torn from somewhere beyond conscious thought.

Afterward, as he lay beside me with wonderment still evident in his expression, I knew he had absorbed far more than the importance of hygiene. He had experienced how presence, attention, and embodied awareness can transform physical congress into something approaching transcendence.

"I design spaces meant to elevate human experience," he mused, trailing fingers along my collarbone with newfound delicacy, "and yet I've never thought about how to bring that same intention to this most intimate architecture between two bodies."

I smiled, recognizing in his words the beginning of a new awareness. I often reflect on how many opportunities for connection are missed simply because we haven't been taught to approach intimacy with the same care and intention we bring to other aspects of our lives. How many partnerships might flourish if participants understood these fundamental principles of presence and attention?

"Architecture and intimacy share more than might be immediately apparent," I replied. "Both require understanding the relationship between structure and flow, tension and release, privacy and revelation."

His thoughtful nod told me the metaphor had resonated. As he dressed to leave, there was a new mindfulness in his movements, an embodied presence I hadn't observed when he arrived. This, perhaps more than the physical pleasure we'd shared, represented the true gift of our encounter. An awakening to the possibilities of conscious presence in a realm where most operate on unconscious habit.

•

The most profound truths about human connection often lie in what remains unspoken, in the delicate spaces between intention and touch, between desire and fulfillment. What fascinated me about the architect's transformation wasn't merely the physical metamorphosis, but the psychological unfurling that accompanied it. His initial embarrassment, like a tightly closed fist, gradually opened into relief, then blossomed into embodied confidence. In that moment, he wasn't simply cleaner; he was more fully present, more authentically connected to his corporeal reality.

Physical intimacy demands a proximity that transcends our carefully maintained social boundaries. When basic hygiene is neglected, our limbic system, that ancient, emotional brain beneath our rational facade, awakens like a sentinel in the night, triggering subtle avoidance responses that sabotage connection before consciousness even registers the cause. This isn't aesthetic snobbery but biological wisdom encoded in our very cells, designed to protect us from invisible threats. A client may drape himself in the most exquisite external signifiers, yet overlook this fundamental prerequisite for genuine closeness, like building a cathedral upon sand.

I've observed, through thousands of intimate encounters, how frequently we invest in elaborately constructed facades while neglecting the essential self that others actually experience. We armor ourselves with designer clothes, expensive accessories, and carefully curated personas, yet somehow forget the foundations upon which all meaningful connection must be built. We construct walls of perfume to mask our humanity, then wonder why we feel so alone even when pressed against another's skin.

The most revelatory lessons emerge not from grand philosophical discourse but from moments of simple vulnerability, those quiet sanctuaries where pretense falls away and we stand revealed in our imperfect humanity. As the architect of my own unconventional life, I've discovered that the essential elements of connection are often more elemental than we imagine, yet more frequently overlooked than we dare admit to ourselves.

In intimacy, as in architecture, what remains unseen holds the greatest significance. The invisible structures of pleasure, like the most breathtaking buildings, require proper foundational elements. Not for their visual appeal, but for their essential function in supporting everything that rises above. Our bodies, these temporary temples we inhabit, speak truths that our elaborate words often obscure. Perhaps this is why genuine connection feels increasingly rare, We have forgotten that before we can truly touch another, we must first be willing to be touched ourselves, to be seen in our unadorned reality, to offer not perfection but authentic presence.

The Lesson:

The most elaborate seduction strategy cannot overcome the impact of basic bodily neglect. This isn't about expensive products or elaborate grooming rituals. It's about the fundamental courtesy of clean skin and fresh breath. Beyond courtesy, however, lies something more profound: an acknowledgment of our animal nature, the recognition that we communicate through subtle chemical signals as well as through words and gestures.

What I've learned through thousands of intimate encounters is that clean skin carries its own intoxicating fragrance, unique to each person and infinitely more appealing than artificial scents layered over neglect. This natural human essence creates an olfactory signature that heightens attraction in ways we process beneath conscious awareness.

Consider hygiene not merely as preparation for intimacy but as an act of presence, a ritual that awakens awareness of your physical self before sharing it with another. When you shower mindfully, feeling water trace the contours of your body, attending to sensation rather than merely completing a task, you activate sensual awareness that enhances all that follows.

The Power of Scent

The invisible governs us more powerfully than the visible. This truth haunts me each time I witness a client's pupils dilate at a scent that bypasses conscious thought, the body's silent confession transcending all practiced seduction. Have you noticed how fragrance dissolves boundaries more effectively than touch, how certain molecular arrangements create immediate presence while others repel regardless of visual appeal?

My international businessman moved between worlds with the liquid grace of mercury, belonging everywhere and nowhere simultaneously. During our previous encounters, I had observed how Western precision in his business dealings melted into Eastern languor once transactions concluded. His most compelling quality, rarer than his wealth or his carefully cultivated cross-cultural fluency, was genuine attentiveness. Where most men designed external presentations, he seemed attuned to interior qualities like a musician hearing harmonics others miss.

The Mediterranean sunset had transformed my apartment into a chamber of amber light when my doorbell announced his arrival. He stood backlit in my doorway, carrying neither the expected flowers nor wine, but a small object wrapped in midnight-blue silk.

"Isabelle," he murmured, my name acquiring unexpected weight in his deliberately maintained accent.

After completing the requisite social choreography, he presented the silk-wrapped object, his gaze intense enough that I understood immediately, this wasn't transactional pleasantry but something carrying deeper significance.

Unwrapping it revealed a small amber bottle adorned with intricate gold Arabic calligraphy spiraling across its surface like frozen music.

"Oud oil," he explained, his eyes never leaving mine. "In my homeland, certain scents aren't merely decorative. They're considered pathways between bodies, bridges across the space that separates us."

The sincerity with which he spoke transcended what might have otherwise registered as orientalist cliché. This wasn't performance; it was invitation into dimensions of sensuality our previous encounters hadn't explored.

"May I?" he asked, carefully removing the stopper.

I nodded, curiosity mingling with professional wariness. My profession has left me with certain occupational hazards regarding scent. Two decades of experience has taught me that feigning pleasure in response to fragrance proves considerably more difficult than simulating other forms of enjoyment. The nose remains stubbornly honest when the body might politely lie.

As the first molecules reached my receptors, all hesitation dissolved. The fragrance unfolded in successive waves, initial notes of cedar and sandalwood giving way to deeper currents of ambergris and musk, with undercurrents so complex they defied categorization. My internal chemistry responded with instant recognition, as though these particular molecules had been seeking mine through centuries.

"This comes from a small distillery outside Muscat," he said, voice softening as one might when disclosing a treasured secret. "The resin ages for over thirty years before distillation."

"It's traditionally applied before intimate encounters," he continued. "To specific points where body heat will release the fragrance gradually throughout the experience."

With practiced movements suggesting ritual rather than routine, he demonstrated first on himself, placing a tiny drop on his wrist, then touching wrists together before pressing them lightly to the pulse points at his neck. Each gesture appeared choreographed yet completely natural, the result of cultural knowledge embodied through repetition.

"May I apply some to you?" he asked, the question calibrated perfectly between professional courtesy and intimate possibility.

I extended my wrists in silent answer. His fingers encircled each with deliberate pressure, firm enough to signal intention, gentle enough to indicate respect. The momentary contact became communication more eloquent than words. He turned my wrists upward to receive a small drop of the precious oil, his thumb pressing briefly to each pulse point, ensuring absorption into my warming skin.

"Now here," he said quietly, indicating the hollow of my throat.

I tilted my chin upward, a gesture of acquiescence that felt unexpectedly vulnerable, exposing this most vital area to his touch. His finger pressed lightly at the base of my throat, delivering a single drop of oil before sliding downward in an unhurried caress that ended at my collarbone. The pathways his touch created seemed to ignite beneath my skin, awakening nerve endings I'd forgotten existed.

"And finally," he continued, his voice deepening slightly, "here." He gestured toward the space between my breasts with a question in his eyes.

I unfastened several buttons of my blouse in silent response. The air against my newly exposed skin felt charged, as if molecules had rearranged themselves in anticipation. He applied a final drop of oil to my sternum, his fingertip lingering just long enough to register the quickening of my heartbeat beneath the thin barrier of skin.

The fragrance bloomed against my body's warmth, interacting with my personal chemistry to create something neither of us could have anticipated, a third presence in the room, invisible but undeniable. Each breath drew this presence deeper into my lungs, into my bloodstream, until the distinction between external and internal blurred completely.

"Beautiful," he murmured, inhaling deeply. His pupils dilated visibly, that involuntary physiological response no amount of social conditioning can suppress.

When he stepped closer, his fingers followed the pathway of oil along my skin as though reading some ancient text written in scent. His lips found the pulse point at my throat, and the heat of his mouth against the oil released new dimensions of the fragrance, notes that had remained dormant until activated by this specific combination of body heat, pressure, and breath.

"In my tradition," he whispered, mouth still pressed against my neck, "we believe scent creates the most profound connection possible between people. It mingles in the air we share, enters our lungs, becomes part of our blood."

The poetry of this concept struck me as unexpectedly profound: this idea that something as ethereal as fragrance could create a more fundamental connection than physical touch. He suggested we move to my bedroom, adding, "Would you mind if we dim the lights further than usual? Scent is experienced more intensely when visual input is reduced."

In the resulting half-light, other senses heightened dramatically: the rustle of clothing, the changing quality of our breathing, and most of all, the enveloping presence of the oud oil that intensified as our body temperatures rose.

He undressed me with ceremonial deliberation, pausing at each newly revealed expanse of skin to lower his face and inhale deeply. This wasn't the performative appreciation I've grown accustomed to, the predictable compliments and practiced caresses. Instead, he seemed to be memorizing me through scent rather than sight, creating an olfactory map of my body that existed independent of visual appeal.

When he revealed my breasts, they seemed to transform under his gaze, no longer merely parts of my body but instruments of some ancient ritual we were both remembering rather than discovering. His hands cupped their weight as one might hold precious water from a sacred well – with reverence that transcended desire, though desire pulsed between us like a living creature.

His mouth found my nipple with the certainty of a blind man reading braille – instinctively understanding the story written in my flesh. The wet heat of his tongue traced secret alphabets around the sensitive aureola before drawing the hardened peak between his lips. He suckled with such exquisite precision that I felt myself dissolving at the edges, the boundary between pleasure and existence blurring into meaninglessness.

"Your nipples speak secrets," he murmured, his breath cooling the wetness his mouth had left behind, creating a shiver that seemed to rearrange my internal architecture. "They confess what your professional mask would conceal." To demonstrate this betrayal, he delivered a precise, knowing bite that hovered at the exquisite threshold between pleasure and pain, followed by such tender suction that tears formed at the corners of my eyes – not from discomfort but from the unbearable perfection of the sensation.

When he finally stood naked before me, I beheld him not merely with eyes but with the ancient recognition that exists in the marrow of women's bones. His erection arose not as vulgarity but as primal architecture – a column of flesh both thunderously present and ethereally beautiful in its naked purpose. The swollen head glistened with the first sacred waters of desire, the visible testimony of what invisible currents passed between us.

The curve of his cock – for it curved upward as though seeking some celestial destination – contained an unspoken question that only the hollow spaces of my body could properly answer. In that moment of mutual witnessing, I understood how the reproductive act transcends reproduction itself, becoming instead the physical expression of cosmic forces that care nothing for our small identities and everything for the momentary dissolution of separateness they might create.

He positioned himself above me like a storm cloud pregnant with lightning. The solid weight of his manhood pressed against my inner thigh, leaving a wet trail of anticipation that marked my skin like invisible calligraphy. The space between our bodies vibrated with potential energy that made my sex open like a night-blooming flower, unfurling petals already glistening with the dew of arousal.

I could feel emptiness as a positive presence – a vacuum demanding to be filled, a question formed in flesh awaiting its answer. My inner walls contracted around this absence, rehearsing the embrace they would soon perform. Yet instead of plunging into the welcoming darkness my body offered, he remained suspended above me, his face lowered to the hollow of my throat.

For several timeless moments, we existed in perfect tantric balance, united not through physical joining but through the more profound communion of synchronized breath. My pelvis lifted with instinctive wisdom, allowing my slick labia to graze against the underside of his shaft – a momentary contact that contained such concentrated pleasure it seemed to pause the universe's expansion for the space between heartbeats.

"Breathe me in," he instructed softly. "And I will breathe you."

This simple exchange of breath created an altered consciousness that transcended ordinary arousal. The oud oil's complex fragrance combined with the musky scent of my arousal to form a chemical duet our bodies conducted without conscious participation.

When he finally entered me, it was not merely a physical act but a cosmological event – the moment when separate galaxies finally collide after billions of years of gravitational courtship. He pushed inside with the inexorable patience of continental drift, each millimeter of penetration rewriting the geography of my awareness. The stretching fullness as his considerable girth parted my flesh created a pleasure so complete it transcended the boundary between ecstasy and anguish.

My body received him as temples receive worshippers – with secrets revealed only to those who enter with proper reverence. The ridged head of his phallus dragged against inner landscapes that normally lay dormant, awakening nerve centers that connected to chambers of sensation I had forgotten existed despite my professional expertise.

A sound emerged from somewhere beneath my conscious mind – a primal vocalization that belonged neither to Isabelle the professional nor to any version of myself I recognized. It was the voice of the feminine principle itself acknowledging penetration by its cosmic counterpart.

He paused when fully sheathed within me, the base of his cock pressing against my clitoris with exquisite precision while his full length touched places so deep they seemed connected to my very core. "I can feel your pulse around me," he murmured, his observation causing involuntary contractions that confirmed his words. "Your body speaks a language more honest than words."

He withdrew with ceremonial deliberation before returning to me with renewed purpose, establishing a language of penetration and retreat that seemed to tell the oldest story in existence. His movements alternated between deep, soul-reaching thrusts that touched the very gate of my womb and shallow, teasing strokes that concentrated exquisite attention at my entrance where sensation gathers most densely.

As his rhythm found its perfect expression, he whispered against my heated skin in his native tongue – ancient syllables that required no translation as they vibrated from his lips directly into my flesh. The unknown words carried meaning beyond semantic understanding, speaking directly to the most primitive layer of my brain.

His hands reached beneath me to cup the flesh of my buttocks, fingers pressing into muscle with possessive knowledge as he tilted my pelvis to receive him at an angle that targeted the most responsive territories of my sex. His cock found the hidden constellation of my pleasure with astronomical precision, the swollen head dragging across the subtly ridged landscape of my g-spot with each withdrawal.

My nipples stood erect as monuments to arousal, aching for contact even as his mouth descended to claim one hungry peak. He suckled with perfect pressure, teeth and tongue working in concert to create sensation that traveled directly to my sex like an underground river suddenly surfacing. Meanwhile, his cock maintained its relentless exploration below, the dual penetration of mouth and phallus creating echo chambers of pleasure that amplified each other in feedback loops of increasing intensity.

The tempo of our coupling intensified like a gathering storm, his hips meeting mine with the force of tectonic plates colliding. My professional distance had long since evaporated like morning mist under the harsh truth of undeniable desire. I wrapped my legs around his waist, ankles locking at the small of his back, my heels pressing into the taut muscles of his buttocks to urge him deeper still.

"Take your pleasure from me," he commanded, his voice dropping to a register that seemed to vibrate directly against my cervix. "I want to witness you undone."

I felt his gaze burning into mine – not the empty stare of men who look without seeing but the penetrating observation of one determined to witness transformation. I allowed my hand to descend between us, finding the swollen bud of my clitoris already slick and exquisitely sensitive.

The first circle of my fingers against this concentrated center of feminine desire sent violent tremors cascading through my internal landscape. My sex clutched his thickness with hungry desperation, inner muscles rippling in patterns beyond conscious control. He responded by driving into me with renewed determination, the head of his magnificent cock finding internal territories that made stars explode behind my eyelids.

The dual sensation – his substantial presence stretching me while my fingers worked the sensitive pearl with increasing urgency – created a tension that wound tighter with each passing moment. My thighs began to tremble, the first harbinger of approaching cataclysm, as sweat gathered at the hollow of my throat where our mingled scents collected most intensely.

"Your body is ready to surrender," he observed with intimate knowledge that transcended our brief acquaintance. "I can feel you gathering, preparing to dissolve."

His words, so precisely aligned with my internal reality, created the final bridge between sensation and release. My orgasm arrived not as external event but as fundamental reorganization of my being – a momentary death of the limited self as boundaries dissolved under pleasure's unstoppable assault. Wave after wave of ecstatic contractions seized my womb and sex, each one triggering fresh pulses that rippled outward to finger and toe.

My internal spasms triggered his own surrender, the exquisite grip of my muscles finally shattering his remarkable control. I felt him swell impossibly larger within me before erupting with volcanic force, his essence flooding my depths in hot, rhythmic pulses I could feel against my quivering walls. His face, normally so composed, transformed in that moment of release – all cultural barriers dissolved under the universal expression of male ecstasy.

"Allah," he gasped, the sacred name escaping as involuntary prayer. When our eyes met through the haze of mutual completion, I saw not triumph but wonder – the humbled recognition that some experiences transcend even the most sophisticated understanding.

As we lay joined, aftershocks still rippling between us, I became aware of how the scent had transformed, our shared fragrance now enriched with the musky aroma of sex. Neither of us collapsed into the typical post-orgasmic stupor; instead, we remained alertly present, continuing to breathe each other in, his softening cock still pulsing occasionally inside me as my inner muscles fluttered around him in diminishing contractions.

The moments that followed maintained the same quality of attentive presence that had characterized our entire encounter. Rather than drifting into separate reveries, we remained connected through breath and scent, his fingertips occasionally brushing places where the oil had been applied, reactivating the fragrance in gentle pulses.

"Your skin transforms it beautifully," he said after a long, comfortable silence. "Oud responds differently to each person's chemistry. With you, it becomes something I've never smelled before."

"In the West," I observed, "we spend billions trying to eliminate natural human scent, then billions more trying to replace it with synthetic approximations."

His quiet laughter vibrated against my shoulder. "Yes, an odd contradiction. In my tradition, natural human scent isn't something to be eliminated but rather enhanced, complemented, celebrated."

"The most powerful aphrodisiac," he added after a thoughtful pause, "is often simply paying complete attention. Noticing what most overlook."

In my years of professional intimacy, I'd observed how rare genuine presence has become. So many engage in physical connection while remaining mentally elsewhere.

This man had demonstrated an alternative approach, one that engaged every aspect of consciousness in a unified experience.

When he eventually rose to dress, he left the bottle of oud oil on my nightstand, a gift that represented far more than its considerable monetary value. After he departed, I sat at my dressing table, applying a small drop of the precious oil to a blank page in my client journal. Long after the specific details of our physical connection might fade, this scent would remain, capable of triggering the complete sensory memory with a single inhalation.

•

I carry within me now a secret architecture of understanding. Chambers excavated by this encounter that altered my relationship to the invisible. The amber bottle stands on my dressing table like a talisman, not displayed as conquest but positioned where only I will notice it, a silent witness to dimensions of pleasure modern consciousness has forgotten how to name.

What he awakened in me was not new knowledge but ancient remembrance, the neurological pathways that connect scent directly to the limbic brain, bypassing the rational filters that so often diminish our most profound experiences. Like subterranean rivers flowing beneath the conscious mind, these channels carry messages too primal for language, too essential for interpretation. I had studied these principles in university classrooms, diagrammed them in academic exercises, but never before had I witnessed their orchestration with such deliberate artistry, such intuitive mastery.

His approach, this fusion of ancient wisdom with present connection, revealed how thoroughly we have surrendered to the tyranny of the visual. We modern lovers, inheritors of a fractured sensory heritage, have trained ourselves to want what we can see, neglecting the whispered invitations of scent that might guide us toward more authentic communion. We catalog bodies according to visible attributes while remaining blind to invisible compatibilities that might transform mere coupling into transcendence.

The amber liquid he left behind, both gift and challenge, has become my silent teacher. I've begun incorporating its wisdom into my professional practice, noticing how those most receptive to olfactory dimensions often achieve depths of connection that visually-fixated lovers never discover. Like a musician suddenly granted access to octaves previously beyond hearing, I find myself perceiving new harmonies in encounters that once seemed merely physical.

What haunts me, what follows me through Monaco's perfumed evenings, is the recognition that true sensuality may exist not in what we consciously display but in what we unconsciously emanate, those molecular confessions our bodies whisper despite our intentions. Perhaps the most profound intimacy awaits those brave enough to close their eyes and open these other channels of awareness, to return to forms of knowing that preceded language itself.

I sometimes wonder if our ancestors, lacking our technological extensions but possessing fully awakened senses, experienced connections more genuine than our sophisticated but fragmented modern encounters. Were they more wholly present in their bodies, more fluent in these subtle vocabularies of scent and breath? Did they recognize, as we have forgotten, that the skin communicates in dialects beyond touch, that proximity creates conversations beyond hearing, that true communion often occurs in dimensions we have trained ourselves to ignore?

The amber bottle has become for me not merely vessel of fragrance but container of possibility, a reminder that beneath the visual surface of experience, invisible currents flow between bodies that science can measure but not fully explain. In reclaiming this awareness, I've discovered territories of connection that exist not at the endpoint of desire but in its very atmosphere, the charged space where separate beings momentarily dissolve not just physically but chemically, not just through touch but through transformation of the very air between them.

The Lesson:

Our sense of smell, the most direct connection to our limbic brain, remains the most neglected dimension of contemporary sexuality. This oversight represents the abandonment of an entire channel of intimate communication that provided our ancestors with crucial information about compatibility and health.

Through observation across thousands of encounters, I've noted a strong correlation between olfactory awareness and capacity for pleasure. Those attuned to scent typically experience more profound and nuanced sexual responses than those fixated exclusively on visual stimuli.

Consider how you might incorporate olfactory awareness into your intimate life. Rather than masking your natural fragrance, explore approaches that enhance your unique olfactory signature. Clean skin allowed to maintain its subtle natural aroma often proves more arousing than artificial scents that create olfactory confusion.

When we integrate olfactory awareness into sexual experiences, we access ancient pathways of pleasure that bypass conscious thought, creating more immediate and authentic connection.

The Power of the Pause

Time exists differently in the spaces between sensations. It revealed itself on a night when Monaco's lights punctured the darkness like stars fallen to earth, scattered across the velvet landscape below my windows.

I had just finished watching his documentary, a revelatory study of a prima ballerina's final performance, when the doorbell announced his arrival. The film's emotional resonance still vibrated through me, its artful silences more eloquent than its movements. His work had seduced me long before his body ever could. The way he manipulated time itself, stretching moments, compressing hours, knowing precisely when to sustain a shot beyond comfort, spoke of a mastery that transcended his professional medium. Each viewing left me with the curious sensation of having been touched intimately, though we had yet to cross that threshold.

When I opened the door, he stood like a sentence awaiting punctuation: complete in structure but suspended in meaning until the final mark is placed. His filmmaker's eyes held mine with the same patient focus he applied to his craft, noting every microexpression that might betray my response to his latest work.

"The sequence where she removes her pointe shoes for the last time," I said, stepping aside to welcome him. "Those three seconds of stillness before the camera moved to her face...that's where I found myself holding my breath."

Relief flooded his features, displacing the professional anxiety that had creased the corners of his eyes. "The pause," he replied, following me into my apartment. "Always the most powerful moment, if you know when to use it."

We moved to the terrace, where Monaco's nightscape provided a fitting backdrop for our discussion. The rosé in our glasses caught the ambient light as we spoke of his evolving technique, the confidence with which he now employed silence as a narrative device. His hands conducted invisible stories in the air between us: fingers orchestrating moments, palms cupping seconds, wrists pivoting to reframe reality with the fluidity of his cinematic vision.

"Most people don't understand that editing is mostly about what you remove, not what you keep," he confided, leaning slightly closer. Evening light silvered the threads emerging at his temples, evidence of countless hours spent in darkened editing suites. "It's knowing when to let the audience linger in a moment, when to make them wait."

"Like anticipation in intimacy," I suggested, meeting his gaze without artifice.

"Exactly like that."

The atmosphere between us thickened with possibility, the evening air transformed into something almost tangible with unspoken intent. Neither of us moved to diminish the distance. This, too, was part of our ritual during his infrequent returns to Monaco, this measured approach, this deliberate delay. In his presence, I became acutely aware of how rarely I experienced true anticipation in my professional encounters, how seldom a client understood the power of suspended fulfillment.

His hand finally crossed the space between us, but instead of the expected progression, he merely pressed his middle finger against the inside of my wrist. My pulse quickened beneath his fingertip, an autonomous response no amount of professional experience had taught me to control. Such minimal contact should not have commanded my body's attention so completely, yet heat bloomed everywhere except where he actually touched me, a phantom pleasure mapping my nervous system with inverse logic.

"The most powerful edit," he murmured, "cuts away just as the viewer leans forward."

With this principle clearly established, he withdrew his finger, leaving my skin humming with absence. I rose from my chair, understanding without words that our evening was transitioning to its next sequence. He followed at a calculated distance. Close enough that my body registered his proximity, yet not close enough to satisfy the craving his single touch had awakened.

My bedroom welcomed us with amber light that pooled in the hollows and planes of our bodies as clothing gradually yielded to intention. He stood behind me, his presence registered through senses beyond touch: the subtle displacement of air, the faint scent of sandalwood and clean skin, the almost imperceptible sound of his controlled breathing. His fingers found my zipper, drawing it downward with cinematographic deliberation. The metallic whisper seemed amplified in the quiet room, each tooth surrendering with an individual surrender that stretched seconds into miniature eternities.

Cold air kissed my exposed spine, but his hands did not replace the fabric they had displaced. Instead, his warm breath descended the newly revealed terrain, his lips hovering millimeters from my skin. Close enough that I could feel their heat, yet denied their actual touch. My dress hung suspended from my shoulders, neither removed nor restored. I existed in editorial limbo, a frame frozen between before and after.

The sensitive flesh between my shoulder blades tingled with expectation, my nipples hardening beneath silk that suddenly felt abrasive against their heightened sensitivity. Moisture gathered between my thighs, my body's involuntary preparation for what it sensed was inevitable, yet remained tantalizing out of reach. I felt my sex swell and open like a night-blooming flower, petals unfurling in the darkness, seeking the touch that hovered just beyond their reach.

"Beautiful," he whispered, circling to face me. "Now remain just like this."

His eyes absorbed the partial revelation of my body while his hands hovered millimeters from my collarbone, close enough that the fine hairs on my skin rose to meet him, reaching across impossible distance like supplicants toward salvation.

"The anticipation," he said softly, "is everything."

When his fingertips finally alighted on my skin, the contact was so precisely calibrated that a sound escaped me. Not the practiced response I often offered clients but something startled from a deeper, less choreographed part of myself. His touch traveled the geography of my collarbone with cartographer's attention, then vanished completely.

My body betrayed me, swaying toward the withdrawn pleasure. His mouth curved in quiet recognition of my involuntary response. This, too, was part of his art, observing the effects of his curated absences, the way the eye seeks what is suddenly removed from frame.

"Patience," he instructed, stepping back to create a new composition between us.

He unbuttoned his shirt with meticulous care, each movement a complete narrative with beginning, middle, and end. I recognized the technique from his films, extending a sequence just beyond where convention would dictate the cut, making the viewer acutely conscious of passing time.

As the fabric parted to reveal his torso, softly curved with the gentle roundness of a man devoted to his art rather than his physique, I moved toward him. He captured my wrists with gentle authority, his thumbs finding the pulse points where my heartbeat betrayed my composure.

"Not yet," he said. "First, we learn to appreciate emptiness."

My bed received me as he guided me backward, his control of our physical narrative never faltering. He knelt before me, lifting my foot with unexpected reverence. The removal of my shoe became ceremonial, his thumbs pressing into the arch with precision that located nerves I hadn't known existed. Just as pleasure began to radiate upward; he stopped completely, hands withdrawn, pressure vanished.

In that suspended moment, absence became its own presence between us. My skin prickled with heightened awareness, each nerve ending straining toward where sensation might next appear. This negative space, this deliberate withholding, created tension more exquisite than continuous touch could generate.

When his hands claimed my ankles again, sliding upward along my calves with excruciating patience, my nerves sang with amplified response. Each centimeter he traversed awakened a corresponding internal topography I rarely accessed with clients who rushed toward obvious destinations. He paused again at my knees, his restraint visible in the tightened muscle of his jaw.

"The hardest part of editing," he said, voice rough-edged with desire, "is knowing exactly when to cut away."

His hands continued their ascent, raising my dress as they mapped my thighs. Again he stopped, this time just short of where my body silently pleaded for his touch. The emptiness between his fingertips and my center of arousal vibrated with potential, with unmanifested pleasure held in perfect suspension.

"And when to return," I whispered, recognizing the mastery in his approach.

His smile, rare and transformative, acknowledged our shared understanding of this language. His mouth found my inner thigh at last, no longer teasing but devouring. The wet heat of his tongue worked upward with devastating precision, each lash sending electric jolts to my center. When he reached the silk barrier of my underwear, already darkened with evidence of my arousal, he pressed his open mouth against me, his hot breath penetrating the thin fabric. My hips lifted involuntarily toward his face, abandoning dignity for raw need.

Instead of removing the final barrier between his mouth and my sex, he simply pressed his tongue firmly against the damp silk, creating maddening friction that stimulated without providing direct contact. The fabric transformed into an instrument of exquisite torture, both barrier and conductor of sensation. I could feel the heat of his mouth through the delicate material, the pressure of his tongue finding my swollen clitoris with unerring accuracy despite the obstacle. Just as my breathing shortened into desperate gasps, he withdrew completely, leaving only cool air where his burning mouth had been.

As clothing yielded completely to our progressing narrative, he maintained this pattern: touch and retreat, pressure and release, fullness and emptiness. Each sensation was allowed to bloom fully before vanishing, flowers opening and disappearing in the hothouse of our encounter, establishing a counterpoint of fulfillment and yearning that cultivated hunger within every cell of my body. By the time our bodies joined, I vibrated with arousal rarely achieved even in my extensive experience, my nerves suspended in a state of heightened receptivity that transformed ordinary contact into transcendent communication.

His entry was deliberate, controlled. A slow penetration that allowed me to experience each incremental stretching, each millimeter of accommodation. The exquisite friction as my body yielded to his intrusion left me gasping, my inner walls gripping him with a hunger I rarely allowed myself to acknowledge in professional encounters. My wetness welcomed him, easing his passage while simultaneously heightening every sensation. His thick hardness parted me like a vessel cleaving water, creating waves of pleasure that rippled outward from our point of connection. When fully sheathed within me, so deep I could feel him pressing against territories seldom reached, he remained absolutely motionless, suspending us in perfect stasis.

"Here," he whispered against my ear, "is where we hold the frame."

Everything stopped: his movement, his breathing, time itself. We existed in perfect conjunction, neither advancing nor retreating. Pleasure plateaued at a sustaining peak, neither crescendoing nor diminishing but simply existing in extended present tense. My muscles contracted around him involuntarily, seeking the friction he deliberately withheld. I could feel every vein and ridge of his cock pulsing inside me, my body memorizing his exact shape as though creating an internal cast of his presence.

When he finally resumed movement, each thrust was punctuated by a carefully timed pause, a rhythm that transformed ordinary intercourse into something orchestral, each note given its full value before the next was introduced. He would withdraw almost completely, the swollen head of his cock lingering just inside my entrance, where nerve endings clustered in anticipation, before driving forward again with devastating slowness that allowed me to experience the fullness as if for the first time.

The angle of his penetration deliberately targeted that spongy, ridged territory along my anterior wall, applying precise pressure that made my vision blur and my thighs tremble. I felt myself opening to him in ways beyond the merely physical, my usual professional boundaries dissolving under his methodical deconstruction of pleasure itself.

"Feel how different," he murmured, adjusting slightly to create new pressure against neglected internal landscapes, "when absence precedes presence."

To demonstrate, he withdrew completely, suspended above me in a constellation of near-touches. The clock surrendered its mechanical certainty. One moment elongated beyond its natural boundaries, stretched until time lost coherence. In this liminal emptiness, where arousal typically wanes, mine instead intensified, the void itself becoming a species of pleasure more acute than any physical contact could render. When he finally entered me again, the sensation was so acute that my back arched involuntarily, a cry escaping that held no performance in its rawness.

He established a new cadence then: three deep, measured thrusts followed by complete withdrawal, a pattern that built mathematical tension in my nervous system. My swollen labia glistened with arousal, achingly empty during each retreat, then gloriously stretched with each return. The slick sounds of our connection filled the air, a liquid symphony of desire that punctuated each reunion of our bodies. Each cycle increased the duration of absence, three seconds, then five, then eight, the Fibonacci sequence of deprivation. My hands clutched at his buttocks, trying to prevent his withdrawal, nails leaving crescent indentations in the soft flesh, but he maintained sovereign control of our rhythm.

My clitoris, ignored at first, then attended to with devastating accuracy by his thumb during certain penetrations before being abandoned again, had become a focal point of such acute sensitivity that even the whisper of air across it during his withdrawals elicited involuntary spasms through my pelvis. Each deliberate circle of his thumb sent spirals of almost unbearable pleasure radiating through my core, only to be denied just as the sensation threatened to crest into climax.

When he turned me onto my stomach and entered me from behind, the new angle allowed him to press against previously unexplored depths. His hardness filled me completely, reaching places inside that made stars explode behind my eyelids. His chest pressed against my back, his breathing ragged in my ear as his control began to fray at the edges. My face pressed into the pillow muffled sounds I rarely allow clients to hear: authentic, unfiltered responses to pleasure that transcended my professional performance.

His fingers slid between my legs from the front, finding my clitoris with unerring accuracy while he remained still inside me. The dual sensation, his hardness filling me completely while his fingertips circled that exquisitely sensitive bundle of nerves, created a feedback loop of pleasure that threatened to unravel my composure entirely. Just before I would have tipped over the edge, he withdrew both his cock and his fingers, leaving me suspended in agonizing pleasure-without-release.

"Trust the emptiness," he instructed, his voice strained with his own willed restraint.

The pattern continued until anticipation itself became a form of fulfillment, with my body learning to experience desire as its own pleasure rather than merely the pathway to release. I became a creature composed entirely of sensation, my consciousness contracted to the point where our bodies joined and separated. When orgasm finally approached, it wasn't the familiar cresting wave but something more architectural. A structure built of presence and absence, of fullness and emptiness, each component essential to the integrity of the whole.

Our shared climax, when it arrived, wasn't the desperate collision I'd grown accustomed to with other partners, but a perfectly timed convergence, a montage of sensation cutting seamlessly between separate experiences to create something greater than either could achieve alone. My internal muscles contracted around him in rhythmic waves that milked his own release, the pulsing of his cock inside me triggering secondary spasms that extended my pleasure far beyond its expected boundaries. I felt each hot pulse as he emptied himself inside me, each surge triggering another cascading wave of contractions that seemed to possess a will beyond my control.

His face, normally composed behind his filmmaker's analytical gaze, contorted with naked vulnerability as he emptied himself inside me, his careful control finally and gloriously abandoned. The orgasm radiated from my center in concentric waves, washing through my thighs, my abdomen, my breasts, finally reaching my extremities until even my fingertips seemed to pulse with its echo. The spasms continued long after the initial peak, aftershocks reverberating through nervous systems recalibrated to register nuances typically lost in more conventional encounters.

In the quiet aftermath, he traced meandering constellations on my damp skin, his touch now continuous, the lesson in pauses complete. "The difference between good editing and great editing," he murmured against my shoulder, "is understanding that the cut itself creates meaning. The juxtaposition of presence against absence tells the true story."

My thoughts drifted to the countless clients who approached pleasure as destination rather than terrain: men who rushed toward release as if intimacy were a task to be completed rather than an experience to be inhabited. How rarely I encountered someone who understood that desire itself, properly cultivated, could become more satisfying than its resolution.

"And which parts will remain on the cutting room floor?" I asked, curious about how he might frame this encounter in memory.

"Nothing," he replied without hesitation. "This is the director's cut, the complete vision, preserved exactly as it unfolded."

I smiled into the darkness, recognizing the professional wisdom that had transformed into intimate art. Monaco continued its luminous performance beyond my windows, but my attention remained fixed on the spaces between breaths, between heartbeats, the pauses that had somehow become the most eloquent moments of our encounter.

•

I watch my hand hover above my wineglass now, suspended in mid-air, and think of him. How strange that he transformed even the smallest moments of my daily rituals: this breath before sipping, this delicious second of anticipation that now contains its own pleasure.

We speak so easily of desire as hunger, as flames, as currents. Yet he showed me that desire is also architecture, spaces defined as much by emptiness as by structure. I think of ancient Japanese gardens where a single stone's placement is determined by the emptiness it creates around itself. He touched me the same way, each contact designed to honor the void that would follow, each absence curated to heighten what came next.

The soul grows weary of constant sweetness. My profession has shown me this truth a thousand times: how the steady diet of pleasure eventually dulls the palate. My filmmaker's genius lay in his understanding that pleasure must occasionally withdraw to truly devastate upon its return. Each time he pulled away, my body arched toward the vanished contact, nerves awakening from their slumber, skin becoming a constellation of heightened awareness.

I saw him later that year, through the blue light of my television, accepting his industry's highest honor. "For masterful understanding of rhythm and timing," the presenter read. In my darkened apartment, I raised my glass to secrets those applauding hands would never know. How thoroughly those skills had translated beyond his frames of celluloid.

Then came that terrible morning, the industry newsletter open on my screen, his face suddenly bordered in black. Highway collision. Instantaneous. No lingering farewell, no gradual diminuendo. Just brutal, sudden silence. For a man who orchestrated pauses with such exquisite precision, the universe offered only blunt, graceless interruption.

I waited, absurdly, for his return. For some continuation after this most profound pause. My body remembered the pattern: withdrawal followed by presence, absence creating hunger for return. But this time, the emptiness remained, expanded, took residence in places I had thought impervious to such occupation. I, who had cultivated professional detachment as others might cultivate rare orchids, found myself inhabited by an absence more substantial than any presence had ever been.

We rehearse separation in these small withdrawals, these artful pauses between touches, never understanding we practice for deeper losses. Perhaps all pleasure contains this bitter seed, this knowledge that everything returns to silence eventually. The filmmaker taught me the power of the pause, but failed to prepare me for the one pause that permits no resumption, no eventual return of contact.

Even now, my skin sometimes wakens in darkness, remembering his particular rhythm of approach and retreat. My body still carries the ghost-prints of his hands, still waits for the completion of a sequence interrupted mid-frame. I find myself leaning forward unconsciously, like his audience must have done during those extended shots he refused to cut. Waiting, breath suspended, for the resolution that never comes.

The Lesson:

Continuous pleasure eventually becomes background noise to the nervous system. The strategic introduction of pauses, moments where stimulation is temporarily withdrawn, resets sensory awareness and intensifies subsequent sensation. This principle can revolutionize intimate encounters when applied with intention.

Begin by slowing your default tempo. Before removing clothing, before moving to the next stage of intimacy, pause. Allow anticipation to build in that suspended moment. When touching your partner, periodically lift your hand entirely away from their skin for several seconds before resuming contact. The return of sensation after absence creates a magnified response that continuous touch cannot achieve.

Practice edging, bringing yourself or your partner to the threshold of climax, then pausing, retreating slightly before continuing. This technique not only prolongs pleasure but dramatically intensifies the eventual release. Remember that the brain's pleasure centers respond more powerfully to intermittent rewards than to constant stimulation.

Most importantly, approach these pauses not as interruptions but as essential components of the experience, negative space that defines and enhances what surrounds it. The pause itself becomes a form of communication, a moment of heightened awareness that transforms physical sensation into profound connection.

The Language of Touch

Hands remember what minds forget. This truth revealed itself to me long before I understood its significance, before I recognized how fingers retain histories that words cannot capture, how skin harbors memories that language fails to preserve. My profession has transformed me into an unwitting scholar of tactile communication, able to read intentions, histories, and desires through the silent eloquence of flesh against flesh, that most ancient dialect that preceded all others.

The request materialized through my discrete messaging service: a professor of linguistics sought not conventional pleasures but an exploration of touch as language. His academic interest in what he called "haptic communication" awakened my curiosity enough to accept this unusual proposition. After two decades of intimate encounters, the opportunity to articulate what my hands had learned through thousands of exchanges offered its own unexpected seduction.

Monaco surrendered to rain that afternoon, transforming its typically brilliant landscape into impressionist brushstrokes of gray. Water struck my windows with percussive insistence as I arranged my apartment, not for seduction but for exploration. I selected fabrics of varying textures, oils of different viscosities, their amber depths catching light as I poured them into shallow porcelain dishes. I cleared sufficient space for what would essentially become a laboratory of physical communication, though one where the boundaries between science and art would inevitably dissolve.

He arrived, rainfall clinging to his wool coat and eyeglasses, tiny crystalline universes that refracted light as he moved. Tall and angular, with hands I immediately noticed: long-fingered and expressive, gesturing in unconscious counterpoint to his speech as if conducting an invisible orchestra. They betrayed his profession: slightly ink-stained at the cuticles, with the particular callus on the middle finger that comes from years of handwriting. Yet they moved with an intuitive grace that suggested potential beyond his academic bearing, a dexterity that whispered promises his words would never make.

"Most professionals misunderstood my request," he explained as he accepted herbal tea rather than my usual offering of wine. His voice carried the particular accent of the perpetual expatriate. Traces of multiple countries creating a transnational blend that belonged everywhere and nowhere simultaneously. "They assumed I was using academic interest as pretext for conventional services."

"Perhaps because few consider touch itself worthy of scholarly attention," I replied, settling into my armchair as thunder emphasized my words with cosmic punctuation. "Western philosophy has long privileged the distance senses, sight and hearing, while treating touch as primitive and unreliable."

His eyes brightened with intellectual recognition, a flush spreading beneath the scholarly pallor of his cheeks. "Precisely! Yet touch predates language evolutionarily and developmentally. We communicate through contact before we master words."

"And often more honestly," I added, watching how his body leaned forward in unconscious affirmation of his interest, the space between us charged with unacknowledged currents. "Hands rarely lie, even when words construct elaborate fictions."

Our initial conversation unfolded with the particular pleasure of minds recognizing unexpected kinship. As rain transformed the world outside into watercolor impressions, we established parameters for our exploration: a structure that would allow systematic investigation while preserving space for discovery. The intellectual dance created its own form of foreplay, ideas touching and withdrawing, approaching and retreating in patterns that mirrored more primal rhythms.

"Shall we begin with fundamentals?" I suggested, moving to sit beside him on my sofa. The proximity altered our dynamic immediately, like a chemical reaction triggered by reduced distance. I poured warming oil into my palms, the scent of sandalwood rising between us like an invisible veil. "If touch constitutes language, then it must contain analogous elements, vocabulary, syntax, emphasis, dialects."

He nodded, extending his hands toward mine with the openness of a true researcher, curious rather than expectant. I began with what might be considered isolated phonemes of touch, individual contacts that form the building blocks of tactile expression. The first brush of my fingers against his upturned palm sent a visible current through him, his pupils dilating in involuntary response.

"The fingertip," I demonstrated, drawing a single finger across his upturned palm with deliberate slowness, watching how the simple contact sent blood rushing to the surface of his skin, "communicates precision and specificity. It asks questions, seeks pathways, expresses curiosity." I watched how his breathing shifted slightly, his focus intensifying, the rise and fall of his chest quickening almost imperceptibly. "The full palm, by contrast, makes statements. It claims knowledge rather than seeking it."

I pressed my palm against his, feeling the heat that bloomed between our hands, demonstrating the difference between questioning and declaring through physical contact. His eyes narrowed slightly, processing this distinction not merely intellectually but somatically. His body understanding before his mind could analyze.

"Different pressure creates different meaning," I continued, varying the force behind identical movements, feeling his pulse quicken beneath my touch. "Light pressure suggests possibility; firm pressure expresses certainty." I implemented these variations across his forearm, watching how his pupils dilated in response to firmer contact, the body registering information before the mind processed it, desire preceding comprehension.

"And location fundamentally alters meaning," I explained, using identical circular motions at different points, wrist, palm, inside elbow, each creating visibly different responses. The hollow of his elbow proved particularly responsive, his breath catching when my fingers lingered there, discovering the secret geography of sensitivity that mapped his form. "The same 'word' spoken in different locations conveys entirely different messages."

His analytical mind engaged fully with these distinctions. But gradually, I watched intellectual understanding give way to something more primal, his responses shifting from thought to instinct as our exploration deepened. A flush had begun to spread across his throat, rising toward his cheeks in a tide of blood that betrayed what his scholarly composure attempted to conceal.

"Let me demonstrate syntax," I suggested, moving from isolated touches to sequences that created narratives of approach and withdrawal, tension and release. "Just as words form sentences through arrangement, touches create meaning through progression and rhythm."

I guided his arm to rest on my thigh, affording better access for demonstration while creating a new circuit of awareness between us. My flesh warmed beneath the weight of his forearm, my skin tingling with heightened sensitivity. My fingers composed phrases of sensation, alternating pressure with feather-light contact, creating pauses that functioned as commas or periods within tactile sentences. His breathing deepened as his focus narrowed to these points of connection between us, the academic detachment in his gaze gradually melting into something more primal.

"Remarkable," he murmured, scientific curiosity momentarily overcoming physical response. "There's semantic content being conveyed without a single word."

"Now notice how the same physical movement changes meaning when the emotional context shifts," I continued, executing identical patterns while deliberately altering my facial expression and body language, from nurturing to seductive, from comforting to commanding. The atmosphere between us thickened with each transition, air becoming something palpable we swallowed with each breath.

His eyes widened at this demonstration, a visible tremor passing through his body. "Pragmatics," he whispered, the academic term emerging as something like a prayer. "The social context of utterances shaping meaning."

"Precisely," I replied, pleased by his understanding even as I noted how his intellectual framework provided necessary scaffolding for his growing arousal. "Touch never occurs in isolation from other communicative channels."

As our exploration progressed, I suggested moving to my bedroom where fuller expression would be possible. He followed without hesitation, his researcher's curiosity having overcome initial awkwardness. The rain continued its liquid percussion against windows as I dimmed lights to reduce visual dominance, allowing tactile sensation greater prominence. The shadows transformed the familiar landscape of my room into something mysterious, the bed a continent waiting to be discovered.

"May I?" I asked, reaching for the buttons of his shirt after removing my own outer garments. With his nod, I began creating expanded access for our tactile conversation, not as prelude to conventional intimacy but as extension of our linguistic exploration. Yet my fingers trembled slightly against the buttons, my own desire beginning to color what had begun as demonstration.

His chest revealed itself as I parted fabric, lean but surprisingly defined, with sparse dark hair across pectorals that rose and fell with increasingly rapid breaths. The heat emanating from his exposed skin carried the sweet musk of arousal, a scent language communicating directly to my most primal brain. I guided him to recline on my bed, where I could demonstrate more complex tactile expressions, his body supine before me like text awaiting interpretation.

"Notice how different parts of the hand communicate distinct intentions," I explained, alternating between fingertips, palms, knuckles, and nails across the landscape of his torso. Each variation elicited markedly different responses, the subtle arch of his back when nails lightly grazed his ribs, drawing rosy lines across pale skin; the settling deeper into the mattress when palms spread firm pressure across his shoulders, releasing tension he hadn't known he carried.

"The body develops fluency in receiving touch just as it does in giving it," I told him, watching how his responses evolved, becoming more nuanced as he learned to distinguish subtler variations in my communication. His nipples had hardened under my attention, dark peaks rising from the pale terrain of his chest. "Receptive vocabulary expands through exposure."

His hands eventually began reciprocating, initially with academic precision, attempting to replicate what I'd demonstrated, moving with the careful exactitude of a student practicing penmanship. I closed my eyes to focus completely on his tactile "speech," providing feedback through my own physical responses, allowing small sounds of pleasure to escape when his touch found particularly eloquent expression.

"Your touch reveals your thinking," I observed when I opened my eyes again, meeting his gaze directly. "You're translating concepts into contact rather than speaking directly through your hands."

He laughed softly, the truth landing. "How does one move beyond translation?"

"The same way one becomes fluent in any language," I replied, placing my hand over his and guiding a more intuitive movement across my collarbone, where my skin rose to meet his touch like water responding to moon. "Through immersion. Through forgetting you're speaking a language at all."

This perspective appeared to liberate something in him. His touch gradually transformed, losing its deliberate quality and discovering natural eloquence. No longer merely replicating patterns I'd shown him, his hands began expressing authentic intention, curiosity, appreciation, emerging desire that communicated itself through increasing pressure, through lingering contacts that conveyed reluctance to break connection.

As clothing yielded further to exploration, our tactile conversation deepened. His fingers discovered the dip of my waist, the subtle flare of hip, the varied textures of my skin, reading my body's topography with increasing confidence, mapping territories of greater sensitivity with explorer's attention. I demonstrated how the same motion carried different implications when applied to different landscapes: how circular movements that relaxed tension at the shoulder became charged with erotic potential when spiraling toward the inner thigh, how the same pressure that soothed at the back could awaken hunger at the breast.

My hands reciprocated his explorations, mapping the territories of his body, discovering the particular sensitivity at the juncture of neck and shoulder that made him gasp when teeth gently grazed the skin there; the responsiveness of nipples that surprised him with their intensity, his sharp intake of breath when my tongue circled the hardened peak; the changing landscape of his abdomen as breathing patterns shifted with arousal, muscles tensing and releasing beneath my wandering fingers.

"The most sophisticated touch contains both statement and question simultaneously," I explained as my fingers descended toward the unmistakable evidence of his arousal straining against remaining clothing, the fabric tented with desire that could no longer be concealed. "It both offers and inquires."

When my hand finally enclosed him, after removing the last barriers between us, his sharp intake of breath spoke volumes about the difference between intellectual understanding and embodied experience. The velvet hardness of him pulsed against my palm, heat radiating through my fingers as I explored his length with appreciative attention. His cock twitched against my hand, communicating without words or conscious intention, blood speaking to blood in the most ancient conversation.

"Notice," I instructed softly, demonstrating variations in grip, rhythm, and direction, watching how his face contorted with pleasure as I found particularly effective combinations, "how different approaches fundamentally alter sensation. There is no single 'correct' touch, only different statements in different contexts."

His ability to remain present, to experience sensation while maintaining awareness, impressed me. Many clients surrender entirely to feeling, losing reflective capacity in the flush of arousal. He inhabited the rare space between abandonment and analysis, experiencing fully while still perceiving patterns and meanings. His hands gripped the sheets when particular sensations threatened to overwhelm him, the tendons standing out in sharp relief against his skin.

When I straddled him, our exploration having evolved naturally into more explicit intimacy, I continued our tactile education. "The entire body speaks through contact," I explained, guiding him inside me with deliberate slowness, feeling the exquisite stretch as my body accommodated his substantial girth. The heat of him reached places words never could, filling emptiness I hadn't recognized until that moment. "Even internal touch communicates distinct intentions."

I began demonstrating how different movements create varied sensations despite identical physical connection: how a subtle rocking motion emphasizes external stimulation while deeper movements access interior sensitivity, how changing angle redirects pressure against different internal landscapes. His hands found my hips, fingers pressing into muscle with newfound confidence. Where earlier they had moved with academic precision, they now expressed authentic desire, no longer mimicking patterns but discovering their own eloquence in the language of possession and pleasure.

"You're becoming fluent," I acknowledged, genuine pleasure coloring my voice as his touch discovered pathways to authentic response, as my body answered his unspoken questions with unmistakable affirmation.

Then I felt it, the sudden change in his breathing, the unexpected tightening of his grip, the involuntary upward thrust of his hips. Before I could adjust our rhythm or offer guidance, his body seized in premature release. A flush spread across his chest as his eyes widened in surprise and embarrassment, his climax arriving like an unexpected guest, far earlier than either of us had anticipated. I felt the hot pulse of his release inside me, his cock throbbing with each wave of pleasure that claimed him.

"I'm sorry," he whispered, intellectual composure momentarily shattered by physical reality. "I didn't—"

I placed my finger gently against his lips, stopping his apology. "This too is communication," I said softly, feeling the final tremors of his orgasm subsiding within me. "Bodies speak truth when minds would prefer fiction. There's no failure here. Only information."

His expression revealed the peculiar vulnerability that follows unexpected release, that moment when carefully constructed persona yields to biological reality. For a man who lived primarily in his intellect, this surrender of control clearly represented unfamiliar territory. The flush had spread to his face, staining his cheeks with evidence of emotional exposure more revealing than physical nudity.

"Touch includes moments of acceleration and delay," I continued, maintaining our physical connection as I felt him begin to soften inside me, creating gentle internal movements that prolonged his pleasure while preventing immediate withdrawal. "Just as conversation includes pauses, interruptions, and unexpected turns."

Rather than separating or treating the moment as conclusion, I guided his hand to the center of my pleasure, where blood had gathered in expectant hunger. "Now we simply shift dialects," I suggested, showing him how fingers could continue our conversation where other parts had temporarily finished speaking. The first contact of his fingers against my swollen, slick flesh drew a gasp from me, nerves singing with heightened sensitivity.

His touch, initially hesitant with lingering embarrassment, gradually regained confidence under my guidance. I demonstrated pressure variations and rhythmic patterns that maintained our intimate dialogue despite the change in physical expression. His academic curiosity resurfaced, intellectual engagement providing bridge across momentary awkwardness. The combination of his fingers exploring externally while his softening cock remained inside me created a delicious fullness that sent tendrils of pleasure spreading through my pelvis.

"Notice how my body responds differently now," I instructed, arching slightly as his fingers found a particularly effective rhythm against my clitoris, electricity gathering at my center with increasing intensity. "Earlier arousal changes sensitivity. Touches that might have been merely pleasant before now create more intense response."

His fascination with this sensory education helped him move beyond self-consciousness, his fingers becoming increasingly eloquent as they explored this new form of communication. When I guided his mouth to my breast, showing how the combination of manual and oral stimulation creates compound sensation, he applied his newfound tactile knowledge with remarkable adaptability. The wet heat of his mouth closing around my nipple while his fingers maintained their rhythm below sent shocks of pleasure traveling between these points of contact, creating internal constellations of sensation.

"Multiple points of contact create harmonies rather than merely melodies," I explained between increasingly shallow breaths as pleasure built within me, coiling tighter with each circle of his fingers. His hands and mouth worked in counterpoint, creating complex patterns of sensation that demonstrated his rapid learning curve. My hips began moving of their own accord, pressing harder against his touch, wordlessly communicating growing urgency.

When my climax finally arrived, a genuine response that surprised me with its intensity, his eyes watched with undisguised wonder, all embarrassment forgotten in the face of this new discovery. My inner muscles contracted rhythmically around his still-present cock as waves of pleasure radiated outward from where his fingers maintained perfect pressure. The sensation built beyond what I had anticipated, my professional boundaries momentarily dissolving as genuine abandon claimed me. After thousands of professional encounters, I've learned to distinguish between physical response and authentic pleasure. This moment contained elements of the latter, a testament to the unusual nature of our exchange.

As our breathing gradually settled, we lay together in the dim light of late afternoon, rain still playing its gentle percussion against windows, creating a liquid boundary between our intimate world and the city beyond. His hand rested on my hip, thumb describing small unconscious circles that spoke of continued presence without demand. Our bodies remained connected, though the nature of that connection had transformed from urgency to reflection.

"I've interviewed dozens of experts on nonverbal communication," he said eventually, his voice thoughtful in the ambient glow. "None articulated the systematic nature of tactile language as clearly as you've demonstrated today."

I smiled, appreciating his ability to return to intellectual framework without losing the embodied experience we'd shared. "Perhaps because most research examines touch in public contexts, where it's necessarily abbreviated. The complete vocabulary emerges only in intimate spaces."

He was quiet for a moment before adding, "And I suspect few researchers discuss the communicative aspects of… timing difficulties."

"Most people mistake bodily responses for personal failures rather than valuable data," I replied, shifting slightly to better see his face, feeling the pleasant soreness where our bodies had joined. "What you experienced simply demonstrates that intellectual control sometimes yields to embodied reality, itself an important aspect of tactile communication."

His expression relaxed further, the last vestiges of embarrassment dissolving. "I suppose academic detachment has its limits."

"Those limits," I suggested, my fingers tracing the line where his chest hair narrowed toward his navel, "often mark the territory where genuine discovery begins."

"The implications are profound," he mused, his fingers still moving in that unconscious pattern against my skin, creating ripples of subtle pleasure that maintained our connection. "If we conceptualized touch as language rather than merely sensation, we might approach physical intimacy entirely differently."

As our session drew to its natural conclusion and he prepared to leave, dressing with a new physical awareness that transformed even this mundane activity, I found myself reflecting on what we'd discovered together. While I had guided our exploration, I too had gained new insights into the communicative potential of touch, articulating through demonstration what had previously existed as unconscious knowledge.

At my door, rain having finally subsided to gentle misting, he took my hand in parting. The pressure of his fingers against mine spoke volumes: gratitude, respect, and lingering pleasure communicated more eloquently than his accompanying words of appreciation.

After he had gone, I stood at my window watching Monaco emerge from its liquid veil. Streetlights illuminating rain-slicked streets into rivers of gold. I contemplated how many intimate relationships suffer not from lack of desire but from impoverished tactile vocabulary. Lovers speaking in rudimentary touch-phrases when they might compose poetry through contact. My own body still hummed with the afterglow of pleasure, nerves singing with memories my skin would retain long after conscious recollection faded.

•

What fascinates me most about these encounters is how knowledge finds a home not merely in the mind but within the secret chambers of our flesh. When the linguist first arrived, his curiosity was purely cerebral, touch as theoretical language to be dissected and cataloged. Yet as evening deepened around us like darkening wine, I watched understanding migrate from his head to his hands, from concept to blood and nerve. His transformation reminded me of watching ice melt into water, something rigid and defined dissolving into fluid possibility.

I've seen this metamorphosis countless times behind my doors: the beautiful moment when thinking surrenders to feeling, when touch escapes the cage of intention to become its own wild poetry. His fingers, initially moving with the hesitancy of a scholar afraid of misquotation, gradually found their own voice, discovering an eloquence his extensive vocabulary could never articulate. It is always this way with bodies; they know truths our minds struggle to confess.

The Western world has largely forgotten what my grandmother in La Trinité understood instinctively, that before we speak with tongues, we converse through skin. I remember how she would cradle my face between palms textured by olive harvests, communicating entireties of love without a single syllable. Yet somewhere between childhood and sophistication, we severed ourselves from this primal wisdom, relegating touch to medicalized or sexualized contexts that drain it of its natural eloquence. We became like musicians who have forgotten how to play without sheet music.

I sense this amnesia deepening with each passing year in Monaco. New clients arrive with increasing hesitancy, their hands betraying a peculiar uncertainty, as if they are travelers who have forgotten their native language. When we communicate primarily through glass screens that never yield or warm to our touch, do we gradually unlearn the dialect our ancestors spoke so fluently? The awkward, truncated gestures of otherwise articulate people suggest a new form of illiteracy spreading silently among us.

I encountered the linguist years later at a conference in Vienna where spring had dressed the city in blossoms that fell like snow across ancient cobblestones. He approached after my presentation, accompanied by a woman whose connection to him required no explanation. Their bodies conversed in a private language developed over time: the unconscious synchronization of their movements, the way his hand found the small of her back without looking, how she leaned almost imperceptibly toward him when another speaker approached.

"Your insights fundamentally changed my research," he told me, introducing his companion as both colleague and lover. "We've been exploring touch as a complete communicative system in its own right, not merely supplementary to spoken language."

As they described their work, I watched the more compelling conversation happening beneath their words. A tactile dialogue composed of seemingly incidental contacts. His thumb briefly circled her wrist while she spoke; she responded by shifting her weight subtly toward him; his shoulder settled against hers in acknowledgment. This wordless exchange contained more intimacy than their formal explanations, like a melody playing beneath recited text.

Their unconscious fluency made clear to me why my unusual vocation carries meaning beyond the pleasure it provides. In a world increasingly divorced from physical presence, where screens mediate our connections and distances compress through technology while paradoxically expanding in our experience, I preserve something ancient and essential. Each client who leaves my apartment with greater awareness of their embodied existence carries forward a heritage that predates all our sophisticated technologies and philosophies.

The most profound moments in my profession have never involved elaborate technique or performance, but rather those rare, sacred instances when two people momentarily dissolve the boundaries between self and other through the simple miracle of attuned touch. In these suspended moments, we remember what we have always known beneath our forgetting: that before language, before civilization, before all our complex systems of meaning, we communicated most honestly through the press of skin against skin, through the ancient grammar of desire that needs no translation.

The Lesson:

The body speaks a language older than words, yet receives almost no formal education. How curious that we force children to recite conjugations of irregular French verbs, yet never teach them the difference between a touch that questions and a touch that declares. Through my years in this most intimate of classrooms, I've discovered that physical fluency has little to do with technical virtuosity and everything to do with the courage to be fully present in one's skin.

To rediscover your own tactile voice, begin by slowing down enough to inhabit each gesture completely. Experiment with the infinite gradations between light and firm, from contact so delicate it barely disturbs the tiny hairs on skin to pressure that anchors and grounds. Play with time as a musician plays with tempo, stretches of continuous contact followed by tantalizing absence, predictable rhythms shattered by sudden improvisation. Notice how identical movements can speak entirely different truths depending on their execution. How a single fingertip traveling the landscape of an inner arm might ask a question, offer comfort, or ignite desire based on nothing more than tiny variations in pressure, pace, and intent.

Remember that like all true conversation, touch involves both speaking and listening. When being touched, try silencing the voice that immediately plots your response or analyzes the technique. Instead, let sensation write itself directly onto your awareness without translation. Receive before you reply. The most transcendent physical dialogues occur when neither person is performing or calculating. When hands are allowed to speak their own truth without the mind's constant editorial interference.

The most beautiful love letters I've ever witnessed contained no words at all, just the exquisite calligraphy of fingertips writing poems across the landscape of another's waiting skin, messages that eyes cannot read but bodies never forget.

Part 2: Psychology & Connection

His hands moved with practiced expertise across my skin, yet I felt nothing beyond mechanical response. Despite his evident skill, despite my body's automatic reactions, something essential remained untouched. Then our eyes met accidentally, a moment of unplanned connection, and suddenly every sensation intensified a hundredfold. In that instant of genuine presence, the geography of pleasure transformed completely.

This peculiar alchemy, how momentary authenticity can transmute ordinary touch into transcendent sensation, reveals the exquisite paradox at intimacy's core. Our bodies and minds are not separate territories but a single, seamless landscape where psychological connection amplifies physical pleasure beyond recognition.

Yet how desperately we guard against true vulnerability even as we hunger for it. I've watched billionaires who command global empires tremble at the prospect of being truly seen by another human being. I've felt my own carefully constructed professional distance dissolve unexpectedly in moments of startling authenticity. We construct elaborate defenses against the very connection we most desire, creating intimacy's central contradiction.

In the chapters that follow, we explore the erotic power of genuine presence, the strange courage required to surrender control, the distinctive pleasure that emerges when boundaries are not eliminated but consensually crossed. Here you'll discover how the mind itself becomes the most powerful erogenous zone when properly engaged, how psychological attunement creates physical responses no technique alone could generate.

I offer these observations not from clinical distance but from the wisdom of a body that has experienced thousands of encounters, cataloging with scientific precision which elements transform mechanical coupling into meaningful connection. The most profound revelation? That the courage to be truly known creates sensations more intense than any physical skill could ever provide.

The Connection Beyond the Physical

A child's red balloon drifted skyward outside my window, freed from some small hand along the harbor. I watched its ascent, untethered yet not truly free, still bound by invisible forces guiding its journey. How we romanticize such escapes, I thought, imagining liberation in what is actually disconnection. The balloon was not free but lost, severed from purpose, from the joy it was created to bring, from the small hands meant to hold its string.

How often we mistake detachment for freedom.

It was one of those late autumn evenings when Monaco's light possesses a particular quality, softer than summer's glare yet more defined than winter's pallor. The sea had transformed into beaten copper beneath the setting sun while shadows stretched like liquid across my apartment floor.

Into this gilded hour arrived the quantum physicist.

He moved with precision, each gesture economical as if conserving energy for thoughts that required it more. Silver threaded through his dark hair, suggesting both wisdom and a certain untamed quality rarely found in men of science. His eyes, observant, curious, seeking, held the particular intensity I've come to recognize in those who spend their lives pursuing what cannot be easily seen. My body responded to this intensity with its own silent awakening, a subtle dampening between my thighs that caught me by surprise with its immediacy.

"The nature of my work," he explained after preliminary pleasantries, "involves accepting that particles can remain connected across vast distances, influencing each other instantaneously in ways that defy our conventional understanding of space and time." He smiled then, a brief softening of his otherwise serious demeanor. "It requires believing in connections that transcend physical explanation."

Something in his phrasing captured my attention. This notion of connections that exist beyond physical constraints. How curious that a man who devoted his life to understanding the universe's invisible bonds should seek me out, a woman whose profession is often reduced to the merely physical when it encompasses so much more.

His fingers circled the rim of his wine glass with the same precise attention I imagined he brought to his experimental apparatus. "I've spent twenty years studying quantum entanglement," he said, his gaze now meeting mine directly. "Two particles, once connected, remain influenced by each other regardless of distance. Einstein called it 'spooky action at a distance.'" A moment's pause.

"I've always wondered if human connections might operate according to similar principles."

The vulnerability beneath his intellectual framing was unmistakable. How many of us clothe our deepest questions in the language of our expertise? His was a soul seeking confirmation that connection transcends the physical, that intimacy operates on planes beyond the merely corporeal. This, I realized, would be an encounter not merely of bodies but of minds seeking similar truths through different languages.

I approached him with unhurried deliberation. His breath caught almost imperceptibly as my fingers followed the line of his jaw, a small data point suggesting deeper currents beneath his composed exterior. His skin carried the faint scent of sandalwood and something more elemental, like petrichor, the earth's exhalation after rain.

"Perhaps," I suggested, my voice deliberately soft, "we might explore this question of connection through direct observation rather than theory."

His smile revealed a different facet of the serious scientist, a flash of playfulness, a willingness to step beyond the rigors of his discipline. "The scientific method does demand empirical evidence," he conceded, his hands finding my waist with surprising certainty.

When our lips met, I perceived immediately that his approach to kissing revealed the same attention to detail evident in his conversation, methodical yet somehow undiminished by this precision. Each point of contact between us seemed to generate its own field of awareness, a heightened sensitivity that spread outward from our joined mouths. I guided him toward a deeper surrender, showing without words how intention can transform a kiss from mechanical process into communion.

My tongue teased the seam of his lips until they parted, granting me access to the warm, wet territory beyond. The taste of him, wine-dark and slightly mineral, flooded my senses as our tongues met, first tentatively, then with increasing boldness. His hands tightened at my waist, pulling me closer until I could feel the hard evidence of his desire pressing against my abdomen. My nipples hardened in immediate response, the thin silk of my blouse suddenly an unbearable barrier between his chest and mine.

"Remarkable," he murmured against my lips, "how something as simple as this creates such cascading effects throughout the entire system."

I smiled at his framing, the scientist still present even as the man began to awaken to sensation. "The body is the most complex system you'll ever explore," I replied, taking his hand and placing it against the pulse point at my throat. "And unlike your particles, it responds to observation."

His fingers lingered there, registering the quickening rhythm beneath my skin. Something shifted in his expression. A recognition that he stood at the threshold between abstract knowledge and embodied understanding. I've witnessed this moment countless times: when intellect gives way to sensation, when the mind that knows surrenders to the body that feels.

I led him toward my bedroom where afternoon light had softened into the golden glow of early evening. With deliberate movements, I began unbuttoning his shirt, revealing skin that rarely saw sunlight, the pale landscape of a man whose natural habitat was the laboratory rather than the beach. Yet there was beauty in this pallor, in the vulnerability of a body unaccustomed to being seen.

"In your work," I asked as my fingers skimmed the unexpected definition of his chest, feeling his nipples harden beneath my touch, "do you find that observation changes the behavior of what you study?"

His breath deepened as my touch moved lower, tracing the thin line of dark hair that disappeared beneath his waistband. The muscles of his abdomen contracted involuntarily beneath my exploratory fingers. "The observer effect," he confirmed, voice slightly strained. "The act of measurement inevitably alters what's being measured."

"Then consider this research," I whispered, my lips finding the sensitive hollow between his collarbones, my tongue tasting the salt of his skin. "Observe how your body responds when I do this."

A sound escaped him, half laugh, half gasp, as my tongue painted patterns against his skin. My teeth grazed his nipple, and his hands flew to my hair, fingers threading through the strands with sudden urgency. His academic control was slipping, revealing something raw and hungry beneath.

His hands, initially hesitant, found greater certainty as they moved across the silk of my blouse, learning the topography beneath. When I guided those hands to the buttons, he needed no further instruction, revealing me with the same careful attention he might bring to unveiling a new experimental apparatus.

"Beautiful," he murmured as my lace-covered breasts spilled into his waiting palms. His thumbs circled my hardened nipples through the delicate fabric, creating electric currents that shot directly to my sex. I felt myself growing slick and swollen beneath his touch, my body's ready response to his careful exploration.

I stepped away briefly, allowing him to fully witness me in the amber light as I removed my bra with deliberate slowness. His eyes darkened visibly as my breasts were fully revealed, their weight settling naturally in the evening air. His Adam's apple bobbed as he swallowed hard, his gaze traveling the length of my body not with the objectifying assessment I've sometimes encountered but with reverent attention, as if memorizing a landscape essential to his understanding of the world.

"Physics teaches us that solid matter is mostly empty space," he said softly. "Atoms are vast voids with tiny particles creating the illusion of solidity through force fields and probability patterns." His fingers reached out to caress the curve of my hip, slipping beneath the waistband of my skirt with newfound boldness. "And yet, nothing has ever felt more substantive, more real, than this moment of connection."

This observation, this recognition of the paradox between scientific understanding and lived experience, created an unexpected intimacy between us. In that moment, I understood precisely what he sought: not escape from his intellectual understanding but integration with his embodied existence. The marriage of knowing and feeling that eludes so many who dwell primarily in the mind.

As we moved together onto my bed, I guided him to lie back against the pillows, positioning myself above him with deliberate grace.

"Sometimes," I suggested, "surrender precedes discovery. Let yourself experience before analyzing."

His eyes closed briefly as I drew feather-light patterns across his chest, awakening nerve endings long neglected in his pursuit of abstract understanding. The scientist momentarily receded, allowing the man beneath to emerge, a being of flesh and desire rather than calculation and theory.

When my lips followed the path my fingers had traveled, his breathing altered, deepening into the rhythm of arousal that transcends education, profession, and intellect, the ancient cadence of the body remembering its primary purpose. I moved with unhurried deliberation, allowing each sensation to bloom fully before introducing the next, creating a continuity of pleasure rather than isolated moments of stimulation.

My mouth traced the contours of his abdomen, tongue exploring the shallow indentation of his navel while my hands worked at his belt buckle. The metallic sound of his zipper descending seemed unnaturally loud in the quiet room. Beneath the fine wool of his trousers, his erection strained against the thin cotton of his underwear, a damp spot already visible at its tip. The evidence of his desire sent a corresponding flood of warmth between my own legs.

"The difference," he gasped as my mouth journeyed lower, teeth grazing his hipbone, "between theoretical knowledge and direct experience is..." His words dissolved into a sound more primal as my tongue traced the hard outline of his cock through cotton, feeling it twitch and swell further beneath my attention.

I paused, looking up at him with a smile. "Perhaps analysis can wait?"

His answering laugh contained a note of surrender I found unexpectedly moving, this brilliant mind allowing itself to be fully present in sensation. I continued my exploration, freeing his erection from its confines. The velvet hardness of him filled my palm as I stroked him once, twice, watching a pearl of moisture form at the tip. My tongue darted out to taste it, salt and musk and something uniquely his, before taking him fully into my mouth.

The sound he made, part groan, part reverence, cascaded through me, intensifying my own arousal. I could feel myself growing wetter, my inner muscles clenching around emptiness as I took him deeper. My tongue swirled around his length as I established a rhythm, using my hands in counterpoint to my mouth.

Using my practiced skill, I brought him to the threshold of release before retreating, establishing the pattern of approach and withdrawal that builds not just physical intensity but emotional investment. His hands fisted in the sheets, then in my hair, his control visibly fraying with each withdrawal.

When I finally moved up to straddle him, the expression on his face had transformed. The composure replaced by something more vulnerable, more present. I lifted my skirt, revealing that I wore nothing beneath, my sex already glistening with evidence of my desire. His eyes widened at the sight, his cock twitching visibly in response.

I guided him to my entrance with deliberate slowness, watching his eyes widen at the sensation of my heat against his sensitive tip. Inch by exquisite inch, I lowered myself onto him, feeling my body stretch to accommodate his substantial girth. The fullness as he filled me completely drew a moan from deep in my throat.

"Tell me what you feel," I whispered, remaining motionless for a moment, savoring the perfect connection where our bodies joined.

"Everything," he answered simply, his hands finding my hips with sudden urgency.

I began to move, establishing a rhythm that responded to his breathing, to the tension in his body, to the almost imperceptible signals that indicated his pleasure. This is the language I've spent decades learning to read, the subtle communications of the body that tell more truth than words could ever express.

The slick sound of our joining filled the room as I rose and fell above him, each downward motion sending him deeper inside me. My internal muscles gripped him tightly each time I lifted, creating a velvet friction that made his eyes roll back. I could feel the tension building within my core, a familiar tightening that promised explosive release.

His hands traveled up from my hips to my waist, then higher to cup my breasts with unexpected tenderness. His thumbs circled my nipples before pinching them lightly, sending jolts of pleasure-pain directly to my clitoris. The juxtaposition of strength and gentleness in his touch suggested a man comfortable with complexity, with holding opposing forces in equilibrium. I leaned into his caress, allowing my own pleasure to build visibly, knowing that for a man like him, my authentic response would create a feedback loop enhancing his experience.

"There's a theory," he managed between increasingly ragged breaths, his hips now rising to meet each of my downward movements, "that consciousness itself arises from quantum processes in neural microtubules."

I smiled at this quintessential moment, the mind still seeking to understand even as the body surrenders to sensation. "And what does your consciousness tell you now?" I asked, deliberately contracting my inner muscles around him, squeezing his length in a rhythmic pulse that made his eyes widen.

His response was nonverbal. A groan that seemed to emerge from somewhere deeper than thought. His hands tightened on my hips, fingers digging into my flesh as he guided me into a more urgent rhythm. My clit rubbed against his pubic bone with each movement, adding another layer of sensation that had me gasping with building pleasure.

What happened next transcended my expectations. As his climax built, he reached up to pull me down against his chest, creating full-body contact that transformed our connection from merely sexual to profoundly intimate. His arms encircled me completely, his face buried in my neck, our bodies moving in perfect synchrony. One hand slipped between us, his thumb finding my swollen clitoris with unerring accuracy, circling it with the precise pressure that made my thighs begin to tremble.

In this moment of complete presence, something shifted between us, a connection that seemed to exist both within and beyond our physical joining. I felt myself responding not just to the friction of our bodies but to the complete surrender of this man usually so contained within his intellectual framework.

My own pleasure crested unexpectedly, my inner walls clamping down on him in rhythmic waves. White-hot sensation exploded outward from my core, radiating through my pelvis, my spine, my limbs, until even my fingertips seemed to pulse with its echo. I cried out, a sound of surprise and surrender that came from somewhere beyond conscious thought.

His release followed immediately, as if triggered by mine. A perfect synchronicity. His cock pulsed inside me, filling me with wet heat as he groaned my name against my throat. His entire body tensed beneath mine, then shuddered in waves that matched the continuing aftershocks of my own climax. For several transcendent moments, the boundaries between our separate selves seemed to dissolve completely.

We remained thus entwined, breath mingling, hearts racing in parallel rhythms, the distinction between giver and receiver temporarily suspended. In twenty-four years of professional intimacy, I've experienced this transcendent connection rarely: this sense of merging that extends beyond physical pleasure into something approaching communion.

When we finally separated, he continued to hold me close, his fingers weaving abstract patterns along my spine. The silence between us felt charged with unspoken recognition, not awkwardness but a shared awareness that something unexpected had transpired.

"I've spent my career studying the fundamental forces that bind the universe together," he said eventually, his voice carrying a new softness. "Gravity, electromagnetism, the strong and weak nuclear forces. But there's something else, something science hasn't fully mapped, that creates connection between conscious beings."

I raised myself on one elbow to look at him, struck by the unguarded wonder in his expression. "Perhaps some forms of connection aren't meant to be fully understood through observation alone," I suggested. "Perhaps they must be experienced."

His smile then, part scientist, part newly awakened sensualist, contained a wisdom beyond academic knowledge. "The most profound discoveries often begin with admitting what we don't know," he acknowledged. "Perhaps human connection operates according to principles my equations haven't yet captured."

As twilight deepened outside my windows, we talked with unusual openness, about his work exploring the universe's hidden architecture, about my observations of human intimacy across thousands of encounters. Though our fields of expertise differed dramatically, we found unexpected resonance in our shared fascination with connection, how particles and people alike seem driven toward relationship, toward influence that transcends distance and circumstance.

"My colleagues would be amused," he confessed later as he dressed to leave, movements more relaxed than when he had arrived, "to know that an afternoon with a courtesan provided more insight into quantum entanglement than a month in the laboratory."

I laughed at the irony, appreciating his ability to find meaning rather than mere release in our encounter. "Perhaps physical intimacy is itself a form of research," I suggested, "exploring connections that exist beyond conventional understanding."

His parting kiss carried a depth that transcended the transactional nature of our arrangement, a genuine acknowledgment of shared discovery.

As I watched him walk toward his waiting car, his posture seemed subtly altered. Still the precise movements of the scientist but now integrated with the more fluid awareness of the embodied man.

The encounter left me contemplating the many dimensions of connection we experience but rarely acknowledge: how bodies communicate in languages far more ancient and profound than the words we use to analyze their interactions. Perhaps, I thought as Monaco's evening lights began to glimmer, this was the true gift of my unusual profession: bearing witness to moments when human beings transcend their ordinary boundaries, briefly touching something essential that exists beyond explanation.

•

I have known many men, but few whose touch has lingered like a half-remembered dream, whose presence has continued to unfold inside me long after physical separation. Fifteen years have passed since that first afternoon with my physicist, yet time itself seems to bend around our connection, compressing and expanding like the quantum fields he studies.

We meet still, when Mediterranean seasons turn and the light across Monaco's harbor shifts to certain hues that remind me of that first golden hour. Sometimes our bodies tangle in ancient rhythms; other times we simply talk, our words creating invisible bridges between his universe of equations and my landscape of human desires.

"You've become my control experiment," he told me once, Mediterranean sunlight fracturing across his espresso cup, his eyes crinkling with the smile that now emerges more freely. "The constant variable in an otherwise chaotic equation."

His words held no clinical detachment, only the tender recognition of something rare, how we've created between us a gravity neither sought yet both needed, an orbit of mutual recognition that has witnessed our separate evolutions while maintaining its essential pattern.

What fascinates me is how the scientist in him prepared the man for transcendence. His mind already dwelled in realms where particles remain eternally connected across impossible distances, where time folds upon itself, where observation creates reality. The universe had been whispering secrets to him long before my body did.

Last month, as we shared wine beneath a sky bruised purple with approaching night, he confessed that his colleagues have begun questioning his latest research. "They think I'm approaching mysticism," he said, his fingers painting absent patterns on my wrist where pulse meets skin. "Perhaps I am."

I recognized in his voice what I've witnessed countless times. How genuine connection transforms us molecule by molecule, rearranging not just our bodies but our perceptions. The man who once sought empirical evidence for connection beyond physics now embodies that very mystery, his theories expanding to contain what his body discovered in our shared silence.

We are changed by everyone we truly touch. This truth shimmers at the heart of both his quantum theories and my intimate observations. Like subatomic particles that, once having danced together, remain eternally responsive to each other's movements, we carry within us echoes of every soul that has truly seen us.

What remains between us isn't memory but presence, a connection that exists outside time, that needs no physical proximity to maintain its silent influence. In the spaces between our meetings, I sometimes feel the ghost of his touch when I stand beside the sea at certain hours, as though the same invisible forces binding electrons across vast emptiness maintain the bridge between our separate lives.

The Lesson:

Genuine intimacy transcends technique and requires presence, that rare quality of being fully engaged in the moment without distraction. This presence creates a feedback loop: when you are completely attentive to your partner, they feel truly seen, which deepens their response, which in turn heightens your experience.

The most profound sexual connections occur when partners temporarily suspend goal-orientation and immerse themselves in the unfolding experience. This isn't about achieving specific positions or performing particular acts but about cultivating awareness of the subtle energies passing between bodies in communion.

Try this: Before your next intimate encounter, set an intention to remain fully present throughout. When your mind begins to wander, analyzing performance, worrying about appearance, planning unrelated activities, gently return your attention to physical sensation and emotional connection. Notice the texture of skin beneath your fingertips. The rhythm of shared breathing. The unspoken communication happening beneath words.

This mental presence transforms ordinary physical acts into extraordinary connections, creating experiences that resonate beyond the bedroom into your broader relationship. When we approach sexuality as an opportunity for genuine connection rather than merely physical release, we access dimensions of pleasure and intimacy that our culture rarely acknowledges but that human beings have recognized throughout history.

The Power of Presence

Absence precedes presence. Perhaps this is why I found myself in Kyoto that autumn: to discover the negative space around which genuine connection forms. The maple leaves had begun their passionate transformation, their metamorphosis from demure green to brazen crimson mirroring my own journey from Monaco's polished artifice to Japan's disciplined authenticity.

The traditional ryokan breathed with centuries of whispered secrets. Its wooden beams had witnessed countless surrenders to presence long before the tyranny of perpetual digital availability colonized human attention. From my tatami-matted sanctuary, I gazed upon the garden where moss-covered stones created an undulating landscape in miniature, a physical meditation on the beauty of deliberate arrangement, of placement as profound as object.

My client, a Silicon Valley architect of virtual worlds, had summoned me across oceans, perhaps instinctively understanding that the intimacy he sought couldn't manifest within Monaco's glittering confines. In our previous encounters, his body had occupied my bed while his attention remained tethered to the persistent glow of devices. I had come to know the subtle tension in his shoulders when notifications illuminated his periphery, the almost imperceptible pause in his breathing when digital summons reached his consciousness. His climaxes, though physically adequate, had always seemed partial, as if some essential part of him remained elsewhere, unreachable through mere physical stimulation.

The irony whispered through the paper-thin walls of this ancient structure: a man whose fortune derived from fragmenting human attention had journeyed to a culture that had elevated presence to art. What exquisite tension in this contradiction. What delicious possibility in this collision of worlds.

The bronze resonance of a temple bell announced his arrival as evening shadows lengthened across the garden stones. He stood framed in my doorway, his customary confidence subtly undermined by the ryokan's simple yukata robe that had replaced his armor of tailored suits. Without his usual digital extensions, his hands appeared curiously vulnerable.

"This place is extraordinary," he observed, eyes darting around the spare elegance of my room. "Though I don't think I've been without Wi-Fi this long since the nineties."

His fingers performed their habitual pantomime, reaching for phantom devices, mapping emptiness where screens should be. This unconscious choreography revealed his addiction more eloquently than words ever could.

"There's a certain luxury in unavailability," I replied, gesturing toward the cushions flanking the low table where ceramic flasks of sake awaited us. The moonlight filtering through rice paper screens transmuted the simple setting into something sacred, a stage for communion rather than performance.

As I poured warm sake into shallow cups, I recognized an opportunity for initiation into presence. This man who existed primarily in simulation could perhaps discover embodiment through ritualized attention.

He accepted the sake cup with both hands, a gesture he had clearly learned for this journey. I observed his gaze darting around the room, perpetually gathering data, analyzing, categorizing. Without explanation, I rose and moved to the ornate wooden chest near my futon. From a drawer, I withdrew a length of black silk, part of a kimono sash I had acquired in Gion. His expression registered momentary alarm as I returned and positioned myself behind him.

"What are you—"

"Shh," I whispered, letting the cool silk glide across his palms before lifting it toward his eyes. His body tensed, that instinctive resistance of the perpetually vigilant to surrender control, but he made no move to stop me as I bound the fabric securely around his head, plunging him into manufactured darkness.

"Now tell me what you taste," I continued, my voice dropping to just above a whisper, close enough that my breath caressed his cheek.

His brow furrowed in concentration. "Rice, obviously. Something floral? And… minerals, maybe?" He analyzed the liquid as he might examine code: detached, taxonomic, seeking to categorize rather than experience.

"Not what you think it contains," I clarified. "What you actually experience on your tongue, against your palate, as it travels down your throat."

Silence claimed him. I watched his features soften as analytical mind yielded to direct sensation. When he spoke again, his voice emerged from someplace deeper than cognition.

"Heat. Subtle sweetness. A kind of… expanding sensation?"

"That's presence," I whispered, allowing my lips to brush the delicate spiral of his ear. "Direct experience, undiluted by analysis or categorization."

The sake's warmth unfurled within me, dissolving boundaries between professional purpose and personal pleasure. I reached for the simple knot securing his yukata, untying it with ceremonial deliberation. The cotton parted, revealing the landscape of his body, territory mapped by ambition's relentless demands.

"Keep your eyes closed," I instructed, my fingertips discovering the contradiction of his form: soft skin stretched over the artificial hardness of muscles cultivated in climate-controlled gymnasiums rather than through labor with purpose. "Simply feel what is happening without naming it."

A sound escaped him. Not language but its precursor, the vowel of surrender that precedes articulation. His consciousness hovered at the threshold between habitual cognition and pure sensation. I guided him backward until he lay supine on the traditional futon, moonlight transforming his skin to alabaster.

"Trust your skin to see for you," I murmured when his eyes fluttered open, seeking reassurance in the visible world. He complied, swallowing expectation as my hands continued their patient exploration.

My own robe I released without ceremony, the fabric sliding from shoulders to floor in one fluid descent, leaving nothing between my skin and the autumn air. The night air claimed my nakedness, each pore awakening to atmospheric caress before I lowered myself beside him. Our bodies formed a calligraphy of contrast: his angles against my curves, his tension against my fluidity, his pallor against my warmth.

"What do you feel?" I asked, guiding his palm to the slope where my waist curved into hip.

"Warmth," he answered, voice breaking on the simplicity of truth. "Softness. A kind of... living silk."

This departure from technical vocabulary revealed his crossing of the threshold between thinking about experience and dissolving into it. I rewarded this submission to presence by bringing my body fully against his, creating a constellation of contact points from sternum to ankle. His gasp contained genuine wonder, as if this elemental connection constituted revelation rather than return.

I cradled his face between my palms, my thumbs resting lightly on his eyelids to discourage premature sight. "There is no code to write here," I whispered. "No algorithm to perfect. Only moment flowing into moment."

My mouth found his in unhurried exploration, a kiss existing as complete experience rather than prelude. The sake's subtle sweetness lingered on his tongue as we breathed in tandem, exchanging more than oxygen. My teeth captured his lower lip with gentle precision, the slight pressure drawing blood to the surface, heightening sensation through controlled restriction.

His hands discovered my back, fingers counting vertebrae like prayer beads, each touch simultaneously question and answer. When his palms curved around my breasts, I arched into their unexpected reverence. Where previous encounters had been characterized by efficient expertise, this touch contained the humility of genuine exploration, as if he were encountering feminine form for the first time, despite his wealth of sexual experience.

My nipples hardened against his palms, their sudden rigidity a stark contrast to the soft fullness beneath them. This duality of softness and hardness mirrored the contradiction in his own body. His thumbs traced circles around the darkened areolae, creating spirals that narrowed toward the center but never quite reached their destination. The deliberate denial made my breath catch, my body arching involuntarily to seek what was withheld.

"Even anticipation is a form of presence," I whispered, guiding his mouth to where his hands had awakened such hunger. The wet heat of his tongue against my nipple sent electric current racing through neural pathways that connected directly to my sex. I felt myself growing slick with desire, the physical evidence of arousal gathering between my thighs like dew on morning petals.

I straddled him with deliberate slowness, my hair falling around us like a veil that further isolated this moment from all external concerns. His hands discovered my thighs, not directing but witnessing their curve and tension. My body hovered above his, creating a moment of exquisite suspension, neither separation nor connection but the sacred space between intention and fulfillment.

The garden beyond our screen had surrendered to darkness, moonlight illuminating only the white stones placed with ancient intention among shadowed moss. Within our cocoon of awareness, I positioned him at my entrance, extending anticipation until it blossomed into its own form of fulfillment. His breath caught, suspended between inhalation and release, as I allowed gravity to deliver me onto him in incremental surrender.

The initial joining, that exquisite threshold where separation dissolves into unity, I transformed from moment into eternity. Each millimeter of penetration registered as distinct universe, the gradual parting of flesh creating friction that ignited nerve endings in sequence rather than symphony. The subtle resistance that sweetens surrender, the spreading warmth as bodies recognize one another at the cellular level. These moments existed as complete experiences rather than transitions.

His cock stretched me deliciously, the rigid heat of him a perfect counterpoint to the liquid warmth that welcomed him. I felt my inner muscles adjusting to accommodate his substantial girth, the slight burning sensation at the edge of comfort only heightening my awareness of our connection. When he was finally seated to the hilt within me, my body gripped him in rhythmic pulses that were both voluntary and instinctive, ancient wisdom residing in flesh that remembered what the mind had forgotten.

His gasp transcended physical pleasure, emerging from someplace where sensation meets meaning. I guided his hands to where our bodies joined, allowing him to witness our temporary dissolution of boundaries not just from within but through touch. With careful fingers, he explored the stretched tissue that encircled his base, his touch reverent as he discovered the silken wetness that eased our connection. Tangible evidence of desire that no technical sophistication could fabricate.

When I finally enveloped him completely, the fullness radiated beyond the physical point of connection, awakening filaments of pleasure throughout my pelvis in gloriously attentive response. I felt him throbbing inside me, each pulse of blood through his erection creating subtle expansions that my body registered with exquisite sensitivity. This internal dialogue, his pulse, my response, created a silent conversation more intimate than words could articulate.

Rather than establishing the predictable rhythm of conventional coupling, I remained nearly motionless, creating instead subtle internal adjustments that demanded his complete attention to perceive. The muscles sheathing him contracted in patterns both deliberate and involuntary, each pulsation a silent question that required his total presence to answer.

His breathing deepened as habitual expectations yielded to this unfamiliar approach, his need for control dissolving into the novel pleasure of pure receptivity. The tension in his face, that perpetual readiness for the next demand, the next innovation, the next crisis, melted into an expression I had never witnessed during our previous encounters: wonder.

"Feel everything," I instructed, my voice barely disturbing the air between us. "Not just where we join, but the air against your skin, the pressure beneath your shoulder blades, the weight of my thighs alongside yours."

When I finally began to move, it wasn't the linear progression toward climactic resolution but a circular exploration that emphasized connection over conquest. My pelvis described perfect ellipses, creating sensations that varied in location and intensity with each revolution. His hands ascended my spine, each fingertip recording the subtle shifting of muscles beneath skin as I moved above him.

The swollen bud of my clitoris found delicious friction against his pubic bone with each forward rotation, sending jolts of pleasure that made my inner walls clench around his shaft. Each tightening drew a corresponding groan from deep in his throat, a call and response pattern that required no conscious orchestration. My wetness increased with each circuit, the slick sounds of our connection providing sensual percussion to our wordless symphony.

The moonlight caught beads of perspiration forming along my collarbone, transforming ordinary secretion into luminous adornment. I leaned forward, allowing these droplets to fall like silent rain upon his chest, this liquid connection creating yet another sensory bridge between our forms.

"Open your eyes," I whispered when I sensed his breathing accelerate toward the familiar patterns of approaching release.

He obeyed, his gaze meeting mine with startling clarity. Nothing calculated or guarded remained in those depths. In that moment of connection, visual, physical, energetic, something transcended the professional nature of our arrangement. Pure presence shimmered between us, that rarest of human gifts: consciousness fully inhabited, experience directly apprehended without distortion.

His hands found my hips, not to control but to stabilize as sensation threatened to dissolve form entirely. I altered my movement, transitioning from circular to vertical oscillation, deepening his penetration while maintaining the deliberate pace that prevented descent into mechanical habit.

I lifted until only his swollen head remained captured within me, then descended with measured deliberation, taking him deeper with each stroke. The sensation of being repeatedly filled after emptiness created a rhythm of presence and absence that echoed our larger lesson. Each downward motion brought him against that sensitive spot on my anterior wall, that ridged territory that responds so enthusiastically to precisely applied pressure.

The precise moment when pleasure transitions from localized sensation to systemic experience announced itself in the sudden synchronization of our breathing: inhalation matching inhalation, exhalation answering exhalation. I recognized the familiar tightening at the base of his abdomen, the subtle lift of his pelvis seeking deeper connection, the almost imperceptible tremor in his thighs that heralded imminent surrender.

Between us, my clitoris had become a focal point of almost unbearable sensitivity, each movement sending shockwaves through my nervous system. The dual stimulation, internal fullness and external friction, created a complex harmony of sensation that built toward inevitable crescendo. I felt my inner muscles beginning to contract rhythmically, the prelude to a release that would claim every fiber of my being.

"Stay with me," I murmured, maintaining eye contact as wave after wave of intensity gathered within my own body. "Be here for this."

The release, when it arrived, moved through us like a current finding conductive material, reorganizing cellular memory and neurological pattern. My sex gripped him in powerful spasms, each contraction triggering corresponding pulses in his cock as he emptied himself into me. I watched his consciousness expand beyond the narrow confines of goal-oriented pleasure into something more encompassing. A state where distinction between giving and receiving momentarily dissolves into pure being.

Afterward, as moonlight painted silver choreography across our entangled forms, silence reigned with perfect sufficiency. His hand wandered across my shoulder in patterns without purpose, each touch containing a quality of wonder previously absent from his efficient caresses.

"I think I understand why you brought me here," I said eventually, my voice barely disturbing the night's perfection.

He nodded, expression thoughtful in the half-light. "I needed to learn something I couldn't download or delegate." A smile touched his lips as he added, "Though I never expected the lesson to be about attention itself."

"Most of what we seek through endless acquisition and achievement," I replied, resting my palm against his chest to feel the steady percussion of his heart, "already exists within our capacity to be fully present."

"That's the paradox, isn't it?" He spoke with unexpected insight. "We create technology to connect us, then use it in ways that ensure we're never truly present with each other."

"Or with ourselves," I added softly.

As night deepened around our island of connection, I observed how his body had transformed, not physically, but energetically. The perpetual subtle vigilance that had characterized his presence previously had yielded to a quality of relaxed awareness I suspected was foreign to his daily existence.

Later, as he prepared to return to his own room, he paused at the threshold where golden light from the corridor met the silver moonlight of my chamber. For once, his hands remained still, making no unconscious motion toward phantom devices.

"Will you teach me more of this?" he asked, his question containing layers of meaning beyond the obvious request.

"Presence cannot be taught," I replied with a smile. "Only practiced."

Understanding illuminated his features as he nodded before disappearing into the corridor, leaving me alone with the moon and the whisper of ancient cedars beyond my window. In the perfect stillness that followed his departure, I recognized that I too had received a gift: the rare satisfaction of offering something more valuable than physical release. In this traditional room where countless seekers had discovered presence before the digital age fractured human attention, we had briefly recovered what technology so often obscures: the irreducible wonder of embodied consciousness, fully awake to its own existence.

•

I often walk through Monaco's Japanese Garden in those liquid hours between appointments, when light shifts and shadows lengthen like thoughts uncoiling. It was there, last week, I watched cherry blossoms commit their annual suicide – so beautiful in their voluntary dissolution, their petals spiraling downward to kiss the water's surface before surrendering to its embrace. Each pale tear created momentary poetry against the dark pond before dissolving, and suddenly I was back in that tatami-scented room, watching my Silicon Valley lover discover his body for perhaps the first time.

How strange that it took a journey across oceans to help him find what lived within his own skin all along. I remember the trembling of his fingers that first evening – not the confident trembling of anticipation but the anxious pulsing of an addict deprived of his drug. Those same hands that created empires of code grew uncertain without screens to anchor them. Yet by our final night, they had rediscovered their primal intelligence, moving across my body with the unhurried wisdom of someone who has remembered how to taste time rather than merely measure it.

The truth whispers between the lines of my encounter journals: some of the wealthiest men I've known are the most desperately impoverished – rich in everything except presence, that most precious of currencies. They come to me expecting revelation through elaborate technique, then seem startled to discover that the simplest touch, fully given and completely received, contains more power than the most acrobatic encounter performed while mentally elsewhere.

I've loved thousands of bodies in my years of intimate profession. I've witnessed beauty in each, though sometimes beauty that required careful excavation to reveal. Yet I've noticed something curious – those most alive to pleasure are rarely those with the most partners or most practiced techniques. They are, instead, those rare souls who have somehow preserved or recovered the child's gift of complete absorption – those who can lose themselves entirely in the texture of skin against palm, in the perfect hollows where neck meets shoulder, in the subtle symphony of synchronized breath.

Have you noticed how we navigate relationships now, always half-present, half-elsewhere? We float above our bodies like reluctant ghosts, tethered to distant concerns by invisible strings of obligation and distraction. In bed with one lover, we're already composing messages to another, planning tomorrow's meetings, revisiting yesterday's slights. We've become virtuosos of division, experts in the art of being simultaneously everywhere and nowhere.

My Silicon Valley architect taught me as much as I taught him. Through his transformation, I glimpsed again the miracle that first drew me to this unusual vocation – how presence, freely given, can transmute the lead of ordinary contact into gold. How flesh meeting flesh with complete awareness becomes not merely pleasure but sacrament. How time itself changes texture when we stop trying to outrun it.

Sometimes I wonder who we might become if we approached all of life with the presence we occasionally stumble into during exceptional lovemaking – those rare moments when thinking yields to pure experience, when the line between self and sensation momentarily dissolves. Perhaps we've been seeking transcendence in the wrong temples, creating ever more complex technologies of connection while forgetting the most direct path: this breath, this touch, this moment, completely inhabited.

The Lesson:

Presence is the most potent aphrodisiac, yet remains our most neglected erotic skill. When we bring complete attention to intimate encounters, ordinary sensations transform into extraordinary experiences, not through special techniques but through the quality of our awareness.

Most sexual dissatisfaction stems not from inadequate performance but from fragmented attention. Notice how often your mind wanders during physical intimacy: planning future activities, replaying past encounters, evaluating your performance, or simply drifting into unrelated thoughts. Each of these mental departures diminishes pleasure by creating distance between sensation and awareness.

I frequently instruct clients to close their eyes during intimate encounters, not merely as romantic gesture but as neurological intervention. Vision dominates our sensory processing, consuming approximately 30% of our brain's cortical resources. When we close our eyes, we liberate enormous neural capacity that can redirect to other sensory channels. Touch becomes more vivid, scent more nuanced, subtle sounds suddenly perceptible. The mind, freed from visual processing, can immerse more completely in bodily sensation.

To cultivate presence, begin with conscious breathing. Before intimate contact, take three deep breaths together, synchronizing your respiratory rhythm with your partner's. This simple act creates physiological alignment that facilitates deeper connection. During intimacy, when you notice your mind wandering, gently return attention to physical sensation: the texture of skin, the pattern of breathing, the points of contact between bodies.

Remember that presence cannot be achieved through effort, paradoxically, trying hard to be present creates its own form of distraction. Instead, cultivate receptivity. Allow sensations to arrive without grasping or analyzing. When thoughts arise, acknowledge them without judgment, then gently return attention to the direct experience of your body.

The most profound sexual experiences emerge not from complicated techniques but from moments of complete presence, when thinking yields to direct experience, when the boundary between self and sensation momentarily dissolves.

The Exploration of Boundaries

The line between professional and personal existence grows permeable in Monaco, more so than anywhere else I've lived. Here, where wealth creates its own demarcations, where entire lives unfold in spaces smaller than some Americans' garages, we learn to partition ourselves with invisible skill. We craft boundaries not from walls but from nuances: a shift in posture, a change in vocabulary, the careful modulation of eye contact.

This preoccupation with boundaries occupied my thoughts when Alexandra requested my services. Her message held the clipped precision of corporate communication, mentioning her position as compliance officer for a multinational financial firm. In three terse paragraphs, she revealed more about herself than perhaps she realized: a woman whose professional identity had been built upon establishing limits for others, now seeking to explore her own.

Her arrival confirmed my analysis. She materialized at my door like a corporate apparition, all clean lines and controlled energy, her charcoal suit cut with architectural precision, her dark hair secured so tightly at the nape of her neck that it seemed to pull her features into sharper relief. Even her handshake communicated boundaries. Firm enough to establish presence but brief enough to prevent connection.

"Research suggests that those who maintain strict boundaries in their professional lives often benefit from safely exploring their personal limits elsewhere," she explained when I inquired about her specific interest in my services. The academic framing of her response revealed her nervousness more clearly than trembling hands ever could.

This intrigued me. The compliance officer seeking non-compliance, the boundary-setter longing to discover what lay beyond her own carefully constructed perimeters. As I guided her into my living room, I observed how her eyes inventoried each detail with professional assessment, calculating distances, evaluating exits, establishing a mental map of unfamiliar territory.

"I spend my days establishing what others cannot do," she continued, settling into my armchair with perfect posture. "I'd like to discover what I can."

Her words crystallized something I've observed repeatedly in my years of intimate anthropology: how often we become imprisoned by the very structures we create to protect ourselves. The expert in limitation had herself become limited: a poignant irony I've encountered in various forms across two decades of professional intimacy.

"Boundaries exist for important reasons," I replied, pouring wine into crystal glasses that had witnessed countless similar negotiations. "But we rarely question whether they still serve the purpose for which they were created. Tonight we'll explore which ones protect you and which merely confine you."

I offered her the wine, but instead of placing it in her hand, I held it to her lips, a small reconfiguration of expected dynamics. The momentary widening of her eyes revealed her recognition of this minor threshold already being tested. After the briefest hesitation, she parted her lips, allowing me to control this initial exchange.

"Let's establish something important first," I said, my free hand finding the small of her back as she drank. "What boundary do you know you won't want to cross tonight? Establishing this firmly might free you to explore everything else more fully."

She considered this with analytical precision. "I don't want to be restrained," she finally said. "I need to know I can move freely."

"That boundary is established and will be honored absolutely," I confirmed, setting aside her glass. "Now, may I remove this?" My fingers found the first pin anchoring her severe chignon.

Her permission came as a slight nod, the barest relaxation of her jawline. As I extracted each pin with deliberate care, her transformation began, dark waves cascading over shoulders that remained professionally squared.

This simple act, the literal loosening of a tightly controlled exterior, often serves as prelude to more significant surrenders.

"Your professional life is spent clarifying what exists on either side of a line," I observed, my fingers now weaving through her freed hair. "But the most interesting territory often lies directly on the boundary itself, where certainty dissolves into possibility."

I stepped closer, confounding her spatial expectations. In business, people maintain precise distances; in intimacy, these distances collapse in carefully choreographed stages. Her breathing changed as I entered the zone typically reserved for confidential conversation, then shifted again as I moved closer still, into the realm where breath mingles and molecules transfer between bodies.

"The richest experiences happen when we linger at thresholds rather than rushing across them," I continued, my lips now close enough to her ear that my words became physical sensations as much as auditory information. "When we fully inhabit the borderland between yes and not-yet."

My mouth found the tender hollow beneath her earlobe, and her sharp intake of breath confirmed my theory: those most bounded in daily life often experience heightened sensitivity when those boundaries begin to dissolve. My lips continued their deliberate cartography along her jawline, approaching but not claiming her mouth, dwelling in the electric territory of almost.

When I finally withdrew slightly, her eyes had darkened, pupils dilating with the brain chemistry of emergent desire. I unbuttoned my blouse with unhurried movements, watching her gaze track my fingers' progression.

"Professional interactions require us to pretend bodies don't exist," I said, slipping the silk from my shoulders. "We construct elaborate fictions of disembodiment, as if humans were merely talking heads floating above invisible flesh."

Her eyes traveled across my exposed skin with a hunger that contradicted her still-perfect posture. This delicious contradiction, desire constrained by habit, created its own exquisite tension. I stepped forward again, taking her hand and guiding it to the clasp of my bra.

Her fingers, so assured with contract clauses and regulatory compliance, fumbled slightly with this unfamiliar mechanism. I placed my hand over hers, not to assist but to connect, to transform what might have been embarrassment into shared experience. When the garment finally yielded, her exhale carried notes of accomplishment and awakening desire.

"Now stand," I directed.

She rose with ingrained elegance, her body maintaining the careful alignment taught in corporate seminars on executive presence. I moved behind her, hands sliding inside her suit jacket, easing it from her shoulders with a sommelier's reverence for fine vintage. Beneath, her silk blouse, the precise burgundy of aged Bordeaux, revealed the heat rising from her skin.

"May I continue?" I asked, fingers finding the first pearl button at her throat.

"Yes," she whispered, the single syllable carrying complex harmonics of nervousness and anticipation.

I worked each button with deliberate slowness, a temporal recalibration that transforms efficiency into sensuality. When the silk parted completely, revealing a black lace bra architectural in its precision, I didn't immediately remove the blouse. Instead, I allowed it to hang open: another threshold state between dressed and undressed, between professional presentation and intimate revelation.

My hands moved to her waist, finding the hidden closure of her skirt. The whisper of the zipper descended between us like a confession. The garment released its hold, slipping over her hips to pool around stiletto heels that had carried her through countless boardrooms. She stood now in lingerie as structured as her corporate life, precise black lace engineered to shape and contain.

"Your body exists under protest," I observed, circling to face her. "Constrained by proper fabric, held in approved postures, denied its own voice."

My palms glided over the controlled curves of her waist, the disciplined arch of her back. The heat between my fingers and her skin kindled something primal between us, a current that flowed from my core to hers, igniting nerve endings long dormant beneath corporate armor.

"Tonight," I continued, my voice dropping to a whisper that seemed to caress her skin rather than merely reach her ears, "we'll rediscover what exists beneath these carefully maintained borders."

I guided her back against the bookcase that spanned my living room wall: leather-bound volumes pressing against her shoulder blades, philosophy and psychology witnessing our unfolding exploration. My body aligned with hers, creating points of contact that disrupted her lifelong training in appropriate distance.

"Close your eyes," I suggested, watching her internal debate before compliance. This voluntary relinquishment of visual control, this willingness to exist in momentary darkness, represented another threshold crossed.

With her sight suspended, her other senses heightened. My mouth found hers not in the direct collision of cinema but through incremental approach. Breath first. Then the lightest grazing of lips. A gentle tasting that slowly deepened as her awareness concentrated into this single point of connection. My tongue teased the entrance to her mouth, requesting rather than demanding, awakening rather than claiming.

When she yielded, opening to me with a soft, surrendered sigh, the wet heat of our tongues meeting sent liquid lightning coursing through my veins. My hand found the nape of her neck, fingers tangling in hair now freed from corporate constraint, applying just enough pressure to deepen our connection without triggering her need for autonomy.

I drew back slightly, my hands continuing their patient excavation of her body beneath professional armor. When I unhooked her bra, the soft sound of her moan seemed to surprise her, as if hearing her own voice express unfiltered pleasure was itself a boundary crossed.

"Sounds, too, are often kept behind carefully constructed walls," I murmured, cupping the newly liberated weight of her breasts, feeling nipples harden against my palms. The transformation of flesh under attention, this involuntary response beyond conscious control, represents one of the body's most honest communications. "What other expressions have you been silencing?"

My mouth descended to taste these awakened peaks, tongue circling with deliberate pressure that transformed rosy areolas into tightened peaks. The heat of my mouth against her skin drew forth another sound, deeper, rougher, emerging from some primal place where corporate titles held no meaning. I drew her nipple between my teeth, applying the precise edge of pressure that balances pleasure against exquisite almost-pain.

Her head fell back against the books behind her, throat exposed in unconscious offering. The elegant column of her neck, that vulnerable pathway housing voice and breath and life itself, presented itself in silent invitation. I accepted, my mouth tracing the blue-veined pathway where her pulse throbbed visibly beneath delicate skin.

My hand slid lower, fingers slipping beneath black lace to discover the wetness that corporate armor concealed. The silken evidence of her desire coated my fingers, her body's undeniable truth-telling where words might equivocate. I found her swollen with need, sensitive flesh engorged with blood rushing to meet my touch.

"Your body speaks with perfect eloquence," I whispered against her collarbone. "Listen to what it's telling you."

Her hips moved instinctively toward my touch, the body making its own declarations independent of the brain's careful censorship. I worked in slow circles through silken folds, learning the specific topography of her desire, the particular pressure that made breath catch in her throat, the rhythm that caused her thighs to tense in anticipation of greater pleasure.

"Boundaries exist in the body as well as the mind," I told her, my fingers continuing their deliberate exploration. "Tension held in muscle and fascia, pleasure denied through habitual contraction. These, too, can be gently released."

I withdrew my hand, raising wet fingers to her lips. Another threshold: the tasting of her own arousal, the metabolic evidence of desire she could no longer deny. After momentary hesitation, her lips parted, tongue meeting my fingers with surprising boldness. The warmth of her mouth around my fingers, the gentle suction as she accepted her own essence, these created mirrored arousal between my own thighs, wetness gathering in sympathetic response.

"Turn around," I instructed, guiding her to face the bookcase.

She complied, hands instinctively finding the shelves for support, her body now presented to me in new architecture: the elegant curve of spine, the twin dimples above her tailbone, the controlled strength of thighs still bisected by the black lace I had yet to remove. I knelt behind her, drawing the final garment down legs that maintained their perfect corporate stance despite the intimacy of the moment.

"Wider," I suggested, and her feet shifted apart on my plush carpet, creating access to the most carefully guarded frontier of her physical territory.

From this position of apparent supplication, I held surprising power. My hands gliding up the backs of her thighs, my breath warming the sensitive skin now exposed to my attention. The scent of her arousal rose to meet me, that primal perfume no expensive fragrance could ever replicate, the chemical signature of desire in its purest form.

When my tongue finally found its way between her legs from behind, her sharp cry mingled with the sound of hardcover books shifting as her hands gripped the shelves with new urgency. The taste of her exploded across my palate, salt and musk and subtle sweetness combining into a flavor uniquely hers. I worked with focused attention, tongue alternating between gentle exploration and more insistent pressure, creating patterns of sensation that dissolved cerebral control.

"Don't analyze," I instructed between deliberate tastes. "Just feel."

Her body began to move with instinctive rhythm against my mouth, corporate discipline yielding to mammalian memory. My hands gripped her hips, supporting and guiding this rediscovered motion. The wet sounds of my mouth against her most intimate flesh filled the room, a percussive counterpoint to her increasingly vocal responses.

When I sensed her approaching climax, felt it in the trembling of her thighs, the changing cadence of her breath, the increasing flood of wetness against my tongue, I paused, rising to press against her back, my still-clothed lower half meeting her naked vulnerability.

"Not yet," I whispered, hands reaching around to cup her breasts, thumbs circling nipples that had forgotten their confinement beneath structured lace. "Pleasure exists most powerfully in anticipation, in the exquisite tension before release. Let's explore that threshold a while longer."

I guided her away from the bookcase toward the baby grand piano that occupied the corner of my living room. Another threshold to cross, another redefinition of objects and their purposes. When the cool polished wood met the heat of her skin, she gasped, the unexpected temperature differential awakening new nerve endings.

"Lean forward," I directed, watching as she bent at the waist, forearms coming to rest on the closed keyboard cover. The position presented her to me with sculptural perfection, the curves of her body offering counterpoint to the piano's own geometry, creating visual harmonies to complement the sounds we were about to compose.

I stepped out of my remaining clothes, retrieving a small ceramic jar from a nearby shelf. Inside, an oil of my own creation, sandalwood and neroli, with subtle notes of clary sage, awaited our ceremony of boundary dissolution. I warmed it between my palms before allowing it to drizzle along the channel of her spine, watching it pool momentarily in those sacred dimples before my hands began working it into her skin.

Beginning at her shoulders, where professional tension maintained its strongest hold, I worked with the focused attention of a surgeon, identifying and releasing knots of resistance that had accumulated through years of corporate vigilance. Her sighs deepened as muscles surrendered decades of vigilant contraction, the physical embodiment of boundaries beginning to dissolve beneath my touch.

When my oiled fingers finally returned to the molten center of her desire, they met with even greater heat and wetness than before. The slickness between her thighs had intensified, her body producing its own lubrication in abundant preparation for deeper pleasure. I worked with deliberate precision, experimenting with pressure and rhythm, noting each shift in her breathing, each involuntary motion that signaled heightening pleasure.

"Some boundaries," I observed, my voice low and steady as my fingers continued their focused attention, "exist not as protection but as habit, limitations we've forgotten to question."

I introduced a second finger, then a third, stretching slightly, awakening nerve endings long denied variation. The tight resistance of her entrance yielded to my gentle insistence, internal muscles gripping my fingers with hungry pulses. Her response was immediate. A full-body shudder that vibrated through the piano strings beneath the lid, creating ghostly harmonics that seemed to emanate from the instrument itself.

"Let me hear you," I encouraged as my fingers established a rhythm that matched her deepening breath. "Give voice to what your body already knows."

The sounds that emerged then were symphonic. Primal notes that had never found expression in boardrooms or corporate retreats. With each thrust of my fingers, each deliberate curl against the textured ridge within, her vocalizations grew less constrained, her body's motion more fluid against the piano's polished surface.

My fingers found the spongy, ridged territory along her anterior wall, that often misunderstood region where pleasure concentrates beneath the surface. Each deliberate stroke against this sensitive landscape drew forth deeper sounds, more abandoned movements. My free hand slid around her hip, finding the swollen bud at the apex of her sex.

As I worked internal and external pleasure points in counterpoint, her universe contracted to these twin centers of sensation. The corporate strategist, the professional boundary-setter, dissolved into pure physical response: the ultimate threshold crossed from thinking to being. The pulsing bundle of nerves beneath my circling thumb swelled further with each deliberate stroke, as hungry for attention as her voice was now for expression.

The slick sounds of my fingers moving within her filled the room, liquid evidence of boundaries dissolving, of control surrendering to desire. Her inner muscles clenched around my fingers with increasing urgency, the prelude to imminent release. The wetness coating my hand spoke more honestly than any verbal acknowledgment could. A physical confession of need beyond corporate constraint.

When orgasm finally claimed her, it arrived not as a destination but as a transformation, waves of release radiating from her core, dissolving boundaries between us, between mind and body, between control and surrender. Her inner walls contracted rhythmically around my fingers, each pulse sending fresh wetness flowing over my hand. Her cry contained notes I suspect she had never heard from her own throat, a primal song unconcerned with professional propriety or controlled presentation.

As aftershocks subsided, I withdrew gradually, supporting her trembling body against mine. We remained joined in this tableau against the piano, my arms encircling her waist, her breath gradually slowing to normal cadence. When she finally straightened and turned to face me, her eyes held a new quality, clarity without analysis, presence without performance.

"Now," I said simply, taking her hand and guiding it between my legs, where my own arousal had built through attention to hers. The wetness she discovered there seemed to surprise her. Tangible evidence that giving pleasure generates its own reciprocal desire. "Your turn to explore."

Her fingers moved with surprising confidence, as if this new territory, once feared, had suddenly become navigable through direct experience rather than theoretical understanding. She discovered through touch and response what brought me pleasure, her analytical mind now applied to this most intimate form of problem-solving.

I guided her to kneel before me, my back now against the piano, one leg lifted to rest on the bench. Her tongue, initially tentative, found growing boldness as my responses encouraged exploration. The first touch of her mouth against my sex sent electric current racing through my body, the warm, wet heat of her tongue against my most sensitive flesh creating sensation that arched my back and pulled sound from my throat.

I watched the compliance officer transform into curious adventurer, moving beyond prescribed boundaries into the territory of instinctive connection. Her tongue traced exploratory patterns: broad strokes alternating with focused attention, each movement growing more confident as she cataloged my responses. When she found the rhythm and pressure that drew the most abandoned sounds from me, she maintained it with the same focused determination that likely made her exceptional in the corporate realm.

My hand found her hair, not directing but connecting. Fingers tangling in dark waves now freed from severe constraint. The sight of her between my thighs, this woman who spent her days enforcing limits now passionately engaged in transcending them, created its own visual arousal that heightened physical sensation. My breathing shortened, muscles tensing as pleasure built toward inevitable peak.

When release finally claimed me, it was her eyes I noticed most. Watching my face with wonder as pleasure reconfigured my features, as carefully maintained professional control yielded to genuine ecstatic surrender. In that moment of shared vulnerability, a new understanding passed between us, a recognition that boundaries, properly understood, can become gateways rather than barriers.

Afterward, as we dressed in comfortable silence, I observed the subtle but significant differences in her movements, still precise but more fluid, as if some internal constraints had been gently loosened. She gathered her hair back, but instead of recreating the severe chignon of her arrival, she secured it in a loose arrangement that softened her features.

"What will you take from this?" I asked as she prepared to depart.

She considered the question with the same thoroughness she likely applied to regulatory compliance issues, but her answer emerged from a different place, not calculated but realized.

"The understanding that boundaries need regular examination," she replied, a new quality of openness softening her features. "Some protect us, while others simply imprison us in habits we've outgrown."

As she stood at my threshold, literal and figurative, I recognized in her the beautiful complexity that defines human experience: our need for both structure and freedom, for both boundaries and their transcendence. In her journey from corporate constraint to embodied awareness, she had discovered what many spend lifetimes seeking, the boundary between limitation and liberation is itself an illusion, a line drawn in sand rather than carved in stone.

•

What continues to fascinate me about human intimacy is how often our greatest growth occurs not by shattering boundaries but by approaching them mindfully: that delicate caress along the edge of comfort where we discern which borders truly protect us and which merely imprison us within the familiar. Alexandra's situation perfectly crystallized this paradox: a woman who constructed impenetrable professional perimeters yet found herself longing for dissolution in her most intimate moments.

I have watched this pattern unfold countless times across the landscape of bodies and souls that have graced my bed, this curious transference where those who enforce structure in daylight hours crave its absence when darkness falls. The anthropologist in me recognizes it as the inevitable consequence of our compartmentalized culture, where success demands the fragmentation of self into discrete territories of being. This division cuts more deeply through women like Alexandra, for whom authority requires twice the fortification to receive half the respect.

The true alchemy of our encounter wasn't in eliminating her boundaries but in rendering them transparent enough to be seen, examined, and consciously navigated. As she stood at the threshold between habitual limitation and unexplored possibility, I watched her face transform with that exquisite realization that some borders exist to protect the precious inner landscape while others merely prevent its flourishing.

In my years of intimate cartography, I've come to believe that we are most nakedly ourselves not when boundaries dissolve completely but in that sacred moment of choosing which thresholds to maintain and which to cross with full awareness. It is this discernment, this conscious navigation of limits rather than their unconscious acceptance or reckless disregard, that constitutes the most profound art of both pleasure and becoming.

Each time I witness this transformation, I'm reminded that meaningful intimacy creates sanctuary by honoring limits while inviting us to dance along their edges. Like moon-pulled tides kissing the shore without consuming it, we approach each other's boundaries not to conquer but to commune—finding, in that liminal space between separation and union, the truest expression of both desire and respect.

Perhaps this is why my profession continues to reveal unexpected wisdom despite its marginal status in proper society, because the border itself, when approached with reverence rather than demand, becomes not an ending but a luminous beginning, a doorway rather than a wall, a place where souls might meet in the exquisite space between what is and what might be.

The Lesson:

Meaningful intimacy requires clear communication about boundaries before they are approached. This conversation isn't a clinical negotiation but can be one of the most intimate exchanges possible, the vulnerable sharing of desires and limits that creates safety for exploration.

Begin by identifying your own boundaries, not just what you don't want but what you do want to experience. Recognize that some boundaries are absolute while others may be contextual, shifting based on trust, circumstance, and evolving desire. The most enlightening approach is to ask yourself: "Is this boundary protecting me or limiting me?"

When communicating boundaries with a partner, specificity serves better than generality. Rather than simply stating what you don't want, articulate what form of touch, approach, or interaction would feel comfortable and pleasurable. This positive framing transforms boundaries from walls into doorways.

Remember that boundary exploration should be gradual rather than sudden. The edge, that territory where comfort meets unfamiliarity, often contains the richest potential for discovery. Lingering at this threshold, approaching it with awareness rather than rushing past it, can transform limitation into liberation.

The Gift of Vulnerability

Armor isn't only made of metal. It forms in layers of silence, in the calcification of fear into discipline, in the practiced art of appearing invulnerable when the flesh beneath remains as tender as a child's dream.

This truth crystallized for me during an encounter that began with an ending: the final evening of a sun-drenched Mediterranean spring weekend. Monaco had done its work on him, softening the edges of a man who commanded thousands but struggled to command his own heart. I watched him now from my terrace as he gazed out at the harbor, his military bearing momentarily surrendered to contemplation, his silhouette carved against the dying light like a monument to controlled power.

The American General had arrived three days earlier with the efficient precision that characterized his professional life, a man accustomed to having his orders followed without question, to reviewing operations rather than participating in them. His approach to pleasure mirrored his approach to warfare: methodical, objective-oriented, with territories to be conquered rather than explored. His hands had mapped my body like terrain to be subdued, each caress executed with tactical proficiency that brought satisfaction without revelation.

"Do you ever find it difficult," I asked, joining him at the balcony's edge as the evening light transformed everything it touched into liquid gold, "to switch between who you are there and who you might be here?"

It was our third evening together, the final night of his brief respite before returning to duties that waited with implacable demand across borders.

The air between us hung heavy with unspoken possibilities, the last chance for something beyond the choreographed pleasure we had shared thus far.

He turned toward me, his profile momentarily outlined in gold against the deepening blue of the Mediterranean. The light caught the silver at his temples, evidence of his forty-eight years, most spent in service to a flag and country an ocean away. His eyes, the color of weather-beaten slate, held a weariness that his posture refused to acknowledge.

"They don't teach courses in that transition at West Point," he replied, a ghost of humor briefly animating his expression before the habitual mask of command resettled. "The switch stays permanently in the 'on' position after a while."

I studied him, this man whose body I had come to know intimately yet whose inner landscape remained largely unmapped. His physicality spoke of disciplined strength, of a lifetime's adherence to standards visible in every controlled movement. The architecture of his chest, the precise geometry of his shoulders, the careful economy of his gestures, all testified to a man who had made himself into a living fortress. Yet in unguarded moments, I had glimpsed something beneath the military precision, a gentleness at odds with his chosen profession, a depth belied by the purposeful simplicity of his speech.

"Perhaps," I suggested, pouring ruby Châteauneuf-du-Pape into crystal glasses that caught the fading light like captured fire, "the greater challenge isn't the transition but the integration. Finding how all the parts of yourself might coexist rather than compete."

He accepted the offered wine with a nod of appreciation, his fingers briefly brushing mine, a contact that sent unexpected electricity coursing through my skin. Like so many aspects of our encounters, this touch seemed simultaneously intentional and carefully bounded, the perimeter of pleasure patrolled with vigilant attention.

"Integration suggests these parts belong together. I'm not sure that's true in my case." He took a measured sip, his throat working in a rare moment of exposed vulnerability. "Some things you compartmentalize for good reason."

Something in his tone had shifted—a hairline crack in the smooth facade of his professional persona. It was a rare opening, a door briefly ajar, revealing chambers usually sealed by duty and expectation. Such moments are fleeting, and they deserve our full attention.

"What makes you doubt that?" I asked, keeping my voice deliberately neutral, creating space without pressure. My body leaned imperceptibly toward his, instinctively seeking the heat that radiated from him even through the barrier of his tailored clothing.

He took a measured sip of wine before answering, his gaze returning to the harbor where luxury yachts bobbed like expensive toys in the gentle swell. The Mediterranean light bathed his features in amber warmth, softening the hard lines that responsibility had carved around his mouth and eyes.

"There was an incident last month. A training exercise that went wrong." His voice remained steady, but a subtle tension appeared at the corners of his eyes, tiny muscles contracting with memory. "Two young soldiers were injured. Not critically, but it was… preventable."

This small disclosure, hardly dramatic by civilian standards, represented a significant departure from his previous careful compartmentalization. I remained silent, allowing the moment to breathe, understanding that premature response might cause the door to swing closed again. My hand rested on the balustrade, close enough to his that our knuckles almost touched, an invitation without demand.

"I visited them in the hospital," he continued after several heartbeats. "One couldn't have been more than twenty. Reminded me of my son at that age." He paused, rotating the wine glass between precise fingers. "He was scared but trying not to show it. Keeping up the brave face for the general." A humorless smile briefly touched his lips. "I wanted to tell him it was okay to be afraid. That I was afraid too, at his age. Still am, sometimes."

"But you didn't," I observed softly, my voice barely audible above the distant sounds of the harbor below.

"No." He shook his head. "That's not what generals do. We project confidence, certainty. The moment doubt becomes visible, the whole chain of command starts to fray."

Here was the crux of his division, the man required to project invulnerability who nonetheless carried human fragility within him. The weight of this contradiction was suddenly visible in the set of his shoulders, in the subtle tension around his mouth, in the way his fingers tightened almost imperceptibly around the crystal stem of his glass.

"Perhaps," I said, moving closer until our arms touched, the heat of his skin sending tendrils of warmth through the thin silk of my dress, "there are places where those rules needn't apply. Sanctuaries where different truths can safely emerge."

His eyes met mine, held for a moment longer than comfort would dictate. Something shifted in that gray landscape, a thaw in winterbound terrain, the first intimation of spring in fields long fallow. His scent reached me: a complex mélange of expensive cologne, clean sweat, and something uniquely his, a molecular signature that had already imprinted itself on my memory.

"Is that what this is? A sanctuary?" The question hung between us, weighted with implications beyond the professional transaction that had brought us together.

I considered my response carefully, understanding its potential significance. My hand moved to cover his where it rested on the balustrade, my fingers sliding between his with deliberate intent.

"It can be," I answered simply. "If you choose to use it that way."

Something shifted in his expression. A momentary softening around his mouth, a flicker of contemplation replacing the habitual alertness. The silence between us felt charged with possibility rather than expectation, with the electric potential that precedes revelation.

"May I show you something?" he asked finally, setting his glass on the marble balustrade.

I nodded, curious about this unexpected shift. He turned slightly, angling his left arm toward the fading light. My eyes traced the familiar scar I had noticed during our previous encounters, the long, pale line running from wrist nearly to elbow, a topographical reminder of mortality on a body otherwise suggesting invincibility. I had seen it, of course, when his body was laid bare before me on previous nights, but had maintained the professional courtesy of not inquiring about wounds that were not freely discussed.

"Kandahar, 2010," he said quietly. "IED took out our lead vehicle. I was in the second." His fingertips traced the raised tissue with a curious tenderness, as if greeting an old adversary with newfound respect.

Though I had observed this mark on his flesh before, this was the first time he had acknowledged it, the first time he had transformed it from private history into shared knowledge. The intimacy of this disclosure, more revealing than the complete nakedness we had already shared, sent a shiver of understanding through me.

"You've seen it, I know," he continued, his fingers continuing their journey along the scar's path. "But you've never asked."

"Some questions feel like trespassing," I replied simply, allowing my fingers to join his in this tactile exploration of memory. The scar tissue felt smooth beneath my touch, a testament to both damage and healing.

He nodded, appreciation flickering across his features. "Most people either pretend not to notice or immediately demand the story, as if my scars exist for their entertainment."

"And what do they mean to you?" I asked, maintaining respectful exploration, allowing him to control the degree of revelation even as my touch claimed gentle knowledge of his wounded history.

His expression shifted, becoming both more distant and somehow more present, as if looking simultaneously inward and outward across a divided landscape. "They're complicated... these marks." His fingers entwined with mine, guiding my touch along the scar's path, sharing the texture of damage like a blind man reading braille. "When it first happened, the scar represented failure. I should have anticipated the attack, should have protected my men better."

I remained silent, creating space for him to continue at his own pace, my body leaning slightly against his in a gesture of attentive presence.

"Later, it became proof that I had purpose. That my survival wasn't accidental but necessary. The medic who worked on me in the field died three days later. His life for mine." He swallowed visibly, the movement of his throat suggesting words unsaid. "I carry that weight in this scar."

The evening light caught the subtle topography of the healed wound, highlighting its raised edges against his tanned skin. I raised his wrist to my lips, pressing a kiss against the beginning of the scar, a benediction for both the wound and the man who carried it.

"The strange thing about scars," he continued, voice dropping as if sharing a confession, "is how they become another form of armor. The tissue thickens, becomes less sensitive. It's nature's way of protecting vulnerable places." He looked up, meeting my gaze directly, the gray of his eyes darkening with unspoken desire. "But that protection comes at a cost. What's beneath becomes... sealed away."

I understood then what he was truly revealing, not just the physical marking but what it represented: pain locked within thickened skin, vulnerability protected by strategic numbness, experience transformed into barrier rather than opening. My hand moved to the side of his face, fingers tracing the strong line of his jaw where tension habitually gathered.

"The fear never really goes away," he admitted, turning slightly to press his lips against my palm. "It just gets… contained. Controlled. The stubbornness for life that gets you through the initial trauma hardens into something else over time. Something less flexible."

"Like emotional scar tissue," I suggested gently, moving closer still until our bodies pressed together from chest to thigh, his heat penetrating the thin silk of my dress to warm flesh already awakening to possibility.

"Exactly." His eyes held a quiet wonder at being understood. "Professional armor over personal wounds. Necessary in the field, but…"

"But perhaps not everywhere," I finished for him, my lips close enough to his that our breath mingled in the narrowing space between us.

He nodded, a subtle gesture that conveyed profound acknowledgment. "There are others," he said after a moment's pause. "Less visible."

The statement hung between us. This acknowledgment of internal injuries carried beneath impeccable uniform and military bearing. I recognized the significance of what he was offering, not just the history of his physical wound but the emotional territory it represented. My body responded with instinctive hunger, desire kindled not merely by his physical presence but by this rare willingness to be truly seen.

"Thank you," I said softly, "for showing me what they mean to you." My lips brushed his in the barest suggestion of a kiss, an invitation rather than a demand.

"Perhaps Monaco has worked its magic," I suggested with a gentle smile, drawing back just enough to see his expression. "This place has a way of dissolving boundaries we maintain elsewhere."

"Or perhaps it's the company," he countered, his eyes meeting mine with unexpected directness. His hand moved to my waist, fingers splaying to claim the curve with deliberate possession that sent heat pooling low in my abdomen.

The current that passed between us in that moment transcended the professional connection we had established over previous evenings. Something more authentic had entered our shared space: a truth beyond transaction, beyond the careful choreography of arranged intimacy. His desire, no longer contained behind ramparts of control, reached for me with tangible heat.

I took his hand then, the wine forgotten on the balustrade, and led him inside my apartment where gathering darkness was held at bay by amber lamps. Unlike our previous progressions toward the bedroom, this transition held different promise, not merely physical release but potentially deeper connection. His fingers tightened around mine, the strength in his grip revealing the hunger his disciplined exterior had previously concealed.

"Tonight," I suggested, stopping in the center of my living room where gold light pooled on polished floors, "perhaps we might begin differently."

Curiosity flickered across his features. "What did you have in mind?"

"A trade," I replied, turning to face him fully. "Vulnerability for vulnerability."

His eyebrow lifted slightly, the gesture of a man accustomed to negotiating terms. "That seems... unbalanced. You're not the one paying for services."

"Genuine connection is always mutual," I explained, my fingers working at the top button of his shirt with deliberate patience. "And always valuable, regardless of financial arrangement." The first loosened button revealed the hollow of his throat, the strong column of his neck where pulse beat visibly beneath tanned skin.

He considered this, the soldier's habitual assessment of terrain and risk visible in his contemplative silence. His hands came to rest on my hips, neither pulling me closer nor holding me at distance, simply establishing connection while decision formed. Finally, he nodded. A decision reached through consideration rather than impulse.

"I'll start, then," I said, stepping closer until our bodies pressed together, the hard planes of his chest meeting the softer curves of my breasts through increasingly inadequate layers of clothing. "Something I rarely share with clients: when I was eleven, my father left our family without explanation. For years afterward, I believed it was somehow my fault. That I had failed some essential test of worthiness without realizing it."

The disclosure was true, drawn from personal history rather than professional calculation. I watched something shift in his expression, surprise giving way to recognition, to a different quality of attention. His hands moved from my hips to my back, drawing me closer in wordless acknowledgment.

"That must have been... difficult," he said finally, the inadequate words nonetheless carrying genuine empathy.

"It was," I agreed simply. "Now you."

He drew a measured breath, his military bearing momentarily emphasized as though preparing to issue orders in uncertain territory. Then, deliberately, he allowed his shoulders to relax, his chest to soften from its habitual rigidity. His hand came to my face, fingers tracing the curve of my cheek with unexpected tenderness.

"I have nightmares," he admitted, voice dropping as though the confession might be overheard despite our privacy. "Not constantly, but regularly enough. Always the same theme: I give an order, and someone I care about dies because of it." His gaze dropped briefly, then returned to mine with renewed determination. "My son has enlisted. Begins officer training next month. The nightmares have been more frequent since he told me."

The weight of this disclosure settled between us, not just the admission of vulnerability but the specific nature of his fear, so directly connected to his professional identity and personal relationship. I reached for his hands, enfolding them between both of mine, offering simple human contact as recognition of his courage.

"Thank you for trusting me with that," I said softly, pressing my lips to the center of his palm—where life and heart lines cross like ancient maps.

Something in his posture yielded further, a subtle but significant surrender of the rigid control he typically maintained. His free hand moved to my face, fingertips tracing the curve of my cheek with featherlight precision. When his lips found mine, the kiss carried a different quality than our previous encounters. Less controlled, more questioning, genuinely exploratory rather than performative.

His mouth opened against mine, tongue seeking entry with a hunger previously held in careful check. I welcomed this exploration, my lips parting to allow deeper connection. The taste of him, wine and male heat and undefinable essence, flooded my senses, creating a hunger that transcended professional engagement. His hands tangled in my hair, cradling my skull with delicious tension between gentleness and demand. My body arched against his, seeking more complete contact, the silk of my dress suddenly an intolerable barrier.

We moved to my bedroom as night claimed Monaco completely, transforming my windows into perfect mirrors that reflected our forms as we undressed each other with newfound reverence. Unlike previous encounters where efficiency had characterized his approach to lovemaking, tonight he moved with deliberate patience. Each button of my blouse released with focused attention, each newly revealed expanse of skin greeted with both visual appreciation and tactile exploration.

"You're beautiful," he whispered as the silk slipped from my shoulders, exposing the black lace beneath that contrasted with pale skin. His hands skimmed my collarbones, descended to cup my breasts through the delicate fabric, thumbs circling nipples already tightened with anticipation. The rough texture of his palms, a soldier's hands, accustomed to weapons, created exquisite friction against sensitive flesh.

I unbuttoned his shirt with matching deliberation, revealing the terrain of his chest inch by measured inch. Unlike the previous nights where nakedness had been merely practical preparation, tonight each unveiling carried ritual significance. The powerful architecture of his torso emerged from hiding: broad shoulders tapering to narrow waist, muscles defined without vanity, skin bearing the marks of a life lived in sun and danger. A scatter of dark hair across his pectorals narrowed to a line that disappeared beneath his waistband, drawing the eye with silent invitation.

His own disrobing held similar unhurried quality, each garment set aside with characteristic precision yet without the sense of completing preliminary requirements. When we finally stood naked before each other, the moment carried ceremonial weight, not merely physical revelation but a different kind of exposure, a willingness to be truly seen.

"What are you thinking right now?" I asked as we moved to my bed, the sheets cool beneath heated skin.

He paused, considering the question with the same seriousness he might give a strategic assessment. "That I feel both more vulnerable and more present than I have in... I'm not sure how long."

"And how is that?" My fingers traced the strong column of his neck, feeling his pulse quicken beneath my touch.

"Unsettling," he admitted. "But also... alive." His hands moved to my waist, drawing me against him with newly unleashed hunger.

This single word—alive—contained multitudes, suggesting territories of experience long abandoned in service to duty and protocol. When his body covered mine, the weight and heat of him created a different kind of sanctuary than we had shared previously. Where our prior encounters had carried a certain military precision: effective, controlled, with clear objectives, tonight his approach transcended strategy.

The solid wall of his chest pressed against my breasts with deliberate pressure, creating exquisite friction as our skin welcomed the sweat beginning to form between us. His thigh wedged between mine, creating pressure against my center that drew involuntary movement from my hips. I felt myself opening to him, not just physically but emotionally, the professional boundaries I maintained with careful vigilance yielding to something more authentic.

His mouth found mine with newfound hunger, no longer kissing with technical competence but with authentic desire that sought connection rather than conquest. I tasted wine and something more elemental: the distinctive flavor of a man allowing himself to truly want, to need, to surrender the careful restraint that had characterized him before. His tongue explored the warm cavity of my mouth with the same thorough attention he would soon bring to more intimate territories.

"I want to feel everything," he murmured against my neck, his breath creating patterns of heat and cool that sent shivers racing across my skin. "Not just what's permitted."

My response transcended professional engagement, emerging from genuine appreciation of his courage. My hands mapped the landscape of his back, tracing the subtle topography of muscle and scar tissue, a body shaped by both discipline and damage. I discovered a second scar beneath his left shoulder blade, a small depression that spoke of embedded shrapnel perhaps never fully removed. My fingers lingered there, acknowledging without words this additional evidence of vulnerability carried beneath his uniform.

His mouth traveled downward with unhurried deliberation, discovering the sensitive hollow between my collarbones, the gentle swell of my breasts, the subtle contraction of my abdomen as his tongue traced patterns that seemed to ignite nerve endings previously dormant. Unlike our previous encounters where he had approached my body with almost tactical efficiency, tonight he explored as if encountering new territory, his focus complete rather than divided.

When his lips closed around my nipple, the wet heat of his mouth sent currents of pleasure spiraling outward. His tongue circled with exquisite precision, while his hand mirrored the motion against my other breast, the dual sensation creating a symmetry of pleasure that made my back arch instinctively toward him. I heard myself make sounds rarely offered to clients, authentic, unfiltered responses that emerged from a place beyond professional calculation.

"The sounds you make," he whispered against my heated skin, "they're different tonight."

"Because this is different," I acknowledged, truth replacing performance.

His journey continued downward, his strong hands parting my thighs with gentle insistence. The anticipation of his mouth between my legs created its own delicious torture, each kiss placed on inner thigh bringing him closer to where heat pooled with increasing urgency. My fingers tangled in his short hair, not directing but connecting, creating additional pathways for sensation to travel between us.

When his mouth finally found the center of my desire, the first touch of his tongue against slick flesh drew a gasp from deep within me. Unlike his previous methodical approach to pleasuring me, tonight his exploration carried a quality of genuine discovery. Each stroke, each subtle change in pressure seemed guided by my responses rather than predetermined technique. The flat of his tongue created broad pressure before narrowing to focused attention on the swollen bud where sensation concentrated like light through a magnifying glass.

The contrast between his military strength and this exquisite tenderness created its own erotic tension. His hands, capable of command, of controlled violence when duty required, now cradled my hips with reverent care, his thumbs tracing small circles against my hip bones as his mouth worked with dedicated focus between my thighs. The juxtaposition of power restrained and power expressed heightened every sensation.

My fingers found his short-cropped hair, neither directing nor controlling but simply connecting as pleasure built in concentric waves. His tongue discovered a rhythm that seemed perfectly calibrated to my responses: firm, consistent circles that occasionally dipped lower to gather wetness before returning to the sensitive bundle of nerves that had become the center of my universe. When he slipped first one finger, then two inside me, curving upward to find the textured ridge of internal tissue that so many men overlook, the dual stimulation sent electricity racing through my limbs.

"Yes," I breathed, abandoning any pretense of professional detachment. "Just like that."

I felt myself approaching that exquisite threshold where control dissolves completely. Yet rather than surrendering immediately to the rising tide, I gently guided him upward. "I want to feel you inside me," I murmured, needing this connection to complete our transformed intimacy.

He moved above me with fluid grace that belied his military bearing, his body finding position between my thighs as if we had rehearsed this choreography for years rather than days. His hardness pressed against me, the velvety head sliding through wetness that testified to my arousal. The first press of him against my entrance created a moment of exquisite anticipation; that suspended instant before joining where possibility exists in perfect tension.

When he finally entered me, the penetration carried almost ceremonial significance, a connection that transcended mere physical pleasure to become something approaching communion. He filled me completely, his considerable length and thickness creating a delicious stretching sensation that made me momentarily breathless. But unlike previous nights where he would have immediately established rhythm, tonight he remained perfectly still, fully seated within me, our bodies joined in sacred stillness.

"Feel that," he whispered, his forehead pressed against mine, our breath mingling in the narrow space between our lips. "Just this moment. Nothing else."

The intimacy of this suspended animation, this deliberate pause to simply exist in perfect connection, affected me profoundly. I felt tears gathering unexpectedly at the corners of my eyes, not from sorrow but from the strange poignancy of authentic union so rarely experienced in my professional life.

When he finally began to move, it was with measured restraint that contained its own power: each thrust deliberate, unhurried, reaching depths that seemed both physical and emotional. I watched his face above mine, fascinated by the emotions that now moved across features previously held in careful neutrality. Pleasure mingled with something deeper. A vulnerable wonder, a surrender of control that paradoxically seemed to intensify rather than diminish his masculine presence.

My legs wrapped around his waist, pulling him deeper still, my heels pressing against the muscled curve of his buttocks. Our bodies found rhythm together, giving and receiving, advancing and yielding, in patterns that seemed to write themselves rather than following prescribed choreography. His hands cradled my face with unexpected tenderness even as our movements gained urgency, the contrast between gentleness and intensity creating its own exquisite tension.

The symphony of sensation built between us: the slick heat where our bodies joined, the friction of chest against breasts, the mingled sounds of pleasure that seemed to create their own intimate music in the amber-lit darkness of my bedroom. My fingers traced the corded muscles of his shoulders, feeling them flex and release with each powerful movement. His mouth found mine in kisses that grew increasingly urgent yet remained present, not the distracted collisions of approaching climax but genuine connection maintained even as pleasure mounted.

I felt him begin to establish a faster cadence, his control fraying at the edges as sensation overtook strategy. Yet in this moment of approaching abandon, I sensed a subtle retreat. His gaze shifting focus as if withdrawing to safer internal terrain.

"Stay with me," I encouraged, my palms against his cheeks guiding his eyes back to mine. "Stay present."

His eyes opened fully, meeting mine with startling clarity. Something new inhabited his gaze, a naked truth beyond performance or expectation. "I'm here," he whispered, the simple words carrying complex meaning.

In this moment of shared vulnerability, alchemy occurred between us. Pleasure deepening beyond physical dimensions, intensifying through emotional presence rather than technical variation. He shifted angle slightly, his pubic bone pressing against that exquisitely sensitive external point with each movement, creating dual waves of sensation that radiated through my entire body. His hand slipped between us, fingers finding precise rhythm against my center while he maintained the perfect cadence of his thrusts.

The combined stimulation pushed me toward a pleasure so intense it bordered on transcendence. I felt it building from somewhere deeper than physical architecture alone, a gathering force that originated in connection rather than mere stimulation. My inner muscles began to contract around him with increasing urgency, each pulse drawing an answering throb from his hardness within me.

"Let me feel you," he urged, voice rough with his own approaching release. "Show me everything."

The permission contained in these words, this invitation to complete abandonment, unleashed something primal within me. Release claimed me with devastating totality, contractions pulsing through my center and radiating outward in waves that seemed to dissolve boundaries between physical sensation and emotional surrender. I heard myself cry out, a sound pulled from somewhere beyond conscious control, beyond professional modulation.

My release triggered his own, his rhythm faltering momentarily before establishing three final, powerful thrusts that seated him completely within me. His face transformed with pleasure that held something of pain's intensity, his controlled features yielding completely to authentic experience. I felt the pulse of his climax deep inside, each throb of his release triggering aftershocks in my still-sensitive flesh.

For several suspended moments, we existed in perfect communion. Neither general nor courtesan but simply man and woman, joined in authentic connection that transcended the circumstances of our meeting. His weight pressed me into the mattress, yet I welcomed rather than merely accommodated this temporary surrender to gravity. Something had broken open between us, some essential barrier had yielded to allow true meeting in territory neither of us frequently traversed.

As our breathing gradually steadied, he shifted to avoid crushing me completely, yet maintained our connection by gathering me against his side. His arm cradled me with surprising tenderness, my head finding perfect resting place in the hollow beneath his collarbone where heartbeat gradually returned to measured cadence. The gentle stroke of his fingers through my hair carried none of the efficient detachment that had marked the conclusion of our previous encounters.

"That was..." he began, then stopped, searching for adequate terminology.

"Different?" I suggested, my fingers tracing patterns across his chest.

"Completely." His hand covered mine, stilling its movement. "I've had sex countless times. That felt like making love."

The observation, so simple yet profound, touched something deep within me. In my profession, I've witnessed countless variations of physical connection, yet relatively few moments of genuine intimacy. His recognition of the difference spoke to an emotional intelligence perhaps underutilized in his military career.

We talked then as we never had during previous evenings, about his childhood in rural Pennsylvania, about the mix of pride and terror he felt regarding his son's decision to follow his path, about moments in combat that had marked him beyond physical scars. I listened without judgment, offering presence rather than advice, creating space for expressions rarely permitted within military hierarchy.

When he eventually dressed to return to his hotel, something had shifted in his demeanor. Not a complete transformation, but an integration of aspects previously kept rigidly separated. The general's bearing remained, evident in his posture and economical movements. Yet it now coexisted with a new quality, a certain openness that allowed his humanity to become visible alongside his authority.

At my door, he paused, hand resting lightly on the frame. "Thank you," he said simply, "for creating a space where different rules applied."

"The courage was yours," I replied truthfully. "I merely witnessed it."

After he had gone, I returned to my terrace where our wine glasses remained, the liquid now dark and still in the midnight air. Monaco continued its luminous display below, the harbor lights reflecting in fractured brilliance across the gentle Mediterranean swell. Something lingered in the space he had occupied. Not just memory or impression but a reminder of intimacy's true nature.

What distinguished our final evening was not exceptional technique or novel approach but the willingness to bring authenticity into our shared experience. His small act of vulnerability, showing me his scar, sharing his fears, had transformed pleasure into connection, transaction into genuine exchange.

In a world that rewards armor and penalizes its absence, such moments of courageous revelation become increasingly precious. Perhaps this represents my profession's deepest value, not the physical release we ostensibly provide, but the rare sanctuaries we create where armor can be safely set aside, where the defenses necessary in daily combat might briefly yield to the fundamental human need for authentic connection.

•

Through countless intimate encounters, I've observed how emotional presence and physical pleasure dance together, inseparable twins, one flowing naturally from the other in perfect correlation. The General's experience beautifully illustrated this sacred principle. His military training had taught him to compartmentalize emotions for necessary reasons, to make life-or-death decisions without interference, to lead while burying doubt deep beneath duty's surface. Yet when those essential professional boundaries calcified into emotional armor he carried everywhere, they transformed into invisible barriers to his deepest pleasure.

I've witnessed this pattern with remarkable consistency across professions demanding emotional containment, surgeons whose hands remain steady in blood but tremble in tender caresses, judges who deliver verdicts without flinching yet cannot surrender to their own sensual verdicts, executives who command boardrooms but remain perpetual strangers to their own desires. The very discipline making them exceptional in their fields often diminishes their capacity for surrender in intimate contexts. These individuals experience physical pleasure, most achieve satisfying sexual release, but transcendent dimensions remain locked behind carefully maintained defenses, treasures they cannot reach through their own fortifications.

When emotional barriers dissolve, even momentarily, something exquisite happens within the body's ancient systems. The vigilant sympathetic nervous system, perpetually scanning horizons for threats, yields to the parasympathetic system governing our capacity for pleasure. Breathing deepens like a sea finding its natural rhythm after storm, blood flows more generously to erogenous tissues awakening them to sensation, nerve endings become hypersensitive to the slightest touch, registering whispers where before they required shouts. The body, no longer standing guard at ramparts of self-protection, inhabits pleasure fully rather than merely visiting it on brief reconnaissance.

His willingness to reveal that scar, such a small disclosure when viewed objectively, represented profound surrender of the rigid control defining his existence. This wasn't manufactured vulnerability or calculated performance, but an authentic moment of truth-sharing that created alchemical conditions for deeper connection. The transformed intimacy that followed wasn't about novel technique or position but about presence. That rare courage to be fully there, undivided, in shared experience.

I sometimes wonder about the General, what lingered with him after our encounter. We touch each other in ways neither predicted nor fully understood, leaving fingerprints on souls that may not be recognized until years later, if ever. Some seeds find fertile ground; others blow away on the next morning's breeze. The mystery of our influence on one another remains one of life's most beautiful uncertainties.

This explains why the most memorable encounters in my profession rarely feature sexual acrobatics or technical prowess. The moments that linger, that transform both participants in ways neither anticipated, invariably contain this element of authentic revelation, where carefully maintained performance of self yields, however briefly, to genuine presence. The veil parts, and for one perfect moment, we truly see and are seen.

In our world that increasingly rewards armor and punishes its absence, creating spaces where vulnerability safely emerges becomes revolutionary. Perhaps this represents the true value of my unusual profession: not the physical release we ostensibly provide, but the rare sanctuaries we create where armor can be temporarily set aside, where fortifications necessary for daily battles might yield to our fundamental human need for connection.

The pleasure emerging from such courage transcends the merely physical, touching something essential, reminding us that beneath our carefully constructed personas, general or courtesan, surgeon or teacher, we share the same fundamental yearning: to be truly seen, if only for a moment, in all our beautiful imperfection.

The Lesson:

Vulnerability awakens pleasure in ways that technical perfection never can. This seems counterintuitive in a culture that equates vulnerability with weakness, yet I've witnessed its truth hundreds of times in my profession. The most extraordinary experiences of pleasure aren't orchestrated through sexual virtuosity but emerge when we dare to lower our shields, even slightly.

The beauty of this approach lies in its simplicity. Profound connection doesn't require grand emotional revelations or psychological excavation. Small, authentic disclosures, the kind that feel slightly uncomfortable but not overwhelming, often create the most fertile ground for deepened pleasure. A simple "I feel nervous" or "I've never shown anyone this scar" can transform an encounter from performance to communion.

If you're someone accustomed to maintaining control, consider starting with physical vulnerability. Allowing your partner to touch you in ways that require surrender, perhaps having your face cradled or your eyes covered, can create pathways toward emotional opening. The body often leads where the mind hesitates to follow.

For those receiving such vulnerability, your response shapes whether the opening deepens or closes. Avoid rushing to reassurance or reciprocal disclosure. Instead, offer the gift of witnessing. Simple acknowledgment through touch, presence, or quiet affirmation. Sometimes the most profound response is simply creating space where another's truth can exist without judgment.

The correlation I've observed remains consistent: physical pleasure expands in direct proportion to emotional presence. This doesn't mean abandoning all boundaries, the General didn't need to share his entire military history or break down in emotional catharsis. His simple disclosure, that moment of authentic sharing, created sufficient opening for deeper connection. Think of vulnerability not as removing all armor but as opening a single necessary clasp, allowing breath to flow more freely through the places where we've been bound.

Part 3:
Female Pleasure & Empowerment

My first client who truly understood female pleasure was, surprisingly, a mathematician. A man who approached the female body as sophisticated topology rather than simple geometry. "The clitoris isn't a button," he explained with elegant precision as his fingers demonstrated his understanding, "but a complex three-dimensional structure that responds to field equations rather than single-point stimulation." As my body arched involuntarily beneath his touch, I realized he'd discovered through analysis what most never grasp through years of experience.

Female pleasure remains poorly mapped territory, charted primarily by explorers who cannot feel its contours from within. Despite decades of supposed sexual liberation, women's bodies are still approached through outdated understanding that prioritizes male experience. The resulting cartography contains shocking omissions, misidentified landmarks, and paths that circle endlessly without reaching actual destinations.

In my profession, I've witnessed this disconnect countless times: men genuinely believing they're providing pleasure while their partners simulate response out of kindness, obligation, or simple efficiency. This mutual disappointment stems not from lack of desire or effort, but from fundamental misunderstanding of female anatomy and psychology.

The chapters that follow correct these ancient errors, offering precise guidance through territories often shrouded in unnecessary mystery. We begin with physical accuracy, the exact location of structures typically missed or misidentified, but extend into the psychological dimensions where agency and surrender create their own erotic voltage.

I've felt my body respond to touches so precisely calibrated they seemed to bypass conscious thought, activating pleasure centers I hadn't known existed until that moment of discovery. That such sensations remain inaccessible to many women reflects not their capacity for response but the inadequate maps they've been given. Consider what follows not merely education but liberation, a reclaiming of pleasure too long misunderstood.

The Elusive Pearl

The Mediterranean revealed itself that afternoon as a living canvas of impossible blue, each wave catching light in a rhythm so hypnotic I found myself arrested at my own window. Even after years of gazing upon it from my Monaco apartment, this sea retained its capacity to astonish, to transform ordinary moments into meditations on beauty. That particular day, the water's surface scattered sunlight in diamond brilliance, creating liquid constellations that shifted with each passing moment.

It was this spectacle that captivated him first when he crossed my threshold, my marine biologist with his Scandinavian inflections and eyes already searching past me toward the horizon. His attention, diverted by beauty, revealed more about his true nature than any practiced introduction could have.

"The visibility must be exceptional today," he remarked, momentarily forgetting the social choreography of greeting me. "You can almost see the underwater topography from here."

I studied him as he studied the sea, a tall man with skin weathered by salt and sun, body lean from days moving across research vessels. His hands particularly intrigued me, strong yet precise fingertips accustomed to handling delicate specimens now fidgeting slightly as he returned his attention to our imminent encounter. Those hands would soon explore territories more mysterious than any ocean trench, would discover secrets his scientific training had never prepared him to uncover.

"The sea is my favorite companion," I offered, watching tension dissolve from his shoulders as conversation drifted toward waters he knew well. "It holds so many secrets beneath its surface."

"That's what drew me to marine biology," he admitted, moving further into my apartment with newfound ease. "The contrast between what appears visible and what remains hidden. Like how this sunlight changes the color completely." He gestured toward the window. "It reminds me of pearls. How light reveals their true nature by penetrating and bouncing between all those translucent layers of nacre. The luminescence comes from light seeking to uncover what the pearl is trying to conceal."

I smiled at the unintended parallel, feeling heat bloom low in my belly at the perfect metaphor he had unknowingly provided. "Perhaps that's true of pleasure as well. How the right touch transforms something anatomical into something transcendent."

His eyes met mine with sudden recognition, the scientist beginning to understand that today's exploration would bridge his world of marine biology and the more mysterious waters of human connection. I saw his pupils dilate slightly, the first physical betrayal of desire rippling beneath his composed exterior.

We stepped onto my balcony where the sea breeze carried salt and hints of distant gardens. Over wine, he spoke with infectious enthusiasm about Mediterranean tide pools and the surprising complexity of seemingly simple organisms. His hands sketched invisible shapes in the air, anatomical diagrams of sea creatures and ocean currents, moving with the same precision they would soon apply to more intimate geographies.

I observed the subtle currents beneath his scientific composure: the forward shift when speaking of desire, his gaze dropping to my lips before deliberately returning to my eyes. The pattern suggested a man who had scheduled this appointment with clear expectations of his own pleasure, viewing female satisfaction as a pleasant but secondary achievement.

"I hope you don't find this presumptuous," he said after finishing his wine, "but I've been thinking about this meeting for weeks." His fingers drummed gentle rhythm against his glass. "I've imagined what it would be like to... to be with someone who understands the art of pleasure."

I recognized the unspoken assumption in his words, that our encounter would follow the conventional script where his satisfaction formed the ultimate destination. In that moment, like a navigator suddenly changing course, I decided what this man truly needed wasn't what he thought he wanted.

"In my profession," I said, rising from my chair and approaching him with deliberate slowness, "I've observed that many men approach a woman's body as if navigating without charts. They may eventually find their own satisfaction, but often through a journey that leaves vast territories of female pleasure unexplored."

Curiosity momentarily overrode desire in his expression. "That seems..." he hesitated, seeking the precise term, "...inefficient."

"Exactly," I nodded, standing now between his knees, close enough for him to inhale the bergamot and vanilla notes of my perfume, close enough to feel the heat radiating between our bodies. "And entirely unnecessary. Would you like to learn something that will transform every intimate encounter you have for the rest of your life?"

The scientist in him couldn't resist this offer of rare knowledge, though I noticed a momentary stiffening in his posture: that familiar male pride bristling at the suggestion he might not already know everything about a woman's body. His jaw tightened briefly, a fleeting resistance I've witnessed countless times.

"I'm quite familiar with female anatomy," he said with a professional's confidence, the defensive note in his voice betraying him. But his eyes told a different story. Curiosity warring with ego, the researcher's hunger for discovery battling against masculine pride.

I simply held his gaze, saying nothing, letting the silence work between us. After a moment, his scientific nature triumphed over pride.

"Yes," he finally answered, shoulders relaxing as he surrendered to curiosity, "I'd like to learn." His pupils dilated visibly as I took his hand and led him inside, intellectual hunger merging with physical desire.

The day's light had mellowed to a burnished gold when we reached my bedroom, each shadow now elongated and precise, like ink lines drawn by a meticulous hand. Objects seemed to glow from within: the curve of a pillow, the drape of silk sheets, the outline of his body as he stood uncertainly beside my bed. Confusion briefly crossed his features. He had expected to be the recipient of pleasure, not a student of it. Yet his natural curiosity quickly overcame initial disorientation.

"I believe in beginning with observation," I said, fingers moving to my blouse buttons with unhurried precision. "The most important discoveries often come from patient looking."

His gaze followed my hands with the concentration of someone memorizing a new species. With each button I released, his breathing deepened almost imperceptibly. The fabric parted beneath my fingers, revealing first the hollow of my throat, then the subtle curve where collarbones meet, then the swelling beginnings of my breasts. I maintained perfect eye contact as I slipped the garment from my shoulders, letting it whisper to the floor in a pool of silk.

When I stood before him in simple black lingerie, I watched him cataloging details: the topology of curves, the textures of exposed skin, the geography of shadow and light. Yet something beyond scientific interest emerged in his expression, a warmth transcending analysis. His hands clenched slightly at his sides, the first involuntary sign of restraint being tested.

"May I?" he asked, reaching toward me with a researcher's reverence.

"Not yet," I replied, taking his hands in mine. Surprise registered in his eyes, but he didn't resist. "First, I want you to understand why we're here. Many men leave encounters like this with momentary satisfaction but nothing lasting. I'm offering you something more valuable: knowledge that will serve you and every woman you're ever intimate with."

Something shifted in his gaze. A recognition that this wasn't proceeding according to expected script, yet the possibility of gaining rare insight clearly intrigued him. I guided him to sit beside me on the edge of the bed, close enough that our thighs pressed together through our clothing, close enough that I could feel the heat of him through the fabric.

"The female body contains a secret that shouldn't be a secret at all," I continued, my voice dropping to intimate register, creating vibrations I knew he could feel as much as hear. "A center of pleasure that many men spend their entire lives misunderstanding or overlooking entirely."

His professional curiosity sharpened, drawing him closer, his gaze steady and searching. "I'm listening," he said, though the faint catch in his breath gave him away—this was no longer just intellectual inquiry, but something warmer, more vulnerable, beginning to stir beneath the surface.

I took his hand in mine, bringing his fingers to my lips. "Today, I want to teach you something specific," I murmured against his skin, allowing my lips to linger on each fingertip, my tongue darting out to taste the salt of his skin. "Something many men seek but never truly find."

His eyes locked with mine, a flush spreading across his cheekbones. "I'm eager to learn," he whispered, voice roughening at the edges.

Holding his gaze, I guided his hand between my legs, pressing his palm against the black silk still covering me. The fabric was already damp with my arousal, the heat of my sex radiating through the thin barrier. His eyes darkened as he felt the wetness beneath his palm, his throat working as he swallowed hard.

"Feel that warmth," I whispered, my voice dropping to a register I reserved for moments of genuine desire. "That's anticipation. That's response."

His throat constricted visibly, scientific detachment yielding to primal hunger. I watched his nostrils flare as he caught the scent of my arousal, that sweet musk that no perfume can replicate. With deliberate slowness, I slid the silk to one side, revealing myself to both his touch and his gaze. The naked want in his eyes as he looked directly at my exposed flesh sent liquid heat pulsing through me, made my inner muscles clench with anticipation.

"Now," I said, taking his index finger and guiding it with precision, "this is where careful observation becomes crucial."

I placed his fingertip directly on my clitoris, that small paradise so often bypassed. His pupils expanded instantly at the intimate contact, breath escaping in a soft hiss. My hips lifted involuntarily toward his hand, a movement as ancient as the tides he studied.

"This," I explained, voice already thickening with arousal, "is what poets call the pearl, what anatomists call the clitoris, what countless women wish their lovers could locate with confidence."

I detected a flash of recognition in his eyes as he studied where our bodies connected. He nodded with affected confidence, as if confirming something he already knew, though his hesitation betrayed him.

"Of course, the clitoris," he said with academic pronunciation, a terminology shield against admitting uncertainty. Then, more honestly: "Though it's... positioned differently than I imagined." His thumb moved cautiously, as if approaching an unfamiliar specimen, then brushed against the sensitive hood.

The sudden jolt of pleasure made me gasp involuntarily, my back arching, my sex growing even wetter beneath his touch. His eyes widened at my unrestrained response, professional composure momentarily abandoned.

"I've read about this structure, naturally," he added quickly, scientific vocabulary a thin cover for his evident surprise at my reaction. "But textbooks don't quite..." He paused, struggling between maintaining his expert persona and acknowledging the gap between theoretical knowledge and practical understanding.

I saw the moment he surrendered to genuine curiosity, his features softening as he let go of pretense. "Show me exactly," he whispered, voice stripped of professional distance, "how to touch you here."

"Size and sensitivity are inversely proportional here," I managed as he repeated the motion with deliberate intent. His touch, tentative but curious, triggered visible responses that seemed to fascinate him. "The concentration of nerve endings here surpasses any equivalent structure in the male body."

My thighs parted further, an unconscious invitation as his exploration gained confidence. The subtle scent of my arousal intensified, filling the narrow space between us. His breathing deepened, the front of his trousers visibly straining with his own mounting desire. This visual evidence of his arousal intensified mine: that exquisite feedback loop where giving and receiving pleasure become indistinguishable.

Under my guidance, his explorations grew bolder. I showed him how to vary pressure: light, teasing circles that had me squirming, followed by firmer strokes that made my breath fragment into soft gasps. His gaze never left my face, watching intently as different techniques produced different responses. My nipples had hardened visibly beneath black lace, tight peaks straining against the delicate fabric.

Without prompting, he lowered his head and captured my nipple with his mouth, the warmth of his lips pressing through the delicate fabric of my bra. This unexpected initiative, the wet heat of his tongue against the sensitive peak, sent electric current directly to where his fingers continued their discovery. I rewarded this creativity with a moan that seemed to affect him physically, his hips unconsciously pressing forward against empty air, seeking friction that wasn't yet available.

"You're learning quickly," I breathed, reaching to free his evident arousal from confinement. The sound of his zipper descending seemed unnaturally loud in the quiet room. When my fingers found him, he was already fully hard, his cock straining upward, hot and silken against my palm. I encircled him, feeling the pulse of blood beneath the surface, the slight twitch as my grip tightened. His thickness pulsed against my palm as I stroked him in rhythm with his circles on my pearl. "Feel how giving pleasure creates its own reward?"

He groaned agreement, scientific precision momentarily faltering as sensation claimed some of his concentration. But his fingers never lost their place, continuing their exploration with increasing skill even as his own desire mounted.

"Circles," I murmured, guiding his motion with subtle movements of my hips. "Gentle but consistent. Think of ocean currents. Continuous movement without overwhelming force."

His erection strained against my palm as he adopted the suggestion with remarkable aptitude, his touch becoming more intuitive with each passing moment. The focused intensity in his eyes, that same concentration I'd observed when he described marine specimens, now turned entirely to my pleasure, though his own was clearly building. When my breathing quickened, he noticed immediately, maintaining the precise rhythm that had triggered the response.

"Now slightly faster," I guided, my words fragmenting as sensation built inside me like a gathering wave. My hand moved faster on his length in tandem, feeling the velvet-soft skin sliding over rigid hardness. "Just like that…" I gasped as he found the perfect pressure.

His free hand slipped beneath my bra, pushing the lace aside to discover bare flesh, thumb circling my nipple in mirrored rhythm to his lower attention. The dual stimulation heightened everything, pushing me toward the precipice. I felt inner muscles beginning to contract in anticipation, felt the gathering wetness at my core.

"I can feel you responding," he murmured, voice rough with desire and wonder. "The way your body tenses, the change in your breathing…" Even in mounting passion, the scientist in him observed, cataloged, learned.

"I didn't expect this," he whispered, his voice revealing wonder rather than disappointment. "I thought I was coming here for…"

"For your own satisfaction?" I finished. "You'll have that too. But first, understand that giving this kind of pleasure is its own profound reward."

His eyes, dark with desire, showed he was beginning to comprehend this truth not just intellectually but viscerally.

I guided him to lie back on the bed, my hand still encircling his impressive hardness. Straddling his thighs, I showed him how to use his thumb to maintain contact with my pearl while his long middle finger slipped inside me. The penetration made me cry out. A sound of pure, unfiltered pleasure as his finger entered me. The wetness of my arousal welcomed him, easing his passage while simultaneously heightening every sensation. He could feel my inner walls clutching at him, my body's instinctive urge to draw him deeper.

"Feel that texture," I instructed, voice breaking as his finger curled upward. "That slightly ridged area…"

He found the subtle ridged terrain of my internal pleasure point with surprising accuracy. His eyes widened with discovery.

"Another pearl," he murmured, his scientific mind making the connection as he massaged the spot with perfect pressure. His thumb continued its circles outside while his finger worked within, creating harmony of sensation that had me rocking shamelessly against his hand.

"Yes," I managed, as he applied concurrent pressure to both locations. "Internal and external..."

My words dissolved into urgent sounds as waves of pleasure radiated outward from these dual centers. My body responded with increasing urgency, inner muscles gripping his finger as he explored. My free hand braced against his chest, nails leaving crescent impressions as sensation built toward inevitable release.

What amazed me was his patience. The way he maintained precise stimulation without rushing, without disrupting the building wave. His own arousal was evident in the hardness throbbing against my thigh, yet he remained focused on my pleasure with remarkable discipline. His scientific mind had transformed this encounter into a study of my responses, and he proved an exceptionally attentive researcher.

When orgasm finally claimed me, it wasn't the polite climax I sometimes enacted for clients' egos, but a genuine storm that arched my back and tore uninhibited sounds from my throat, a surrender to elemental forces that momentarily dissolved consciousness itself. My inner muscles contracted rhythmically around his finger, squeezing in waves as pleasure pulsed outward from my core, radiating through my limbs until even my fingertips tingled with the aftershocks.

As tremors subsided, I opened my eyes to find him watching me with undisguised wonder, his fingers still inside me, feeling the rhythmic contractions gradually slow.

"That was..." he paused, searching for adequate words, his erection still rigid and urgent against my thigh, "...like witnessing a perfect natural phenomenon."

I laughed softly, moving to straddle him fully. "Nature's most intimate miracle," I agreed, positioning his thickness at my entrance, still slick and sensitive from release. I held him there for a moment, letting him feel the heat and wetness of me just barely taking his tip. "And entirely reproducible under the right conditions."

His eyes darkened as I sank down onto him in one fluid motion, taking him deep inside me. The fullness after sensitivity created a delicious aftershock of pleasure, my body stretching to accommodate his size. I could feel every ridge and vein of him as he filled me completely, the connection so intense that we both froze for a moment, suspended in the perfect sensation of joining.

"The perfect scientific discovery," he gasped, his hands finding my hips, fingers pressing into soft flesh with an urgency he could no longer disguise.

I leaned forward, breasts grazing his chest as I began to move. "Now," I whispered against his ear, "apply what you've learned."

With remarkable presence despite obvious arousal, he reached between us, thumb finding my still-sensitive pearl as I rode him. The dual stimulation, his thickness filling me while his thumb circled that crucial point, quickly rebuilt the sensation I'd just experienced. Most men would have been too lost in their own pleasure to maintain such attentiveness, but he watched my face with the same intensity he'd shown all afternoon, adjusting pressure and rhythm according to my responses.

I moved above him in undulations reminiscent of the sea outside my window, teaching him through my body how penetration alone rarely provides enough stimulation. The wet sound of our joining filled the room. That unmistakable rhythm of bodies merging and separating, of flesh meeting flesh in ancient conversation. The way he applied this lesson, maintaining contact with my pearl as our bodies joined, showed how thoroughly he'd absorbed the earlier instruction. His free hand discovered my breast, rolling the nipple between thumb and forefinger with exquisite pressure that bordered perfect pain.

When I contracted around him deliberately, his eyes widened with pleasure. "Feel that?" I asked, repeating the internal caress, squeezing him with muscles hidden deep within me. "Women can create sensation too."

His response was a sound drawn from somewhere beneath language, primal and raw. I increased my pace, the slick friction between us building new waves of pleasure. The air filled with our mingled essences: the salt of skin, the essence of arousal, the faint sweetness of my perfume caught in the afternoon heat.

Just as he approached his own release, he astonished me by stilling my hips momentarily and adjusting our position so his pubic bone pressed more firmly against my pearl with each thrust. This intuitive adaptation, applying what he'd learned without instruction, pushed me toward a second climax I hadn't anticipated. As we came together, his hand tangled in my hair, pulling my mouth to his in a kiss that swallowed our shared sounds of pleasure.

I felt him pulsing inside me, his cock twitching as he emptied himself in hot spurts. The sensation triggered my own release, my inner walls clenching around him rhythmically, milking every drop as waves of pleasure crashed through me.

For a moment, the boundaries between us collapsed. Scientist and courtesan no longer separate entities but a single circuit of sensation. Our bodies communicated in a language more ancient than words, each response flowing between us like current seeking completion. In that sacred space where separate selves briefly dissolve, we discovered truth that reason alone could never reveal.

Afterward, as afternoon light faded to dusk, we lay in comfortable silence. His fingers still mapped my body occasionally, returning to the places he had discovered, as if committing the topography to memory.

"This wasn't what I expected when I made the appointment," he confessed, his voice soft in the gathering darkness. "I thought I was coming here for... well, for my own pleasure primarily."

"And did you find it?" I asked.

His smile was genuine and slightly wondering. "Yes, but in a completely different way than I anticipated. Discovering how to give pleasure has been more satisfying than simply receiving it."

"That's the lesson most men never learn," I replied, touching his face. "The greatest satisfaction often comes from understanding your partner's pleasure as thoroughly as your own."

"In my research," he continued thoughtfully, "I've observed how certain stimuli can trigger remarkable responses in simple organisms. But I've never fully appreciated how complex and beautiful the human response can be—and how rewarding it is to be the one who understands how to elicit that response."

I turned toward him, placing my hand over his heart. "The difference, perhaps, is that while you merely observe your marine subjects, here you both observe and participate. The scientist becomes part of the experiment."

His smile contained both satisfaction and new understanding. "The most rewarding research I've ever conducted."

As darkness settled over Monaco, transforming the Mediterranean into endless obsidian, we continued our exploration, his touch now informed by knowledge, my responses deepened by his genuine attention. What had begun as instruction had evolved into mutual discovery, each of us mapping the territories of the other with increasing familiarity and wonder.

•

The body contains a diary of our most intimate truths, written in the language of nerves and sensation. What transpired with the marine biologist revealed how pleasure exists as a conversation between knowledge and surrender. I watched understanding transform physical sensation before my eyes, from his first clinical touch to the moment his fingertips discovered the terrain that made my back arch involuntarily. This transformation never fails to move me, when intellectual comprehension dissolves into embodied knowledge, when scientist becomes poet.

The greatest mysteries hide in plain sight. The pearl of pleasure, obvious once revealed, elusive when sought without guidance, becomes the perfect metaphor for human connection. How many women's bodies have been mapped incorrectly, their treasures bypassed in the rush toward more obvious destinations?

He returned six more times before leaving Monaco. Each visit transformed him, his approach evolving from methodical to intuitive. By our third meeting, he arrived with sketches that might have been created by a Renaissance master. By our fifth, he had begun to innovate. I observed this evolution with the peculiar satisfaction that remains my profession's greatest reward: witnessing understanding born and nurtured into wisdom.

What moved me was his essential transformation. The man who initially sought service became a student of reciprocity, his satisfaction increasingly derived from what he could elicit, from sounds escaping my throat, from quickening breath, from tremors revealing pleasure too deep for performance. His confidence grew not from conquest but from connection, the quiet assurance that comes when one truly sees another's experience.

On our final evening, as Mediterranean twilight painted my apartment in violet shadows, he confessed our encounters had fundamentally altered his approach to intimacy. "I've spent my career studying how organisms respond to their environments, but I never thought to apply that same curiosity to understanding human pleasure. Now I can't imagine approaching intimacy any other way."

There exists no greater satisfaction in my professional life than witnessing the birth of awareness in another. When we learn to bring pleasure to someone else, to truly understand their needs without ego, we develop a quality of presence that enriches all aspects of life.

The elusive pearl, once discovered, becomes a touchstone for all future explorations. In guiding him to this center of feminine pleasure, I offered something beyond momentary satisfaction, a gift that would enrich every future intimate connection. Unlike physical pleasure, which fades, knowledge deepens with each application. The greatest lover is not the one who performs most impressively but the one who listens most attentively, who approaches the body not as conquered territory but as sacred landscape.

I imagine him now, bringing his knowledge to distant shores, to women who may never know the origin of his rare understanding. Knowledge of pleasure travels beyond its origin, multiplying joy in widening circles, not momentary release but the capacity to create pleasure anew with each connection.

Every woman's body speaks its own language. Some prefer direct declarations, others metaphorical whispers. The most profound truth I've learned from thousands of intimate encounters is this: there exists no universal map, only the willingness to explore with reverence. The questions we ask with our fingers, our lips, our eyes become the most genuine expressions of desire, more honest than any performance of passion.

Pleasure reveals itself most fully not in technical mastery but in surrender to the present, the willingness to navigate without certainty. The pearl may be elusive, but the search itself transforms both seeker and sought, allowing us to recognize that the greatest mystery lies not in finding what we seek but in becoming capable of truly seeing what has been before us all along.

The Lesson:

The clitoris, that exquisite center of female pleasure, remains curiously elusive in far too many intimate encounters. Its significance cannot be overstated: most women require direct stimulation of this area to reach orgasm, yet I've been astonished by how many otherwise knowledgeable men cannot confidently locate it. This disconnect between anatomy and attention creates a chasm that countless women silently endure.

Finding this "elusive pearl" requires both knowledge and attentiveness. It typically appears as a small, rounded structure nestled at the top of the vulva where the inner labia meet, though, like all aspects of human anatomy, its appearance varies considerably between women. Some are more prominent, others more hidden; some emerge boldly from beneath their protective hood when aroused, while others remain more mysteriously concealed. This natural variation means that visual identification alone often proves insufficient. Exploration guided by touch, response, and communication becomes essential.

What many don't realize, and what I find myself explaining with surprising frequency, is that this structure contains more specialized nerve endings than any equivalent area in the male body, all concentrated in an astonishingly small space. This density of sensation means that touch here should generally be more delicate than intuition might suggest, particularly at first. As arousal builds, this sensitivity often allows for firmer pressure, but beginning with gentleness honors its remarkable responsiveness.

The most satisfying approach combines visual awareness with attentive touch and, most importantly, a willingness to adjust based on response. Begin with gentle exploration of the entire vulva, allowing arousal to build naturally before focusing more specifically on this sensitive region. Most women respond beautifully to circular motions either directly on or slightly to the sides of the clitoris, with pressure that gradually increases as arousal deepens. Consistency often matters more than variety: finding a rhythm that resonates and maintaining it typically proves more effective than continuous variation.

I cannot emphasize enough the importance of communication in this exploration. Every woman's body speaks its own dialect of pleasure, some prefer direct contact, others indirect; some respond to firm pressure, others to feather-light touch. When uncertain, simply ask. A quiet "Is this good?" or "Show me what you like" transforms uncertainty into shared discovery.

The Inner Landscape

Electricity haunts the air after rain, invisible yet potent, awakening skin to whispered possibilities. The mist clung to Monaco's mountains that spring afternoon, a translucent veil transforming my apartment into an island of intimate seclusion. The persistent downpour had finally relented, leaving behind that peculiar charge that makes every surface vibrate with heightened sensitivity, as if the world itself were newly awakened to touch.

He materialized at my door with the precise punctuality of those who measure life in profit margins, his handshake betraying nothing of the yearning that had brought him to my threshold. No courtship rituals, no flowers, no champagne, only the stark honesty of acknowledged need. The Romanian builder moved through my space with eyes that calculated load-bearing capacities and structural vulnerabilities, his gaze a professional assessment that unconsciously extended to my form.

His hands captivated me immediately: large, powerful instruments marked by years of labor before wealth had elevated him to command rather than execute. They rested on his thighs like dormant creatures, calloused palms facing upward in unconscious supplication. Despite directing luxury developments across Eastern Europe's emerging playgrounds for the wealthy, he seemed determined to fortify himself against vulnerability, erecting invisible barriers between us with his clipped sentences and averted gaze.

"You mentioned seeking understanding about female pleasure," I said finally, abandoning indirect approaches. His eyes momentarily met mine before retreating to study my carpet's pattern as if it contained some essential architectural wisdom.

"There are techniques... anatomical structures," he managed, the words emerging with visible effort through his Romanian accent. "I've not been... successful in this area."

The clinical framing revealed volumes. Here was a man who approached intimacy as a structural problem rather than a shared expedition—viewing the female body as territory to be conquered through precise technique, rather than a living landscape to be discovered through mutual exploration. Yet beneath this detachment, I sensed a genuine desire to understand—perhaps even a quiet ache, a frustration with his own limitations that professional pride made difficult to admit, let alone overcome.

"I imagine in your work," I ventured, "there are foundations that appear solid on blueprints but require different approaches once excavation begins."

Something shifted in his posture. Not relaxation but recognition, a subtle acknowledgment of common ground. "Yes," he replied, the single syllable carrying neither elaboration nor emotion, yet containing universes of potential understanding.

In my bedroom, afternoon light spilled through gauzy curtains, transforming ordinary air into gilded possibility. The tension remained in his shoulders as I approached him, his expression a masterpiece of contained anxiety masked by professional distance.

"Perhaps we should begin," I suggested, my fingers finding the buttons of his precisely pressed shirt.

He nodded once, permitting my assistance while neither participating nor preventing. As fabric parted, his body revealed itself exactly as I had anticipated, powerful rather than sculpted, bearing testimony to his journey from labor to leadership. The contrast fascinated me. Weathered hands against the relatively unmarked expanse of his chest, a man who had traversed worlds, who straddled the physical and administrative domains with equal authority.

My fingertips discovered the boundary where these different territories met, dancing across the subtle transition. Beneath my touch, I felt him suppress a shiver, the first betrayal of desire concealed beneath careful composure. His skin radiated heat that contradicted his cool demeanor, volcanic warmth beneath the surface of apparent indifference.

When my nails whispered across his chest, tiny bumps rose in their wake, his nipples hardening against his conscious will. The body's honesty cannot be counterfeited. This, I have learned through countless encounters. No matter how disciplined the mind, flesh speaks its truth without artifice.

I recognized in his rigidity that particular tension of men accustomed to overseeing rather than being overseen. Years of intimate anthropology have taught me that such men require specialized approach, blueprint language before poetry, structure before surrender. Yet often beneath this careful restraint lies an ocean of unexpressed passion, awaiting only permission to surface.

"Your body tells the story of someone who built his empire from the ground up," I murmured, my touch clinical enough for his comfort yet intimate enough to awaken response. My fingers discovered a raised ridge of scar tissue along his lower ribs, a record of construction days before he commanded others to lift and carry. I traced this history with deliberate attention, honoring the journey inscribed in his flesh.

As my hands moved lower to free him from remaining constraints, he lifted his hips in mechanical cooperation, physically present yet emotionally distant. Still, his arousal stood undeniable, magnificent contradiction to his emotional withholding. The sight of him already hard beneath fabric both thrilled and challenged me. Here was desire without surrender, hunger without acknowledgment.

"I'd like you to notice the temperature difference between my hands and your skin," I instructed, employing the empirical language that might penetrate his defenses. My palms glided over the taut plane of his abdomen, feeling the subtle contraction of muscle beneath my touch, registering the barely audible catch in his breath as my fingers ventured dangerously close to where his desire strained toward me.

His eyes finally met mine with startling directness, intensity momentarily displacing professional detachment. This, I've discovered, often marks the first fissure in the armor of the profoundly reserved: intellectual engagement preceding emotional surrender.

I removed my own clothing with deliberate ceremony, each garment relinquished as deliberate offering rather than practical necessity. Throughout this unveiling, I continued speaking in measured tones about nerve pathways and pressure points, creating narrative bridges between clinical understanding and embodied experience.

"I'd like to show you something," I said, taking his hand in mine as I arranged myself against the pillows. "But I need your complete attention."

My words penetrated where touch alone could not reach. His eyes settled on mine with newfound presence, his focus narrowing to this moment, this discovery, this exchange between teacher and willing student.

"Touch requires awareness," I told him quietly. "Observation alone isn't enough for this particular exploration."

Taking his hand, I guided it downward across the landscape of my body. Over the subtle rise of ribcage, the gentle valley of my waist, the soft swell of my abdomen. His palm followed my direction, fingers still tentative as I led them through the silken thatch that marked the entrance to more intimate territory.

His touch remained methodical, almost clinical, fingers mapping without intuition, exploration without genuine discovery. Yet paradoxically, this very mechanical approach sent unexpected currents of pleasure through me, the stark contrast between his intellectual distance and the deeply intimate act created a tension that hummed between us, charging the narrow space between our bodies with dangerous potential.

"Like this," I whispered, placing my hand over his, applying gentle pressure to demonstrate both location and motion. The heat of his palm against my most sensitive flesh sent a ripple of genuine pleasure cascading through me, not from any particular skill in his technique but from the exquisite vulnerability of guiding uninitiated fingers, of witnessing transformation from hesitant exploration to awakening expertise.

His eyes darted briefly to where our hands joined, then away again, a builder uncomfortable with terrain that defied blueprint precision. Yet his breathing had deepened perceptibly, a flush spreading across his pale chest. Between his thighs, his arousal strained upward, the swollen head glistening with evidence of his own desire. His body spoke eloquently what his face refused to acknowledge, the hunger that professional reserve could not entirely contain.

"Feel how tissues respond to different pressures," I instructed, guiding his fingers in circular motions against my swelling flesh. "There's intelligence in resistance, in flexibility, in moisture."

Though silence remained his shield, his breathing changed subtly. Deepening as his fingers began following patterns I'd established. When I released his hand, he continued the motion, his touch gradually becoming more present, more responsive to the evidence of my pleasure. The sight of his strong, calloused fingers against my pink flesh created visual poetry that heightened awareness of every sensation, the slight roughness of his skin catching against my smoothness, the precision of his movements contrasting with the liquid heat building within me.

"Good," I affirmed quietly, rewarding his progress by arching toward his touch.

A flush crept across his cheekbones, first visible evidence that the man behind the methodical exterior was engaging beyond mere technical exercise. I allowed my breath to quicken, my responses to grow less controlled, providing the feedback his practical mind required to gauge success. There exists a particular triumph in witnessing composure fracture beneath desire's pressure, in watching restraint dissolve into genuine hunger.

When his thumb found my clitoris, whether by design or fortunate accident, electric current shot through me, drawing an involuntary tremor from my thighs. His eyes flickered to my face at this unfeigned response, and for a heartbeat, I glimpsed something feral behind his scientific detachment, primal need carefully contained within civilized boundaries.

"Now," I said, capturing his hand and redirecting his fingers to my entrance, "we approach the territory you need to understand."

I showed him how to enter me, first with one finger, then two, directing the angle of his wrist with explicit instruction. The sensation of being filled by his strong fingers while guiding their movement created cascading pleasure that transcended the merely physical. There exists an exquisite vulnerability in this instruction, openly displaying not just one's body but one's most intimate responses.

His expression remained neutral, but his pupils had dilated dramatically, the pulse visible at his throat accelerating. The body betrays what the face conceals. This truth has been confirmed through thousands of encounters.

"Feel along the front wall," I instructed, adjusting his position with my hand over his. "Not so deep...it's closer to the entrance than many expect, typically one to three inches inside."

He made the adjustment silently, his exploration remaining mechanical yet somehow intensely erotic in its very precision: the slow, methodical way he explored my inner landscape like a cartographer mapping uncharted territory. I closed my eyes, surrendering to the sensation of his fingers moving within me, instinctively seeking greater pressure against that sensitive internal zone.

"There's a difference in texture you're seeking," I explained, fighting to keep my voice steady as pleasure built beneath his touch. "A slightly ridged area, more textured than surrounding tissue."

His movements paused as he explored with deliberate attention. I felt the subtle change in pressure as he located the spot we sought. My breath caught, an involuntary sound escaping my lips as his fingertips pressed against that sensitive internal ridge.

"There," I confirmed, not needing to manufacture the catch in my breath. "Do you feel the textural distinction?"

After a moment, he spoke, the first unprompted words since we'd crossed my bedroom threshold. "Yes." Then, with builder's precision: "Textured. Like specialized concrete."

The unexpected comparison made me smile despite its clinical delivery. Something about this juxtaposition, construction terminology within the context of intimate exploration, created its own unique eroticism. His fingers now pressed with greater confidence against that sensitive zone, and I felt my internal muscles flutter around them, responding to the precisely applied pressure.

"Exactly. Now apply more pressure. You don't have to worry about being too gentle here."

He hesitated briefly before complying. The increased pressure sent waves radiating outward from my core: sensation entirely different from clitoral pleasure, deeper and more diffuse, rising from somewhere central in my body. My back arched involuntarily, thighs tensing, toes curling against silk sheets as pleasure built with startling intensity.

"That's the correct response," I confirmed, my voice transformed by genuine arousal. "Now curve your fingers as if beckoning someone toward you."

His technical mind served him well in implementing this directive, fingers curling against that internal ridge in the "come hither" motion that intensified building pressure. My breath shortened, internal muscles beginning to clutch rhythmically around his fingers. Prelude to the distinctive release that differentiates this type of stimulation.

"Sometimes," I managed between increasingly ragged breaths, "this can trigger a release of fluid, different from typical lubrication."

Though he gave no verbal acknowledgment, I sensed a new intensity in his focus. The construction foreman turned executive confronted with empirical evidence of phenomena previously encountered only in medical texts he'd once awkwardly consulted. His movements maintained their controlled precision, testament to his capacity for methodical execution even as my responses grew increasingly uninhibited. The builder in him, accustomed to maintaining unwavering concentration during complex procedures where a single mistake could compromise structural integrity, applied that same disciplined attention to maintaining the rhythmic pattern that intensified my mounting pleasure.

Pleasure built with intensity that bordered exquisite discomfort before transforming into waves of sensation. I felt the distinctive internal clutching that precedes this specific type of climax, followed by the warm gush of fluid against his hand. His eyes widened perceptibly, composure finally cracking before empirical evidence so unmistakable. Something shifted in his expression. The pragmatic skepticism of a man who deals in concrete realities yielding to genuine wonder, as though witnessing the physical manifestation of a blueprint he'd studied without truly believing.

As contractions subsided, he withdrew his hand with unexpected gentleness, his eyes moving between my flushed face and his glistening fingers with fascination. His silence now carried different quality. Not emotional withdrawal but profound absorption, focused attention of someone processing significant revelation.

"That's what we were seeking," I said finally, breaking the silence between us. "A different kind of pleasure, a different kind of release."

He nodded, flush still visible on his cheekbones. I recognized this moment of vulnerability, the builder confronted with results that transcended mere measurements, that touched something primal beyond pragmatic understanding.

"Would you like to experience how this feels from a different perspective?" I asked.

I guided him onto his back, feeling the subtle shift in his movements, less rigid now, as though his body was beginning to surrender, following mine with an increasing openness. His magnificent erection stood proud against the flat plane of his abdomen, the swollen head flushed a deep pink, a single bead of moisture at its tip catching the afternoon light like a perfect crystal, its delicate sheen a quiet testament to the moment's intimacy. There was undeniable beauty in this physical honesty, the raw truth of desire laid bare, existing independently of his usual careful emotional restraint, as if his body was speaking a language he could no longer control or conceal.

"This position allows precise control of angle and pressure," I explained, straddling him with slow deliberation until I hovered just above him, our bodies separated by mere millimeters of heated air. "I'll demonstrate how to create contact with the same area you just discovered."

Anticipation vibrated between us, his body visibly tense beneath mine, abdominal muscles contracting as if bracing for exquisite impact. I lowered myself with excruciating slowness, taking him inside me inch by careful inch, watching his face for subtle signals his words would never reveal. The delicious stretching, the gradual filling, created its own pleasure entirely different from what his fingers had evoked. I adjusted my posture with practiced precision, ensuring his shaft pressed against my anterior wall exactly where I needed the pressure.

His breathing changed immediately, sharp intake followed by deeper exhalation than I'd yet heard from him. His lips parted slightly, first visible crack in his carefully maintained facade. His hands came to rest on my thighs, neither directing nor restraining, merely establishing tangible connection. The heat of his palms against my skin sent ripples of sensation traveling upward, combining with internal pressure to create complex symphonies of pleasure.

"Note the difference in sensation when I change angles," I continued, shifting slightly forward, then back, observing the subtle changes in his expression with each adjustment. When I found the perfect position, his shaft pressing firmly against that sensitive internal ridge, a genuine sound escaped me, unplanned and unfiltered. His eyes flew to my face at this authentic response, pride or wonder briefly illuminating his otherwise guarded features.

I began moving in rocking motion rather than conventional rhythm, maintaining constant pressure against my anterior wall while creating exquisite friction for us both. Heat built between our bodies, my skin growing slick with perspiration that caught the filtered light. Each movement sent waves radiating outward from our connection, my breasts swaying gently, my hair falling forward to create intimate curtain around our joined faces.

His eyes closed, perhaps finding sensation easier to process without visual vulnerability. I accepted this temporary retreat, understanding that for some, journey toward connection requires such momentary withdrawals. Yet his body betrayed deeper engagement than his expression revealed, his hips began moving beneath mine with increasing urgency, rising to meet my downward motion with rhythm that spoke of awakening hunger.

I guided his thumb to my clitoris, demonstrating the circular motion that would complement our connection. "Dual stimulation," I explained. "Internal pressure combined with external touch."

He followed instruction with surprising attentiveness for a man clearly approaching his own release. The precise pressure of his thumb, not too firm, not too gentle, suggested a construction foreman's understanding of applied force, intuitive calibration that served him perfectly in this intimate context. This dedication to technique even as pleasure mounted revealed something essential about him. Professional commitment to completion that transcended personal gratification.

The combined sensation of his thick shaft pressing against my internal sweet spot while his thumb circled my clitoris created spiraling tension that built with unexpected swiftness. My movements became less measured, more instinctive, inner walls clutching around him, drawing him deeper. Moisture gathered where our bodies joined, creating slick evidence of mutual arousal that amplified each sensation.

Each time our bodies connected, the impact sent shockwaves through me, pressure against that sensitive internal spot creating pleasure entirely different from direct clitoral stimulation: deeper, more diffuse, yet no less intense. Sounds escaped me beyond professional performance, primal vocabulary that transcended language's precision. His eyes opened at these vocal signals, watching my face with wonder mingled with his own mounting need.

When climax finally broke through me, it came in waves of contracting muscle and pulsing sensation, each peak followed by momentary ebb before building again with renewed intensity. My thighs trembled against his hips, back arching to maximize pressure exactly where I needed it. Through pleasure's haze, I felt his rhythm falter, his breathing grow ragged, the careful control he had maintained beginning to fracture beneath his own approaching release.

His hands finally gripped my hips with genuine urgency, guiding my movements with newfound purpose. This moment of assertion, this surrender to instinct over intellect, was perhaps our encounter's most profoundly erotic aspect. I yielded to his guidance, allowing him this moment of control, watching with fascination as his head pressed back into the pillow, tendons standing in sharp relief as pleasure overtook his carefully maintained reserve.

When he came, it was with a single, deep groan that seemed torn from somewhere beneath scientific detachment. His hips lifted us both momentarily from the bed, the power of his release evident in tension that claimed his entire body. For that brief, unguarded moment, I saw him completely: not the reserved builder but simply a man experiencing pleasure beyond analysis or control.

As aftershocks subsided, he lay perfectly still, eyes closed, one arm draped across his forehead. The silence between us had transformed. No longer the tense quiet of discomfort but the emptied space that follows significant revelation. His chest rose and fell with gradually slowing breaths, perspiration making his skin glow in softening afternoon light. Even in repose, his body maintained a certain dignity that seemed intrinsic rather than imposed.

After several minutes, he spoke, his voice carrying new quality, less controlled, slightly roughened. "Thank you." Two simple words suggesting deeper meaning than mere courtesy.

I rested beside him, respecting the space his silence created while maintaining physical connection his body seemed to welcome. Eventually, he added five more words, delivered with precision suggesting careful mental composition: "That was... instructive and unexpected."

I smiled, appreciating both understatement and effort such acknowledgment required from him. "The best discoveries often are."

•

In the Romanian builder's hands, those calloused instruments of creation, I discovered a mirror reflecting back ancient truths I had long suspected. Like moonlight glancing off disturbed water, his approach illuminated the secret cartography of desire. He came to my body not with the imperious march of conquest but with the hushed reverence of a pilgrim approaching sacred terrain. What mysterious alchemy this presented: that in his very restraint, in his willingness to approach pleasure as humble scholar rather than entitled victor, he accessed chambers that more experienced yet less surrendered explorers have passed blindly for centuries.

I have, since this encounter, been drawn to construction sites throughout Monaco, particularly one overlooking Port Hercules. There, beneath unforgiving afternoon sun, workers peel away layers of earth that once appeared uniform and unremarkable. With each careful excavation, they reveal the startling complexity concealed just beneath appearance, varying densities of soil telling tales of ancient floods, stone formations holding memories of geological epochs, remnants of structures from civilizations now remembered only in fragments. In this ordinary sight, I recognized my life's work made visible, the careful revealing of hidden territories that exist beneath conventional perception.

What appears simple under casual gaze contains labyrinths of extraordinary intricacy, each secret passage responding uniquely to different pressures, temperatures, approaches. I find myself moved not by the infinite variations between bodies but by their profound commonalities, these shadowed chambers that exist in each of us, waiting to vibrate with recognition when approached with genuine attention. Like musical instruments crafted from different woods but tuned to the same scale, we carry unique expressions of shared potential.

How peculiar and telling that knowledge surviving centuries in Eastern traditions, passed mother to daughter, teacher to student through generations, suddenly became "discovered" by Western researchers decades ago, only to be followed by tedious debates about whether these territories exist at all. This controversy speaks volumes, not about female anatomy, but about our cultural fear of women's complex pleasure. How we prefer our maps with obvious legends and direct pathways, yet the body's ancient wisdom resists all attempts at such clean reductionism. The most profound territories will never surrender to those who approach with clipboards and skepticism.

The qualities that elevated my builder from laborer to creator, his patience with resistant materials, his attention to subtle variations, his respect for natural properties, his willingness to adapt plans when reality differs from expectation, these served him perfectly in the realms of intimate discovery. Perhaps herein lies the deepest secret of connection: that the greatest gift we offer is never virtuoso performance but authentic presence, the willingness to explore another's unique architecture without rushing toward predetermined completion.

In building pleasure, as in creating structures that endure, the invisible foundations often matter more than obvious facades. What remains unseen, these subterranean networks of nerve and desire, supports all visible expressions of pleasure. The master builder, like the consummate lover, understands that what cannot be immediately perceived must nonetheless be acknowledged, respected, and incorporated into the complete design. For it is often in the negative spaces, the pauses between notes, the shadow between objects, the silence between words, that the most profound revelations await those patient enough to perceive them.

The Lesson:

The territory so clinically termed the "G-spot" exists not as some mythical button awaiting discovery, but as a region of responsive tissue with its own characteristics and requirements. Nestled along the anterior vaginal wall, typically one to three inches inside, this area feels distinctly different under attentive fingers, its texture more ridged or textured than surrounding tissue, like finding a subtle change in terrain beneath seemingly uniform surface.

What I've learned through countless explorations is that this landscape responds less to speed than to pressure. The "come hither" motion that my builder executed with such precision creates the firm, consistent contact this region craves. Many men approach with excessive gentleness, not realizing that firmer pressure, gradually applied and attentively adjusted, often awakens the most profound response.

For those navigating this territory during intercourse, certain positions naturally create better access: the woman astride but leaning slightly backward, her body angled downward during rear entry, or a strategically placed pillow beneath her hips in more conventional arrangements. These adjustments aren't merely technical; they transform ordinary connection into extraordinary discovery.

I often remind clients not to be alarmed by certain responses that might seem concerning without proper context. The initial sensation of needing to urinate that some women experience represents not a problem but a precursor to deeper pleasure when exploration continues. Similarly, the release of fluid that sometimes accompanies this type of climax, something my builder witnessed with such open fascination, is entirely natural, a physical expression as worthy of celebration as any other aspect of arousal.

Above all, I've observed that the most satisfying discoveries happen when exploration is approached with the simple desire to understand rather than to achieve. The builder who studies terrain before breaking ground invariably creates structures of greater beauty and durability than one who rushes toward completion.

The Empowering Ride

Power shifts between bodies like light through water, never resting in a single place for long. This truth came alive for me one spring afternoon through an encounter with a woman who had mastered the art of partnership with creatures far more powerful than herself, yet struggled to claim that same mastery in the intimate wilderness of her own desire.

She arrived at my door framed by Mediterranean sunshine, her form revealing a body shaped by years of disciplined movement. Even before she spoke, I recognized the distinctive posture of an equestrian: that centered gravity, that particular alignment of hip and spine that remains imprinted by countless hours in the saddle. Her handshake possessed both firmness and sensitivity, the mark of hands accustomed to communicating through the subtlest pressure.

"I train dressage horses along the coast," she confirmed as she accepted the rosé I offered, her eyes reflecting a confidence I've rarely witnessed. Yet beneath this professional assurance flowed an undercurrent of uncertainty that only surfaced when our conversation turned toward intimacy.

Something about her awakened a childhood memory I had long suppressed, my own contradictory relationship with horses. As a young girl in La Trinité, I had adored them, filling sketchbooks with their powerful forms. Then inexplicably, as adolescence claimed me, that love transmuted into irrational fear, a visceral tightening in my chest at their proximity, as though my awakening body had suddenly recognized the danger in what I once loved. This woman before me had moved beyond such fear, had learned to partner with that power rather than submit to or flee from it.

"There's something about controlling a creature that could easily overpower you," she remarked, rolling the stem of her glass between fingers marked by calluses I longed to explore with my tongue. "It's not about domination, it's about partnership, about finding the perfect balance between guidance and surrender."

Her words hung between us, weighted with implication. Though she had sought me out for professional guidance in intimate matters, I sensed she already possessed the wisdom she sought. Her request, when finally voiced, emerged with charming hesitancy, a flush climbing her throat like morning light over water.

"I've always preferred men to be... in charge," she admitted. "But recently, I've been curious about taking a more active role. I just don't know how to begin."

The dichotomy intoxicated me: this woman who commanded half-ton animals with confident precision, yet surrendered her pleasure to others' direction. I set aside my glass, the crystal catching light as I leaned forward.

"Tell me," I asked, "when you're training a horse, are you ever truly passive?"

Her laugh, rich and sudden, transformed her face, revealing a sensuality her professional demeanor had carefully contained. "Never. Even in apparent stillness, I'm constantly communicating through weight shifts, through breath, through intention."

"Perhaps," I murmured, my voice descending to where secrets are shared, "intimacy operates by similar principles."

I rose from my chair with deliberate slowness, watching how her pupils dilated as I approached. This suspended moment, this electric void between desire and fulfillment, contains a potency that often surpasses physical contact itself. I deliberately prolonged this exquisite tension, allowing anticipation to build between us like electricity before lightning strikes.

My fingers found her wrist, not where social courtesy dictates a handshake, but where life pulses visibly beneath the skin. The juxtaposition captivated me, how the same hands that controlled powerful beasts housed such delicate vulnerability in their blue-veined undersides. Her pulse quickened beneath my touch, her blood singing secrets her voice hadn't yet confessed.

"Close your eyes," I instructed softly. "Feel with your entire body, not your vision."

Her eyelids lowered, dark lashes settling against high cheekbones, transforming her immediately from observer to experiencer. Without sight, her remaining senses heightened: nostrils flaring to capture my scent, head tilting toward my breathing like a flower following sun. I guided her through my apartment with gentle pressure at her lower back, her body responding with intuitive grace to my silent direction.

In my bedroom, where afternoon light filtered through ivory curtains, I finally allowed our mouths to meet. The contact jolted through her like current through wire, a visible shudder traversing her form. Her lips parted beneath mine, initially yielding but quickly growing hungrier, her hands finding my waist with a tentative pressure that swiftly intensified. I felt the precise moment when instinct overtook hesitation, her body remembering what social conditioning had suppressed.

We separated, breath mingling in the diminished space between us. The room seemed to hold its breath, air thickened with possibility. I began disrobing, maintaining unbroken eye contact as each garment surrendered to gravity. This ceremonial unveiling, this deliberate exposure, created a charged silence broken only by the whisper of fabric and her increasingly uneven breathing.

"Beauty isn't in perfection," I told her, standing naked before her widening gaze. "It's in authenticity."

Her eyes journeyed across my landscape, lingering at the valleys and peaks that made me flesh rather than fantasy. When I motioned for her to join me in nakedness, her fingers hesitated at her buttons, anxiety flickering across her features like shadow.

"Undress for yourself," I encouraged. "Feel the pleasure of your own emerging skin."

She shed her careful exterior with growing confidence: jacket, blouse, riding pants surrendering to gravity in a cascade of abandoned restraint. As layers fell away, so too did her professional persona, revealing the sensual woman normally hidden beneath discipline. Her body told stories her words hadn't, the elegant musculature of thighs shaped by years astride horses, faint tan lines mapping boundaries between public and private selves, a crescent scar on one shoulder speaking of falls and recoveries.

When she finally stood before me unclothed, I witnessed the universal female hesitation: that moment of vulnerability before another's assessment. I approached slowly, raising my hands as one might toward a creature requiring reassurance, and placed my palms against the elegant architecture of her collarbones. The contact seemed to anchor her, her breathing deepening as my fingers admired the junction where neck becomes shoulder.

"Magnificent," I whispered, a truth rather than flattery.

I drew her toward my bed, sheets of raw silk chosen for their sensory conversation with naked skin. As I reclined, I guided her above me, her knees pressing into the mattress on either side of my hips. In this position, she towered above me, immediately taller yet simultaneously more exposed. Her spine aligned instinctively, years of equestrian training asserting themselves even in this unfamiliar territory.

"Your body remembers how to balance," I observed, my hands discovering the taut strength of her thighs. "These muscles know how to grip, how to guide, how to control movement."

Recognition illuminated her expression, the sudden understanding of how one mastery might inform another. I felt her weight shift as she settled more confidently against me, our vulvas meeting in electrifying contact that drew synchronized gasps from our lungs. The slick heat of her desire made itself known against mine, her arousal undeniable where our bodies met. Her fingers splayed across my ribcage, claiming territory with newfound purpose.

"Move as your body suggests," I instructed, my words emerging with the husky texture that only true arousal can create. "Listen to what brings you pleasure."

Her initial movements carried the tentativeness of first explorations, small shifts seeking sensation without commitment. I kept my hands on her thighs, offering presence without direction, creating sanctuary for her discovery. Gradually, like ice yielding to spring, hesitation melted into intuition. A rhythm emerged from somewhere deep within her body's memory, a languid undulation that created liquid friction where our centers joined.

The descending sunlight transformed perspiration gathering at her clavicle into molten gold. I watched, transfixed, as self-consciousness dissolved into pure sensation, her attention turning inward to the building pleasure at her core. Her head fell back, exposing the vulnerable column of her throat, her chestnut hair cascading down her back in waves that swayed with increasing urgency.

"That's it," I encouraged, my fingers pressing more firmly into the dense muscle of her thighs. "Your body knows."

A sound escaped her. Not the performative noises of practiced sexuality but something primal and unfiltered. The honest vocalization of a woman discovering her own capacity for pleasure, raw and unedited by expectation. Her thighs began trembling against mine, not from weakness but from intensifying sensation.

I reached up to cup her breasts, which moved with her rhythm like ripe fruit heavy on the branch. My touch forced a sharper inhalation, her cadence faltering momentarily before resuming with greater determination. My thumbs circled her nipples with deliberate pressure, drawing them into taut peaks. I watched, entranced, as rose-colored flushes bloomed across her chest, climbing toward her throat. Desire mapping itself visibly across her skin.

My hand slid between our bodies, finding the wet heat where we connected. Her swollen lips glistened with evidence of her arousal, slick and hot against my fingers. The additional stimulation drew a sharp cry from her lips, her movements growing more urgent. I guided her fingers to join mine.

"Show me," I whispered. "Show me how you create your own pleasure."

This suggestion, to pleasure herself while being witnessed, simultaneously thrilled and terrified her; I could read both emotions warring across her expressive face. After brief hesitation, her fingers joined mine, finding the swollen bud of her clitoris. The intimacy of this shared touch, the doubling of sensation where our hands met, created new dimensions of pleasure between us.

Her carefully maintained composure, that professional discipline, began fragmenting beautifully. Her movements abandoned calculation for instinct, guided now by the ancient wisdom of the body rather than the constraints of the mind. I observed, mesmerized, as pleasure consumed her consciousness, narrowing her universe to pure sensation. The wet sounds of our bodies meeting filled the air between us, a primal music accompanying her increasingly urgent movements.

Her thighs quivered against mine, her rhythm growing erratic as she approached the precipice. I grasped her hips, providing stability as her control unraveled, supporting her journey without directing it. This represents the most exquisite balance in intimate education, offering framework while creating sanctuary for abandon.

When climax claimed her, it arrived with unexpected force. Her body arched dramatically, head thrown back, inner muscles contracting visibly as waves of pleasure rippled through her. A sound tore from her throat that contained no trace of self-consciousness, pure, uncensored ecstasy. I held her firmly, anchoring her through waves of pleasure that visibly transformed her. The extraordinary vulnerability of witnessing a controlled woman's complete surrender moved me profoundly.

Aftershocks pulsed between us as she collapsed against my chest, her skin slick with exertion, her breathing ragged against my neck. I enfolded her in my arms, acknowledging through touch the trust implicit in her abandonment of control. We remained intertwined as her breathing gradually steadied, her heartbeat finding calmer rhythm against mine.

When she finally raised her gaze to mine, her face held wonder, as if territories previously unimagined had suddenly appeared on her internal map.

"I never knew," she confessed, voice slightly raw, "that I could feel so... powerful in surrender."

I brushed damp strands from her flushed face. "The greatest paradox of pleasure is that true power often emerges when we release the need to control everything except our own desires."

As afternoon light surrendered to evening, I guided her through variations of this position: subtle shifts in angle that stimulated different regions, ways to leverage her thigh strength, how leaning forward or backward transformed sensation entirely. With each discovery, her confidence visibly expanded, her body awakening to possibilities long dormant.

She proved remarkably adaptable, her athletic form quickly incorporating suggestions, her natural grace finding expression in this intimate choreography. When she later straddled me face-to-face, commanding our rhythm with newfound assurance, I witnessed her complete transformation, from hesitant novice to confident explorer, from passenger to pilot of her own pleasure.

"In dressage," she shared afterward, fingers absently drawing patterns on my skin, "we speak of 'collection'—the horse gathering its power under the rider, creating potential energy that can be directed."

"Yes," I replied, watching evening light play across the topography of her body. "In intimacy too, we collect ourselves, our awareness, our desire, our intention, before channeling that energy toward pleasure."

She nodded thoughtfully. "I've always been comfortable with physical aspects of sex, but somehow relegated myself to the role of responder rather than initiator."

"Cultural conditioning runs deep," I observed. "We're taught contradictory lessons about desire. To be desirable but not too desiring, to please but not to seek pleasure too openly."

"It feels revolutionary," she said with quiet wonder, "to simply claim what brings me joy."

I watched her dress with new embodiment, each movement more fluid, more conscious than when she had arrived. This transformation, this reclamation of bodily autonomy, represented the true value of our encounter. Beyond technique, beyond physical release, she had recovered a part of herself previously surrendered to convention.

"Remember," I told her at my door, evening shadows lengthening across my apartment, "you already possessed everything needed. Like your work with horses, mastery comes not from domination but from partnership, with your lover, yes, but primarily with yourself."

•

What captivated me deeply in our encounter was the paradox she embodied: a woman who could command half-ton beasts with the subtlest pressure of her thighs, yet doubted her authority to command her own pleasure. Her body held wisdom her mind refused to recognize, as though pleasure and power existed in separate kingdoms that could never share borders.

Throughout my years as an observer of intimate truths, I've traced a curious pattern across the territories of human desire. Those who control every element of their waking hours, the executives, the surgeons, the architects of empires, often discover unexpected liberation in momentary surrender. Meanwhile, those who habitually yield to others' direction sometimes blossom most dramatically when finally rising to command. We seek in darkness what daylight denies us; we hunger in private for what we publicly disavow.

The woman-on-top position crystallizes this exquisite contradiction. Unlike arrangements where she might orchestrate from beneath—subtle movements concealed beneath the surface like a hidden conductor of an invisible symphony—this orientation renders her simultaneously most exposed and most empowered. Every movement, every expression is visible, unshielded by shadow or distance. There is no place to hide, and yet, paradoxically, this very exposure grants her command. To be completely witnessed while completely sovereign creates an alchemical transformation, turning vulnerability from weakness into its own form of power. A radiant, embodied defiance of every narrative that has ever equated openness with submission. In that space, she becomes both performer and audience, giver and receiver, the axis around which the entire experience revolves.

I watched this metamorphosis unfold within her: how the professional discipline that kept her spine rigid through years of training dissolved into fluid grace when she finally claimed her pleasure without apology. Her body, accustomed to silent communication with creatures who detect the slightest tension, already possessed every instrument needed for this intimate orchestra. The subtle shifts of weight, the deliberate pressure of thighs, the intentional contraction of internal muscles, all these techniques of the riding arena translated perfectly to this more intimate arena, once given permission.

When I guide women toward this exploration, I offer something beyond technique, beyond momentary satisfaction. I invite them to experience physically what we all seek emotionally: that rare equilibrium where vulnerability becomes strength, where exposure creates connection rather than shame, where commanding one's pleasure allows a different kind of surrender. True mastery in intimacy, as in horsemanship, comes not from dominance but from partnership, with one's lover, yes, but primarily with oneself.

The woman astride her partner embodies intimacy's most beautiful paradox: Fully seen, fully unbound. She neither dominates nor submits but exists in that rare space where power flows between bodies like light between mirrors, multiplied rather than divided. What appears as contradiction, to be completely vulnerable while completely in control, reveals itself as the deepest truth of human connection, where opposites not only coexist but create something greater than either could alone.

The Lesson:

When a woman rises above her partner, she claims something beyond mere physical advantage. The practical benefits are considerable, of course: the freedom to find perfect angles, to determine depth and pace, to access pleasure directly rather than through translation. But the true revelation lies in the psychological shift this position invites.

For women unaccustomed to such visibility, begin by focusing inward rather than worrying how you appear. Close your eyes if necessary, allowing sensation to guide you rather than performance. Lean forward to increase pressure where you need it most, sit upright to feel fullness differently, or arch backward to discover sensations you didn't know existed. Your thighs, those powerful muscles developed through years of movement, become instruments of precision, capable of creating subtle variations that change everything.

Remember that your pleasure isn't selfishness but generosity. The greatest gift you can offer is your authentic response. If uncertainty surfaces, place your partner's hands on your hips momentarily for reassurance, then gradually reclaim the composition as confidence builds.

For partners beneath, resist the impulse to direct through upward movement (unless explicitly welcomed). Instead, become the steady ground from which exploration can safely launch. Your hands should communicate appreciation rather than correction, support rather than force or control.

The real challenge here rarely involves physical technique but the courage to be completely witnessed while completely in charge. Yet this apparent contradiction holds the position's true magic: discovering that vulnerability and power aren't opposing forces but complementary currents in the same flowing river.

The Multi-Orgasmic Path

Pleasure, I've found, rarely follows a linear trajectory. It spirals and undulates, rises and falls, reaches plateaus before ascending to greater heights. The traditional view of sexual satisfaction as a singular peak followed by inevitable decline has always struck me as unnecessarily limiting, a strange economic model applied to the boundless realm of human sensation.

This philosophy materialized in physical form when he arrived at my Monaco apartment at precisely four o'clock on a crisp autumn afternoon. The economics professor had contacted me with unusual specificity about his interests, not merely in experiencing pleasure but in understanding its architecture, its potential for sustaining and repeating rather than simply peaking and subsiding.

The Mediterranean light at this hour possessed that perfect quality, not the harsh brilliance of midday nor the golden nostalgia of sunset, but the clarified luminance of late afternoon that transforms ordinary objects into something ethereal. It caught in the silver threads at his temples, evidence of a life spent in deep thought rather than mere passage of time. His eyes, observant, analytical, yet somehow gentle, took in my apartment with the careful assessment of someone accustomed to noticing patterns others might miss.

"Your message intrigued me," I said after preliminary pleasantries and wine had established a comfortable atmosphere between us. "This interest in sustained pleasure cycles isn't something most articulate so precisely."

His smile revealed a subtle charm absent from his formal demeanor. "My work focuses on economic peak-trough cycles: how systems rise, fall, and potentially rise again rather than simply collapsing after a single climax." A slight flush colored his cheeks as the academic terminology brushed against more intimate implications. "I've always suspected similar principles might apply to... more personal experiences."

"The body is indeed an economy of sensation," I replied, appreciating his intellectual framing of desire. "Most people approach pleasure as a limited resource to be consumed quickly, when it might better be understood as renewable energy that can be cultivated and sustained."

Something in my phrasing seemed to release tension he'd been carrying. His posture softened, professional reserve yielding to genuine curiosity. "Exactly. Yet most literature on the subject seems either overly clinical or wrapped in mystical language that obscures practical application."

I moved to sit beside him, close enough that our knees almost touched, creating a circle of shared intimacy without yet entering it physically. "Perhaps because we're conditioned to view orgasm as culmination rather than transition. An ending rather than a turning point."

His eyes met mine with newfound intensity. "And you see it differently?"

"I see possibilities where others see limitations," I answered, my hand finding his with deliberate purpose. "The body contains multitudes if we learn to listen rather than merely direct."

The transition from conversation to touch unfolded with natural grace. His fingers interlaced with mine, the simple contact creating currents that traveled up my arm and settled like liquid warmth in my belly. When our lips finally met, I recognized immediately a quality rare among my clients: he kissed not as prelude but as complete experience unto itself, each moment fully inhabited rather than merely advancing toward some predetermined destination. His tongue parted my lips with gentle insistence, tasting of the wine we'd shared and something darker, more essentially himself.

Rather than guiding him directly to the bedroom, I led him toward what appeared to be a sculptural art piece in my living space, a customized Varier Ekstrem Chair, its impossible curves and protrusions upholstered in supple black leather rather than the standard fabric. I had commissioned this particular modification, including a discreet cross bar support between its abstract legs for additional stability during more vigorous activities. Most visitors mistook it for avant-garde sculpture until I revealed its true purpose.

"Most people approach furniture with predetermined notions of how bodies should interact with objects," I explained, trailing my fingers along one of its sensuous curves. "This piece liberates us from such limitations. There is no 'correct' way to engage with it."

He circled it with academic curiosity, his analytical mind visibly attempting to categorize this object that defied conventional classification. "Norwegian design," he observed with appreciation. "Terje Ekstrøm's work, though I've never seen one executed in leather."

"I find traditional furniture often limits possibilities," I replied, appreciating his knowledge of design. "This piece was created specifically to challenge how we think about our bodies in space."

As clothing yielded to intention in the warm afternoon light filtering through gauzy curtains, I observed his body with appreciative attention, lean yet strong, bearing the subtle asymmetries that make human forms infinitely more fascinating than sculpted ideals. A slight curve to his shoulders from years bent over academic papers, a small appendectomy scar like a parenthesis on his abdomen, hands more elegant than one might expect from someone who worked primarily with abstractions.

My dress fell away under his surprisingly deft fingers, revealing the black lace beneath that contrasted starkly with my skin. His breath caught visibly as he took in my form, his arousal evident against the confines of his trousers. When I helped him remove those final barriers, his cock sprang free, magnificently hard, the head already glistening with the first pearly drop of his desire. I couldn't resist tasting him, my tongue collecting that salty essence as his fingers tangled in my hair with sudden urgency.

"Today," I murmured as we approached the unconventional chair, its organic shapes providing both challenges and opportunities, "we'll explore principles of extension and recurrence. How pleasure can build upon itself rather than deplete its resources."

"I'm in your hands," he replied, his academic confidence tempered by vulnerability that made the surrender all the more compelling.

I began with touch designed not to arouse immediately but to awaken: fingertips discovering the landscapes of his body with cartographer's precision. Most sexual encounters rush toward obvious erogenous zones, neglecting the body's capacity for whole-system response. My approach instead honored the entirety of his form. The sensitive hollow behind his knee, the often-neglected terrain of his inner wrist, the extraordinary responsiveness at the nape of his neck.

His breathing deepened as my exploration continued, his skin flushing with blood drawn toward the surface by deliberate attention. When my hand finally enclosed his throbbing erection, the contact drew a sound from his throat that contained surprise despite its inevitability, as though the directness after such meandering approach intensified the sensation beyond expected parameters. His cock pulsed against my palm, velvet skin stretched taut over iron hardness, the ridge around the head pronounced and sensitive to my circling thumb.

"The first principle," I explained, my touch establishing a rhythm deliberate enough to build sensation without hastening conclusion, "is recognizing the space between arousal and culmination. Most rush toward the latter without fully inhabiting the former."

His eyes, which had drifted closed in pleasure, opened to meet mine with remarkable presence. "The plateau phase," he observed, academic knowledge finding physical confirmation. "Often treated as mere transition rather than destination itself."

"Precisely." I varied pressure and tempo, demonstrating how pleasure could intensify without necessarily advancing toward release. My hand moved in long, languid strokes from base to tip, occasionally twisting gently around the sensitive head, watching his abdominal muscles contract with each subtle variation. "In economic terms, think of it as sustainable growth rather than boom-bust cycles."

The academic metaphor, so aligned with his professional framework, seemed to help him integrate intellectual understanding with physical experience. His body responded with increasing sensitivity as I guided him toward heightened arousal while deliberately maintaining distance from its tipping point. The resulting tension manifested visibly, his abdominal muscles tightening, his breathing growing shallow, his hands clutching at the sheets in sweet restraint.

When I finally brought him to the threshold of climax through precisely calibrated touch, I paused completely, a cessation that drew a groan of both protest and relief. The momentary emptiness resonated between us like a held breath, creating space for sensation to reset without diminishing. His cock twitched against his stomach, angry and red with unspent need, a bead of clear fluid escaping from the tip.

"This pause," I explained as his breathing gradually steadied, arousal receding just enough to create distance from inevitability, "is where possibility lives. The body interprets it not as denial but as postponement, intensifying neural pathways for the next approach."

Understanding bloomed across his features, theory and practice converging into embodied knowledge. When my touch resumed with renewed deliberation, his response carried heightened intensity, nerve endings reawakening with amplified sensitivity. I guided him toward threshold again, this time through different approach, my mouth replacing hands, creating contrasting sensation that engaged different receptors while building upon existing arousal.

I took him between my lips with exquisite deliberation, my tongue tracing the pronounced vein that ran along his underside. The taste of him, mineral tang and cedar warmth, something uniquely male, flooded my senses as I took him deeper, my throat opening to accommodate his length. His hands found my hair, not guiding but simply connecting, fingers tensing with each downward movement of my mouth. I felt his thighs begin to tremble beneath my palms, the telltale tightening that precedes release.

Again I paused at the critical moment, allowing him to experience the exquisite suspension between desire and fulfillment. His breath came in ragged gasps, his body trembling with contained energy. The professional composure he had arrived with had completely dissolved, revealing the elemental being beneath academic identity. This transformation, this surrender of constructed self to authentic experience, represents perhaps the most profound victory in intimate education.

"The economics of scarcity would suggest this delay diminishes resources," I observed, my fingers lightly tracing patterns across his chest as his breathing stabilized once more. "But the economics of sensation operates by different principles. Each approached threshold that isn't crossed immediately doesn't deplete but rather compounds potential energy."

"Like charging a battery beyond its expected capacity," he managed, his voice roughened by desire.

"Exactly."

On the third approach, I straddled him with deliberate slowness, taking him inside me with exquisite precision. The sensation of fullness as he entered me elicited authentic response, a pleasure not performed for his benefit but genuinely experienced. His hardness pressed against internal landscapes with perfect pressure, my slick heat enveloping him completely. I couldn't suppress the moan that escaped me as he filled me entirely, stretching and completing me in equal measure.

I established a rhythm designed to build his arousal methodically while simultaneously attending to my own response. I rose and fell above him with measured grace, each downward movement taking him fractionally deeper, each upward motion creating exquisite friction against my most sensitive internal territories. The dual awareness, maintaining conscious presence while surrendering to mounting pleasure, created a complexity of sensation beyond simple stimulus and response. When I felt him approaching threshold again, I slowed completely, remaining motionless above him despite the almost painful desire to continue.

"Focus on your breathing," I instructed, my voice revealing the effect his body was having on mine despite my professional experience. "Imagine drawing energy from pelvis to core, from spine to crown."

He complied with remarkable presence, his inhalations deepening as his focus shifted from external stimulation to internal awareness. I felt subtle changes in his body beneath mine: a releasing of tension in certain muscle groups while others engaged differently, a redistribution of energy I could sense through our connected forms.

When movement resumed between us, something had fundamentally shifted in our encounter. His hands found my hips with newfound confidence, not merely receiving pleasure but actively participating in its orchestration. Our rhythm developed its own intelligence, responding to subtle cues exchanged through pressure, breath, and unconscious vocalization. My body arched above his, breasts swaying with our movement, nipples tight with arousal. His thumb found my clitoris, circling with unexpected precision, adding another dimension to the pleasure already building within me.

The approach to his first release built differently than the previous ascents, not steeper but somehow deeper, engaging more systems simultaneously. When climax finally claimed him, it manifested not as terminal event but as transformative wave, pleasure radiating visibly through his entire form. His face in that moment of culmination contained a vulnerability so profound it bordered on the sacred: ego temporarily dissolved, identity momentarily surrendered to pure sensation. I felt him pulsing inside me, his cock jerking against my inner walls as his seed flooded my depths. The heat of his release, combined with the continued pressure against my most sensitive points, triggered my own orgasm, a cascade of contractions that milked him further, our bodies locked in perfect communion.

The extraordinary aspect of this release, what distinguished it from conventional understanding, was its lack of finality. Instead of the typical descent into detachment that follows male orgasm, he remained present, his eyes opening to meet mine with both gratitude and curiosity. His breathing, though initially ragged, regulated more quickly than typical, his body retaining a remarkable responsiveness despite apparent release.

"That was..." he began, words failing academic precision.

"The first summit," I completed for him. "Not the mountain's peak."

Remaining joined, I leaned forward to brush my lips against his, a connection that reinforced continued intimacy rather than concluding it. My body still surrounded his softening presence, maintaining our circuit of energy exchange. This interim phase, typically treated as conclusion, formed instead a critical transition in our exploration.

"Most men consider this the end," I murmured against his ear, my breasts brushing his chest with deliberate lightness. "But it's merely an inflection point in the greater curve."

What happened next revealed the extraordinary potential of the male body when liberated from conventional understanding. Instead of withdrawal and extended recovery, I felt him beginning to respond again within me. Not immediately, but far sooner than standard sexual scripts would suggest possible. This renewal emerged not from youth, he was well into his fifth decade, but from the careful cultivation of arousal and circulation we had established.

My fingers traced slow patterns across his chest, awakening nerves through deliberate, non-genital touch. I engaged his full sensory system: the taste of skin, breath against his neck, subtle shifts in pressure where our bodies met. This whole-body approach rekindled arousal across multiple channels, bypassing the limits of direct recovery.

His second hardening within me unfolded gradually, an organic response to sustained attention rather than determined effort. I felt him swelling inside me, stretching me anew, filling spaces that had barely registered his absence. The remarkable aspect was not merely this physical recovery but the qualitative difference in sensation it created: a deeper, more resonant pleasure that built upon previous experience rather than attempting to replicate it.

"The body remembers," I explained as he fully awakened inside me once more, his expression registering wonder at this unexpected renewal. "Each culmination creates new pathways for the next, if we allow continuity rather than conclusion."

Our movement together resumed with altered quality, slower, more deliberate, informed by the knowledge of where this path could lead. His hands explored my body with newfound appreciation, no longer driven by urgent need but by genuine curiosity about mutual pleasure. His palms covered my breasts, thumbs circling nipples that had remained sensitized throughout our connection. This circle of giving and receiving, of simultaneous attention to self and other, created a resonance that amplified sensation beyond what either could have generated alone.

The approach to his second peak unfolded with remarkable difference from the first. Where initial arousal had built with familiar urgency, this secondary ascent developed more gradually, engaging deeper tissues and more distributed nerve networks. I felt the changes in his breathing, in the tension patterns across his musculature, in the subtle shifts of his pelvis beneath mine.

"This time," I instructed as I felt the familiar signals of approaching culmination, "focus on drawing the energy upward rather than releasing it outward."

His eyes, which had maintained remarkable contact with mine throughout our connection, registered both understanding and determination. When climax approached again, his conscious breathing redirected energy through visualized pathways, transforming what might have been localized release into full-body experience. This second culmination manifested differently. Less externalized but somehow more profound, pleasure distributed throughout his system rather than centralized and expelled. His cock pulsed inside me with diminished fluid but somehow greater intensity, waves of contraction that seemed to originate from deeper within his core.

The Ekstrem Chair proved its worth magnificently during this phase, its unconventional curves supporting our bodies in configurations impossible on traditional furniture. One particularly inspired moment found him seated on what might be considered the chair's "back" while I straddled him facing away, the chair's protrusions providing perfect support for my knees while its cross bar offered leverage for my hands. The leather's supple texture against our skin provided subtle tactile counterpoint to our connection, while the chair's inherent flexibility accommodated our movements without resistance.

The view he had in this position must have been magnificent. My back arched, hair cascading between my shoulder blades, the place where our bodies joined visible with each rise and fall of my hips. I reached between my legs to touch myself, fingers circling my swollen clitoris while he watched, adding another layer to his visual stimulation. His hands gripped my waist, guiding my movements with increasing confidence, occasionally reaching around to cup my breasts or trace the sensitive line where hip meets thigh.

What followed surpassed even my experienced expectations. The circular path we had established, arousal, threshold approach, conscious redirection, renewed building, continued beyond conventional assumptions about male capacity. A third ascent began developing, each cycle requiring slightly longer cultivation but yielding increasingly complex sensations.

Throughout this exploration, I maintained my own awareness of pleasure without making it central to our exchange. My body responded authentically to our connection, experiencing waves of satisfaction that complemented rather than competed with his journey. This balance, tending another's experience while honoring one's own, represents perhaps the most sophisticated skill in intimate exchange.

When his third culmination finally approached, the previous patterns had prepared his system for extraordinary experience. This peak, when it arrived, transcended conventional categories of pleasure. His entire body participated in the release, muscles contracting in wave-like patterns from feet to scalp. The sound that escaped him contained surprise and wonder alongside satisfaction. The voice of someone discovering capacities within himself previously unimagined.

Afterward, as afternoon light gave way to early evening, we lay together in comfortable silence. His expression held the particular quality I've come to recognize in those who have experienced genuine transformation, a recalibration of understanding that extends beyond physical pleasure into new self-knowledge.

"I've studied systems theory extensively," he said eventually, his voice carrying newfound depth, "but never fully appreciated how it might apply to my own body. The conventional model of male sexuality as linear and finite seems remarkably limiting in retrospect."

I traced patterns on his chest, feeling the steady rhythm of his heart beneath my fingertips. "Most limitations exist primarily in belief rather than biology. The body contains far greater potential than cultural narratives acknowledge."

"What fascinates me," he continued, academic curiosity seamlessly integrated with embodied discovery, "is how this cyclical approach creates a fundamentally different experience, not just multiple identical events but progressively deeper and more complex sensations."

"Like compound interest rather than simple return," I suggested, adopting his economic framework.

His laugh, warm and genuine, filled the space between us. "Exactly. The yields increase with each cycle, defying conventional diminishing returns."

As evening gathered beyond my windows, transforming Monaco's landscape into constellation of lights reflected on dark water, I found myself appreciating this rare synthesis of intellectual understanding and physical experience. Too often, these domains remain separated, mind analyzing what body experiences without true integration. His capacity to build bridges between these territories created possibilities for pleasure that transcended ordinary boundaries.

He glanced appreciatively at the Ekstrem Chair as we dressed, its impossible geometry now forever associated with extraordinary sensation. "I'll never look at Norwegian design the same way again," he observed with a smile that combined intellectual appreciation with newly embodied knowledge. "What appears challenging and even uncomfortable at first glance can offer remarkable possibilities when approached with openness."

As he prepared to leave, his movement expressed a fluidity that hadn't been present upon arrival, a centeredness that suggested altered relationship with his physical form. This transformation, this embodied integration of new knowledge, represents the true value of such encounters, far beyond momentary pleasure.

"I find myself wondering," he said at my door, professional confidence now softened with genuine warmth, "how these principles might apply beyond the bedroom—to creativity, to intellectual work, to relationship itself."

"That," I replied, "is precisely the question worth exploring."

His smile as he departed contained both gratitude and new curiosity, a researcher with fresh territories to investigate, beginning with his own expanding capacity for experience.

•

In the quiet aftermath of our encounter, I found myself contemplating how theory and flesh had merged into unexpected harmony. His economic mind, accustomed to cycles and patterns, provided the perfect vessel for transcending the linear prison most men construct around their pleasure. His body followed where concept led, revealing chambers of sensation that had always existed but remained locked behind doors of misunderstanding.

The multi-orgasmic journey fascinates me not for its physical achievement but for how it illuminates our cultural mythology. We live surrounded by stories that tell us pleasure must follow prescribed arcs, yet beneath these narratives pulse older truths: that energy need not be spent but can be circulated, that emptiness can feed rather than deplete fullness, that culmination might serve as gateway rather than conclusion.

I have witnessed this revelation transform countless men. Their eyes afterward contain a particular wonder, not merely satisfaction, but the profound astonishment of having transcended a limitation they never recognized as arbitrary. Like prisoners who discover their cell door had never actually been locked.

What moves me most is how these transformations extend beyond the bedroom, seeping into all aspects of existence like dye through fabric. Men who learn to circulate rather than merely expend energy often approach creativity, emotional challenges, even spiritual inquiry with similar principles, finding resources where conventional wisdom insists none exist.

In these explorations, pleasure becomes not mere technique but philosophy embodied. The recognition that our most basic assumptions about capacity might be nothing more than stories we've been told. The body becomes not opponent to intellect but its most sophisticated instrument, capable of registering truths too subtle for conscious thought to grasp.

The multi-orgasmic path beckons us toward territory most never glimpse, not because it lies beyond reach but because we've been told not to seek it. In this discovery, we find not what is new but what has always existed, awaiting only our recognition and remembrance.

The Lesson:

The multi-orgasmic journey begins with recognizing that pleasure operates in waves rather than straight lines. For men particularly, this means distinguishing between the localized genital events we typically call orgasm and the full-body experiences possible when energy circulates rather than simply discharges.

Start by cultivating awareness of your arousal patterns. Notice the subtle sensations that precede the "point of no return": the moment where climax becomes inevitable. This threshold awareness creates space for choice rather than automatic progression. When you approach this edge, consciously shift your breathing from upper chest to lower abdomen, imagining energy moving upward through your spine rather than outward through your genitals.

Physical techniques support this conscious redirection. When approaching threshold, try applying gentle pressure to the perineum (the area between genitals and anus) while simultaneously contracting pelvic floor muscles. This physical action, combined with visualization of rising energy, helps redistribute intensity throughout your system rather than concentrating it toward release.

Between cycles, maintain connection through whole-body touch rather than focusing exclusively on genital recovery. The skin contains millions of receptors that can awaken secondary arousal pathways while primary systems reset. Conscious breathing during this transition phase accelerates renewal by improving circulation and oxygenation to all tissues.

Remember that multiple orgasms aren't identical repetitions but evolving experiences. Each successive peak typically feels qualitatively different, often less externally explosive but more internally profound. This progression isn't about achievement or performance but about expanding your capacity for sustained pleasure and presence.

Part 4:
Rhythm & Technique

His fingers moved across my skin with musician's precision, finding rhythms my body responded to before I consciously recognized them. Each touch seemed perfectly calibrated, pressure neither too firm nor too gentle, timing neither rushed nor delayed. I found myself responding with abandon unusual in my professional encounters, surrendering to expertise so complete it transcended technique to become artistry.

Later, watching him dress in the amber light of Monaco's sunset, I asked what had informed his remarkable approach. "I conduct orchestras," he explained with elegant simplicity. "My life is devoted to finding the perfect tempo for each composition, to recognizing when to build tension and when to offer release." In that moment, I understood how mastery in seemingly unrelated domains might transform intimate experience.

Technique without presence creates hollow performance; presence without technique often stumbles into unfulfilled potential. The chapters that follow explore specific approaches that consistently awaken profound response: not as mechanical formula but as foundation for creative exploration. Like music, intimate rhythm cannot be reduced to metronomic precision but must breathe, discover, and adapt to each unique encounter.

I offer these insights from thousands of hours observing which touches consistently awaken response, which rhythms build sustainable pleasure, which variations intensify sensation rather than merely changing it. I've cataloged with scientist's precision and poet's appreciation the subtle differences between competent touch and transformative contact.

Yet throughout this exploration of specific techniques, remember that all skill ultimately serves feeling rather than replacing it. The most exquisite touch applied without attunement becomes merely efficient; the simplest contact offered with complete presence can dissolve boundaries between bodies more effectively than any elaborate approach. What follows is not an instruction manual but an invitation to creative mastery, technical foundation that supports rather than supplants authentic connection.

The Rhythm of Connection

New York vibrates unlike any other place, a perpetual crescendo of eight million lives colliding in magnificent cacophony. I had come for a charity gala where Monaco's elite mingled with Manhattan's, and chosen to extend my stay afterward, surrendering to the city's seductive chaos. My hotel suite overlooking Central Park offered a sanctuary from the urban symphony below, yet I found myself eager to step back into its intoxicating rhythm.

The message had arrived the morning after the gala, an elegantly worded invitation from a European conductor whose orchestra had performed the previous evening. During our brief conversation at the reception, I had detected something compelling beneath his poised exterior. An acquaintance had whispered my profession to him, and rather than the usual awkward withdrawal or prurient interest, he had regarded me with genuine intellectual curiosity. "Perhaps," he had suggested with disarming directness, "we might continue our discussion of physical harmonics in a more private setting."

As evening descended, I prepared to meet him on his terms, in his temporary home, a historic townhouse in Washington Mews, just north of Washington Square Park. I selected a dress that whispered rather than announced its quality, applied perfume to strategic pulse points, and slipped a small leather satchel into my bag, containing not just evening essentials but a change of clothes for the following day. I had planned to explore downtown Manhattan after our encounter, regardless of how late the night extended. A habit born of practicality; in my profession, one learns to anticipate various scenarios without appearing presumptuous. With my preparations complete, I summoned a taxi.

Manhattan traffic congealed around us as we approached the Village. Two blocks from my destination, we encountered an impassable barricade. A film crew had commandeered the narrow streets. Surrendering to circumstance, I paid the driver and stepped onto the pavement, heels clicking against concrete as I navigated the final distance on foot.

The unexpected walk through Greenwich Village's evening energy recalibrated my senses. I absorbed the quartets of students in animated debate, the mingled aromas of competing restaurants, the spontaneous jazz drifting from a basement window. By the time I located the discreet entrance to the Mews, a hidden lane of former carriage houses transformed into some of the city's most exclusive residences, my body had synchronized with New York's accelerated heartbeat.

His door opened before I could knock, as if he had been attuned to my approaching footsteps. Standing in the warm light of the entrance, the conductor's presence registered immediately, a man who existed within music rather than merely creating it. His physicality betrayed his profession before he spoke. He moved with an unconscious economy that suggested precise internal metering, each gesture containing the exact energy required, nothing wasted, nothing arbitrary.

"You walked the final distance," he observed, noticing my slightly flushed complexion. "New York has intervened with its usual disregard for plans." His accent caressed the consonants, transforming ordinary English into something more melodic.

He welcomed me into a space that perfectly embodied its occupant, a harmonious blend of historic architecture and modernist furnishings. A grand piano dominated one corner, its lid open like a great black wing. Sheet music rested on the stand, dense with notation and personal markings in blue pencil.

"Walking served me well," I replied, accepting his invitation to sit. "One should approach certain encounters gradually, allowing anticipation its proper development."

The subtle widening of his pupils confirmed he understood my meaning. He poured wine into crystal glasses. A Barolo that suggested confidence in his selection. When our fingers brushed during the exchange, I felt his subtle tremor, that exquisite contradiction between his commanding presence and an underlying sensitivity. The most compelling men always contain this duality: control veiling vulnerability, strength housing gentleness.

He moved to the windows, pulling aside heavy curtains to reveal the intimate enclosure of the Mews. Gas lamps cast a silvery glow across the historic cobblestones, creating an interplay of light and shadow dancing along the secluded laneway. "A peculiar sanctuary," he observed. "In this alcove, the city's rhythm changes. Listen. You can still hear its pulse, but transformed, like a theme played by different instruments."

"And every city has its signature rhythm," I replied, joining him at the window. "Monaco moves in elegant adagio, Paris waltzes, but New York—"

"Perpetual allegro vivace," he finished, his smile revealing unexpected warmth. "Always slightly ahead of the beat."

"Would you like to experience it?" he asked, already moving toward a side door. "The Mews has a quality at night that can't be appreciated from behind glass."

I followed him outside, where the evening had draped itself in deep indigo. The cloistered laneway existed as a pocket of stillness amid Manhattan's unceasing clamor. Cobblestones beneath my heels, historic façades rising on either side, it felt like stepping into a different era, a parallel New York hidden within the familiar one.

We stood together in the narrow passage, not quite touching. The surrounding buildings shielded us from direct streetlight, creating an intimate penumbra. I became acutely aware of his proximity: the heat radiating from his body, the subtle cedar notes of his cologne intermingling with something uniquely his own, the almost imperceptible sound of his breathing gradually synchronizing with the distant urban rhythm.

He closed his eyes, head tilted slightly as if in concentration. I watched his hand rise, fingers extended, conducting an invisible orchestra.

"Listen," he said softly. "The baseline of traffic on Sixth Avenue... the percussion of the subway beneath our feet... the occasional woodwinds of human voices..."

I closed my eyes as well, allowing my senses to recalibrate. Gradually, the seemingly random urban sounds began organizing themselves into patterns: rhythmic structures emerging from chaos, a complex metropolitan symphony conducted by invisible forces.

"You're hearing it now," he observed, eyes still closed but somehow aware of my shift in perception. "The city's heartbeat."

When I opened my eyes, I found him studying me with an intensity that had nothing to do with music. Our gazes locked for a moment too long to be casual. Caught in this unintended revelation, he cleared his throat slightly.

"Force of habit," he explained, pivoting back to safer territory. "I hear rhythms everywhere—in traffic patterns, in speech cadences." A weighted pause as he gestured vaguely toward the city beyond us. "Even in the spaces between words."

The deflection was transparent, yet graceful, his retreat to musical terminology a professional mask hastily repositioned. But the momentary slip had revealed something more compelling than his polished exterior: genuine desire unfiltered by performance.

In that moment, I felt seen beyond the surface, not merely observed but recognized. The sensation pierced deeper than casual appreciation, striking something fundamental within me.

"The pause is where tension builds," I offered, deliberately allowing silence to follow my words, creating a void that demanded filling.

"In music, we call that *fermata*—a held note or rest." His voice dropped to a register that seemed to vibrate directly against my skin. "The suspension of forward movement that creates yearning for resolution."

As we turned to walk back toward his door, he suddenly stopped. A mischievous expression, so incongruous with his usual composure, transformed his features.

"Wait," he said, raising one hand. "I want to show you something else."

Without warning, he clapped his hands sharply, the sound cracking like a whip in the confined space. The acoustic properties of the narrow passage caught the sound, bouncing it between the façades in perfect diminishing repetition. Once. Twice. Three times. Four, before fading into silence.

His face lit with childlike delight. "Perfect natural reverberation. The Mews creates its own echo chamber." He gestured toward me. "Try it."

I hesitated, feeling suddenly self-conscious, but his expectant gaze disarmed my reluctance. I clapped once, firmly. The sound ricocheted between the buildings, repeating exactly as it had for him.

He closed his eyes, listening with complete concentration until the final echo dissolved. When he opened them again, his expression held a satisfaction that bordered on ecstasy.

"I discovered this by accident my first night here," he confessed. "I've been conducting in the finest concert halls across Europe, but this humble passage has acoustics that would make architects weep."

The shared moment of play, this unexpected break from sophisticated interaction, revealed something endearing about him. I found myself charmed by this glimpse of spontaneity beneath his disciplined exterior.

"We should go inside," he said finally, the professional demeanor returning but now softened by this flash of boyish enthusiasm. "Though I'm tempted to bring my violin out here at midnight."

His hand moved to mine with such calibrated intention that I felt my breath catch. Not the tentative touch of uncertainty nor the presumptuous claim of entitlement, but the knowing contact of someone who understands the instrument before attempting to play it. His thumb discovered my pulse point, applying the perfect pressure to feel its quickening rhythm.

"Your heartbeat is accelerating," he noted, satisfaction curving his mouth subtly.

"The conductor notices everything," I acknowledged, turning my hand to interlace our fingers. This simple connection ignited nerve endings that extended far beyond our point of contact.

I guided him toward the bedroom, where city lights created shifting constellations across the waiting sheets. The anticipation between us had condensed into something almost tactile: a third presence in the room, vibrating with possibility.

"May I?" he asked, reaching for the zipper at my back.

I turned, offering access. Instead of immediately unzipping, his fingers followed the ridge of my spine, each vertebra receiving individual attention. The space between touch and intent created a sweet ache of expectation. When he finally drew the zipper downward, the sound cut through the silence like a sustained whisper.

"There is a rhythm to unveiling," he murmured, his breath warming the newly exposed skin at my nape. The dress loosened, slipping from my shoulders and cascading to the floor in a whisper of fabric. "Too fast, and one misses the beauty of anticipation. Too slow..." His fingertips grazed the indent where waist transitions to hip, barely making contact yet sending currents of electricity through hidden pathways, "...and the tension becomes almost unbearable."

Standing before him in black lace that concealed nothing yet denied everything, I reached for his tie with deliberate slowness. "Perhaps unbearable tension has its place in the composition."

The silk surrendered to my fingers as I loosened the knot. His scent intensified with his rising desire, creating an olfactory chord that awakened something primal within me. I wanted to devour and be devoured, yet the exquisite tension of restraint heightened every sensation.

With the same measured patience he had demonstrated, I unbuttoned his shirt, revealing a body more defined than his formal attire had suggested. When my palms met the unexpected warmth of his chest, feeling the accelerated thudding beneath my touch, his sharp intake of breath punctuated our unfolding score.

"Every instrument requires different handling," he murmured as his fingers threaded into my hair, applying just enough tension to send shivers cascading down my spine. "A different touch, a particular pressure, to produce its most beautiful sounds—each body its own music, waiting to be played."

"And how does one learn the proper technique?" My voice emerged husky as my hands mapped the terrain of his torso, discovering unexpected textures and contours.

"One listens," he replied, guiding me to the bed with gentle pressure. "With complete attention."

The sheets received us like cool water, our bodies creating hollows in the expensive Egyptian cotton. He positioned himself above me, maintaining a maddening distance: only his knees bracketing my thighs, his arms caging my shoulders. This deliberate withholding of contact created an exquisite yearning in the negative space between us.

"In music," he explained, his voice resonating at a frequency that seemed to vibrate directly against my most sensitive places though he had yet to touch them, "silence is as important as sound. The negative space gives meaning to the notes."

To illustrate, he finally lowered his mouth to mine in a kiss of such consuming depth that it seemed to reach beyond physical contact, only to retreat a heartbeat later, hovering just beyond reach. The departure devastated more profoundly than the contact had exhilarated. When I arched upward instinctively, seeking to reclaim his mouth, his hand on my hip pressed me firmly against the mattress.

"Patience," he commanded softly. "Feel the anticipation build."

His mouth traveled along my jaw, down the vulnerable column of my throat, lingering at the hollow where my pulse throbbed visibly. Each point of contact felt precisely calibrated for maximum effect, each withdrawal timed to intensify desire rather than satisfy it. He was composing upon my flesh, transforming nerve endings into strings that vibrated at his slightest touch.

When he finally removed the lace barrier between his mouth and my breasts, the sensation of his tongue circling my nipple after such prolonged anticipation elicited a cry that seemed to please him, judging by the subtle curve of his lips against my skin.

"Beautiful," he murmured. "Such a pure note."

My hands clutched his shoulders, the muscles shifting beneath my fingertips like animate marble. Each time my movements suggested impatience, he would withdraw slightly, decreasing sensation until I yielded to his orchestration. This surrender, this relinquishing of control to his mastery, awakened something untamed within me. I found myself responding not merely physically but with my entire being, all professional distance dissolving until only raw, authentic response remained.

When his mouth traveled lower, blazing a molten path across my abdomen, his hands parted my thighs with gentle insistence. The first contact of his tongue against my sex delivered such perfectly calibrated pressure, neither too forceful nor too tentative, that I gasped, arching involuntarily. Instead of intensifying, he retreated slightly, establishing a pattern of approach and withdrawal that drove me toward magnificent madness.

"Listen to your body," he instructed, his breath hot against my pulsing center. "It knows what tempo it needs."

The liberation in this permission, to follow my internal rhythm rather than conform to expected pace, intoxicated me. I surrendered to the wave-like cadence he established, each crest higher than the last, each temporary retreat creating space for the next advance to reach greater intensity.

His tongue moved in patterns that seemed to follow some internal musical notation, quick, light staccato touches that made me quiver, alternating with long, sustained strokes that built pressure deep within my core. When his fingers joined this orchestration, curving inside to discover the spot that made colors bloom behind my closed eyelids, I felt myself begin to fracture, to dissolve into pure sensation.

"Not yet," he whispered, somehow sensing my approach to climax and deliberately withdrawing, leaving me suspended at the exquisite threshold between anticipation and fulfillment. The emptiness ached, a void demanding to be filled.

I reached for him with desperate hands, guiding him above me. His body radiated heat like stone baked in summer sun. The rigid evidence of his desire pressed against my thigh, yet still he maintained that maddening composure, that absolute mastery over our shared tempo.

When I encircled him with my hand, feeling velvet skin stretched taut over hardness, a shudder disrupted his controlled exterior, a momentary fissure in his maestro's composure that satisfied something deeply feminine within me. His breath caught, his eyes closed briefly, his hands gripped the sheets beside my head.

"Now," I urged, positioning him at my entrance, where I had become slick and swollen with wanting.

He entered me with excruciating deliberation, each increment of penetration meticulously controlled. The gradual stretching, the progressive fullness, created sensations so intense they approached sublime torment. When he was finally sheathed completely within me, we both remained motionless, suspended in perfect tension, a fermata in our carnal composition.

"Now," he whispered, his forehead pressed against mine, our breath mingling in the narrow space between our lips, "we find our rhythm together."

What followed transcended any previous experience. A physical dialogue where dominance and submission flowed between us like counterpoint melodies. He established a cadence, deep and measured, maintaining it until my body fully synchronized with his. Just as I adapted completely to his rhythm, he would shift, sometimes accelerating until each thrust forced small, helpless sounds from my throat, other times slowing to an almost unbearable languor where each movement became a separate universe of sensation.

During one such deceleration, I moved instinctively against his controlled pace, seeking to reclaim the intensity he had deliberately withdrawn.

"Impatient," he observed, his voice carrying an unexpected edge. Without warning, his palm connected with the curve of my buttock: a precise, measured strike that startled more than hurt. The sound resonated in the quiet room, as crisp and definitive as the downbeat that commands an orchestra to attention.

My gasp of surprise mingled shock with unexpected pleasure. The momentary sting bloomed into spreading heat, blood rushing to the surface of my skin as nerve endings awakened to a different category of sensation.

He remained perfectly still within me, waiting for my response. The pause lengthened, became deliberate, another fermata in our carnal composition. I could feel his restraint, the tension in his body as he held himself in check, allowing me space to object if I wished.

I answered by pressing back against him, a silent request for continuation. His hand caressed the heated skin where he had struck, the gentleness of this touch contrasting exquisitely with the sharpness that had preceded it.

"There is music in contrast," he murmured, delivering another precise strike to the opposite side. "The dynamic range between pianissimo and fortissimo—" His hand connected again, slightly harder, "—between tenderness and intensity."

Each carefully measured blow seemed to bypass normal sensory pathways, forging direct connections between skin and core: raw, electric conduits of sensation. I found myself responding with an unfamiliar, almost involuntary surrender, each strike dissolving another layer of control, of narrative, until I existed purely as sensation, as instinctive response. My mind emptied, making room for something primal and expansive. The burning afterglow of each impact heightened my sensitivity to the exquisite fullness of him inside me, layering the intensity of pain with the softness of penetration, creating a symphony of contrasting pleasures: sharp and tender, forceful and yielding, destructive and deeply creative all at once.

"Feel how the tension builds through contrast," he instructed, his voice strained with the effort of his control. "The secret lies in the transitions—moving from one sensation to another without losing the underlying pulse."

To demonstrate, he gradually increased our pace, his movements becoming more forceful, more demanding, until we moved together in perfect synchronicity. My body responded with escalating urgency, internal muscles tightening around him as pleasure coiled ever tighter at my core. Then, just as I approached the threshold of release, he slowed dramatically, his thrusts becoming deep, deliberate, achingly measured.

The plateau he created by denying immediate climax transcended mere pleasure, a sustained note of ecstasy that reverberated through every cell. My hands clutched at his back, nails pressing half-moons into his skin. "Please," I gasped, the word both surrender and demand.

"Not yet," he countered, his thumb finding the epicenter of my pleasure as he continued his measured thrusts. "Feel how much deeper it can go."

This orchestrated delay transformed building pleasure into something approaching sacred agony. My consciousness narrowed to the point where our bodies joined, to the exquisite friction that promised salvation yet withheld it masterfully. Tears formed at the corners of my eyes, not from pain but from the unbearable intensity of sensation sustained beyond what I had thought possible.

When he finally accelerated again, adding pressure from his thumb in perfect counterpoint to his thrusts, the climax that had been building for what seemed like eternity crashed through me with catastrophic force. It manifested not as the brief, localized spasm of ordinary release but as total systemic surrender: muscles seizing, breath suspending, boundaries of self momentarily dissolving.

I heard myself cry out, a sound scarcely recognizable as my own, as waves of ecstasy radiated outward from my core to my extremities. The intensity fragmented consciousness, reality reduced to pure sensation.

His own release followed, not with uncontrolled abandon that typically characterizes male climax, but with deliberate, powerful thrusts timed to prolong and intensify my pleasure. Even in this most primal moment, he maintained that remarkable orchestration, that mastery of rhythm that transformed mere coupling into transcendent communion.

Afterward, as we lay entangled in damp sheets, the city lights painting abstract patterns across our cooling skin, I found myself altered in some fundamental way. He had not merely played upon my body but had somehow, briefly, changed its very orchestration, remapping neural pathways to create new possibilities of sensation.

"What are you thinking?" he asked, his fingertips describing idle patterns along my shoulder that nevertheless seemed to follow some internal musical structure.

"About mathematics and music," I admitted, too languid in the aftermath of such complete pleasure to construct a more sophisticated response. "About how rhythm is really just ratio and relationship."

"You're thinking quite intensely," he observed with a smile containing a hint of professional pride. "Both are languages of pattern. Ways of making sense of time and movement." He propped himself on one elbow, studying my face with the same attention he had given my body. "But there's alchemy beyond the mathematics. A moment when calculation yields to pure feeling."

"The difference between technical proficiency and art," I suggested.

"Precisely." His hand found mine, our fingers interlacing naturally. "You can teach technique, but the intuitive understanding of rhythm—that's innate."

"I'm not entirely convinced," I countered. "I think sensitivity develops through practice and awareness. It's about learning to pay attention to subtle cues."

He considered this, expression thoughtful. "Perhaps you're right. Perhaps it's less about innate ability and more about willingness to listen deeply."

This insight touched something I'd observed repeatedly throughout my career: how the most satisfying connections often occurred with individuals who approached intimacy with genuine curiosity and attentiveness. Technical skill mattered less, ultimately, than this quality of presence, this capacity to respond authentically to the unique rhythm of each encounter.

"What was that piece you were humming earlier?" I asked, recalling a melody I'd heard him unconsciously vocalize while his lips traveled across my abdomen.

"Was I humming?" He looked genuinely surprised. "It must have been Debussy. Claire de Lune. It often comes to mind when I'm experiencing something particularly beautiful."

The compliment, delivered with such unaffected sincerity, warmed me. In a profession where flattery often serves strategic purposes, genuine appreciation retains its power to touch.

Later, as night deepened toward dawn, the conductor moved to the piano. Without preamble, his fingers found the keys, offering a brief, improvised melody that seemed to capture the essence of our encounter, rising tension, sustained release, and lingering resonance.

"A souvenir," he explained, "more lasting than flowers, less obvious than jewelry."

I stood behind him, resting my hands lightly on his shoulders, feeling the music vibrate through his body before reaching my ears. The intimacy of this gesture, sharing his primary art after sharing his body, struck me as more genuinely revealing than our physical communion.

"It's late," he observed as the final notes faded. "Or rather, early. You should stay until morning."

The invitation contained no expectation, merely practical consideration. I had planned for this possibility. The small satchel I'd brought contained not just perfume and lipstick, but a change of clothing for the following day. In my profession, one learns to anticipate various outcomes without appearing to do so.

"I'd like that," I replied, following him upstairs to a bedroom where antique furnishings contrasted with modern linens.

Morning arrived with soft persistence, sunlight filtering through partially drawn curtains. I woke to find him already dressed, preparing coffee in the kitchen below. He had the focused energy of someone accustomed to early rehearsals, yet moved quietly out of consideration.

Over breakfast, we spoke of music, of Monaco, of New York, conversation that acknowledged without directly referencing the intimacy we had shared. When I mentioned my plans to explore the city that day, he offered a list of hidden locations known mainly to long-time residents.

"Leave your evening things here if you wish," he suggested as I changed into the simple day clothes I had brought, linen trousers and a silk blouse suitable for walking. "No sense carrying them through the village all day."

I accepted this practical kindness, transferring just my essentials to a small shoulder bag. The arrangement contained unspoken permission to return, an open possibility rather than an expectation.

When I finally stepped into the morning light, the Mews looked different. Transformed by what had transpired behind its discreet facades. Each cobblestone seemed to hold secret knowledge, each window to observe with benevolent discretion. I moved through the laneway feeling curiously attached to its intimate geography, knowing I would return by evening, if only to collect my belongings.

The day stretched before me with Manhattan's infinite possibilities. As I walked toward Washington Square, each step on the pavement connected me to New York's awakening energy. I moved now with altered awareness, attuned to rhythms I had previously overlooked: the synchronized stride of morning commuters, the percussive dialogue of construction work, the counterpoint of birdsong against traffic.

From somewhere nearby, a street saxophonist began practicing scales, the notes rising and falling in disciplined progression. I smiled at this unintentional reminder of my evening's lesson: that rhythm underlies everything, that music exists not just in concert halls but in the spaces between buildings, in the cadence of footsteps, in the pause between heartbeats.

•

The experience unfolded between us like a dream suspended between sleep and waking, that liminal state where boundaries dissolve and the senses speak in tongues unknown to daylight consciousness. What science calls "entrainment", that beautiful synchronization of separate rhythms, I have come to recognize as the secret heartbeat of all profound connection. Our bodies spoke to each other through pulses and waves, finding resonance where words would have created only noise.

Years later, while attending a performance of the London Symphony, I found him again, not in flesh but in movement, his hands shaping invisible architectures from which sound emerged like water from stone. Watching him conduct, I recognized the same qualities that had transformed our night together: his total presence, his exquisite sensitivity to response, his mastery of tension and release.

The connection between rhythm and desire runs deeper than conscious thought can reach. Like underground rivers flowing beneath civilizations, this knowledge courses through human experience regardless of time or culture. From West African drums to European waltzes, every society recognizes how shared tempo binds us together in ways both sacred and profane. Our bodies understand what our minds often forget: that synchronization creates not just pleasure but profound connection.

The beauty of his skill lay not merely in technical virtuosity but in his ability to listen with his entire being. While most lovers stumble upon moments of synchrony through accident or instinct, he orchestrated our alignment with the same precision he brought to his symphony. This difference, between chance harmony and conscious attunement, transformed what might have been merely satisfying into something that altered my understanding of what bodies can create together.

In both music and intimacy, the difference between competence and artistry lies not in what one knows but in how deeply one listens. Technical proficiency provides the foundation, but it is the capacity to perceive and respond to the subtlest signals: a quickening breath, a tensing muscle, the barely perceptible flush rising along a collarbone, that transforms mechanical interaction into transcendent communion.

This synchronization exists as both neurological reality and metaphysical truth. The endorphins and oxytocin that flood our systems when we find harmony with another are nature's rewards for discovering connection amid separation. Perhaps this explains why both music and intimate touch have retained their power throughout human history. They offer rare glimpses beneath our isolation, moments when the illusion of separateness dissolves into recognition of our fundamental unity.

In a world increasingly fragmented by distraction, these experiences of perfect timing offer something more precious than pleasure alone. They remind us that beneath our carefully constructed individuality lies a capacity for connection that transcends words, that speaks in the ancient language of rhythm, of breath, of presence. Not in metronomic precision but in responsive attunement to another's essential cadence, we discover what the conductor taught me that night in New York. The most profound music emerges not from separate instruments but from their momentary, miraculous ability to become one voice, one breath, one heartbeat.

The Lesson:

Finding mutual rhythm fundamentally transforms sexual experience from parallel self-gratification to genuine connection. Like dancers moving to the same music, bodies that find synchronicity create something greater than either could alone. This harmony doesn't require identical pace, counterpoint and contrast often create the most interesting compositions, but it demands mutual attunement.

Begin by noticing your own natural rhythm. Before attempting to synchronize with another, become intimately familiar with your body's inherent tempo—its rises and falls, its patterns of tension and release. Some naturally move quickly, building rapidly toward climax; others require a slower, more deliberate acceleration. Neither is superior. Knowing your authentic cadence simply provides the foundation for meaningful adaptation, allowing you to meet another not from mimicry, but from a place of embodied awareness.

Practice conscious, fluid transitions between tempos. One of the most common rhythmic mistakes is an abrupt, jarring shift that interrupts the natural build of pleasure and severs connection. Instead, approach changes in pace with awareness—slow down deliberately to stretch out sensation, or accelerate with a clear, intentional progression that mirrors rising intensity. These nuanced transitions often determine whether an encounter feels fragmented and mechanical or seamless and deeply integrated, like a well-composed piece of music.

Listen with your entire body. True rhythmic connection requires peripheral awareness, attention not just to obvious signals but to subtle feedback: changes in breathing, muscular tension, vocal timbre. Develop this sensitivity by periodically pausing during intimacy, closing your eyes, and focusing completely on these less obvious cues. This practice transforms mechanical motion into responsive dialogue.

Remember that silence and stillness are essential components of rhythm, not its absence. The momentary pause before changing position, the sustained pressure that precedes movement, the suspended breath at the threshold of climax: these negative spaces create the anticipation that makes forward motion meaningful. When pleasure plateaus, consider introducing these deliberate hesitations rather than simply increasing speed or intensity.

The Lingering Caress

The telephone shattered my afternoon solitude. An intrusion of urgency into my contemplation. His voice carried none of the practiced seduction my clients often attempt, but rather the direct clarity of a man accustomed to being instantly understood.

"I'll be forty minutes late. Emergency thoracic case. My apologies."

No excessive justification. Just the concise communication of a surgeon whose daily vocabulary includes matters of life and death.

"Of course," I replied. "I'll be here."

This unexpected gift of time stretched before me like an unfamiliar luxury. I prepared a small meal, my kitchen filling with the fragrance of rosemary and garlic as I roasted vegetables and selected a Barolo that would benefit from breathing.

His knock landed forty minutes past our scheduled time—a small restoration of order after unavoidable delay. When I opened the door, I found him still carrying the invisible weight of his emergency case, dark eyes revealing exhaustion he wouldn't verbally acknowledge.

"Something smells wonderful," he said, movements controlled and precise.

"Just a small offering. I thought you might need sustenance after saving lives."

His smile was genuine, not the practiced charm most men deploy. "What I need is to remember there's a world beyond arterial repair and tissue regeneration." His fingers brushed mine as he took the wine glass I offered, the contact brief but electric, these hands that had been inside a human chest now establishing this delicate connection with mine.

"How do you switch between such different worlds?" I asked. "From the operating room to... this?" I gestured to encompass my apartment, myself, our arrangement.

He considered this with surprising seriousness. "I don't switch completely. That's the secret most doctors won't tell you. We don't fully disconnect—can't, really. But we learn to channel the same focus toward different objectives."

His gaze wandered from my eyes to my lips, then lower to where my silk blouse revealed the subtle curve of breast. The trajectory wasn't lascivious but evaluative: the same precision with which he might study anatomy, now directed toward pleasure.

"And what is your objective today?" I moved closer, challenging his surgical precision with deliberate provocation.

"To make time expand," he said, setting down his glass. "In surgery, every second feels compressed, decisions made in microseconds that affect years of someone's life. Here, I want the opposite. To stretch moments until they become territories we can explore together."

This philosophy surprised me. An articulation of desire more nuanced than simple release. His hand found the small of my back, fingers pressing gently into my spine, creating a focal point of sensation that radiated outward like heat through water.

"I spend my days making incisions with absolute precision," he continued. "Why wouldn't I bring the same attention to pleasure?"

The question hung between us, his hand still resting at the base of my spine, neither advancing nor retreating: simply establishing presence, creating anticipation that pooled like warm honey in my belly.

"Perhaps you might demonstrate this philosophy more... practically."

His response came not in words but in action. His hand rose to my face with devastating slowness, fingertips barely grazing my cheek before sliding into my hair. The gentleness contained such focused intention that I felt myself responding with unexpected authenticity, my breath catching not in professional performance but genuine desire.

"The threshold of sensation," he murmured, his other hand finding my waist, "exists well before most people think to look for it." His thumb brushed against my ribs, creating a whisper of pleasure that seemed disproportionate to such minimal contact. "Here, for instance." His fingertips pressed ever so slightly into my scalp, sending cascades of sensation down my neck like warm rain. "And here."

His mouth hovered near mine without making contact, our shared breath becoming an intimate exchange that preceded any physical connection. When his lips finally met mine, the kiss unfolded with meticulous deliberation, not the urgent claiming most men perform but a gradual building of pressure, an exploration that acknowledged the complexity of even this most basic interaction. His tongue moved with surgical precision, finding nerves I hadn't known existed, creating reactions I couldn't have anticipated.

My hands found the buttons of his shirt, instinctively moving toward the expected progression, but he caught my wrists with gentle firmness.

"Not yet," he whispered against my mouth. "First, let me show you what time can do when we refuse to rush it."

His hands moved to the counter behind me, effectively caging my body without touching it. I felt caught in the magnetic field between his chest and mine, the proximity itself becoming a form of stimulation more intense than many hands-on encounters I'd experienced. He lowered his head to my neck, his breath warm against my skin for long moments before his lips made contact.

When his mouth finally pressed against my pulse point, the delayed gratification had so heightened my sensitivity that I heard myself make a sound of surprise, a response too raw to be rehearsed. His smile against my skin told me he recognized the difference.

"You see?" he murmured, his lips traveling with exquisite slowness along the curve of my shoulder. "Anticipation isn't merely prelude. It's essential composition."

He turned me gently, pressing against my back, his hands sliding beneath my blouse to find bare skin. The contrast between the cool marble counter before me and his warm body behind created a delicious tension, opposing sensations heightening each other. His fingers worked the buttons of my blouse with unhurried precision, each new exposure of skin receiving focused appreciation.

"In the operating room," he said, voice low against my ear as his palms smoothed over my now-bare shoulders, "we follow protocols, predetermined sequences. Here, we can let sensation guide us." His hands slid lower, finding the curve of my breasts still contained in black lace. "Tell me what you feel, not what you think I want to hear."

This invitation to authenticity was itself arousing, more intimate than any practiced seduction. His thumbs circled my nipples through the delicate fabric, creating slow, deliberate spirals of pleasure that radiated outward like ripples across still water. Each pass sent a new wave through me, softening the boundaries between thought and sensation. I leaned back against him, my body instinctively yielding, momentarily abandoning the performance of desire for the raw, unfiltered truth of its genuine experience.

"I feel as though you're mapping me," I said, surprised by the tremor in my voice, "creating a geography of sensation I didn't know existed."

His approval rumbled against my neck as his mouth found the junction where it meets shoulder. "The human body contains landscapes most never bother to explore." His hands slid lower, spanning my ribs, thumbs pressing gently into the spaces between bones. "Here, for instance, these intercostal spaces contain nerve plexi rarely stimulated during conventional encounters."

The clinical terminology delivered in the intimate whisper of a lover created an unexpected frisson: knowledge and desire fusing into something more complex than either alone. His hands continued their measured journey to my skirt, the slow descent of its zipper echoing through my body like distant thunder, each increment of release heightening anticipation.

He guided me to step free of the pooled fabric, his hands finding the backs of my knees with surprising delicacy. "Most rush past these transitional zones," he observed, fingers now climbing the sensitive skin of my inner thighs, raising goosebumps in their wake. "But the body doesn't recognize our arbitrary boundaries between erogenous and ordinary."

Standing in my kitchen in nothing but lingerie and heels, I felt more exposed than if I'd been completely naked. The partial state of undress created its own erotic tension: the promise of what remained to be revealed more potent than complete disclosure.

He turned me to face him, his expression revealing genuine appreciation rather than performative desire. His shirt remained buttoned, creating an imbalance of vulnerability that heightened my awareness. I reached again for his buttons, and this time he allowed my progress, watching my face with studied attention.

"Take me to your living room," he said, with such quiet authority that it felt like invitation rather than command.

In the softened light of my living room, he guided me to the arm of my sofa rather than its cushions, this raised surface allowing him to maintain his standing height while exploring my seated form. The position created another delicious imbalance, forcing me to look up at him, creating a vulnerability that wasn't merely physical but psychological.

His hands framed my face with unexpected tenderness. "Close your eyes," he suggested. "Let's remember that touch preceded sight in our evolutionary development."

I complied, immediately aware of how this voluntary darkness heightened my other senses: the scent of his skin like sun-warmed cedar, the subtle sounds of his breathing, the whisper of air against my skin as he moved around me.

His touch came not where I expected, not at breast or thigh but at my wrist, his fingertips finding the pulse point with clinical precision. "Here," he murmured, "your body tells me stories your words might not."

The contact was so minimal yet so focused that it created a current of sensation traveling up my arm, across my chest, finally settling in a pool of liquid heat between my legs. He seemed to read this progression in my quickening pulse, his smile audible in his voice when he spoke again.

"The body is magnificently honest. No matter what the mind instructs, these involuntary responses reveal true desire."

When his fingers finally found the edge of my lace underwear, I arched toward him involuntarily. Instead of granting the implied request, he withdrew slightly, creating an exquisite frustration that was itself a form of pleasure.

"Not yet," he said, his voice carrying warm amusement at my impatience. "We're still discovering what exists before."

He knelt before me, guiding my knees apart. The position created an intoxicating inversion of power: him physically below yet completely controlling the encounter's progression. I felt the slight roughness of his palms against the soft skin of my inner thighs as he spread my legs wider, exposing me to his gaze despite the lingerie still in place.

"Look at me," he instructed, waiting until I opened my eyes. The eye contact created another circuit of tension, this visual connection somehow more intimate than the physical one about to occur.

Without breaking that gaze, he lowered his mouth to my inner thigh, just above the knee. The warm pressure of his lips against this seemingly mundane expanse of skin created a shocking intensity of sensation, as though he'd activated nerve endings normally dormant during sexual encounters. His mouth traveled higher with tantalizing slowness, each kiss precisely placed.

When he finally reached the edge of my underwear, he paused, his breath warm against the damp fabric, evidence of arousal I couldn't conceal. Still maintaining eye contact, he pressed his mouth against me through the lace, the barrier creating an additional layer of tantalizing friction that made me writhe against him.

The sound that escaped me wasn't performative but primal, recognition that his approach had bypassed my professional filters to touch something authentic beneath. With methodical patience, he drew the fabric down my legs with ceremonial deliberation. Now completely exposed to him, I felt an unusual vulnerability, not the practiced openness of my profession but something truly bare.

When his mouth returned to me, the direct contact was so electrifying after such extended prelude that I gasped, my hand instinctively finding his hair. His tongue moved with surgical precision, finding the exact pressure, rhythm, and location that created maximum response. Unlike the mechanical performance many men deliver, his approach contained genuine curiosity, learning my body's particular language through close attention.

His hands gripped my thighs, preventing the instinctive movement of my hips, forcing me to receive pleasure at his controlled pace rather than seek it at mine. The restriction itself became stimulating. This deliberate denial of control creating a surrender more profound than mere physical submission.

He sensed my approaching climax and withdrew slightly, looking up with a mixture of clinical assessment and genuine desire. "Not here," he said, rising. "I want to feel you when it happens."

The interruption created a curious suspension, pleasure held at its peak without release. He guided me to stand, then turned me to face the sofa, his body pressing against my back with delicious solidity. I heard the subtle sound of his belt buckle, then the whisper of fabric as his trousers joined my discarded clothing. His naked body against mine created a cartography of contact: chest against back, thighs against thighs, his hard length pressing between my legs without yet seeking entry.

His hand slid around to my stomach, fingers splayed wide. "Feel this moment," he instructed, his voice carrying a depth of presence rarely encountered. "Not what's about to happen, not what you think should happen, but what exists right now between us."

When he finally entered me, the penetration occurred with the same measured patience that had characterized his entire approach. He filled me with exquisite slowness, each increment of progression creating its own distinct pleasure. The position allowed for a depth that seemed to reach places within me rarely accessed.

"God," he breathed against my neck, composure finally showing cracks. "You feel even better than I imagined."

His control remained evident in the measured rhythm he established, each thrust deliberate rather than driven by escalating urgency. His hand found the center of my pleasure with the same precision he'd demonstrated throughout.

"Stay with me," he murmured when he felt my breathing quicken. "We'll arrive together."

Our synchronized climax contained a depth rarely achieved in my professional encounters. The physiological release was heightened by the psychological connection his approach had created. I felt myself contracting around him with unusual intensity, each pulse drawing an answering response from his body.

For several moments afterward, we remained joined, his chest pressed against my back, our breathing gradually slowing in tandem. When he finally withdrew, the sensation created its own smaller tremor of pleasure. He turned me to face him, his expression revealing genuine satisfaction rather than merely satisfied ego.

"Thank you," he said simply, tucking a strand of hair behind my ear with unexpected tenderness. "For reminding me that time isn't merely something to be managed but to be inhabited."

His approach had reminded me of dimensions of pleasure my professional routine sometimes obscured. The profound satisfaction available when intimacy is approached with full presence rather than performance. As we returned to our abandoned meal, I found myself contemplating how this surgeon had applied his professional intensity to an entirely different domain, approaching pleasure with the same focused care he brought to preserving life.

"In my training," he said, refilling our wine glasses, "we were taught that in surgery, speed often equals excellence. It's taken me years to realize that in other domains, the opposite might be true."

I raised my glass in acknowledgment of this insight. "To the courage of resisting life's constant acceleration."

His smile as our glasses touched contained a recognition of shared philosophy that transcended our professional arrangement. Despite the exchange of money that would eventually conclude our time together, we had created something authentic between us, a genuine connection forged through mutual presence in pleasure rather than merely its pursuit.

•

I saw him again at a medical conference, his hands dancing through a surgical demonstration with the same exquisite precision they had once mapped my body. In that sterile theater of medicine, I recognized the same man who had transformed my bedroom into a sanctuary of suspended time. How curious that these hands could both seal wounds and open secret chambers of pleasure, as if the body's territories of healing and ecstasy shared invisible borders known only to those who have learned to truly inhabit flesh rather than merely navigate it.

We live increasingly in the tyranny of acceleration: modern prisoners who have come to love our temporal chains. I see it in the eyes of my clients, that perpetual elsewhere-ness, that tragic inability to fully arrive before plotting the next departure. We rush toward climax as if pleasure were merely a destination rather than a landscape to be wandered. We consume meals without tasting them, accumulate experiences without experiencing them, forever fleeing the sacred temple of Now toward the mirage of Then. And what do we become in this endless flight and fury but ghosts passing through our own lives, haunting moments we never fully possessed?

What psychology coldly labels "flow state," I have come to recognize as love's truest form. Not the sentimental love of greeting cards and popular songs, but the profound love that manifests as complete presence, as absolute attention. The surgeon had mastered this rarefied attention through his daily communion with mortality. Where others might have developed a desperate clutching at pleasure, he had cultivated instead the opposite: a capacity to expand moments until they became universes unto themselves.

Here lies the beautiful paradox that continues to stir my thoughts long after our bodies have forgotten each other's contours: the same precision that allowed him to excel in surgery's rigid protocols enabled him to transcend the mechanistic approach to pleasure that leaves so many intimacies feeling hollow. He had discovered what few ever realize, that our professional selves need not be exiled from our intimate chambers, that the walls we build between our various identities often prevent the very integration that might make us whole.

I have known hundreds of bodies, each bringing its own particular music to the eternal dance of desire. But it is not the technically skilled lovers who haunt my memory; it is those rare few who brought their complete selves to the encounter, who understood that the body is not merely an instrument to be played but a text to be read, a landscape to be inhabited, a mystery to be entered with reverence rather than solved with technique.

The lingering caress he taught me remains more than a method for heightened pleasure. It has become, in my thinking, a philosophy for living, this willingness to fully occupy each moment rather than treating it as mere pathway. For perhaps we have misunderstood time itself, seeing it as a straight line carrying us from birth to death, when it might instead be a series of expanding and contracting rooms, each containing infinite space for those patient enough to explore its dimensions. This is the secret the surgeon's hands revealed: that heaven might not be a distant realm awaiting us after death, but rather the exquisite territory of the present moment, available always to those who have learned the art of complete arrival.

The Lesson:

The most profound pleasure emerges not from rushing toward climax but from expanding our awareness through every phase of intimacy. When we consciously resist the cultural imperative toward acceleration, we discover sensations and connections typically sacrificed to urgency.

The practice of lingering, treating each caress as complete rather than merely leading toward something "more important", creates several transformative effects: neurologically, it builds arousal through extended anticipation; emotionally, it demonstrates valuing your partner's experience above immediate gratification; physically, it allows pleasure to suffuse the entire body rather than remaining genitally focused.

To begin cultivating this approach, establish clear intention with your partner. Frame slowness not as frustrating delay but as expansion, an opportunity to discover more within each moment. Practice genuine presence with each touch: fully complete one caress before beginning another, notice the texture and temperature of your partner's skin, follow their subtle responses rather than executing a predetermined sequence.

The most common mistake is treating extended foreplay as merely a longer prelude to the "real event" rather than valuable in itself. Instead, approach each moment of connection as containing its own inherent worth, not merely advancing you toward future satisfaction. This shift in perspective, from seeing intimacy as goal-oriented to experience-oriented, often creates pleasure more profound than any specific technique could produce.

The Art of Arousal

Beneath the skin lies an orchestra awaiting a conductor skilled enough to draw forth its most profound melodies, notes that vibrate not in air but in the secret chambers of body and spirit. This truth revealed itself to me on an evening when time itself seemed suspended, as I stood on the terrace of the Hôtel Hermitage watching Monaco transform into a constellation of earthbound stars. The principality glittered below like a handful of diamonds scattered across black velvet by a careless goddess, each light representing desires contained within walls of stone and glass.

I had prepared for this evening with the ceremonial care usually reserved for ancient rituals, bathing in water scented with verbena and cypress, scrubbing my body until it hummed with anticipation, then leaving it deliberately unadorned. No perfume to mask the subtle alchemy of my natural scent. No undergarments beneath my midnight silk dress to interrupt the conversation between silk and skin. Nothing to dilute the impending dialogue between bodies that hungered for fluency in each other's most private languages. Sometimes nakedness begins long before clothing is removed; sometimes we are most revealed when still concealed.

He arrived several minutes before our appointed hour, an unexpected earliness that somehow expressed more anticipation than impatience. Here was a man whose existence had been dedicated to the pursuit of perfection, to the understanding that beauty dwells in the spaces between moments as much as in the moments themselves, yet who allowed himself this small surrender to eagerness. The sommelier had contacted me with a request that intrigued me beyond the usual propositions, an exploration of "the parallels between sensory response in tasting and physical intimacy." How fascinating, this recognition that the tongue performs dual ceremonies of appreciation, that the palate can be as intimate as the most private territories of the body. Where most men seek mere release or fleeting companionship, he desired a conversation conducted through nerve endings and blood cells, through the ancient chemistry that precedes language and lingers after words have evaporated like morning mist from warming skin.

When our hands met in greeting, I immediately understood his gift, the rare ability to touch not just flesh but the invisible currents that animate it. His fingers enveloped mine not with the casual pressure of social convention but with the intentional precision of an artist approaching an instrument of great value. His thumb pressed deliberately against my wrist where my pulse betrayed my body's immediate recognition of something extraordinary, as if my blood itself could sense the approach of a worthy interlocutor. The corner of his mouth curved upward as he registered the quickening rhythm beneath his touch, that betrayal of the body that no amount of professional composure can disguise.

"Your blood already sings," he murmured, maintaining contact several seconds longer than propriety dictated, his skin burning against mine like a brand fashioned from living flame. How curious, this capacity of simple pressure against skin to create reverberations throughout the entire body, as if he had touched not just my wrist but every hidden center of sensation simultaneously.

"And what melody does it play?" I asked, my voice already carrying the husky edge of awakening desire, that subtle transformation of timbre that signals the body's preparation for pleasure long before more obvious signs emerge.

"A prelude to possibility." His fingers withdrew with such calculated slowness that their departure itself became an act of intimate penetration, an absence more keenly felt than the presence had been. In that momentary void left by his touch, my skin seemed to reach toward where his had been, creating an emptiness that demanded to be filled, a hunger more compelling for having been briefly satisfied then denied. I recognized in that moment the subtle mastery of his approach, how withdrawal can intensify connection, how absence can manifest as the most acute form of presence.

Later, as moonlight flooded the suite's bedroom, transforming ordinary shadows into mysterious cyphers on the wall, he stood behind me, close enough that my skin registered his presence yet maddeningly distant from actual contact. The anticipation itself became a tangible caress, invisible fingers of awareness dancing across my bare shoulders, raising gooseflesh in their wake. My nipples hardened beneath silk without being touched, my body responding to the mere promise of his hands.

"The body knows truth before the mind constructs stories around it," he whispered, his breath scorching against my ear, sending liquid heat directly to my core. "In wine, the lips and tongue register complexity long before we find words to describe it."

When his hands finally claimed me, the contact jolted through my system like electricity seeking ground. The sensation was so intense I nearly cried out, not because the touch itself was extraordinary, but because my entire nervous system had been primed to receive it, every cell stretched taut with expectation.

He guided me to the bed where moonlight spilled across the sheets like liquid silver. "Watch what happens," he murmured, reaching for a crystal glass I hadn't noticed before. The clink of ice against glass punctuated the silence before he drew a frozen cube between his fingers. With scientific precision, he pressed the ice against my collarbone, the cold so intense it burned like fire. Before my skin could recover from this exquisite shock, his mouth followed the wet trail, his tongue scorching against the chilled flesh, creating a contrast so profound it hovered at the threshold between pain and pleasure, making me gasp and arch beneath him.

"Pleasure lives most intensely at thresholds," he explained, his voice deepening to a register that seemed to vibrate directly against my sex without touching it. "The moment cold transforms to heat. When emptiness becomes fullness. When anticipation melts into satisfaction."

He continued this deliberate assault on my senses, ice followed by the burning heat of his mouth, traveling unpredictable paths across my body, awakening nerve endings I hadn't known existed until the mere whisper of air against my skin became almost unbearable stimulation. My nipples ached for his attention, my thighs trembled with the effort of remaining still beneath his careful exploration.

His fingers found the zipper of my dress, drawing it downward with the same precision he would use to decant a precious vintage. The silk slid from my shoulders in a liquid cascade, pooling at my waist before continuing its journey to the floor. My nakedness felt both vulnerable and powerful beneath his gaze, my skin burning under his assessment, my sex swollen and slick with a need that transcended professional performance.

"See how beautifully your body orchestrates desire," he murmured, his palms hovering close enough that I could feel their heat without experiencing their touch. "Vasodilation. Tissue erection. The autonomic nervous system preparing for pleasure before consciousness has named it."

When his mouth finally claimed my breast, he broke from the expected pattern, alternating hot suction with cool exhalations across the moistened peak. The contrast shocked a sound from me, a genuine, untamed moan that emerged from some primal place beyond my professional control. My hips lifted involuntarily, seeking contact that remained tantalizingly beyond reach.

He undressed with the same deliberation he'd demonstrated throughout, revealing a body honed by disciplined attention. His cock stood proudly, its swollen head glistening with evidence of his own arousal, its impressive curve a testimony to blood vessels fulfilling their ancient purpose. I wanted to taste him, to feel the weight of him on my tongue, to draw from him the same uncontrolled responses he had extracted from me.

I reached for him, suddenly desperate for the weight and heat of him against me. He came to me with controlled urgency, our bodies meeting like long-separated continents finding their original connection. The shock of full-body contact after such methodical, partial touches sent lightning through my nervous system, drawing a cry from my lips that contained no artifice.

His mouth claimed mine, tasting of mint and something faintly sweet. His tongue performed its own sophisticated alchemy against mine: deep, penetrating explorations interspersed with teasing withdrawals that left me pursuing his retreat, hungry for more of him than he was willing to give.

When his hand finally slid between my thighs, he found me embarrassingly wet, my arousal coating his fingers as they explored my swollen folds. The evidence of my desire glistened on his fingertips as he raised them briefly to his nose, inhaling my scent with the same concentration he would apply to a rare vintage.

"Your body produces its own wine," he murmured, his voice thick with appreciation. "Complex. Distinctive. Impossible to replicate."

He lowered his hand again, parting my labia with deliberate precision. Instead of providing the direct stimulation my throbbing clit screamed for, his fingers performed an exquisite torture, circling the swollen bud without touching it directly, tracing the sensitive inner edges of my labia, occasionally dipping just inside my entrance before retreating. Each almost-touch built layer upon layer of need until I was lifting my hips in wordless supplication, my body begging for what my pride wouldn't allow me to voice.

My wetness increased with each passing moment, the slick sound of his fingers moving through my folds adding an auditory dimension to my arousal. When he finally, finally, brushed directly against my clit, the contact was so electric that a curse escaped me, my back arching off the bed as pleasure spiked through me with shocking intensity.

"The finest wines reveal themselves in stages," he whispered against my throat, his teeth grazing the sensitive skin over my pulse before biting down with careful pressure. "Each moment offering a different note on the palate. First the initial impression—" his finger circled my entrance again, "—then the middle notes—" he pressed one finger inside me, making me gasp, "—and finally, the finish." He added a second finger, stretching me deliciously as my inner walls clutched at this intrusion.

His fingers plunged deeper, curling upward with unerring accuracy to find the ridged tissue of my G-spot. The pressure was both too much and not enough, sending currents of sensation radiating outward from my core. My internal muscles clenched around him involuntarily, trying to draw him deeper, to keep him exactly where I needed him most. He established a rhythm that destroyed coherent thought: fingers pressing firmly against that perfect spot inside while his palm created friction against my clit with each movement.

"Feel how internal pressure creates external response," he said, watching my face with fierce concentration as his thumb separated from his palm to focus directly on my clit, circling the swollen nub in counterpoint to his fingers' internal rhythm. The dual stimulation was almost unbearable in its intensity, pleasure building in waves that threatened to drown me.

My thighs began to tremble uncontrollably, my breath coming in short, desperate pants. Sweat gathered in the hollow between my breasts and at my temples as tension coiled tighter in my core. I felt myself teetering on the precipice of release, that exquisite moment of suspension before falling.

"Please," I gasped, the word torn from me against my professional instincts, a raw acknowledgment of how completely he had dismantled my carefully maintained control.

Just as orgasm approached, my inner walls beginning their rhythmic contractions, my clit pulsing beneath his thumb, he withdrew completely. The sudden emptiness was so shocking that I cried out in frustration, my hips chasing his touch, my sex clenching around nothing but want.

Before I could protest this cruel abandonment, he moved between my trembling thighs, his magnificent cock jutting proudly from the nest of dark hair at his groin. The swollen head was deep purple with arousal, a bead of pre-cum glistening at the tip. He gripped himself at the base, guiding the thick crown to my entrance, rubbing it through my abundant wetness, coating himself in my desire.

He pressed against me, the broad head stretching my opening without penetrating, the pressure exquisite and maddening. My body yielded gradually, the tight ring of muscle expanding to accommodate his impressive girth. The sensation hovered perfectly between pleasure and discomfort, making me acutely aware of every millimeter of penetration.

"Watch me," he commanded, his voice strained with the effort of his control. "Watch me claim you."

My eyes locked on his face as he thrust forward in a single, measured stroke that seated him to the hilt. The fullness was overwhelming. I could feel every ridge and vein of him as he pressed against my innermost depths, the slight curve of his shaft putting delicious pressure exactly where I needed it. My body stretched around him, accommodating his size yet clinging to every inch.

"So tight," he hissed through clenched teeth, his composure finally showing cracks. "So hot. So fucking wet."

The crude language, so at odds with his usual precision, revealed how deeply I'd affected him. His pupils had dilated to midnight as he registered the heat and pressure of my body around his. His expression transformed, clinical observation surrendering to raw sensation, analysis melting into animal presence. For the first time, I saw his control fracture, revealing the primal hunger beneath his sophisticated exterior.

He withdrew until only the head remained inside me, the sudden emptiness making me whimper, before driving forward again with perfect accuracy. Each thrust seemed to reach deeper than the last, his pubic bone grinding against my clit at the apex of each stroke. The delicious friction of his thick shaft dragging against my inner walls sent sparks of pleasure shooting through my pelvis and up my spine.

I wrapped my legs around his waist, changing the angle to take him even deeper. My heels dug into the small of his back, urging him harder, faster, deeper. My nails raked down his back, leaving red trails that would mark him as mine, however temporarily. The room filled with the unmistakable sounds of sex: the wet suction of his cock moving through my arousal, the slap of flesh against flesh, our increasingly labored breathing creating a primal symphony.

He began to move with exquisite precision, each thrust a deliberate exploration of angle and depth. When he found the position that made my breath fracture and my fingers dig into his shoulders, he maintained it with ruthless discipline, hitting that perfect spot inside me with each measured stroke. The sound of our joining, the wet, obscene symphony of his cock moving through my abundant arousal, filled the room, adding an auditory dimension to our escalating pleasure.

"Your muscles begin their rhythmic contraction," he observed, his voice roughened by his own mounting pleasure, the clinical description at odds with the raw need evident in his eyes. "The flush deepens across your chest and throat. The prelude to climax."

His narration heightened my awareness of these responses, intensifying what was already building toward explosive release. I felt myself tightening around him, wetness increasing as blood rushed to tissues already swollen with desire. My heels dug into the small of his back, urging him deeper, harder, faster.

His control began to fragment as our dance intensified. I watched his own body betray the signs he had cataloged in mine: skin flushing crimson, breathing growing ragged, tendons standing out in his neck as discipline battled instinct. His thrusts became less measured, more urgent, as his body surrendered to its most ancient imperatives.

When his thumb pressed hard against my clitoris while he drove deep inside me, the dual stimulation shattered whatever restraint remained. Orgasm claimed me not as a localized release but as a systemic detonation: muscles contracting from toes to scalp, nerve endings firing in chaotic harmony, consciousness itself momentarily dissolving into pure sensation. Wave after wave of pleasure crashed through me, each one seeming to build on the last until I was sobbing with the intensity, my nails leaving crescent moons in his shoulders.

I felt him watching even as his own climax overtook him, his gaze never leaving my face as his rhythm faltered and control dissolved. He drove deep one final time, his cock pulsing inside me as my internal muscles milked every drop of his release. The raw vulnerability in his expression as he came, this moment of complete surrender from a man so carefully controlled, moved me more profoundly than the physical pleasure itself.

Afterward, as sweat cooled on our skin, he propped himself beside me, fingers wandering across my still-sensitive flesh with scientific curiosity. My body responded to even these casual touches, small aftershocks of pleasure rippling through me with each point of contact.

"Understanding the mechanisms of pleasure only enhances its impact," he murmured against my shoulder, his breath warm against my cooling skin. "Just as knowing how wine affects the palate deepens rather than diminishes appreciation."

As midnight deepened outside our windows, I found myself grateful for this rare integration of knowledge and sensation, this transformation of physical coupling into something approaching sacred inquiry without sacrificing its animal intensity.

•

What lingered with me long after the sommelier departed was not merely the physical satisfaction but the revelation his approach had awakened in me. Like a precious vintage that continues to develop complexity hours after tasting, our encounter left traces that transformed my understanding of desire itself.

His extraordinary intuition about pleasure as orchestration rather than singular sensation revealed itself in every aspect of his approach. While most lovers target specific erogenous zones like explorers rushing toward obvious landmarks, he approached my body as a sommelier would a rare vintage: with patience, attention, and the understanding that proper preparation transforms the experience entirely.

Through his deliberate choreography of sensation, the shocking cold of ice followed by the burning warmth of his mouth, whisper-light touches alternating with firm pressure, he awakened my skin until my entire body became a landscape of receptivity. This approach reminded me of what I once heard a French lover call "l'éveil sensuel", the sensual awakening that must precede profound pleasure, the slow unfurling of sensation that transforms mechanical coupling into transcendent communion.

Most profound was his capacity to truly observe rather than merely see. Just as he could detect the subtle notes of blackberry or oak in a complex Bordeaux, he read the quiet signals my body offered: the catch in my breath when he found a particularly sensitive spot, the almost imperceptible arch of my spine, the changing cadence of my pulse beneath his fingers. In his hands, my body revealed secrets even I had forgotten it kept.

This memory inevitably returns me to my first encounter with the power of physical response, though I wouldn't have described it in those terms then. I was seven years old, walking home from school through the lavender fields near La Trinité, when I wandered from the main path. The summer heat had prompted me to remove my cardigan, leaving my arms bare to the world as I allowed the tall purple stalks to envelop me in their fragrant embrace.

As I moved through the dense growth, the rough stems brushed against my wrists and forearms, creating a tingling sensation that stopped me mid-step with its unexpected pleasure. My cotton skirt caught on the plants, pulling the fabric against my legs in ways that awakened something I had no name for. With each movement, the lavender swayed against me, some stems slipping beneath my skirt, grazing skin normally hidden from the world's touch.

The combination, scratchy stems and velvet blossoms, warm air heavy with intoxicating scent, the play of afternoon sunlight filtering through purple stalks, created something beyond mere physical sensation. My body responded with a rush that momentarily transfixed me, skin prickling despite the warmth, something fluttering low in my belly, a curious and not unpleasant tightness spreading through my chest. This accidental awakening, born purely from sensory immersion, left me momentarily breathless, confused, and strangely exhilarated.

What my encounter with the sommelier illuminated was a truth I had felt instinctively since that childhood afternoon, that physical response often precedes conscious desire, that pleasure begins in nerve endings and blood vessels before the mind has fully registered its presence. That moment in the lavender fields had been my first lesson in how the body awakens to sensation through the simplest of touches in unexpected places, how our flesh carries wisdom our intellect often fails to honor.

His expertise demonstrated a philosophy I've long embraced: that pleasure, like any art form, deserves patient cultivation. The difference between his approach and most others was like comparing the hasty consumption of table wine with the thoughtful appreciation of a grand cru, like the distinction between hearing music and truly listening to it with the whole body.

In our increasingly virtual world, where experience arrives filtered through screens and consciousness is constantly pulled away from the physical, perhaps the most profound act of rebellion is simply inhabiting our bodies completely, honoring the intelligence that resides not in our thoughts but in our very flesh. The true art of arousal, I've found after countless intimate encounters, lies not in technical expertise but in presence, both feeling and witnessing the body's exquisite capacity for pleasure without judgment, expectation, or hurry.

Sometimes, when the Mediterranean heat reminds me of childhood summers, I still close my eyes and remember that field of lavender, nature's first lesson in how the world touches us, and how transformative it can be when we allow ourselves to fully feel it. In this remembering, I find both the innocent awakening of the child and the sophisticated understanding of the woman, the perfect circle of sensual knowledge completing itself across decades of embodied experience.

The Lesson:

Arousal flows through the body like electricity seeking ground, a current that can either disperse into insignificance or gather into transformative power. The secret lies in understanding that our skin is not merely a boundary between self and world but our most expansive sensory organ, containing universes of potential pleasure when approached with proper attention.

The body speaks its readiness in a language more ancient than words: pupils dilating like flowers opening toward light, skin flushing as blood rises to the surface, breath changing rhythm as desire deepens. These signals reveal more truth than any verbal affirmation. Learn to read them as a captain reads the sea, with respect for their honesty and awareness of their power.

Consider the paradox that continuous sensation eventually becomes invisible to consciousness, while change, the transition between states, commands complete attention. This is why the clever lover varies pressure, temperature, and rhythm, understanding that contrast creates awareness where constancy might fade into background.

Remember too that arousal reveals itself through involuntary responses no amount of control can fully master: the hardening of nipples beneath silk, the dampness gathering between thighs, the quickening pulse visible at the throat. These honest messengers often arrive before conscious desire, reminding us that the body possesses wisdom the mind would be wise to follow.

The Taste of Skin

Taste is memory crystallized on the tongue. Long after touch has faded and scent has dispersed, the ghost of flavor lingers, summoning entire worlds from oblivion with a single molecule. This truth reveals itself to me each time I bite into a sun-warmed strawberry and find myself transported to childhood summers, or when the brine of an olive resurrects a forgotten seaside encounter. Our bodies archive these sensory memories, preserving them in chambers more ancient than language, more reliable than photographs.

The irony wasn't lost on me when he contacted me, this man whose entire existence revolved around creating memories for others through taste. A chef whose name had become synonymous with Monaco's gastronomic renaissance, whose palate could distinguish between olives harvested mere kilometers apart, yet who confessed in our initial correspondence that he had lost the ability to savor the most elemental of pleasures.

"A paradox," he'd written in an email more eloquent than most, "that I can identify fifty-seven varieties of salt but have forgotten how to taste a kiss."

The Mediterranean sun had painted my apartment in gold that afternoon as I prepared for his arrival: honey from lavender fields, bread from the artisanal baker on Rue Grimaldi, chocolates from Ecuador with ascending percentages of cacao that would challenge even the most sophisticated palate.

He arrived when the day's heat had begun to soften. When I opened the door, I was struck first by his hands, instruments of his craft that conveyed an entire biography without words. Strong fingers bearing small scars and burns that no professional kitchen spares its practitioners, yet possessing elegant precision in their movements.

His physical presence carried an olfactory autobiography I found unexpectedly alluring. Beneath the crisp scent of recently showered skin lingered trace elements of his profession: whispers of charred herbs, caramelized sugars, and complex umami notes. His cologne, applied with admirable restraint, provided a sophisticated top note without overwhelming its authentic base.

"Your home smells of bergamot and sandalwood," he observed immediately, "but also something unexpected... black tea with cassis?"

"A candle I discovered in a small parfumerie in Èze," I confirmed, pleased by his immediate demonstration of sensory acuity.

We settled with tea in my sitting room, where afternoon light transformed ordinary air into something almost tangible. He held his cup with the reverent precision of someone for whom the act of consumption is never casual, inhaling the steam before sipping, his eyes closing momentarily to process the experience without visual distraction.

"You mentioned something in your message that intrigued me," I began, watching his fingers circle the rim of his cup with unconscious grace. "About having forgotten how to taste a kiss."

"It's a peculiar affliction of specialists," he said after setting his cup down. "We develop extraordinary sensitivity in one domain while becoming blind to others. I can detect when a sauce needs three more grains of salt, yet somehow, I've lost the capacity to simply... experience."

This confession resonated deeply with my own observations of human intimacy. How often we develop expertise that paradoxically diminishes our capacity for authentic pleasure. The businessman who masterfully negotiates million-euro deals yet cannot navigate the simple give-and-take of physical affection; the surgeon whose fingers perform miracles of precision but move mechanically across a lover's skin.

"Perhaps," I suggested, setting aside my cup with deliberate care, "we might approach this as an exercise in sensory recalibration."

His eyes registered immediate interest. He possessed that quality I've always found most compelling in a man, the rare willingness to become a student again, to surrender certainty for discovery regardless of status or achievement.

The Taste of Skin

I led him toward my bedroom, where honey-gold light filtered through ivory curtains. Before he could begin the customary undressing, I placed my palm against his chest, feeling the steady percussion of his heart beneath expensive linen.

"I'd like to try something different," I proposed. "If you're willing to surrender control temporarily."

From my bedside drawer, I withdrew a length of black silk. I approached him with unhurried movements, the fabric suspended between my hands like an offering.

"May I?" I asked, holding it up where the light caught its subtle shimmer.

He nodded, understanding immediately the purpose without explanation.

"The elimination of one sense heightens others," he observed as I moved behind him. "In culinary terms, this would be like tasting in complete darkness."

"Exactly," I murmured, bringing the silk across his eyes with gentle precision. "Though what we're tasting will be considerably more complex than even your most ambitious tasting menu."

I guided him to sit at the edge of my bed, where I began unbuttoning his shirt with deliberate slowness. The revelation of his skin occurred in increments: first the hollow of his throat where pulse visibly flickered, then the upper planes of his chest still pale despite Monaco's persistent sunshine.

I placed myself between his knees, taking his right hand in mine, raising it until his fingers brushed the pulse point at my throat.

"Follow the path I create," I instructed softly, guiding his fingers down the column of my neck to the hollow between my collarbones.

I guided his hand lower, where the first button of my blouse created a natural pause in his exploration. Without instruction, his fingers worked it free with a dexterity that revealed years of fine motor control. Each subsequent button surrendered until my blouse hung open, mirroring his own state of partial dishabille.

"Now," I said, my voice dropping to that register that seems to bypass the ear and vibrate directly against skin, "I want you to use your professional palate. I'm going to offer you something to taste, and I want you to describe it as you would a new ingredient."

I guided his mouth to the inside of my wrist, where perfume mingles with the body's natural chemistry. Pressing my skin gently against his lips, I felt the momentary hesitation of someone transitioning between cognitive frameworks.

"Taste," I encouraged again. "Really taste."

His mouth opened against my skin, lips and tongue moving in careful exploration. The warm wetness of this contact sent an unexpected current through my nervous system, a reminder that despite my professional detachment, my body remains exquisitely responsive to skilled attention.

"Salt," he finally said, voice carrying that particular quality of someone accessing specialized vocabulary. "But different from sea salt... more like the mineral quality of fleur de sel from Camargue. And something almost floral beneath... like jasmine tea."

I moved with deliberate grace, offering the crook of my elbow to his mouth, that tender territory where skin remains sheltered.

"And here?" I whispered as his lips met this new landscape. "What do you discover?"

"Sweeter here," he observed after careful consideration. "With subtle bitter notes, like the relationship between orange flesh and pith."

This reversal, me offering my body as a tasting menu for his blindfolded exploration, created an exquisite tension that transcended conventional power dynamics. With each touch, I was both revealed and revealing, simultaneously guide and subject, controller and offering.

When I placed my breast against his mouth, his professional commentary momentarily dissolved into something more primal, a sharp intake of breath followed by a sound of pleasure too genuine to be performance.

"The nipple," he murmured eventually, recovering his analytical frame though his voice had acquired a roughened edge, "is where sweet meets savory. Like the perfect balance in a dish that bridges categories."

His hands found their purpose in this new context: supporting the weight of my breast, thumb circling sensitive skin with the same care he might give to stirring a delicate reduction. What escaped me wasn't deliberate, just breath and truth: a soft inhale, a helpless sigh, unshaped by intention.

When he finally knelt before me, hands circling behind to support the small of my back, his expression held that perfect synthesis of professional focus and visceral hunger.

"Here," he murmured against the juncture of thigh and pelvic crease, "salt meets sweet in perfect equipoise."

I guided him toward more central pleasures, fingers tangling in his hair as his mouth found the heart of my desire. His technique contained none of the aggressive performance that often characterizes such encounters; instead, he approached with the patient precision of someone carefully building a complex flavor profile.

"Tell me," I encouraged between increasingly shortened breaths, "what you taste now."

He paused momentarily, his head tilted in deep consideration despite the blindfold.

"Ocean," he replied simply. "The primordial sea from which all life emerged."

This unexpected poetry intensified my response beyond what I had anticipated. The image he evoked: ancient waters, original source, fundamental essence, resonated with something deep within my understanding of feminine sexuality.

When climax finally claimed me, it arrived not as the narrowly genital phenomenon most pursue, but as a full-body cascade that seemed to originate simultaneously from every point of contact between us. I heard myself make sounds I rarely produce in professional contexts, authentic vocalizations that emerged from some place beyond performance.

In the trembling aftermath, I removed his blindfold with gentle hands. His eyes blinked against the room's amber light, pupils contracting as vision returned. When his gaze finally focused on me, seeing for the first time what he had previously only tasted and touched, a slow smile transformed his features.

"There you are," he murmured, the simplicity of the observation somehow more intimate than elaborate praise.

I extended my hand to him. "Come," I invited, leading him toward the bed. "Let me taste you now."

He moved with me, his body animated by a new fluidity that hadn't been present when he arrived, as if the rigid boundaries of professional identity had begun to dissolve. When he stretched across my sheets, the last light of day transformed his skin to burnished gold, shadows pooling in the hollows of collarbone and hip.

Beginning at his throat, where pulse still visibly fluttered beneath surprisingly fragile skin, I traced the contours of his body with fingertips barely making contact. When my lips finally pressed against the hollow of his throat, his sharp inhalation revealed how completely he had surrendered to sensation. I tasted salt and cedar, the lingering ghost of cologne beneath the more authentic chemistry that prolonged arousal had awakened in his skin.

When I finally took him in my mouth, the salt-sweet flavor of arousal bloomed across my tongue, that primal taste that transcends individual difference, that connects all human beings to our most fundamental drives. His back arched, head pressing into the pillows as pleasure claimed him with visible intensity.

Like the chef tasting multiple components to create a harmonious dish, I combined different techniques to create a symphony of sensation that gradually dismantled his professional composure. When he eventually reached for me with evident hunger, I moved above him with fluid grace.

"Now," I whispered, lowering myself until our bodies joined in that exquisite convergence of separate flesh, "taste me as I taste you."

I moved above him in undulations reminiscent of the sea he had invoked earlier, creating rhythms that spoke to something more primal than conscious thought. What astonished me most was his continued sensory awareness even as passion mounted. Where most abandon conscious perception as arousal intensifies, he maintained an integration of analytical appreciation and visceral response.

"You taste different here," he observed, his mouth finding the pulse point at my wrist as our bodies continued their rhythmic dialogue. "Salt has intensified, musk has deepened... it's extraordinary..."

When his control finally began to fracture, movements becoming less measured, breathing more ragged, I recognized the threshold where analysis surrenders to pure experience. I wrapped my legs around him, changing our angle to intensify sensation for us both.

"There," I encouraged, recognizing the precise moment when intellectual appreciation gave way to pure sensation. "Stay right there."

When climax finally overtook him, the transformation was extraordinary, all professional distance dissolving into pure presence, all calculation surrendering to embodied experience. His expression contained something approaching reverence, the look of someone encountering mystery rather than mastering technique.

As evening light replaced afternoon gold, he confessed, "This wasn't what I expected. I thought I was coming here for my own pleasure primarily."

"And did you find it?" I asked.

"Yes, but in a completely different way. Discovering how to give pleasure has been more satisfying than simply receiving it."

"That's the lesson most miss," I replied. "The greatest satisfaction often comes from understanding your partner's pleasure as thoroughly as your own."

As darkness settled over Monaco, I found myself contemplating the curious parallels between our professions: both devoted to pleasure, both requiring technical mastery, both ultimately measuring success through the satisfaction of others. Yet his focus on taste, that most intimate of senses, offered a perfect metaphor for what meaningful connection requires: the courage to consume and be consumed, to incorporate another's essence into our own.

"I just remembered something," I said, turning toward him in the deepening twilight. "You mentioned having forgotten how to taste a kiss. I believe we've neglected to address that directly."

I moved closer, propping myself on one elbow. "The kiss is where all sensory experiences converge," I explained, my voice softening with genuine tenderness. "It's the most complex tasting menu of all."

Slowly, deliberately, I lowered my mouth to his. Rather than hungry urgency, this kiss began with the lightest touch, my lips barely brushing his, creating the merest suggestion of contact.

What followed was perhaps the most intimate exchange of our entire encounter, this gradual, unhurried exploration of taste and texture, pressure and pause. His hands remained still, one resting lightly at my waist, the other cradling the nape of my neck. All attention had concentrated in this single point of connection, this ancient gesture that predates even language.

I tasted the lingering sweetness of arousal on his tongue, the faint salt of perspiration at the corner of his mouth, the unique essence that belonged to him alone, that flavor that no one else in the world possessed, as unique as fingerprints, as revealing as confession.

When we finally separated, his eyes remained closed for several heartbeats longer, a moment of internal processing I recognized from earlier.

"Well?" I asked quietly. "Have you remembered?"

His eyes opened slowly, revealing a depth of feeling I hadn't glimpsed before, something approaching genuine connection.

"It's like discovering a forgotten instrument and finding I still know how to play," he murmured. "But the music is richer than I remembered."

The next morning, I found an envelope slipped beneath my door. Inside was a handwritten card containing a simple sentence: "The sweetness lingered long after the taste was gone."

•

I have come to understand, watching the boundaries dissolve between expertise and emotion, that we are all fractured beings who have learned to separate what should remain whole. The chef's extraordinary sensitivity to flavor had somehow become isolated within his professional domain, like a river diverted from its natural course, flowing powerfully but cut off from the sea it once fed.

How curious our modern compartmentalization, the artificial walls we erect between aspects of self. The surgeon whose hands heal but falter in intimacy; the poet who writes of passion yet recoils from real touch; the philosopher who dissects connection while watching life unfold from behind glass, never stepping into the dance.

What fascinates me most in these moments of integration is witnessing the reunion of fragmented selves, when professional mastery embraces personal vulnerability, when analytical brilliance enhances rather than diminishes emotional response. I saw this chef's transformation not as the acquisition of new skills but as the remembering of original wholeness, like water finding its ancient path to the sea after long diversion.

In my more lucid moments, I wonder if this compartmentalization reflects our deeper fear. Not of inadequacy but of our own potential intensity. We divide ourselves because to exist as complete beings might overwhelm us, might require a vulnerability too absolute to bear in a world that rewards specialized performance over integrated presence.

This chef reminded me that wisdom resides not in knowledge but in complete engagement, in willingness to taste life with every aspect of our being rather than merely sample it through carefully selected filters. The extraordinary gifts he had cultivated through years of professional dedication needed only to be invited into his intimate life to transform his capacity for connection.

Perhaps this is what I find most precious about my unusual profession, these fragments of time when I witness someone reclaiming their wholeness, when the artificial boundaries between mind and body, knowledge and feeling, observation and experience momentarily dissolve. In these rare convergences, we glimpse what might be possible if we dared to live completely, to taste with our entire being rather than merely our tongue, to touch with our whole history rather than merely our hands, to see with our full awareness rather than merely our eyes.

The Lesson:

Our bodies speak a language older than words, and nowhere is this more evident than in the chemistry of taste. When we truly attend to another person with our mouths, not just kissing perfunctorily or performing expected techniques, but genuinely tasting, we access primal circuits of connection that bypass our usual defenses.

Try approaching your lover's body as a sommelier might approach a complex wine or a chef might explore an unfamiliar ingredient. Notice how different territories offer unique flavors: the slight saltiness that gathers in the hollow of a throat, the subtly sweet undertone of inner thighs, the complex muskiness that develops as arousal deepens. Each person carries their own unique flavor profile, as distinctive as a fingerprint and infinitely more revealing.

Most importantly, approach this exploration with genuine curiosity rather than technique. The quality of your attention matters far more than any specific method. When you taste with your whole being, when you allow sensation to register fully before your analytical mind categorizes it, you create possibilities for connection that transcend ordinary understanding.

And please, don't neglect the simple power of a thoughtful, unhurried kiss. In our rush toward what culture deems "advanced" intimate acts, we often hurry past this fundamental connection. Yet in many ways, kissing remains our most sophisticated intimate exchange. The place where breath, taste, touch, and scent converge in perfect symphony. Through kissing, we share not just physical sensation but essential nature: our anxieties, our joys, our hunger, our tenderness.

A kiss contains worlds when we're fully present within it. Return to this most basic pleasure with renewed awareness, approaching it not as obligatory prelude but as complete experience in itself. You may discover that what appeared simple on the surface contains depths you've never fully explored.

Part 5:
Deeper Dimensions

I remember him clearly, a quantum physicist whose professional life was devoted to understanding reality's fundamental nature. He arrived at my door with scientist's precision, yet when our bodies finally joined, something unexpected emerged in his expression, a recognition that transcended physical pleasure. "This connection," he whispered, his voice containing wonder rather than satisfaction, "feels like touching something beyond ordinary existence."

The moment has remained with me not for its intensity but for how perfectly it articulated something I've observed repeatedly throughout my years of intimate study: that physical pleasure, at its most profound, can become doorway to experiences that transcend explanation yet remain undeniably real.

The chapters that follow explore intimacy's capacity to touch dimensions beyond the merely physical. Not through mystical abstraction but through direct bodily experience. What happens when awareness fully inhabits sensation? When boundaries between self and other momentarily dissolve? When time itself seems to suspend in moments of complete presence?

We'll traverse territories where Eastern wisdom meets Western embodiment, where ancient practices illuminate contemporary connection. We'll examine how physical vitality enhances pleasure, how anticipation creates its own exquisite satisfaction, how preparation transforms practical necessity into meaningful ritual.

I've felt my consciousness expand beyond its usual boundaries during particularly profound encounters, moments where pleasure became so intense it transcended ordinary categories of experience. These dimensions aren't reserved for spiritual practitioners or tantric masters but remain accessible to anyone willing to approach intimacy with intention rather than habit, with presence rather than performance.

What follows offers no guarantee of transcendence, but it opens possibilities many never consider. How physical connection might become vehicle for experiences that linger in memory not just for their sensual intensity but for how they momentarily revealed something essential about existence itself.

The Body Electric

There exists a quality to Monaco's early morning light that defies easy categorization, crystalline yet warm, revealing yet forgiving. It bathes everything it touches in stark honesty, as though the night has washed away all pretense. I was contemplating this particular quality of illumination, how it transformed my living room into a study of geometric precision, when my door chimed.

Opening it revealed a man outlined against the eastern light, one whose appointment request had specified he would arrive directly from his regular swimming session at the Monte Carlo Beach Club. Standing there with droplets still clinging to his hair and skin faintly perfumed with salt, he presented a startling contrast to my usual visitors. Where most men arrive carefully assembled and meticulously presented, he appeared to exist within his skin rather than behind it. His presence had a rare quality of immediacy, as though there was no distance between his essence and his form, no careful facade separating inner life from outer presentation.

"I hope the swimming doesn't bother you," he said by way of greeting, voice resonant without apology. "I find I'm more... centered, more present after being in water."

I watched as he brushed back hair still damp from the sea, a gesture entirely free of self-consciousness. The movement revealed momentary glimpses of silvered temples contrasting against darker strands, evidence of years lived fully rather than resisted. Though his age placed him firmly in his early fifties, he possessed a physical presence that seemed almost phosphorescent compared to the carefully modulated composure of younger clients. His movements through my doorway, fluid, economical, precisely calibrated to the available space, spoke of a body that knew itself intimately, that inhabited the world with rare certainty.

The scent of sea salt mingled with something distinctly masculine as he passed, not artificial cologne but the honest fragrance of clean skin warmed by exertion. His linen shirt clung slightly to places not fully dried, revealing glimpses of a form maintained through purposeful movement rather than vanity. Each gesture, each shift of weight as he entered my space, contained a quality of deliberate intention that drew my professional attention.

"I find it refreshing, actually," I replied, genuinely pleased by this evidence of embodied existence. "Most men arrive already half-absent, mentally calculating their next appointment or composing emails in their heads."

When I commented on the physical vitality he carried with him, he smiled with unexpected modesty, fine lines deepening around eyes that held both humor and quiet conviction. The expression transformed his features from merely handsome to genuinely engaging.

"Maintaining this instrument isn't vanity," he explained, hand gesturing toward his own form with an elegant economy of movement. "It's responsible stewardship of the only vehicle I'll ever truly possess."

The statement struck me as unexpectedly profound. So different from Monaco's typical aesthetic obsession, the pursuit of physical perfection as social currency or armor against mortality. His perspective suggested a more integrated philosophy, one that honored function alongside form, that recognized the body as both temple and home rather than mere accessory or inconvenient container for the mind.

"Tea?" I offered, another departure from the champagne rituals so many clients insisted upon before even casual conversation. His nod of appreciation, a barely perceptible inclination of his head that somehow managed to convey genuine gratitude, confirmed my intuition: this would be an encounter operating outside my usual professional choreography.

He moved through my apartment with a spatial awareness I found myself studying with professional interest. No hesitant adjustments or awkward negotiations of furniture, just fluid certainty, as though he carried a perfect mental map of his surroundings at all times. His eyes took in my carefully curated space with appreciative attention rather than assessment or judgment. He paused before an abstract sculpture I'd acquired in Kyoto years earlier, a piece more notable for the negative space it defined than its solid form, bronze curves suggesting boundaries around emptiness.

"Fascinating," he remarked, circling it without touching, though his fingers hovered millimeters from its surface, tracing the air as if feeling its energetic presence. "The emptiness articulates the shape as much as the material does."

"Like movement," I responded, finding myself drawn closer to him through this unexpected recognition, "which exists equally in the gesture and the pause between gestures."

The smile that crossed his face suggested recognition of a kindred perspective, a momentary bridge formed between our separate worlds through shared perception. Over tea in my sunlit living room, steam rising in gossamer spirals from porcelain cups, we discussed expectations with unusual directness. The amber liquid caught morning light as he raised his cup, his wrist turning with unconscious grace. The clarity with which he expressed his desires, without either shame or entitlement, struck me as its own form of elegance.

"I enjoy exploration through movement," he stated simply, setting his cup down with precise gentleness. "Discovering what bodies can do together when they're fully present."

Setting aside my teacup, I extended my hand toward him, palm open in invitation. "Then let's begin with presence."

What followed was unlike any encounter I'd experienced in years. Rising from my couch, he drew me toward him in a single unbroken motion that spoke of trained physicality, not the showy strength of gymnasium devotees but something more elemental, more integrated. His hands found my waist with precisionist certainty, lifting me with an effortlessness that momentarily suspended gravity. For a heartbeat, I hovered above the floor, held aloft by strength so controlled it appeared effortless, my orientation shifted just enough to create a delicious disorientation.

"You're lighter than you appear," he murmured, setting me down with deliberate slowness that allowed our bodies to align in passing, creating points of contact that awakened nerve endings I had forgotten existed.

"And you're stronger than you advertise," I countered, suddenly aware of dormant muscles in my own form responding to his proximity, a remembered physicality awakening beneath professional poise.

Rather than progressing directly toward conventional intimacy, he seemed fascinated by the mechanics of our physical dialogue: how my balance shifted when he applied pressure to my lower back, how my breathing synchronized with his when our torsos pressed together, how the architecture of our distinct forms could interlock in unexpected configurations. Each point of connection became its own exploration, each adjustment offering new sensory information. His curiosity was neither clinical nor merely sexual, but something rarer. A genuine appreciation for embodied communication.

His mouth found mine not in the performative kiss so many clients deliver, but in an exploratory tasting that seemed to calibrate his awareness to my responses. His tongue traced my lower lip with such focused attention that the sensation radiated outward, activating nerve pathways that connected to my center with unexpected directness. The salt of sea water lingered faintly on his skin, adding mineral complexity to our exchange. I found myself responding with unplanned intensity, a professional lapse that he noted with visible pleasure.

"There you are," he whispered against my mouth, his breath warm and intimate. "Beneath the performance."

The observation, its accuracy, momentarily startled me. How rarely clients perceive the layers of self I maintain, the subtle distinction between professional engagement and authentic response. This recognition, this seeing beyond carefully constructed facades, created an unexpected vulnerability that both unsettled and intrigued me. His hands framed my face, thumbs tracing my cheekbones with such precision that I felt suddenly, completely seen.

"May I try something?" he asked, already guiding me toward my dining table, a solid oak piece I'd commissioned from a local artisan, its surface polished to a honeyed glow by morning light. When I nodded, he lifted me onto its surface with that same controlled power, positioning himself between my legs with deliberate intention, his thighs pressing against the wood's edge.

"Lean back," he instructed, supporting my gradual recline with one hand splayed across my spine, fingers finding the subtle valley between vertebrae. "Now extend your arms above your head."

I complied, finding myself stretched across my own dining table, suddenly aware of its polished coolness against my shoulder blades, the hard surface transforming from functional furniture to sensual platform. Morning light spilled across my body from the nearby window, creating patterns of illumination and shadow that revealed form through contrast. He unbuttoned my blouse with unhurried focus, each newly exposed centimeter of skin receiving focused attention: a touch, a taste, a careful assessment of response. No territory was rushed through, no sensation treated as merely transitional.

"Your body speaks an extraordinary language," he observed, tracing the subtle curve where my ribs gave way to waist, the depression where hip bone created a natural valley. "Most people mutter. You articulate."

His mouth traveled lower, tongue tracing architectural patterns across my abdomen: spirals, lines, and unexpected angles that created a calligraphy of sensation upon my skin. Meanwhile, his hands explored the terrain of my legs through silk trousers, fingers pressing with perfect pressure into muscle, discovering tensions I hadn't realized I carried until they began to dissolve beneath his touch. The dual sensation, wet heat against bare skin, firm pressure through fabric, created a cognitive dissonance that heightened both. I found my breathing changing, deepening, outside my usual professional control.

He unfastened my trousers with the same deliberate attention, sliding them from my hips in a single motion that allowed his fingers to trace the full length of my legs, from hip to ankle. The cool morning air against newly exposed skin created its own pleasure, a counterpoint to the radiating warmth of his touch. The contrast between temperature, pressure, and texture multiplied the sensory information flooding my system.

"Watch," he said, maintaining eye contact as he knelt between my legs, his gaze holding mine with an intensity that somehow magnified physical sensation through psychological connection. Rather than immediately seeking the obvious destination, he began exploring the neglected territory of my inner thighs: the tender hollow behind my knees, the sensitive confluence where leg meets pelvis. His mouth and hands worked in coordinated counterpoint, creating sensations that spiraled outward from each point of contact like ripples in still water.

When his tongue finally found my center, the contact arrived after such extensive anticipation that my body arched involuntarily, nerve endings primed for sensation that now arrived with devastating precision. His technique reflected the same integrated awareness I'd observed in his movements, nothing mechanical or performative, just perfectly calibrated attention to feedback. He seemed to register every subtle shift in my breathing, every minute tensing of muscle, adjusting his approach with exquisite responsiveness.

"Your capacity for sensation is extraordinary," he murmured against my inner thigh, his breath itself becoming a point of stimulation, warm air caressing skin made hypersensitive by previous attention. "Most people experience pleasure through such a narrow aperture."

I found myself approaching climax with surprising swiftness. A professional rarity that momentarily disoriented me. His perception, again uncanny, registered my proximity to release. The muscles in my thighs had begun their telltale tension, my breath catching in the particular rhythm that precedes surrender.

"Not yet," he said, rising with fluid grace, his self-control as evident in this moment of restraint as in his earlier demonstrations of strength. "We've barely begun mapping possibilities."

He helped me from the table, my legs unexpectedly unsteady beneath me, and guided me toward the bay window overlooking Monaco's harbor. Standing behind me, he created a frame of his body around mine, one hand splayed across my abdomen while the other traced the curve of my neck where it met my shoulder, that vulnerable juncture where tension so often accumulates.

"Look," he instructed, positioning me before the panorama of sea and sky that had become so familiar I had ceased truly seeing it. "When was the last time you actually saw this view? Really saw it?"

The question penetrated deeper than intended, bypassing professional persona to reach something more essential. How easily habitation transforms the extraordinary into mere background, rendering miracles mundane through daily exposure. Below us, sunlight fractured into countless diamonds across the harbor's surface, each wavelet catching light at slightly different angles to create a kinetic mosaic. The geometric precision of yachts against azure water created a study in human-imposed order against natural fluidity. The distant smudge of France beyond reminded me how perspective alters perception, how neighboring nations become mere visual texture from sufficient distance.

His hand slid between my legs from behind, finding me still sensitized from his earlier attention, nerves awakened and responsive. The dual awareness, external vista and internal sensation, created a peculiar cognitive split that somehow enhanced both experiences. As his fingers established a rhythm against my most responsive point, I found my perception of the view before me intensifying: colors more saturated, details more precisely rendered, beauty more acutely felt. The pleasure within magnified the beauty without, creating a feedback loop between body and perception.

"Sensation heightens all awareness," he murmured against my ear, free hand now attending to my breast with the same calibrated precision, thumb circling the nipple through delicate fabric with pressure that generated waves of response. "Pleasure isn't a discrete function, it's an integrated state of being."

I leaned back against his solidity, surrendering to the complex orchestration of sensations he conducted. His now-unclothed form pressed against mine, the evidence of his arousal a heated pressure against my lower back. The glass before us had begun to fog slightly from our combined breath, creating a shifting veil between our private moment and the public world beyond, translucence replacing transparency as our passion literally altered perception.

"Now," he said, turning me to face him with gentle insistence. "I want to try something."

He lifted me with that same controlled strength that had so startled me initially, guiding my legs around his waist as he supported my weight entirely. The position created a new architecture between our bodies: my back against the cool window, his form providing the opposing pressure, gravity itself becoming a third participant in our encounter. The contrast between the cool glass against my back and his warm body against my front created a sensory envelope that heightened awareness of both surfaces.

When he entered me, the sensation was amplified by the unique configuration: deep, precisely angled, activating nerves typically untouched during conventional approaches. The feeling was so complete, so perfectly calibrated to my interior architecture, that my exhale found voice, making a sound something between surprise and revelation. His responding smile confirmed this breach in my usual composure had been both noticed and appreciated.

"There you are again," he said, establishing a rhythm that defied conventional pacing, not the predictable acceleration most men employ, but a complex tempo that incorporated unexpected pauses, subtle variations in depth and angle, moments of complete stillness that allowed sensation to bloom fully before continuing. His control transformed intercourse from mundane friction to sophisticated dialogue.

The glass against my back provided a cool counterpoint to the heat building between us. Through half-closed eyes, I observed his complete presentness: no moment of mental absence, no retreat into fantasy or performance. His entire being remained engaged in our connection, adjusting continuously to my responses with an athlete's trained precision. This quality of attention, so different from the divided consciousness most bring to intimate encounters, created a mirrored presentness in me, a professional guardedness giving way to genuine engagement.

"Change," he said suddenly, disengaging with such control that the transition itself created its own pleasure. He guided me toward my reading chair, a burgundy leather piece positioned beside the bookshelf, and arranged me facing its back, hands gripping the polished wood of its frame. The leather received my knees with cool welcome, providing both support and sensual contrast.

The new position created yet another geometric relationship between our bodies, granting him deeper access from behind while keeping his hands free to explore the varied terrain of my torso. As he entered me again, one hand circled forward to maintain contact with my center, grounding me in pleasure, while the other traced languid patterns along my spine: each stroke seeming to activate dormant neural pathways, awakening sensation in places I hadn't known could feel. His touch balanced strength with exquisite sensitivity, pressure calibrated not to overwhelm, but to invite, to coax, to open.

"Your body understands things your mind hasn't recognized yet," he observed, his rhythm now deepening, becoming more insistent while maintaining that peculiar control that spoke of mastery over his own responses. "Feel how this angle changes everything."

He made a minute adjustment to my posture, a slight alteration in the arch of my back, a barely perceptible shift of hips, that suddenly transformed pleasant friction into exquisite precision. The sensation was so acute, so perfectly targeted to nerves I hadn't known existed, that I heard myself gasp with genuine surprise, professional distance completely surrendering to authentic response.

"How—" I began, the question dissolving into incoherence as he maintained the newly discovered alignment with master-craftsman accuracy, each thrust stimulating internal landscapes rarely accessed with such precision.

"Body knowledge," he answered simply, his voice carrying both effort and certainty. "The intelligence that precedes thought."

His pace intensified finally, responding to signals from my own form that I couldn't consciously control: the involuntary tensing of interior muscles, the changing cadence of my breathing, the infinitesimal movements toward and away from particular sensations. The building pleasure centered not just in the obvious points of contact but radiated through my entire system, nerve endings awakening in unexpected regions: thighs, abdomen, even fingertips tingling with approaching release.

My climax, when it arrived, possessed a totality I rarely experienced professionally, not confined to the genitals but radiating throughout my entire system like an electrical current finding every available pathway. Waves of sensation crashed through my body, each one building on rather than diminishing the last, creating a sustained state of ecstasy that momentarily dissolved all boundaries: physical, professional, psychological. For that suspended moment, I existed purely as sensation, all careful distinctions between self and other temporarily erased.

His own release followed, his carefully maintained control finally yielding to the primary grammar of pleasure. The sound he made, a deep exhalation that seemed to originate from his core, carried no performative element, just the authentic expression of culmination. I felt the pulsing heat of him inside me, his hands gripping my hips with an intensity that would leave temporary evidence of our connection.

In the quietude that followed, we remained joined, his forehead resting lightly against my shoulder blade, our breathing gradually synchronizing into a shared rhythm. The morning light had strengthened, defining the room with greater clarity, illuminating dust motes that danced in the heated air between window and wall. When he finally withdrew, the sensation contained its own smaller pleasure: a postscript to the paragraph we'd written together.

"Most people," he said as we slowly restored order to our clothing and ourselves, his movements retaining that fluid grace even in mundane activity, "never discover what their bodies are truly capable of. They operate within such constrained parameters of sensation and movement."

The insight crystallized something I'd witnessed repeatedly throughout my career but never articulated so precisely: this tragic narrowing of physical possibility, this reduction of embodied potential to standardized choreography. We learn to move through the world in increasingly limited ways, restricting our physical vocabulary to the merely functional, forgetting the body's capacity for expression beyond utility.

"Former Olympic hopeful," he explained when I inquired about his background, hands smoothing his linen shirt with easy precision. "Swimming. Shoulder injury redirected my path. Now I coach others, helping them understand that physical discipline isn't a punishment but path to liberation."

The philosophy resonated profoundly. In my own way, wasn't I engaged in similar work, guiding others toward expanded awareness of their embodied potential? Despite the obvious differences in our professional domains, we shared this fundamental understanding: the body, properly attended to, offers wisdom beyond what the mind alone can access.

As he prepared to leave, gathering his swimming gear with the same fluid economy that characterized all his movements, he asked a question that caught me by surprise: "You're unusually attuned to physical nuance. What developed that awareness in you?"

The inquiry was delivered without prurient curiosity, a professional asking another professional about their training. How refreshing to be seen as a practitioner with expertise rather than merely a provider of services. In that moment, our different worlds seemed less distant, connected through shared understanding of embodied knowledge.

"Dance, initially," I answered truthfully. "Then twenty-four years of intimate observation—thousands of bodies, each teaching me something different about the relationship between movement and pleasure."

He nodded, understanding immediately. "The body never lies," he said simply. "It remains our most honest expression of who we are and what we need."

After he departed, I moved through my apartment with heightened awareness of my own physicality, the slight pleasant ache in muscles rarely engaged, the lingering sensitivity of nerve pathways newly awakened. Some clients leave you with gifts they never intended, this one had reminded me of the joy inherent in embodiment itself, something easily forgotten in a profession where intimate touch can become mechanical through repetition.

Later that week, I joined the swimming club at Monte Carlo Beach. Fifteen years later, I still attend three mornings weekly, one of the wisest professional investments I've ever made. That particular client continued his monthly visits for nearly a decade, always after swimming, our sessions maintaining a vitality rare in long-term professional arrangements. The rhythm of our encounters, both predictable in scheduling and endlessly varied in execution, became an anchoring point in both our lives, a reliable source of genuine connection in professions that often keep authentic intimacy at arm's length.

At forty-six, I can attest that this early lesson served me extraordinarily well. Through changes in my body, the subtle softening here, the increasing strength there, the shifting landscapes of pleasure and response, I have maintained this fundamental connection with my physical self, this refusal to surrender embodied wisdom to abstract intellect. Perhaps the most profound insight from my years of professional intimacy is this: the body remembers what the mind forgets, knows what the intellect denies, speaks truths the voice cannot articulate. In our increasingly virtual existence, this ancient wisdom becomes not outdated but essential. A reminder that beneath our sophisticated constructs, we remain creatures of flesh, designed for movement, touch, and the quiet ecstasy of embodied existence.

•

The body holds memories that the mind forgets, knows truths the intellect denies. I witnessed this paradox illuminated through his movements, this swimmer who arrived still glittering with sea-drops, his presence a rebuke to our modern dissociation. How curiously we separate mind from flesh, as though one could exist without the other's embrace. He embodied the opposite truth: integration so complete that each gesture spoke volumes of consciousness dwelling in muscle and sinew, not merely brain tissue.

During my studies at university, where academic language attempted to categorize mysteries of human connection, I encountered research suggesting those with heightened bodily awareness: dancers, martial artists, swimmers cutting through resistant waters, often access deeper realms of intimate satisfaction. Not from technical prowess or physical endurance, but from that rarest quality: presence that cannot be counterfeited. The ability to inhabit one's skin completely, to receive sensation without the mind's constant filtering and cataloging. My swimmer embodied this research not as theory but as living truth, moving through space as though his body had never learned to lie.

What astonished me most was the seamless translation of physical fluidity into emotional presence. Where others compartmentalize: touching while thinking of tomorrow's obligations, performing while remaining inwardly absent, he offered a singular attention that transformed simple contact into sacred exchange. His consciousness inhabited his fingertips as fully as his thoughts, creating an encounter of such authenticity that it momentarily dissolved my professional boundaries.

This raises questions that echo through my years of observation: Have we lost something essential in our modern flight from embodiment? We increasingly exist as minds occasionally inconvenienced by physical needs, working through machines, socializing through screens, touching through interfaces rather than skin. My clients often display this peculiar detachment, experiencing pleasure as something happening adjacent to them rather than through them, their bodies reduced to vehicles transporting minds from appointment to appointment. This separation diminishes not just sensual satisfaction but the very possibility of genuine human connection.

I have witnessed this truth across thousands of encounters: sexual pleasure exists not separate from physical vitality but as its natural expression flowering from healthy soil. The body functions as an integrated universe where each element influences every other in endless correspondence. The man struggling to maintain arousal rarely experiences localized mechanical failure but receives systemic messages about circulation, accumulated stress, disconnection from the wisdom dwelling in his own flesh.

Through years of professional intimacy, I've observed bodies transform. Some declining through neglect like abandoned gardens, others blossoming through newfound care into unexpected beauty. Those who honor their physical selves through movement that brings joy rather than punishment often discover that pleasure doesn't wither with advancing years but transforms, sometimes ripening into sweeter fruit as experience marries embodied wisdom.

In my own practice, maintaining physical vitality has never concerned preserving youth's temporary advantages or meeting culture's narrow aesthetic demands. Rather, it ensures what I offer emerges from authentic presence rather than mechanical technique, from embodied wisdom rather than performed expertise. The body speaks a language more ancient and truthful than words could capture. A dialect of nerve and blood, muscle and bone communicating directly beneath consciousness, beyond the grasp of our sophisticated self-deceptions.

This swimmer's gift, beyond the extraordinary pleasure our bodies composed together, was this essential reminder: we exist not as minds temporarily inconvenienced by physical form, but as integrated beings whose fullest expression requires honoring both intellect and embodiment in perfect harmony. In our age increasingly dominated by virtual shadows, remembering the irreplaceable wisdom of living flesh becomes not merely personal indulgence but revolutionary act, a quiet insistence that genuine connection happens not through screens that separate but through the ancient, sacred medium of skin meeting skin, presence meeting presence, in the endless present moment where all authentic pleasure dwells.

The Lesson

Your physical vitality directly influences your capacity for pleasure. This isn't about achieving some idealized form or performing athletic feats in bed. Rather, it's about maintaining the fundamental aliveness that makes sensation possible. A body in regular movement, whether through swimming, walking, dancing, or any form of exercise that brings you joy, develops the baseline conditions that enhance every pleasure: healthy circulation, hormonal balance, neural sensitivity, and the muscular control that allows for both expressive movement and receptive stillness.

I've observed this connection thousands of times across my years in Monaco. The body that moves with purpose through daily life also moves with greater responsiveness during intimate encounters. This responsiveness manifests not just in stamina (though that certainly matters) but in the capacity to feel more deeply, to control movements with greater precision, and to remain present with sensation rather than mentally withdrawing from intense experience.

Consider caring for your physical self not as preparation for performance but as cultivation of your capacity for feeling. When you nourish your body with appropriate movement, adequate rest, and proper nutrition, you simultaneously expand your ability to give and receive pleasure. This isn't vanity but respect for the vessel that carries you through life, the only vehicle, as my swimmer so beautifully expressed, that you'll ever truly possess.

I've seen how even small changes in physical activity create dramatic differences in intimate experience. Clients who begin regular movement practices often report that sensation becomes more intense, response more reliable, and pleasure more profound, not because they've learned new techniques but because they've developed greater presence in their bodies. The most sophisticated approach to pleasure means little if the body cannot fully register the sensations being offered.

The Language of Desire

Words failed him in Rome. Ironic, considering he made his living translating them.

I noticed immediately upon my arrival at the Renaissance palazzo overlooking Piazza Navona. The man who greeted me, I'll call him the Translator, retained the precise diction and formal manners I remembered from our previous encounters in Monaco, but something essential had vanished from his demeanor. His movements were mechanical, his conversation practiced yet hollow, as if reading from a script he no longer believed.

As twilight deepened over the eternal city, we shared a bottle of Barolo on the terrace. The ruby liquid caught the dying light, transforming each sip into liquid garnets that warmed my throat and loosened something tightly coiled within me. He spoke knowledgeably about the changing light on distant domes, about the particular quality of Roman autumn, yet his eyes held a distance that suggested his thoughts occupied territory far from his words. When the evening air cooled and the moment approached to move our encounter indoors, I felt his body tense beside me, the muscles along his forearm hardening beneath my fingertips.

"I need to tell you something," he said finally, setting down his glass with deliberate care. "My wife died eight months ago. Cancer."

The words hung between us, heavy with all they didn't say. A lexicon of loss that transcended the boundaries of language.

"This was our apartment," he continued after a moment. "We purchased it together last spring, before her diagnosis. This is my first time returning since the funeral."

Understanding bloomed within me: why he had requested I meet him in Rome rather than Monaco, why tension inhabited his frame like an unwelcome guest. My body responded with a surge of warmth that had nothing to do with desire and everything to do with recognition. I felt the invisible threads connecting our breathing patterns, the synchronization of our hearts that happens when one human truly perceives another.

"I thought—" he faltered, then continued with the precise diction that was clearly his professional refuge. "I thought that perhaps physical connection might help me feel something again. But now that you're here…"

He gestured vaguely toward the door leading inside, the unspoken words clear enough. His bedroom remained as she had left it, a shrine, a wound, a space he couldn't yet reclaim. In that moment, I saw him fully, not the client seeking services but the man adrift in grief's merciless ocean, grasping for any fragment that might keep him afloat.

"We don't have to do anything you're not ready for," I said quietly. "I'm not here to extract something from you that you can't give."

The relief that flooded his face was answer enough, but still he struggled with the professional arrangement between us. His fingers traced the stem of his empty glass, seeking occupation to mask his vulnerability.

"I've already paid for your time, your journey here—"

I placed my hand lightly on his, the heat of my palm absorbing the chill that had settled in his flesh. "My job isn't what most people think it is," I said. "I'm not here to perform particular acts. I'm here to meet you where you are, to offer what you actually need, not what you thought you needed when you made the appointment."

Some tension visibly left his shoulders. We sat in companionable silence as darkness settled fully over Rome, the city lights creating a constellation below that mirrored the stars emerging above. When he refilled our glasses, his hand was steadier, the wine streaming in an elegant burgundy arc that reflected the newfound calm between us.

"There are concepts that simply don't translate between languages," he said finally, his voice finding professional solidity in this familiar territory. "Like the Portuguese 'saudade'—a particular kind of melancholic longing for something absent. No single word in English or Italian captures it precisely."

I watched him, understanding that we had moved into the metaphorical, where he felt more secure. The wine had heightened my senses, making me exquisitely aware of the space between us, charged not with expected eroticism but with something equally intimate.

"And grief?" I asked softly. "Does it have its own language?"

His eyes met mine with sudden intensity, dark pupils expanding in the dim light. "That's precisely it. I've spent my career finding equivalencies between languages, but for this—" he pressed his hand against his chest, "—I have no words."

We sat with this truth between us, the admission itself a kind of intimacy more profound than physical connection might have been. His vulnerability in that moment aroused something in me deeper than desire: a hunger to witness him fully, to hold space for the wordless territory he was traversing. My body responded with an opening that had nothing to do with sexuality and everything to do with presence, my pores drinking in the moment, my breath adjusting to match his rhythm, my skin becoming hypersensitive to the air currents moving between us.

When the night air grew too cool to ignore, he reluctantly gestured toward the apartment.

"We should go inside," he said, his voice tightening slightly. "But I don't think I can—"

"We'll avoid the bedroom," I assured him. "Is there a living room where we might be comfortable?"

Relief softened his features as he led me inside, carefully steering us past a closed door, the bedroom, I presumed, down a short hallway and into a spacious living room dominated by floor-to-ceiling windows. A plush sofa in dove-gray linen faced the panoramic view, positioned to capture Rome's nightscape, an altar to the eternal city's quiet splendor.

From this vantage point, the perspective differed dramatically from the terrace where we'd begun our evening. Here, the intimate details of human activity: the couples strolling, the café tables, the animated conversations, faded into a soft golden glow that melted gradually into the ink-black sky where stars punctuated the darkness. It was a view of Rome that emphasized eternity over immediacy, cosmic perspective over human detail, a visual testament to the insignificance of individual sorrow against the backdrop of endless time.

"Let's sit here," I suggested, moving toward the sofa. From my handbag, I withdrew a small flask of cognac and offered it to him with a smile. "A professional secret: sometimes what people need most is permission not to perform."

He accepted the flask with a grateful nod, taking a small sip before handing it back. The amber liquid burned pleasantly as I took my own swallow, creating a liquid bridge between us more binding than words.

"Tell me about her," I said, settling more comfortably into the cushions, allowing my body to relax into a posture of receptive attention.

He looked startled. "You want to hear about my wife?"

"I want to hear about whatever you need to say."

For a moment, I thought he might retreat behind the professional veneer of client and escort, might insist we must "do something" to justify my fee. Instead, hesitantly at first and then with growing animation, he began to speak. He told me about their meeting at a literary festival in Barcelona, about her work as a novelist, about their shared passion for languages. As he spoke of her courage during treatment, her dark humor in the face of prognosis, her insistence that he continue his work even as she weakened, his body gradually relaxed, hands becoming expressive again, voice finding its natural cadence.

I listened without interruption, offering only nods of encouragement or the occasional question when he faltered. This, too, is intimacy, the witnessing of another's truth without judgment or expectation. My body registered his gradual opening with its own response: warmth blossoming across my skin, breath deepening, muscles softening into authentic receptivity rather than practiced seduction.

"She made me promise to return to Rome," he said finally. "To not let this place become a mausoleum. But I didn't realize how difficult it would be to keep that promise."

"You're here now," I reminded him gently. "That's the first step."

He nodded, eyes fixed on the constellation of city lights that mirrored the stars above. "Yes. Though not in the way I expected to be."

I smiled. "Expectations rarely align with reality. That's why they cause so much suffering."

He considered this, hand resting on the sofa between us. "In my profession, precision is everything. The wrong word choice can change entire meanings. I'm not accustomed to... improvising."

"And yet here we are," I observed, "writing a very different script than the one you imagined when you contacted me."

A small smile touched his lips, the first genuine one I'd seen. "Yes, here we are."

As night deepened around us, the city's glow seemed to dim while the stars brightened, as if Earth and heaven were engaged in a gentle rebalancing of light. I moved slightly closer to him on the sofa, the silk of my dress whispering against the linen upholstery. My body registered his heat before actual contact, nerve endings awakening to the magnetic field that exists between two humans in proximity.

"Sometimes the most intimate thing we can offer another person is our complete presence," I said softly. "Not performance, not technique, just authentic awareness."

His hand found mine in the half-darkness, fingers intertwining with a tentative question. I answered by gently squeezing his hand, a permission granted without words. The simple contact sent electric awareness cascading through me, not sexual arousal but something equally physical, the profound somatic recognition that occurs when two bodies establish honest connection.

"What do you typically do," he asked suddenly, "when clients aren't... performing as expected?"

The question revealed his lingering concern about our arrangement, the professional transaction that typically involved physical exchange. I turned to face him, making sure my expression conveyed neither pity nor clinical detachment.

"In my experience," I said carefully, "people rarely know exactly what they need. They come to me with ideas about physical release or validation or excitement, but underneath those surface desires often lies something else. Something they may not recognize or know how to ask for."

"And what do you think I need?" he asked, a genuine question without challenge.

"Tonight? A witness," I replied. "Someone who can hold space for your grief without trying to fix it or rush you through it. Someone who won't collapse under its weight or reflect it back with their own discomfort. And perhaps..." I paused, weighing my words. "Perhaps permission to feel what you actually feel, not what you think you should feel."

His eyes, when they met mine, held a startling vulnerability. "That sounds... expensive."

I laughed softly at his unexpected humor. "Consider it included in my regular fee."

As we continued talking, the emotional distance between us gradually decreased. I shifted closer, and his arm moved naturally around my shoulders. Against the backdrop of Rome's eternal glow fading into star-filled infinity, our bodies found a configuration of comfort rather than arousal: my back against his chest, my head resting in the hollow of his shoulder, our breathing gradually synchronizing. The contact awakened every nerve in my skin, creating a heightened state of awareness that transcended the merely sexual and entered the realm of pure sensory experience.

This physical connection, devoid of sexual intention yet profoundly intimate, created a sphere of safety between us. In this protected space, words flowed more easily, breaths deepened, and the weight of performance expectations dissolved completely. I became aware of the gentle percussion of his heart against my shoulder blade, the subtle expansion of his ribcage with each breath, the particular quality of warmth that radiated from his body into mine. My own form responded with a softening, a yielding that had nothing to do with submission and everything to do with genuine presence.

"May I ask you something personal?" he said, his voice vibrating gently against my hair, sending barely perceptible tremors along my scalp.

I nodded, though with my usual professional caveat: "I might choose not to answer."

"How did you come to understand people so well? To see what they need rather than what they say they want?"

The question deserved honesty. "Necessity," I replied after a moment. "In my profession, reading people accurately isn't just a skill. It's survival. Beyond that... my work has given me a privileged view into human vulnerability. I've witnessed the gap between what people project and who they really are, between what they think they desire and what truly satisfies them."

"That's quite an education," he observed, his hand finding mine in a gesture that seemed instinctive rather than calculated. His thumb traced absent patterns on my palm, each swirl sending subtle currents of sensation up my arm.

"One you can't get in universities," I agreed. "Though your work must provide similar insights. Translation isn't just about words, is it? It's about understanding the human context those words emerge from."

He nodded, his chin brushing against my hair. "Yes, exactly. It's why machine translation will never fully replace human translators. Algorithms can't grasp cultural nuance, historical context, emotional undertones."

"In that sense," I suggested, "we're not so different. We both interpret languages others struggle to understand."

As we talked, our bodies found subtle adjustments of comfort: his arm tightening slightly around my waist, my hand coming to rest on his knee, my head nestling more deeply into the curve of his shoulder. Each small movement created new constellations of contact, endless variations of touch that spoke without words. This was a different kind of lovemaking, not of bodies seeking pleasure but of souls seeking recognition, the subtle dance of two beings acknowledging each other's essential humanity.

The city lights and distant stars witnessed our communion, a reminder that we existed simultaneously in the immediate present of this sofa, this night, this grief, and in the vast continuum of human experience stretching across centuries. Our connected bodies formed a small but perfect constellation against the backdrop of cosmic time, a temporary alignment that would disperse with dawn yet leave its imprint on both of us.

We remained entwined as he shared memories of his wife that made him laugh and then weep without shame, as I offered perspectives on loss and healing drawn from my own life and those of others I had known. The intimacy we created transcended the physical without denying our embodied nature: each touch, each shared breath, each moment of eye contact weaving connections stronger than mere sexual union could have achieved.

When weariness finally overtook us both, he shifted slightly, his eyes finding mine with a question. The flickering city lights illuminated half his face, leaving the other in shadow, a visual metaphor for the divided state grief creates within the soul.

"Stay," he said simply. "Just like this. I don't want to be alone tonight."

I nodded, understanding perfectly. We adjusted our position on the sofa to allow for comfort through the night, his body curled protectively around mine, a light throw blanket covering us both. The arrangement held nothing of sexual intention but everything of human comfort, the ancient solace of shared warmth against life's inevitable chill. My body relaxed into his with complete trust, skin registering each point of contact as a separate note in a complex harmony of physical connection.

Just before sleep claimed him, he murmured against my hair: "Thank you." Then, after a moment's pause, "I love you."

The words hung in the darkness between us. I remained still, uncertain whether this declaration was meant for me or if he was speaking across the veil to his wife, now part of the eternity visible in the stars outside our window. It wasn't the kind of "I love you" that required a response, and I offered none. Instead, I allowed the phrase to exist on its own terms, perhaps the final missing words in his incomplete lexicon of grief.

As his breathing deepened into sleep, I remained awake a while longer, watching the stars through the window, feeling the gentle rise and fall of his chest against my back. The galaxy sprawled above Rome, indifferent to our small human sorrows yet somehow comforting in its vastness. Eventually, I too surrendered to sleep, my consciousness dissolving into the darkness like sand reclaimed by tide.

Morning arrived with golden light streaming through the windows and the sounds of Rome awakening. I opened my eyes to find him already awake, watching me with an expression of peaceful clarity that hadn't been present the night before. The sunlight caught in his lashes, transformed his skin to warm gold, revealed unexpected flecks of amber in his dark eyes.

"Coffee?" he asked simply.

"Please," I replied.

He disentangled himself carefully and moved to the kitchen while I stretched, smoothing my rumpled clothes and running fingers through my hair. The apartment felt different in daylight, less a shrine to absence and more a space of potential. My body registered the night's unusual intimacy not with the familiar soreness of passionate encounters but with a peculiar combination of relaxation and heightened awareness.

He returned with two steaming cups and handed one to me. "I hope it's strong enough. Italian coffee was one of her passions."

We sat on the sofa where we'd spent the night, watching the morning light transform Rome's architecture from shadowy silhouettes to distinct buildings. Neither of us mentioned his nighttime declaration, understanding instinctively that some moments exist outside the boundaries of discussion.

"What will you do now?" I asked after a while. "Will you stay in Rome?"

He considered this, cupping his hands around the warmth of his coffee. "I need to. Not just because I promised her, but because I need to learn how to be here differently. To stop avoiding and start remembering."

We talked of practical things: what work he had waiting, when he might return to Monaco, how to start sorting through her possessions. The conversation was gentle yet purposeful, containing none of the awkwardness that often follows unexpected intimacy.

When the time came for me to leave, I gathered my things with the practiced efficiency of someone accustomed to graceful exits. At the door, he took my hand, his expression conveying gratitude without the need for elaborate phrases.

"Will you be all right?" I asked.

"Not immediately," he answered honestly. "But eventually, yes."

I squeezed his hand and left.

But I didn't go far. At a small flower market just beginning its morning trade in a nearby piazza, I stopped. Among the riot of colors and scents, I selected a generous bouquet of bright, vibrant blooms, nothing somber or formal, but flowers that seemed to embody life itself.

When I returned to the palazzo and knocked on his door, his surprise was evident.

"You forgot something?" he asked, confusion crossing his features.

I handed him the bouquet. "No. But this apartment needs life in it. She made you promise, remember?"

Understanding dawned in his eyes as he accepted the flowers, their colors startlingly vivid against the muted tones of the hallway. For a moment, I thought he might weep, but instead, he smiled, a genuine expression that reached his eyes.

"Yes," he said. "She did."

I turned to leave, but his voice stopped me. "Isabelle?" I looked back. "What we shared last night—what would you call that, professionally speaking?"

I considered the question carefully. "I wouldn't," I replied. "Some experiences belong only to themselves."

He nodded, satisfied with the answer. As I walked away, I glimpsed him through the closing door, already looking for a vase, already beginning the slow, necessary work of bringing life back into spaces where it had been absent.

In my unconventional profession, I've learned that physical intimacy is sometimes the least significant service I provide. What many clients truly seek, beneath the surface desire for sexual release, is permission to be authentically themselves, to drop the performance of desire or prowess or control, to be witnessed without judgment in their vulnerability.

The Translator had contacted me seeking physical escape from grief. What he discovered instead was the courage to begin speaking its complicated language, not through words, which were his professional domain, but through the more subtle dialect of presence and shared humanity, through a form of connection that left clothes in place while removing the barriers between souls.

•

As I lay beside him in the Roman darkness that night, watching the rise and fall of his chest in slumber, I found myself exploring grief's curious architecture. How it carves secret chambers through our being that no rational understanding can fill, how it transforms familiar landscapes into uncharted territories where we wander without map or compass. My translator was suspended in that exquisite paradox we all eventually face, intellectually comprehending that life continues while emotionally experiencing time as frozen at the moment of his beloved's departure.

Rome's ancient stones seemed perfect witnesses to this particular pain. They have absorbed centuries of human sorrow, standing silent through endless stories of loss and quiet renewal. In the stillness of night, with his breath steady against my back, I remembered something my anthropology professor once shared over espresso after a moving lecture: that many traditional cultures understand what ours often forgets—grief requires witnesses. Not fixers or saviors, but those willing to sit beside us in the dark without rushing us toward the light.

Through years of intimate observation, I've noticed how accomplished professionals like my translator often navigate their deepest sorrows in isolation. They've mastered complex languages, negotiated intricate business transactions, translated the most nuanced literature, yet find themselves without vocabulary for this most universal of human experiences. In grief, even the most articulate become suddenly speechless, discovering the limitations of language at precisely the moment they most desperately need expression.

What transformed our evening wasn't what happened between our bodies but what emerged in the space between them, that sacred territory where connection transcends the physical without denying our embodied nature. By releasing the expectation of sexual performance, freeing him from his anticipated role as desire-driven client and myself from my expected role as pleasure provider, we created sanctuary for something more essential than either of us had anticipated: complete presence with what is rather than what should be.

One day, a letter arrived with Italian postage. My translator had finally entered the bedroom he'd shared with his wife and begun the gentle process of sorting her belongings. "I kept hearing your words," he wrote. "About how sometimes what people need most is permission not to perform. I realized I'd been performing grief the way I thought it should look, rather than allowing myself to experience it as it actually was."

His words touched me deeply, reminding me why I continue this unconventional path despite the misunderstandings it often invites. Beyond physical release, beyond momentary pleasure, I offer something many struggle to find elsewhere: a space where authentic human connection can occur without performance or predetermined script, where one soul might recognize itself in another's gaze.

When I consider the countless intimate moments I've witnessed from positions few will ever occupy, I find myself returning to a truth both simple and profound: the greatest gift we can offer another is not our expertise but our humanity, the courage to be fully present without agenda or armor, creating spaces where souls might safely unfold in all their complicated glory. This remains true whether in a professional encounter like the one I shared with my translator, or in the ordinary intimacies that sustain us through life's infinite succession of losses and discoveries.

Like those ancient Roman stones that have witnessed centuries of human passion and sorrow without judgment, we too can learn to stand in patient witness to one another's truths. In doing so, we create connections that transcend the boundaries of skin, of language, of convention, finding in our shared vulnerability the most profound intimacy of all.

The Lesson:

True intimacy begins with seeing what another person genuinely needs, rather than what convention suggests they should want. I've learned through countless encounters that our deepest connections often emerge not from following familiar scripts but from the courage to set them aside when they no longer serve the moment's truth.

The language of intimacy extends far beyond the physical. It includes the eloquence of silence, the gentle pressure of a hand that seeks nothing in return, the profound communication that occurs when we temporarily step outside our rehearsed roles. In our culture that prizes action and achievement above all, there's something almost revolutionary about offering attentive stillness instead.

This doesn't diminish the value of physical connection. Touch remains one of our most profound languages of comfort and affirmation. But touch exists on a spectrum from the sexual to the simply human, and discerning which quality serves the moment requires both sensitivity and the confidence to defy expectations.

I sometimes suggest to clients a simple practice: The next time you're with someone experiencing profound emotion, whether grief, fear, or even overwhelming joy, resist your instinct to fill the space with words or actions. Simply be present. Notice how much passes between you in shared silence, in the meeting of eyes, in the simple acknowledgment of their experience without attempting to reshape it. This presence forms the foundation for all authentic connection, whether emotional or physical.

In the realm of physical intimacy, this same principle applies. The most memorable encounters arise not from technical precision but from moments of complete presence, when we set aside performance to simply experience one another without agenda or expectation.

The Breathless Embrace

I have always believed that desire lives in the spaces between breaths. It hovers there, invisible yet palpable, like the moment between lightning and thunder, an electric pause promising revelation. This truth revealed itself anew when he entered my life, carrying with him the curious contradiction of one who understands the mechanics of breathing yet had forgotten its poetry.

The Mediterranean light was performing its evening alchemy when he arrived, transforming the air in my apartment to liquid gold. Shadows stretched like dreams across the floor, elongated and mysterious. I observed him through this golden haze, a respiratory therapist whose profession required intimate knowledge of the body's most essential rhythm, yet whose own movement betrayed a certain disconnection, as if his clinical understanding had walled off the wisdom of his own flesh.

When I opened the door, his height surprised me. Not imposing, but significant, like a question that demands thoughtful response. His shoulders carried the slight curve of one accustomed to leaning forward, listening to struggling lungs, a healer's posture. But it was his eyes that captured me, clear and attentive yet holding something unresolved, some quiet hunger not fully acknowledged even to himself.

"The irony isn't lost on me," he said after our initial pleasantries, wine glass suspended between us like an unfinished thought. "I spend my days teaching others the science of breath, yet my last lover told me my kisses felt mechanical." The confession emerged without self-pity or defensiveness, only a certain scientific curiosity. How fascinating, this willingness to acknowledge limitation without shame.

I felt myself drawn toward this paradox he embodied, professional expertise coupled with personal blindness. The same hands that surely measured lung capacity and calibrated oxygen flow had somehow missed the secret language of desire that begins with shared breath. This beautiful disconnect moved me, as imperfections always do.

"Perhaps," I suggested, setting aside my barely-touched wine, "technique requires transmutation to become art."

He nodded, recognition flickering across his features. "The gap between knowledge and wisdom."

I moved toward him, not with the practiced choreography my profession might suggest, but with genuine curiosity. The space between us seemed to compress, becoming dense with possibility. Without touching him yet, I synchronized my breathing with his, a silent calibration. His eyes widened slightly at this deliberate mirroring, this wordless communion.

"Before lips meet, bodies converse through breath," I murmured. "Like musicians finding common tempo before playing together."

His chest rose and fell with mine, our lungs drawing from the same invisible pool of air. I placed my palm against his shirt front, feeling the steady percussion of his heart. The tempo quickened beneath my touch, his body revealing what his composed expression concealed. When his breathing accelerated in response, he immediately attempted to regulate it, professional habit reasserting itself.

"Allow the irregularity," I whispered. "Perfection is the enemy of pleasure."

Something shifted in his eyes then, the scientist yielding slightly to the man. I diminished the remaining distance between us with deliberate slowness, savoring the mounting tension. My hands rose to frame his face, learning the landscape of his features, not with clinical assessment but with artist's appreciation. The slight asymmetry of his jaw, the particular texture of skin near his temples, the almost invisible scar that interrupted his left eyebrow, each detail a letter in some half-forgotten alphabet.

When I finally brought my lips to his, I made contact with exquisite restraint. Barely there, like morning mist against window glass. His immediate response was to press forward, seeking definition, certainty. I withdrew slightly, maintaining that delicate suspension, that liminal state between absence and presence. His eyes questioned mine.

"A kiss resembles a haiku," I breathed against his mouth. "Its power lies in negative space, in what remains unsaid."

Confusion crossed his features briefly, then understanding. I returned to that ghostly contact, lips whispering against his without demand. Gradually, I felt resistance dissolving, felt him entering this unfamiliar territory of the undefined.. His breathing deepened, surrendering its measured cadence. Only then did I increase pressure, allowing connection to ripple outward like stone dropped in still water.

His hands discovered my waist with tentative reverence, as if handling some delicate specimen. As our kiss deepened, his grip gradually firmed, fingers learning the subtle curve where ribs give way to hip. This instinctive calibration, this ability to match physical expression to emotional tone, suggested depths beneath his analytical surface.

I pulled back just enough to murmur, "Invitation, not invasion."

His lips parted in wordless response, understanding transforming to embodied knowledge. I answered this silent offering, my tongue venturing beyond the boundary of his lips, not with conquest's urgency but exploration's care. His swift inhalation told me he grasped the difference between this measured approach and habitual patterns, the difference between language recited and poetry experienced.

We continued this gradual revelation, each new intimacy emerging organically from shared breath. When my tongue finally met his fully, the contact ignited current that traveled beyond merely physical pathways. A sound escaped him, wrenched from somewhere essential, like wind finding voice through narrow canyon. This authentic expression affected me more deeply than any practiced technique, reminding me how honesty transcends performance in matters of desire.

His scientific precision began dissolving into something more primal as I guided one of his hands to the nape of my neck. There, beneath carefully arranged hair, vulnerable hollow awaited discovery. His fingers registered the significance of this territory, applying pressure that somehow reached beyond skin, touching nerves connected to hidden aspects of self. My own hands found purchase in his hair, demonstrating how gentle tension creates counterpoint to softness, how contrast awakens sensation.

"Breathe through your nose," I instructed against his mouth. "Continuity creates deepening."

The respiratory therapist in him recognized the practicality, but the awakening sensualist responded to its effect: our connection maintained without interruption, desire building without circuit-breaking pauses. I showed him alteration of pressure, moments of gentle claiming followed by teasing withdrawal that left him pursuing my retreating mouth, creating rhythmic conversation that hinted at more profound exchanges to come.

Our connection intensified, awareness narrowing to this exquisite present. I guided him backward, our bodies negotiating space without breaking contact, until his legs met resistance. When he sank onto my sofa, I stood between his knees, looking down at his upturned face. This new configuration shifted subtle currents of power between us. My fingers tilted his chin upward, exposing the vulnerable architecture of his throat.

"Physical position writes emotional poetry," I explained, watching understanding dawn in his eyes. From this vantage, I lowered my mouth to his, the angle transforming kiss from mutual exchange to gentle possession. His neck muscles yielded beneath my palm, arousal evident in accelerated pulse visible at his throat.

When I straddled him, settling onto his lap with deliberate slowness, another transformation occurred. His hands found natural resting place at my hips, steadying me as our mouths reconnected. The hard ridge of his arousal pressed against me through separating fabric, his cock straining upward like an eager supplicant between my thighs. The heat of him radiated through the thin barrier of our clothing, pulsing with a hunger that made my sex grow slick with answering desire. Yet rather than hurrying toward obvious culmination, I extended our education in oral eloquence, demonstrating how delayed satisfaction intensifies desire, how anticipation itself becomes form of fulfillment.

I guided his hands to my blouse, permitting him to unveil me one small revelation at a time. Each pearl button slipping free exposed new territory for exploration. His mouth followed unspoken invitation, journeying from my lips to throat, discovering how skin changes character across geography of body: how the place behind my ear quivered under his breath, how the hollow above my collarbone invited deeper attention.

"The body speaks dialect depending on region," I encouraged as his mouth descended to the swell of my breast above black lace. "Listen with your lips."

He proved remarkable student, adapting to changing landscapes as he traveled. When his mouth closed over my nipple through thin fabric, wet heat penetrating barrier, I offered authentic sound, not intended but true response. My areola tightened against his tongue, the sensitive peak hardening to an aching point as he drew it between his lips. His hands cupped the weight of my breasts, thumbs circling the dampened fabric where his mouth had been. This unguarded moment seemed to affect him more profoundly than any practiced seduction, his hands tightening momentarily at my waist, his breathing growing ragged around edges.

As I unbuttoned his shirt, I revealed the power of anticipation. My parted lips hovered just above his skin without making contact, allowing warm breath alone to touch him. His flesh responded with visible awakening, terrain rising to meet explorer not yet arrived. His breathing, once so meticulously controlled, now came unevenly, discipline surrendering to sensation.

"In breath we practice smallest form of giving and receiving," I murmured against his chest, still not touching. "Taking what another releases, making it part of ourselves, offering back transformed."

His hands moved up my back with newfound confidence, fingers following spine's delicate geography, learning secret dialect spoken by shifting muscle and subtle bone. I arched into his touch, offering wordless encouragement for this exploration. In this moment, clinical knowledge served intuition rather than replacing it, his understanding of anatomy providing map while desire supplied purpose.

When I rose to lead him deeper into my sanctuary, our journey became meandering, dreamlike. Against hallway wall, I demonstrated how environment participates in desire, cool surface against my back creating counterpoint to heat of his chest pressing forward. In doorway to bedroom, we lingered, recognizing ancient significance of thresholds, those symbolic boundaries between known and unknown, between intention and fulfillment.

Evening had transformed light to something underwater, something blue and secret. I made no move toward illumination, allowing visual sense to soften, making space for touch and scent and sound to emerge from shadow. We undressed each other with unhurried reverence, fabric whispering to floor in hushed conversation. Our kisses had evolved from earlier lessons: sometimes questioning, sometimes declaring, always discovering.

When we finally lay skin against skin without barrier, I drew his face to mine for what might have seemed repetition but was instead recognition. This kiss carried memory of journey, spoke in language his body now comprehended. My thighs parted in wordless offering, the slick wetness between them an unambiguous invitation. His erection pressed hot and urgent against my entrance, the velvet head of his cock gathering my moisture as it slid along my swollen folds.

"The kiss remains anchor," I whispered into humid space between our mouths. "It prevents mind from abandoning body, keeps consciousness from floating away from pleasure."

As he entered me, our lips maintained communion, sharing breath as bodies joined in deeper dialogue. The slick heat of my arousal welcomed him, muscles embracing his thick length with deliberate, articulate pressure. I felt myself stretch to accommodate him, inner walls gripping as he filled me completely. I showed how oral rhythm might orchestrate deeper movement, how subtle changes in kiss suggested corresponding responses below, creating symphony rather than mere percussion.

His professional understanding found unexpected application as I directed his awareness toward my changing breath, how quickening signaled ascending pleasure, how small catches in rhythm indicated passages of exquisite sensation. When his hand ventured between our joined bodies to circle the swollen bud of my clitoris, I taught synchronization of touch with breath, pressure increasing with exhale, lightening with inhale, creating conversation between air and blood and nerve.

"Feel internal response," I murmured, demonstrating subtle contractions that caressed his hardness from within. Wonder crossed his features at this discovery, this bridge between clinical knowledge and erotic experience suddenly manifesting in unmistakable physical dialogue.

We moved together with growing urgency, yet never surrendering mindfulness. I showed how slight adjustments in angle transformed experience entirely. How lifting my pelvis directed his hardness against anterior wall where sensation concentrated, how pressure of pubic bone against my throbbing clitoris created complementary pleasure.

His hands moved beneath me, cupping my buttocks, angling my body to deepen penetration. In this position, he could witness our joining, that hypnotic visual of flesh disappearing into flesh before emerging transformed, his shaft glistening with the evidence of my desire. This sight seemed to bypass intellectual centers, speaking directly to primitive brain. His movements intensified, thrusts becoming more pronounced while maintaining essential control that separates lover from merely enthusiastic participant.

As tension mounted toward inevitable release, our kisses transformed, becoming less structured, more directly expressive. I kept eyes open, encouraging him to do same, demonstrating how visual connection during pleasure creates intimacy transcending physical coupling. In his dilated pupils, I witnessed moment when technique fully surrendered to experience, when respiratory therapist dissolved completely into man.

When climax blossomed through me, I allowed him complete witness to transformation, the flush spreading across chest and throat, momentary suspension of breath followed by shuddering release, involuntary rhythmic grasping he could feel surrounding him. My inner muscles clenched around his cock in waves of uncontrollable pleasure, drawing him deeper as ecstasy claimed every nerve ending in radiant pulses. This vulnerability, being truly seen in moment of absolute surrender, created its own exquisite intensity, doubling pleasure through shared awareness.

His release followed immediately, triggered by pulsing response of my body around his. With a final deep thrust, he emptied himself inside me, his hot seed filling me as his cock throbbed with each pulse of his orgasm. His expression transformed, control shattering into ecstasy, the scientist yielding completely to primal self. Our mouths found each other through this dissolution, kiss no longer technique but necessity, connecting rather than separating us as pleasure moved through us like weather system, like tide, like something ancient and beyond naming.

In quiet aftermath, as breathing gradually harmonized into slower rhythms, I placed final kiss on his lips, gentle acknowledgment of journey completed. Against his chest, I felt heartbeat returning to measured cadence, his body softening into satisfied contentment, tension draining like water seeking lowest point.

"You understand breathing differently now," I observed, fingers wandering constellation of freckles across his shoulder. "Knowledge transformed to wisdom."

His laughter vibrated against my ear: pure, and unguarded. "Medicine meets mystery," he said, fingers creating abstract patterns against my spine. "I never considered respiration could contain such multitudes."

"Tomorrow's patients benefit from expanded understanding," I suggested, "though perhaps not explicit methodology."

"Indeed," he conceded, smile evident in voice. "Some lessons transcend clinical application."

As night claimed sky outside my windows, we lay entwined in comfortable silence, occasionally exchanging small kisses, lips brushing shoulder, mouth pressing against forehead, continuing conversation our bodies had begun. Even after decades in my profession, I found myself appreciating anew how human connection contains infinite territories awaiting discovery, how pleasure itself is merely consciousness directed toward sensation with appropriate wonder, and how breath, this most fundamental exchange with existence, becomes transformed when approached with reverence rather than mere technique.

•

In the secret chambers of intimacy, where souls momentarily abandon their careful masks, I have witnessed a pattern that repeats itself like ancient myth: the separation of knowing from being, of intellect from sensation. My respiratory therapist was not unique in his fractured existence, carrying in one hand the precise measurements of life's most essential function while the other hand remained ignorant of breath's sensual poetry.

This division runs like a fault line through modern existence. We inhabit bodies that remember what minds have forgotten, carrying wisdom deeper than thought in the architecture of bone and muscle. How strange that we must be taught to breathe consciously when every infant arrives knowing this art perfectly. How mysterious that we must rediscover the kiss as sacred ceremony when our bodies recognize its significance without instruction.

One day, fate carried me and several friends to Monaco's Oceanographic Museum for a lecture on cetaceans native to the area. The marine biologist, a weathered man with salt-white hair and eyes like polished sea glass, spoke of dolphins with reverence usually reserved for mystics. "Unlike humans," he explained, "dolphins must consciously choose each breath. What we do without thought, they do with deliberate intention."

The revelation illuminated our evening like lightning across remembered landscape. Perhaps our deepest connections emerge when we transform unconscious function to mindful exchange, when the automatic becomes deliberate, the habitual becomes ceremonial. What dolphins must do by biological necessity, we might achieve through conscious intention: the elevation of mere breathing to sacred communion.

I have observed this phenomenon through thousands of intimate exchanges: how awareness alchemizes ordinary acts into extraordinary experience. The most profound transformations occur not through exotic technique but through applied presence, the quality of attention we bring to connection. My respiratory therapist carried within himself perfect knowledge divorced from application; our encounter served as bridge between separate aspects of self.

The integration of intellectual understanding with embodied experience creates something greater than either alone could achieve. Knowledge without sensation remains theoretical; sensation without understanding lacks dimension. When these separate territories discover their shared boundaries, new landscapes of possibility emerge.

In our increasingly fragmented world, where minds float disembodied through digital spaces while bodies hunger for genuine contact, perhaps the most revolutionary act remains the simplest: the full-presence kiss, the conscious breath, the moment of complete attention. These appear modest against our cultural obsession with novelty and escalation, yet contain depths rarely explored in more elaborate performances.

The breathless embrace, this kiss that transcends mere physical contact to become genuine communion, teaches us that presence transforms everything it touches. In world increasingly fractured by distraction, genuine attention becomes precious gift. What my respiratory therapist discovered wasn't new information but new integration, the marriage of clinical precision with sensual awareness, transforming separate knowledge into unified wisdom.

When dolphins rise to surface for breath, they do not take this exchange for granted. Each inhalation represents conscious choice, deliberate engagement with life's most essential act. Perhaps therein lies intimacy's deepest lesson: that our most profound connections emerge not from extraordinary circumstances but from bringing extraordinary awareness to ordinary exchanges. The miracle waits, as it always has, in the sacred space between one breath and the next.

The Lesson

If I were to distill what I've learned about kissing after thousands of intimate encounters, it would be this: the kiss contains an entire language of connection, a vocabulary more nuanced than any spoken tongue. It isn't merely prelude to "more important" acts but complete expression capable of creating profound pleasure in itself. When approached with full awareness, kissing initiates a cascade through body and mind alike, awakening pathways that transform ordinary contact into extraordinary communion.

Begin, always, with presence. Before your lips meet another's, establish connection through synchronized breath and sustained eye contact. This attunement, this silent acknowledgment of shared purpose, creates foundation for everything that follows. Approach the first touch with exquisite restraint, barely grazing their lips with yours. This ghost-light pressure awakens nerve endings without overwhelming them, creating capacity to register subtler sensations that might otherwise be missed.

Remember that lips hold one of the body's richest concentrations of nerve endings. This extraordinary sensitivity deserves exploration beyond habitual patterns. Vary pressure from feather-light to firmly claiming; alternate between lingering connection and momentary retreat; explore different regions of the mouth with curious attention. The terrain between upper lip and lower, the sensitive corners where they meet, the textural contrast between outer skin and inner mucosa, each territory offers distinct pleasure when approached with appropriate attention.

Notice how position influences the emotional quality of connection. Standing while your partner sits creates different dynamics than mutual height; pressing someone against a wall differs from holding them in open space. These physical configurations aren't merely practical arrangements but emotional architecture, creating subtle power exchanges that enhance experience when consciously employed.

Perhaps most importantly, maintain the kiss as anchor throughout more advanced intimacy. When bodies join in deeper ways, don't abandon this fundamental connection. The continued communion of breath and mouth keeps consciousness present rather than fragmenting into separate experiences. In this sustained connection, mind and body remain integrated, preventing the dissociation that often diminishes pleasure's potential depth.

In essence, the kiss serves as microcosm of all intimate arts: teaching presence, responsiveness, and the dance between assertion and receptivity. If we approach this seemingly simple act with the reverence it deserves, we discover doorways to connection that extend far beyond physical sensation alone.

The Art of Teasing

My niece's jack-in-the-box arrived from the Black Forest last week, a custom piece I'd commissioned from a German toymaker. As I watched Sasha turn the handle, her small fingers working the mechanism with measured patience, I observed something profound in her delight. Though she knew precisely what would happen, she'd played with it a dozen times already, her eyes widened with genuine surprise when her wooden twin finally burst forth. The waiting itself brought her as much joy as the eventual emergence.

The mechanical inevitability of the toy, turning the handle must release the spring, creates tension precisely because the moment of release remains uncertain. Even as the familiar tune signals the approaching surprise, each note building anticipation, the exact instant still startles and delights. One knows what will happen but not precisely when, and in that suspended space between initiation and culmination lies a specialized pleasure that adults frequently abandon in their haste toward completion.

These thoughts accompanied me across the dark waters of Venice, where I was to meet an art dealer encountered months earlier at a gallery in Monaco. Venice in November exists between states, caught in the liminal space of fading autumn and approaching winter, shrouded in mists that transform the familiar into the mysterious. It is a city that has perfected partial revelation, of beauty glimpsed rather than displayed outright, a place where desire breathes in the spaces between buildings, in the fog that veils and unveils bridges and bell towers with capricious whimsy.

My water taxi cut through evening fog toward a historic canal-side hotel as I contemplated how this man's profession might influence our encounter. An art dealer's existence revolves around cultivating desire for beautiful objects and navigating the interval between aspiration and acquisition. His livelihood depends on understanding that value correlates with patience, that the most coveted pieces are rarely obtained immediately. Would this professional wisdom translate to our intimate hours, or would he compartmentalize, applying such principles to business while abandoning them in pleasure's pursuit? The question hummed in my veins like distant music, its answer waiting like a sleeper about to dream.

The hotel materialized from the mist, centuries-old stone glowing amber in carefully positioned lights. Inside, beneath ceilings painted by hands long turned to dust, I was escorted to a suite where diamond-paned windows framed the Grand Canal. Antique furnishings, a velvet chaise, an ornate writing desk, a bed that had witnessed generations of Venetian passion, created an atmosphere of suspended time, as if the room itself existed in the space between past and present, much like desire exists in the space between imagination and fulfillment. The air itself seemed infused with the residue of ancient longings, of whispered promises, of skin against skin in the dark.

He stood at the window when I arrived, silhouetted against darkening waters, his posture revealing the quiet assurance of someone who assigns value with a single glance. When he turned, the amber light caught silver at his temples, lending him the distinguished air of a Renaissance portrait vivified. There was a stillness about him that seemed to demand stillness in return, a quality of attention that made one feel seen beyond surface, an excavation of essence through the mere act of observation.

"Isabelle," he said, my name in his mouth simultaneously greeting and appreciation, invitation and restraint. "Venice suits you."

He approached without hurry, taking my hand not to kiss it but simply to hold it between both of his, establishing a singular point of warmth in the room's pleasant chill. This deviation from expected ritual, this small subversion of automatic greeting, immediately seized my attention. The unexpected always commands presence more effectively than any practiced gesture. He released my hand only to pour prosecco, pale liquid catching light as it cascaded, miniature galaxies of bubbles ascending and bursting in endless nascence and death.

"I've been thinking about this meeting for weeks," he admitted, offering a glass. "Anticipation has always been my favorite form of pleasure."

His confession established immediate complicity between us. I encounter many who have mastered desire's performance but few who understand its architecture: the construction of tension, the deliberate postponement of release, the satisfaction found not just in culmination but in its strategic delay. His words created a secret territory between us, a landscape only those who worship at anticipation's altar can truly inhabit.

"Tell me," I asked, settling onto the velvet chaise, feeling the fabric's resistance beneath me like a body reluctant to yield its secrets, "do you approach art the way you approach desire, or desire the way you approach art?"

The question pleased him; I perceived it in the subtle adjustment of his posture as he sat beside me, close enough for conversation but not for contact, that precise calibration of distance that itself becomes a form of subtle caress.

"Both require discernment," he replied, swirling prosecco in his glass, light fracturing through crystal into momentary rainbows against his skin. "The ability to recognize value beneath surface impressions. But more importantly, both teach you that immediate possession diminishes pleasure. The paintings I've wanted most desperately, I've sometimes waited years to acquire."

As he spoke, his fingers followed the brocade pattern of the chaise between us, not quite meeting my dress but close enough that I could sense the disturbance in the air, the potential energy of connection withheld. This modest gesture, this deliberate proximity without touching, revealed his intuitive understanding of tension's value. The air between his hand and my thigh became electric with possibility, a charged void that connected more profoundly than contact itself.

"And were they worth the wait?" I asked, watching his hand's movement, feeling my skin respond to its nearness as if already touched, nerve endings awakening to anticipated rather than actual contact.

"Invariably." His smile held quiet certainty, the assurance of one who has transformed waiting into an art form. "Some pleasures improve with anticipation, like wine left to breathe until its full complexity reveals itself to the patient palate."

I sipped my prosecco slowly, letting the glass linger at my lower lip a moment longer than necessary, the cold rim a deliberate contrast to the warmth gathering beneath my skin. His eyes tracked the movement with unspoken intensity, drawn into this small, curated performance of anticipation. His gaze felt almost physical, as if vision alone could traverse the space between us, collapsing the distance between observation and touch.

"May I show you something?" he asked, rising to retrieve his phone. Rather than displaying the expected gallery of artwork, he opened a music application, selecting Debussy. As the first notes of "Clair de Lune" filled the suite, he extended his hand with a subtle bow, a gesture both archaic and timeless in its elegant simplicity.

"Dance with me."

The invitation surprised me, especially given the suite's constraints. Yet as he guided me into a simple waltz, I understood this was neither prelude nor diversion but a deliberate composition, an opening movement introducing themes that would develop throughout our encounter. His hand at the small of my back maintained proper distance, his palm's pressure guiding rather than possessing. We navigated between antique furniture and history-laden walls, discovering unexpected space in apparent confinement, like lovers finding freedom within carefully observed boundaries.

Our dance created an exquisite friction, not of bodies in contact but of proximity charged with intention, each turn bringing momentary closeness before the form separated us again. In that alternation of approach and withdrawal, of connection and space, authentic desire awakened, not the manufactured anticipation I often cultivated professionally, but genuine response to this man's meticulous orchestration. My body became a vessel of contained electricity, currents gathering beneath my skin with nowhere to discharge their building charge.

As the music approached its gentle crescendo, he drew me marginally closer, not enough to disrupt form but sufficient for his breath to warm my neck, to allow the subtle notes of sandalwood, wool, and skin beneath expensive cologne to reach me. My body responded to this almost-touch more powerfully than to many explicit contacts. The space between desire and fulfillment, I reflected, often creates more intense sensation than fulfillment itself. Like the drawn bow before release, when tension contains more power than the arrow's flight.

The piece concluded, our movement slowing. He maintained our position for three heartbeats before stepping back with a subtle smile that contained both promise and deliberate withholding. Without speaking, he moved to the windows, drawing heavy velvet across diamond panes, transforming our space from observed to private through deliberate gestures. The room darkened, shadows deepening into pools of mystery, light now concentrated in smaller territories that emphasized what remained hidden.

"Come," he said simply, extending his hand toward the bedroom, the word being both invitation and gentle command, a bridge between our separate worlds.

The bedroom continued the suite's atmosphere of suspended history: an elaborate wooden headboard carved with classical mythology, freshly pressed linens luminous in the half-light, a single lamp whose warm illumination created more shadow than light. He guided me beside the bed but made no move to undress me. Instead, he stepped back, creating a space electrified with possibility, with paths not yet chosen but clearly marked.

"I would like to look at you," he said, his voice deepened but unhurried, a resonance that seemed to vibrate against my skin rather than merely reach my ears. "Would you show yourself to me? Slowly."

The request contained a delicious inversion, not the man undressing the woman but the woman revealing herself, controlling both sequence and timing of disclosure. He offered me the position of power in our theater of revelation while maintaining his role as appreciator. In this exchange of roles lay a subtle understanding that true power flows between partners like quicksilver, never resting too long in either's possession.

I began with earrings, removing them with purposeful movements to place them beside the bed, the small diamonds catching light like fallen stars against dark wood. My fingers then found the zipper at my dress's back, not immediately lowering it but following its metal path from nape to mid-spine, a cartographer tracing boundaries not yet crossed. His gaze tracked this movement with focused intensity, his stillness amplifying my smallest gestures until they became performances worthy of complete attention.

When I finally pulled the zipper downward, its soft descent seemed magnified in the room's expectant quiet, a whispered promise of revelation. I permitted the dress to part slightly, exposing a glimpse of spine without allowing the garment to fall. His subtle intake of breath rewarded this partial revelation, this first chapter in our unfolding narrative of disclosure.

I turned to face him completely, supporting the dress against my front with one hand while freeing my shoulders from its straps with the other. The fabric adhered to my form through this deliberate restraint rather than through design, creating a silhouette poised between revelation and concealment. I held this position, suspended between states, watching desire accumulate in his expression without any move to reduce the distance between us. The waiting itself became a caress more potent than touch, as if the very air had transformed into an extension of his hands.

When I finally allowed the dress to descend, cool air raised my skin to heightened awareness, a thousand invisible mouths breathing against newly exposed flesh. I stood before him in carefully selected undergarments: black silk and lace that suggested rather than displayed, offering another layer of revelation to be controlled and timed. Each article a veil to be lifted, each disclosure a note in our symphony of gradual unveiling.

His gaze moved over my body without haste, making no demand for further disclosure. He was, I realized, extending our dance of anticipation. Finding satisfaction not in rushing toward nakedness but in savoring each incremental shift from concealed to revealed. Time stretched and contracted around us, minutes expanding into territories vast enough to contain entire worlds of sensation.

"Beautiful," he said softly, the word carrying none of the automatic quality of practiced flattery but the weight of genuine appreciation. "Now, watch me."

He removed his jacket methodically, placing it carefully over a nearby chair. His movements possessed none of the utilitarian speed with which most men undress; each item received attention, each disclosure paced to heighten expectation. While unbuttoning his shirt, he maintained eye contact, establishing a current of tension between his measured movements and my focused presence. This silent dialogue, this communion of anticipation, created a language unique to this moment, this room, this gradual revelation of skin and intention.

When he stood before me in only trousers, I appreciated the aesthetic composition of his form, balanced proportions, subtle definition of muscles beneath skin beginning to show the first softening of middle age. He presented not a young man's perfect sculpture but something more compelling: a body carrying its history with confidence, that had learned complete self-inhabitation. Each scar and asymmetry spoke of experiences that had shaped not just his physical form but the consciousness that inhabited it.

He didn't undress further but stepped closer, his warmth brushing mine without contact. "Turn around," he said, his voice like velvet over skin. I obeyed, offering my back, the unseen terrain we must trust others to witness.

His fingers finally touched, following my shoulder's curve with precisely enough pressure to awaken sensation without satisfying it. This first contact, after such sustained anticipation, sent electricity through me that far exceeded the physical stimulus. My breath caught at the intensity, at this current that seemed to connect his fingertip directly to every nerve ending in my body.

"The moment before touch," he murmured, his finger continuing down my spine, each vertebra receiving individual attention, as if he were memorizing my architecture through touch, "contains all the world's possibility. Once contact happens, possibilities narrow to actualities."

His hand paused at my bra clasp, resting without opening it, heat pooling between skin and palm like gathered light. The other settled on my hip, establishing a second point of contact that emphasized all that remained untouched. My breath quickened at the precision of it: sensation arranged like pieces on a chessboard, promise implied but withheld.

"There's an art collection in Tokyo," he continued, voice low near my ear, breath warming the sensitive hollow behind my lobe, creating ripples of response that radiated outward, "where the most valuable pieces remain in a darkened vault. They emerge only once yearly, for a single viewing day. This practice doesn't diminish their worth but multiplies it."

As he spoke, his fingers released my bra with such delicate precision I barely felt the mechanism yield. The garment loosened without falling, held by my arms' position. Another controlled revelation, another moment suspended between states, another threshold crossed that only revealed new territories for exploration beyond.

He withdrew again, breaking contact, the sudden absence of his touch creating its own phantom sensation, as if my skin continued to feel pressure no longer applied. "Turn around," he directed, his voice commanding not through volume but through certainty.

Facing him, I found his eyes holding heat that contradicted his measured movements, that fascinating duality of control and desire that marks the most compelling lovers. I allowed my bra to fall completely, exposing my breasts to cool air and his focused attention. My nipples hardened instantly, responding as much to his gaze as to the temperature, as if his eyes possessed tactile properties.

"If I were to touch you now," he asked, the question containing its own answer, its own inevitability delayed for pleasure's enhancement, "where would you want my hands first?"

The question surprised me, not because clients don't inquire about preferences, but because the phrasing acknowledged touch as theoretical, still suspended in possibility rather than claimed as immediate right. I considered genuinely rather than from professional calculation, allowing myself to inhabit desire's authentic landscape rather than its performative territory.

"Here," I indicated the curve where neck meets shoulder, often overlooked in the rush toward obvious erogenous zones, that territory where vulnerability and strength intersect in delicate balance. His smile suggested appreciation for this choice, for this expansion of sensual geography beyond conventional mapping.

He approached again, but rather than immediately fulfilling the request, he raised his hand to hover just above the indicated area, close enough that I felt palm-warmth without pressure. He sustained this almost-touch for several heartbeats, building anticipation to nearly unbearable intensity before making contact. The suspended moment contained such exquisite tension that my eyes closed involuntarily, consciousness narrowing to this single point of anticipated sensation.

When his hand finally settled against my skin, the sensation electrified, not because the touch itself was exceptionally skilled or the location unusually sensitive, but because carefully constructed anticipation had prepared my nervous system to respond with extraordinary intensity. A visible tremor passed through me at this simplest contact, my body surrendering its composure in involuntary testimony to his patient mastery.

"And now?" he asked, his hand remaining precisely where directed, warmth building between our connected flesh as if touch itself generated its own temperature, independent of our individual warmth.

"My wrist," I answered, intrigued by this guided exploration, this map of desire he was helping me draw across my own landscape. The vulnerability of asking, of acknowledging desire's specific geography, created its own erotic charge, a current that flowed between question and answer, between request and fulfillment.

He maintained connection at my neck while his other hand encircled my wrist, his thumb finding my pulse with unerring precision, that quiet rhythm that betrays what composure might otherwise conceal. This dual connection, one point anchored and the other gently mobile, created a charged circuit of sensation that traveled the length of my body like current through wire. I noted with professional interest how deliberately he built response through minimal, strategic contact rather than overwhelming stimulation. Like a musician who understands that silence shapes sound as surely as notes do, he grasped that what remains untouched sharpens the awareness of what is—turning each point of contact into something electric, something unforgettable.

Our encounter progressed with this pattern of directed restraint: always providing slightly less than desired, always pausing at the threshold of each new intimacy, always creating anticipatory spaces between actions. When he finally guided me to bed, he positioned me against pillows but remained standing, his gaze traveling my now-exposed form with deliberate appreciation, his eyes consuming what his hands had not yet claimed.

"Close your eyes," he instructed, the command so gently delivered it felt like invitation rather than demand. I complied, surrendering sight, that most dominant sense, to enhance all others.

With vision surrendered, my other faculties awakened with startling intensity. The world transformed into a landscape of sound and sensation, smell and anticipation. I heard his remaining clothes being removed, the subtle symphony of fabric yielding to gravity. I felt the mattress shift as he knelt beside me, the subtle compression communicating his position without sight to confirm it. But I couldn't anticipate where his touch would land, which territory he would claim first. Suspense itself became caress, my skin sensitizing to mere possibility, nerves awakening beneath unmarked areas in anticipation of contact that might never arrive there.

His breath came first, warming my inner thigh, not quite touching but near enough to create awareness of potential contact. The heat of it seeped through invisible layers between us, each exhale a promise without commitment. He remained there, exhaling softly against sensitive skin, for extended moments before allowing his lips the gentlest connection. The kiss, when it finally arrived, sent current through me disproportionate to its physical pressure, a surge that originated at the point of contact but traveled mysterious pathways to awaken response in seemingly unconnected territories.

This pattern continued, bringing me repeatedly to the edge of greater pleasure before withdrawing, building sensation in gradual waves rather than linear progression. His mouth would discover some previously overlooked hollow, some territory generally ignored by less patient lovers, lavishing attention until pleasure coiled tight within me, then retreat completely, leaving emptiness where expectation had built a temple to sensation. Each time I neared release, he would sense it: through subtle muscular contractions, through changing rhythm of breath, through the temperature of my skin, and retreat just enough to sustain desire without fulfilling it.

"Not yet," he would murmur, both gentle and firm, his voice itself a texture against my heightened senses. "There's still more to feel."

What might have frustrated in another context became exquisite under his orchestration. Each delayed release intensified the building sensations, each strategic withdrawal created greater anticipation. By the time he finally positioned himself above me, his hardness pressing against my entrance without penetrating, my body had transformed into an instrument of extraordinary sensitivity. Every nerve ending had awakened from its protective slumber, as if consciousness itself had descended from mind to flesh, inhabiting every cell capable of sensation.

He brushed the head of his cock against my slick folds, gathering my wetness without penetrating. The deliberate denial made me arch upward instinctively, seeking fulfillment he continued to withhold. My sex throbbed with each teasing contact, swollen and aching for the fullness he kept just beyond reach, that exquisite emptiness that demands filling more eloquently than any word could express. He smiled, understanding the power of this moment perfectly, this suspension between desire and fulfillment that contains its own unique pleasure.

"What do you want?" he asked, his voice husky with his own restrained desire, the effort of control audible in subtle tension underlying his words.

"You," I answered honestly, professional distance momentarily forgotten in genuine hunger that surprised me with its intensity. "Inside me."

"How badly?" he questioned, continuing to slide against my slick flesh without entering, creating friction that inflamed without satisfying. The smooth, thick head of his erection pressed against my entrance then retreated, each approach promising fulfillment only to deny it again, like tide advancing and withdrawing without ever completely claiming the shore.

"Please," I whispered, surprising myself with the unfeigned request. My hips lifted involuntarily, seeking to capture him, to end this exquisite torture that had transformed desire from abstract concept to living force that seemed to possess volition independent of my own.

He pressed forward slightly, allowing just his tip to enter before becoming completely still. The partial penetration, this deliberate incompletion, created a maddening tension that made me grasp his shoulders, fingernails marking his skin in unconscious hieroglyphics of need. I could feel him pulsing at my entrance, could feel my own body clenching around emptiness, desperate to draw him deeper, to complete what had been so meticulously prepared.

"Patience," he murmured, remaining motionless, letting me feel the throbbing of his pulse without the relief of movement, that tantric suspension of energy that accumulates rather than releases. "Remember the paintings worth waiting years to acquire?"

The comparison between his cock and priceless artwork might have seemed absurd in another context, but in this moment of suspended desire, the parallel felt perfectly apt, as if the most profound aesthetics manifested not in galleries but in the sacred spaces between joined bodies. I relaxed my grip on his shoulders, surrendering to his timeline rather than my urgency, accepting his mastery of our shared rhythm.

His reward came immediately, a single, deep thrust that filled me completely, drawing an involuntary cry from my lips that seemed to emerge from some primal layer of self normally buried beneath civilization's constraints. The sudden fullness after such extended emptiness overwhelmed my senses. I felt him stretching me, touching places inside that awakened with electric response, territories that yielded their secrets only to those patient enough to approach with proper preparation. Before I could adjust to the sensation, he withdrew almost completely, returning me to the exquisite agony of partial fulfillment, that liminal space between emptiness and completion.

He established a rhythm of extreme contrasts: moments of complete union followed by extended withdrawal, deep penetration balanced with shallow teasing, consistent cadence disrupted by unexpected pauses. Each variation prevented adaptation, keeping my nervous system in constant, heightened alertness. My inner muscles clenched desperately each time he withdrew, greedy for the fullness they had briefly known, like a body suddenly remembering thirst after momentary satisfaction.

When he finally settled into deeper, more consistent movement, the shift itself became another kind of surprise. My body, conditioned to expect interruption, responded to steady rhythm with escalating intensity—like a conversation moving from fragments to fluent narrative. Each stroke reached places casual lovers never touched, not from size but from precision, timing, and the sensitivity he'd cultivated through prolonged anticipation. He had prepared me so thoroughly that even the slightest touch triggered a response that usually required far more.

My climax built differently than usual. Not as a linear progression toward inevitable release but as waves of increasing amplitude, each retreat bringing not diminishment but greater intensity upon return, like ocean swells gathering force through momentary withdrawals. When he sensed my approach, rather than accelerating as most would, he slowed further, intensifying pressure while decreasing speed. The tension coiled tighter, a spring wound to its limit, pleasure bordering on sweet pain that threatened to dissolve the boundaries between opposing sensations.

"Look at me," he commanded softly, his hand lifting my chin to ensure eye contact, to add the dimension of witnessed vulnerability to the physical sensations already overwhelming my system. "Stay with me in this moment."

The connection of gazes added another dimension to physical sensation, preventing escape into private fantasy, into the solitude that often accompanies greatest pleasure. I was fully present, fully witnessed in mounting pleasure that had nowhere to hide. The vulnerability of this exposure intensified everything physical tenfold, as if being seen itself was a form of touch that penetrated more deeply than any physical union. My sex pulsed around him, each throb a precursor to the imminent explosion, each contraction a small death preceding the greater one.

"Now," he said simply, when he felt me once again crossing the threshold that separates ordinary pleasure from transcendence. "Now you can let go."

The permission after such extended anticipation unleashed response beyond ordinary climax: waves originating simultaneously everywhere and nowhere, pleasure so intense it temporarily dissolved self-boundaries, as if my identity momentarily fragmented into pure sensation without container. My cry of release seemed to come from someone else entirely, someone capable of vocalization I had never produced even in genuine pleasure. My body convulsed around his hardness, inner muscles clenching in rhythmic spasms that seemed endless, each contraction drawing him deeper, as if my body sought to absorb him entirely, to erase the boundary between separate selves. His own control finally broke in the same moment, our carefully constructed composition reaching inevitable resolution. His release pulsed hot and deep inside me, each spurt triggering renewed ripples of my own pleasure, creating a conversation between bodies that needed no translation.

Afterward, amid tangled Venetian linens, I recognized how different this completion felt from rushed satisfaction characterizing most encounters. A peculiar fullness pervaded the experience, a sense of having explored sensation's entire landscape rather than merely reaching a destination, of having inhabited territories usually bypassed in the race toward culmination.

"You understand something most have forgotten," I told him, fingers discovering the slight dip at the base of his throat, that vulnerable hollow where pulse visibly marks life's rhythm.

"What's that?" he asked, voice softened with satisfaction yet alert with genuine curiosity.

"That pleasure isn't a solitary moment but a terrain to be traversed. Most approach it as a target to be acquired efficiently rather than a journey to be savored."

He smiled, capturing my wandering hand and bringing it to his lips, each fingertip receiving individual attention, as if our intimacy could continue through these smaller gestures of appreciation. "My profession has taught me that acquisition is desire's least interesting aspect," he said. "The path toward possession creates true value."

As night deepened around our small island of warmth, I appreciated this rare encounter with someone who understood sensuality as composition rather than consumption, who found pleasure not just in climax but in all the exquisite tension preceding it. Like a complex wine that reveals different notes as it opens to air, our connection had unfolded in movements and countermovements, each development enhancing what had come before rather than replacing it.

•

I have always been fascinated by the hidden rivers beneath desire's surface, those secret tributaries that flow beneath conscious awareness, carrying currents stronger than reason can map or contain. What my art dealer revealed to me that Venetian night now seems illuminated by science itself, how our brains become flooded with cascades of dopamine not during constant stimulation but in the spaces between, when anticipation creates chemical symphonies more potent than the notes of fulfillment themselves.

I have known many souls who tried to devour time itself, rushing toward completion as though pursued by invisible demons. Their hunger contains a certain desperation, as if pleasure must be consumed quickly before some unspecified expiration. And I have known those rare beings who understand the vast territory between desire and possession, who inhabit that liminal landscape with the patience of explorers who value the journey beyond any destination. They are becoming increasingly precious in our world of instant gratification, these practitioners of an almost forgotten art.

Sometimes at night, in that suspended moment between wakefulness and dreams when consciousness floats detached from its daytime moorings, I wonder if we have not collectively surrendered something essential in our pursuit of immediate satisfaction. We consume rather than appreciate, possess rather than desire. The art dealer reminded me of something my body had always known: that the deepest pleasures belong to those who resist the rush, who linger in sensation rather than chase its replacement.

Years later, I stood before a partially veiled painting at the Peggy Guggenheim Collection, listening as our guide explained the delicate pigments required limited exposure. Around me, other visitors leaned forward imperceptibly, suspended in that exquisite state between anticipation and revelation, their bodies unconsciously reenacting the ancient posture of desire. When the protective curtain finally withdrew, revealing vibrant color and form, the collective gasp that filled the small gallery spoke of pleasure magnified through strategic denial, through the discipline of withholding that transforms ordinary satisfaction into extraordinary experience.

In that moment, watching strangers experience this orchestrated unveiling, I understood something profound about human desire. We are creatures caught between primitive hunger and sophisticated appreciation, capable of transforming basic needs into elaborate rituals of deferred pleasure. This transformation, this elevation of simple satisfaction into complex orchestration, marks the boundary between mere sexuality and true eroticism. It distinguishes the feast from mere feeding, the composition from mere notes strung together without structure.

The art dealer knew intuitively what scientists now measure in laboratories and what poets have always known: that desire itself contains pleasures that no fulfillment can match, that the space between wanting and having creates unique sensations unavailable to those who cannot tolerate emptiness. Like the negative space that defines a sculpture, the absence of immediate pleasure creates contours that shape a more profound satisfaction. The hollowness of hunger becomes a vessel into which completeness can pour itself more thoroughly than into bodies already filled with lesser satisfactions.

In our culture of instant downloads, next-day delivery, and algorithmic matches, we have largely forgotten how to cultivate hunger, how to nurture anticipation until it blossoms into something richer than mere satiation. We have traded the complex architectures of desire for the quick consumption of pleasure, never realizing what is lost in this bargain. I sometimes think of my profession as a quiet rebellion against this collective amnesia, a sanctuary where the ancient rhythms of expectation and fulfillment can still be experienced in their full, unhurried complexity, where bodies can remember what minds have forgotten.

The Lesson:

I've come to believe that anticipation isn't merely the pathway to pleasure but a unique form of pleasure itself – perhaps even the most sophisticated kind. The space between wanting and having, that exquisite tension where desire stretches but doesn't break, creates sensations that continuous contact can never achieve, no matter how skilled.

Try this sometime: identify the moment when you normally rush forward – when your hand would naturally move from hip to breast, when your mouth would typically seek more intimate territories – and instead, pause. Hold that moment. Let anticipation build like pressure in a sealed vessel. Watch your partner's breathing change, feel your own skin become hypersensitive, and notice how a simple touch, when it finally arrives, carries impact that would have been impossible without that deliberate delay.

Words become crucial in this dance. "Not yet" whispered against heated skin transforms frustration into delicious anticipation. "I want to see how much you can want this" acknowledges desire while extending its domain. The art lies in maintaining certainty that fulfillment will arrive while keeping its exact moment unpredictable – like holding a gift just beyond someone's reach while assuring them it will eventually be theirs.

Remember that this balance requires sensitivity – desire stretched too far snaps into frustration, tension maintained too long collapses into disinterest. The key lies in reading your partner's responses, in distinguishing between the lovely agony of anticipation and the sharp edge of genuine discomfort. But when orchestrated with care, this deliberate delay creates memories that outlast any immediate satisfaction, no matter how intense.

The Proper Preparation

I've often reflected on how civilization itself might be measured by the distance it places between our animal nature and our socialized selves. Like tides retreating from shores, leaving mysterious territories exposed then covered again, we oscillate between primal desires and cultivated facades. Nowhere is this more evident than in the realms we designate as taboo, territories of pleasure that exist on maps drawn with trembling hands, rarely explored with proper reverence.

The Italian archaeologist arrived as evening descended over Monaco, the harbor lights beginning their nightly shimmer against waters turned indigo by the winter twilight. A rare December mistral had swept through earlier, leaving the air crystalline and stripped of secrets, the stars emerging with uncommon brilliance above the Mediterranean. I'd been watching the transformation of light, how the golden glow of late afternoon surrendered to the deepening blue of evening, contemplating how illumination from different angles reveals aspects of familiar landscapes previously hidden in shadow. An apt metaphor, I thought, for the conversation suspended between us, waiting to be voiced.

"I've spent my life excavating ancient cultures," he said after preliminaries had given way to his purpose, his voice carrying the quiet authority of one accustomed to handling civilization's forgotten intimacies. "Uncovering evidence of how previous societies approached pleasure without our modern taboos." His fingers, long and precise, trained to brush away centuries of dust from delicate artifacts, turned his wine glass with methodical care. "Yet in my personal life, I find myself constrained by boundaries I intellectually recognize as arbitrary."

His confession came without preamble, delivered with the same measured tone he might use to discuss Etruscan burial practices: "I've always been drawn to anal pleasure, but my attempts have been... disappointing. I suspect I've been approaching the territory without proper preparation."

That single word—preparation—revealed an understanding many never reach. In my decades of wandering the secret landscapes of desire, I've witnessed how frequently humans rush toward experiences they covet without adequate groundwork, then blame the experience rather than their approach when disappointment follows. This tendency manifests across all aspects of life but becomes particularly pronounced when addressing desires shadowed by cultural discomfort, those regions marked on interior maps with whispered warnings.

"Most excavations fail," I replied, selecting my metaphor deliberately, "when the archaeologist prioritizes discovery over methodology."

The smile that transformed his serious features indicated I'd found the perfect conceptual bridge. Intellect often provides the necessary permission for pleasure, particularly for those whose minds must approve what their bodies have always known.

"Perhaps," I suggested, rising from my chair in a motion that seemed to gather the evening light around me, "we might approach this as you would a significant dig, with proper respect for the methodology required before the treasure can be revealed."

I did not begin where most would expect. Instead of proceeding directly to my bedroom, that chamber where bodies so often meet with frantic urgency but insufficient understanding, I led him to my study, a room few clients ever enter. Floor-to-ceiling bookshelves lined three walls, their spines creating a topography of wisdom accumulated across continents and centuries. The fourth wall gave itself to windows framing Monaco's illuminated harbor and the vast darkness of the Mediterranean beyond, that ancient sea which has witnessed every variety of human desire since the first ships crossed its mysterious depths. Between the central windows stood a glass cabinet holding artifacts from my own international journeys, small sculptures with secrets embedded in stone, ritual objects that had once facilitated forgotten ceremonies, and books too fragile for open shelving, their pages containing knowledge that once changed how humans approached pleasure.

His eyes widened with appreciation as he took in this more intellectual facet of my life, this evidence that my understanding of bodies stemmed from cultivation of mind. I unlocked the cabinet and removed a small object carved from rose quartz, a prehistoric fertility symbol from the Indus Valley, its smooth curves suggesting rather than declaring the contours of feminine anatomy.

"The ancients understood something we've forgotten," I said, placing the cool stone in his palm, watching his fingers curl around it as if receiving communion. "Preparation for pleasure was once considered sacred rather than merely functional."

The weight of the ancient object in his hand created a moment of unexpected intimacy, a connection across millennia to others who had approached pleasure as something worthy of ritual and respect, not furtive grasping in chambers of shame. I watched understanding dawn in his expression as his thumb traced the object's polished curves, how its symmetry spoke of careful attention rather than hasty creation.

"Contemporary society," I continued, my voice finding the register that invites confidences, "has commodified sexual experience, emphasizing destination over journey. We've forgotten that proper preparation isn't merely practical, it's transformative."

From my bookshelf, I selected several volumes, anthropological studies of sexual practices across cultures, anatomical texts with illustrations more honest than pornographic, and philosophical explorations of pleasure that treated the body as temple rather than machine. I laid them open on my desk, creating a scholarly foundation for what would become an embodied education.

"Knowledge," I told him, "is the first element of preparation. We cannot properly approach what we don't understand."

Using the texts and anatomical illustrations, I explained physiological realities rarely discussed outside medical contexts. The rich network of nerves that make anal pleasure possible, the internal structures that can transform discomfort into ecstasy when properly engaged. I spoke without euphemism but also without clinical detachment, maintaining the delicate balance between education and enticement, between illumination and seduction.

"The body," I explained, allowing my hand to trace the contours of an illustration with the same reverence one might touch a lover, "harbors no shame in its design. Every avenue of pleasure serves a purpose in our complete understanding of sensation."

The lights of Monte Carlo glittered against the deep blue of the winter evening sky, creating a backdrop of distant brilliance that seemed to insulate my apartment from the outside world. The unusual clarity of the air after the mistral's passage had created a rare atmospheric stillness that seemed to suspend ordinary time, placing us in a pocket universe where conventional limitations could be examined and potentially transcended, where desires usually kept chained could be allowed to stretch their limbs.

As his intellectual understanding deepened, I observed subtle shifts in his physical presence, a softening of his scholarly rigidity, a new receptivity in how he occupied space, as if knowledge itself were dissolving invisible armor he had worn since adolescence. The mind, properly engaged, prepares the body for its own education; this truth reveals itself repeatedly in my profession, where intellectual permission often precedes physical surrender.

We moved then to my bathroom, a sanctuary of marble and subdued lighting I've designed for both function and sensuality, where water becomes ritual medium rather than mere cleansing agent. From a discrete cabinet, I retrieved items specifically selected for this aspect of intimate education: hygienic tools designed with both effectiveness and dignity in mind, cleansers formulated to respect the body's natural chemistry, and a collection of lubricants varying in consistency and composition, their crystal containers transforming utilitarian substances into elements of beauty.

"The second element of preparation is respect for the body's boundaries and needs," I said, arranging these items with deliberate care, each placement an offering on an altar of potential pleasure. "What appears as restriction often simply indicates insufficient preparation."

I demonstrated practical approaches to hygiene without embarrassment or unnecessary clinical language. There exists surprising intimacy in sharing precise knowledge about bodily care, an acknowledgment of our shared humanity more profound than many more conventionally sexual interactions. Something divine resides in this honesty, this refusal to shroud natural functions in shame.

"Water temperature matters," I explained, adjusting the shower to demonstrate, my fingers playing in the stream until it reached perfect balance. "Too warm causes relaxation but potential inflammation; too cool creates tension that contradicts our purpose." Such minute details, temperature, timing, technique, compose the invisible architecture supporting pleasure that endures beyond momentary sensation, that builds cathedrals from what might otherwise be mere shelters.

We discussed dietary considerations, timing relative to natural bodily rhythms, and the importance of environmental factors in creating states conducive to exploration. Throughout this education, I maintained the delicate balance between practical instruction and sensual anticipation: each piece of information building not just understanding but desire, each explanation clearing paths that desire might later follow without obstacle.

"The distinction between clinical preparation and sensual ritual," I told him as we returned to my living room, twilight now fully surrendered to darkness outside, "lies not in the actions themselves but in the consciousness behind them."

On my coffee table, I arranged the collection of lubricants in cut-crystal containers that transformed utilitarian substances into elements of beauty. Each formulation, water-based, silicone, hybrids with specific properties, became not merely functional but symbolic of a different approach to sensation, different doorways to the same chamber of delight.

"The third element of preparation is patience," I said, warming a small amount of silicone-based lubricant between my palms, the substance transforming from cool gel to liquid warmth through the alchemy of body heat. "Feel the difference."

I took his hand, applying a small amount of warmed lubricant to his fingers. The simple contact, skin against skin, shifted our interaction from theoretical to experiential, from abstract understanding to embodied knowledge. His sharp intake of breath suggested this transition registered as more profound than he had anticipated, this small crossing of boundaries from talking about touch to experiencing it.

"Temperature transforms experience," I observed, guiding his fingers in small circular motions against his opposite palm, creating patterns of sensation that awakened nerve endings long accustomed to utilitarian contact. "What might be merely tolerable when cold becomes pleasurable when warmed. What might cause tension when applied hastily creates welcome anticipation when introduced gradually."

I demonstrated pressure techniques on the inside of his wrist, showing how gentle circular motion followed by more directed pressure creates relaxation rather than resistance. The principles I illustrated on his wrist would translate directly to more intimate territories, building a physical vocabulary he could later access when intellectual overlay might create hesitation. I watched his pupils dilate as understanding moved from abstract to concrete, as theory became tangible beneath his fingertips.

"The body," I explained, my fingers creating expanding circles against his skin, the tiny hairs rising in response as if reaching toward my touch, "responds to consistent patterns more readily than erratic attention. Repetition with slight variation creates both comfort and anticipation, the perfect conditions for exploration."

As my fingers moved from his wrist to his forearm, I observed his breathing deepen, his attention fully present in the sensation rather than analyzing it from intellectual distance. This transition, from thinking about experience to being within it, forms the essential bridge many highly educated clients find most difficult to cross, this surrender of the observing mind to the experiencing body.

"The final element of preparation," I said, my voice dropping to match the intimacy of the moment, finding that register that bypasses conscious mind to speak directly to the body, "is the transition from intellectual understanding to embodied knowledge. Shall we continue this education in a more comfortable setting?"

In my bedroom, amber light filtered through alabaster sconces, creating an atmosphere both warm and diffused, illumination that revealed while still maintaining mystery. I had prepared the space earlier with an intuitive understanding of what the encounter might require: additional pillows arranged for both comfort and strategic positioning, heated towels on the warming rack in the adjacent bathroom, music selected to engage the parasympathetic nervous system without demanding attention. The sheet's Egyptian cotton carried the scent of lavender and cedar, aromas chosen to evoke both cleansing and foundation.

The night had fully descended outside my windows, the distant lights of yachts in the harbor appearing as suspended constellations against the darkness of the Mediterranean. This nocturnal privacy complemented the psychological space I was creating for his exploration, a sanctuary where conventional boundaries could be temporarily suspended in service of discovery, where the excavator might himself become the site of excavation.

I revealed his form layer by layer, each garment removed with the meticulous care of one uncovering a delicate artifact, each movement preserving the integrity of what was being discovered. His suit jacket, the professional armor, came first, shoulders releasing their burden of presentation as the wool slipped away. Next, the tie that had constrained his throat throughout the day, that symbol of civilization's stranglehold on animal nature. Each button of his shirt surrendered under my fingers, exposing strata of his being: first fabric, then the cotton undershirt with its intimate knowledge of his daily warmth, and finally skin with its constellation of sensory receptors awaiting awakening. This methodical unveiling constituted not a prelude to our encounter but its foundation: the first brushstrokes on a canvas of sensation, the preliminary sketches that true artists create before the masterpiece emerges.

When he stood naked before me, vulnerable in that particular way that combines physical exposure with psychological openness, that mutual disarmament that precedes true connection, I guided him to the bed, arranging pillows to support his body in positions that would facilitate the exploration to come.

"Comfort," I explained, positioning a firm pillow beneath his hips, elevating them slightly to create both access and ease, "is not merely a courtesy but a prerequisite. Physical tension in any part of the body communicates itself everywhere. Proper support allows surrender."

I began with a full-body massage using warmed oil infused with sandalwood and cedar, scents selected to evoke grounding rather than excitation, to create foundation rather than ecstatic flight. Beginning with his shoulders and working methodically downward, I created a progression of relaxation that prepared him for more focused attention. My hands learned the particular topography of his body: where tension had created mountains, where natural hollows invited deeper touch. The oil transformed from separation to connection, from barrier to medium of communication.

"Notice," I instructed as my hands worked the muscles flanking his spine, creating rivers of sensation that flowed toward his core, "how sensation changes when you breathe into areas of tension rather than away from them. The same principle will serve you in all forms of pleasure that initially present as intensity."

His breathing synchronized with my movements, establishing the foundation for the parasympathetic dominance necessary for the exploration to come. When my hands reached the base of his spine, I felt the subtle arching response, that unconscious invitation the body offers when the mind finally surrenders its vigilance, when intellect yields to sensation's wisdom.

Only then did I reach for the lubricant I had placed on the warming stone beside the bed. The brief separation created its own tension, a momentary pause in contact that heightened awareness of its resumption. I warmed additional lubricant between my palms, the transparent substance catching amber light as it transformed from gel to liquid, functional preparation becoming sensual ritual through attention and intention.

"Communication," I said softly as my hands returned to his body, "remains essential throughout exploration. But this communication need not be verbal. Your body will speak if I listen properly."

I started with external massage, gradually focusing on the area around his opening. Each circle of my fingers created concentric waves of sensation, establishing patterns his nervous system could anticipate and welcome. The gradual approach, never moving directly to the center but spiraling inward, allowed his body to invite rather than just permit exploration. Goosebumps rose across his skin, that primal response signaling the boundaries between self and environment dissolving.

When my finger finally breached the threshold, the moment arrived not as invasion but as natural progression: a boundary crossed through invitation rather than persistence. His sharp intake of breath followed by a long, vocalizing exhale told me his experience registered as revelation rather than intrusion. The sound emerged from someplace deeper than his throat, as if originating from the exact point where our bodies connected.

"Stay present with the sensation," I instructed, my free hand making soothing circles at the base of his spine, creating countercurrents of pleasure that distributed attention rather than focusing it too intensely. "Notice how it transforms when you breathe into it rather than away from it."

I maintained perfect stillness, allowing his body to accommodate this crossing of boundaries both physical and psychological. The subtle pulses around my finger, his body's unconscious communication, guided my understanding of his experience more precisely than words could convey. This silent dialogue between bodies reveals truths that language often conceals behind euphemism or technical terminology.

Only when these pulses gave way to relaxation did I begin exploratory movement, gentle rotations followed by carefully directed pressure designed to awaken nerve networks rarely engaged. When my fingertip discovered his prostate, his involuntary response, a full-body arc accompanied by a sound unlike any he had made previously, a cry that seemed torn from some primal depth, confirmed that preparation had created the conditions for genuine discovery. His hands clutched at the sheets, gathering fabric as if trying to anchor himself against waves of unexpected pleasure.

"There," I confirmed softly, maintaining gentle pressure against this hidden center of sensation, this internal pearl so rarely touched with proper reverence. "Feel how sensation radiates beyond its source? How it connects to places you didn't know were linked?"

I established a rhythm of stimulation that alternated between direct pressure and peripheral attention, creating waves of sensation rather than focused intensity. With my free hand, I reached beneath him to encircle his cock, which had grown impressively hard and slick with excitement, a glistening testament to pleasure's ability to manifest physically even when the source remains hidden. The dual stimulation, internal pressure against his prostate synchronized with the rhythmic stroking of his shaft, my palm gliding from base to tip in unhurried appreciation, created a circuit of pleasure that integrated rather than compartmentalized his response. His erection pulsed in my hand, veins carrying blood to sensitive tissues grown tumescent with desire, heat radiating against my palm.

His reaction transcended conventional patterns. The sounds emerging from him grew deeper, more primal, as if originating from caverns rarely explored, suggesting access to aspects of his sensual capacity previously unexplored. His hips began to move of their own accord, pressing back against my finger while simultaneously thrusting into my encircling hand, creating two complementary rhythms that harmonized rather than competed. The wetness at his tip spread beneath my thumb as I circled it deliberately across the sensitive glans, drawing forth a moan that seemed wrenched from someplace deeper than his throat, a sound that existed before language, from when pleasure and survival were indistinguishable.

"Allow the entirety of the experience," I encouraged as I felt the tension of approaching release building within him, muscles tightening in preparation for that momentary dissolution of self. "Release expectations of how pleasure should manifest or express itself."

When climax finally claimed him, it appeared not as the localized, familiar experience to which most men are accustomed, but as successive waves that seemed to originate from his core and radiate outward through his entire being, transforming his physical form into a vessel for sensation. His cock pulsed violently in my hand, spilling hot release across his stomach and my fingers in rhythmic jets that synchronized perfectly with the internal contractions gripping my finger still buried inside him. The pearlescent fluid caught amber light, transforming utilitarian reproduction into evidence of transcendence. His cry, a sound of astonishment as much as release, filled the room, vibrating between walls as his body vibrated beneath my touch. The pulses around my finger continued long after conventional orgasm would have subsided, each wave slightly less intense but somehow deeper than the one before, ripples expanding outward from the center of a pond where a stone of perfect weight had broken surface tension.

In the quiet aftermath, as his breathing gradually returned to normal, I maintained connection. Physical withdrawal, when performed without proper care, can disrupt the integration of experience, can transform communion back into separation too abruptly. Only when the final tremors had subsided did I begin a careful retreat, following the same principles of patient attention that had guided entry, my finger withdrawing with the same deliberate care with which it had entered, transforming necessary ending into its own form of pleasure.

I cleansed him with warmed towels, each movement continuing the care that had characterized our entire encounter. This attention, this refusal to treat practical necessity as mere function, maintained the atmosphere of ritual that transforms physical acts into meaningful experience. The warm cloth moved across his skin like benediction, removing evidence but preserving memory.

When he finally turned to meet my gaze, I recognized the expression that accompanies genuine discovery: a particular quality of wonder combined with recalibration of previous understanding, that moment when known maps must be redrawn to accommodate new territories. His eyes held questions his voice couldn't yet formulate, mysteries of the body that expand rather than resolve with exploration.

"There exists knowledge," I said softly, arranging pillows to support him in his newly relaxed state, his body now liquid where it had been solid, "accessible only through direct experience. No amount of intellectual understanding can substitute for embodied discovery."

The smile that slowly transformed his features spoke of territories not merely visited but incorporated into an expanded understanding of his own capacity for pleasure. In that moment, I was reminded again of why I chose this unusual path. Not merely to provide physical release but to offer glimpses of what lies beyond culturally maintained limitations, brief but profound expansions of what we believe possible.

"I've attempted this before," he confessed as we lay in the gentle aftermath, his voice carrying the quiet wonder of one who has seen familiar landscapes from unprecedented angles, "but the experience was so different as to seem entirely unrelated to what just happened."

"The difference," I replied, "wasn't in the act itself but in the approach. Proper preparation transforms, not just the physical experience but its very meaning."

Beyond my windows, the night had deepened. Monaco's harbor gleamed with the distant lights of luxury vessels and shoreline buildings, their reflections rippling across the dark water, doubled and distorted beautifully. This transformation of the familiar daylight landscape into something mysterious yet beautiful seemed to mirror his internal experience, territories once known now revealed in entirely new aspect through the proper approach, illuminated differently by this altered relationship to pleasure.

•

I have witnessed it countless times, this sacred dance, when intellectual understanding dissolves into embodied wisdom like salt into warm sea, leaving no separation between knowledge and experience. It haunts me still, the transformation in his eyes when revelation claimed him, the moment when all my words were vindicated by his body's ecstatic reality. Like a mask slipping to reveal the true face beneath, his journey from hesitation to discovery mirrors a pattern I've witnessed across twenty-four years beside Monaco's glittering waters, how we blossom in proper soil when given both accuracy of knowledge and tenderness of guidance.

What fascinates me most is this ancient alchemy, the transmutation of the forbidden into the sacred through nothing more complex than careful attention, how fear becomes wonder through unhurried touch. We are creatures of shadow and light, of secret chambers locked unnecessarily, our pleasures often sequestered behind walls of misunderstanding. Yet how easily these barriers dissolve when approached with loving patience, when touched by hands that expect neither rejection nor immediate surrender. I think sometimes of the archaeologist's fingers, how they unearthed pottery fragments with the same reverence they later explored his own hidden territories: the tools identical though the landscapes differed, the methods unchanged though the discoveries belonged to different orders of existence.

Several months after our encounter, a package arrived from northern Italy, a small, carefully wrapped archaeological reproduction of a Roman oil lamp, its rust-colored clay still carrying the scent of earth from which it was formed. Its surface depicted embracing figures in a position unmistakably related to our exploration together, captured in silhouette with that peculiar timelessness of ancient art. The accompanying note read simply: "You have taught me that proper preparation illuminates territories I once thought forever dark. The method of the careful excavator applies to personal archaeology as well."

I placed this lamp in my study, where sometimes in the lavender twilight I light it and contemplate how knowledge crosses between realms, how wisdom in one domain can illuminate another like moonlight reflecting on different facets of the same sea. His gift spoke to something I've observed repeatedly throughout my years in this profession: that proper preparation transforms not merely specific acts but our entire relationship to pleasure itself, our map of what is possible expanding with each boundary gently crossed.

The magic lies not in technique but in presence, the sanctuary where learning occurs through the body rather than merely the mind, where we become simultaneously teacher and student of our own sensations. How many of us rush through life collecting sensations without experiencing them? Like tourists who photograph everything yet see nothing, we pass through pleasure's landscapes without inhabiting them, our bodies merely vehicles rather than temples of experience. The archaeologist reminded me of what I've observed repeatedly through countless encounters: that proper preparation, attentive, thorough, unhurried, transforms not just our intimate encounters but potentially every significant experience, every moment where sensation might transcend mere function.

I often watch visitors to Monaco's Oceanographic Museum moving hurriedly from exhibit to exhibit, their eyes already seeking the next marvel before fully absorbing the present one, capturing images but missing the wonder. Then occasionally I notice someone different, standing transfixed before a single display, absorbed in its details, receiving its full impact as if the moment might never end, as if that particular wonder might never be offered again. The difference lies not in what they see but in how they see it. The quality of attention brought to the experience, the willingness to allow wonder rather than merely collect it.

What continues to fascinate me as time weaves its patterns through my life is how preparation, this seemingly mundane prerequisite we so often resent, contains such transformative power. Our culture's fixation on immediate gratification has taught us to rush toward pleasure as if it might escape, yet in doing so, we often bypass the very conditions that would make that pleasure profound. Like travelers so focused on destination they miss the journey entirely, we forfeit depth for speed, wonder for completion, communion for conquest. I sometimes wonder how many chambers of potential delight remain unexplored in most lives, not because they contain no treasure but because the approach has lacked the excavator's patient reverence, the pilgrim's willingness to approach sacred thresholds with proper humility.

Perhaps in this lies wisdom worth carrying beyond intimate chambers into the larger world: that honoring any experience by creating optimal conditions for its unfolding might be both the most countercultural and ultimately satisfying choice we can make. In a world characterized by convenience and acceleration, by the constant reaching for what comes next, the willingness to prepare properly, to approach pleasure as something worthy of ritual rather than merely consumption, may be the most profound rebellion of all, the most sacred reclamation of our embodied humanity.

The Lesson:

Proper preparation is alchemy, transforming what might otherwise be merely tolerated into a journey of genuine discovery and pleasure. Like the careful excavation that precedes the unearthing of treasure, thoughtful groundwork allows us to receive new sensations as gifts rather than intrusions.

Begin with understanding. Knowledge illuminates the path, dispelling shadows of uncertainty that might otherwise trigger tension. Knowing the body's landscape: its sensitive networks, its responses, its internal architecture, provides both practical guidance and the confidence to explore. I've found that many approach unfamiliar intimate territories armed with myths rather than facts, their anxiety born from imagination rather than reality.

Next, honor your body through mindful physical preparation. For casual exploration, gentle external cleansing creates both physical and psychological readiness. For deeper journeys, consider internal preparation using plain, lukewarm water. Remember that nature designed our bodies with wisdom, the goal is natural cleanliness, not clinical sterility. Aggressive approaches often disrupt the very balance they seek to maintain.

Listen to your body's rhythms and timing. Like the Mediterranean tides that shape Monaco's shoreline, our bodies follow cycles that, when respected, create natural windows for exploration. Forcing pleasure against these rhythms rarely yields satisfaction; following them often reveals unexpected depths of sensation.

Approach lubrication not as optional but essential. Unlike other intimate activities where the body provides its own moisture, these particular landscapes require additional care. Choose lubricants specifically designed for this purpose, those with staying power and gentle formulations. Apply with generosity; in this context, abundance serves pleasure better than restraint.

Create an environment that whispers invitation rather than demands performance. The space around us shapes the space within us: comfortable temperature, gentle lighting, perhaps music that soothes without commanding attention. I've noticed how profoundly external conditions influence our capacity to remain present, particularly when exploring territories that might initially trigger vigilance rather than relaxation.

When the moment for exploration arrives, patience becomes your greatest ally. Begin with gentle touches that familiarize rather than demand, creating expanding circles of pleasure that gradually approach the center. Allow boundaries to dissolve through invitation rather than insistence. The initial crossing should feel like a natural progression, never an invasion, the smallest touch, thoroughly lubricated, introduced with exquisite attention to response.

For those receiving, conscious breathing offers perhaps the most powerful tool for transformation. Deep, unhurried breaths tell your body that all is well, allowing tension to dissolve and pleasure to enter. Though it might seem counterintuitive, bearing down slightly during initial moments of pressure can help muscles relax rather than resist, a paradox of surrender I've observed countless times.

For those giving, attention to response, both spoken and unspoken, creates the necessary dialogue for pleasure to unfold. Follow your partner's pace, not your anticipation or desire. This patience directly transforms the experience; rushing converts potential ecstasy into mere endurance.

Remember that true care extends beyond the moment of exploration itself. Gentle cleansing, emotional reassurance, physical comfort afterward: these elements complete the circle, honoring the vulnerability shared and creating associations that transform the unfamiliar into the welcomed.

Consider how this philosophy might illuminate other aspects of intimacy as well. So many realms of pleasure remain unexplored not because they hold no potential for delight but because previous approaches lacked the preparation necessary for discovery. When approached with care and attention, what many consider forbidden territory becomes instead a landscape of unexpected revelation, not replacing other forms of intimacy but expanding our capacity for sensation in all its magnificent diversity.

Part 6:
Integration & Closure

In the violet hour between night and dawn, as Monaco's lights still glittered against the Mediterranean darkness, he asked a question that penetrated deeper than our physical connection had. "How do you maintain such presence," he whispered against my hair, "when intimacy makes most people retreat into performance or fantasy?" The question illuminated something essential about pleasure's ultimate paradox: how experiences seemingly focused on bodily sensation might ultimately transform our relationship with consciousness itself.

All journeys circle back to themselves, though we return changed by territories traversed. In these final chapters, we integrate the physical, psychological, and spiritual dimensions of intimacy into coherent whole. The symphony reaches completion when each element finds its proper place, when sound harmonizes with touch, when surrender complements control, when preparation culminates in presence.

I've watched powerful men weep unexpectedly after particularly profound encounters, not from emotional distress but from momentary recognition of beauty they'd spent decades avoiding. I've felt my own carefully constructed professional boundaries dissolve in fleeting moments of connection so authentic they seemed to touch something eternal within the temporal.

This integration extends beyond momentary pleasure to infuse all aspects of life with greater awareness, attunement, and appreciation. The capacity to remain present during intense sensation, neither retreating from nor grasping at experience, creates ripples that extend far beyond the bedroom. The ability to communicate desire directly yet without demand transforms relationships beyond the merely sexual.

As our exploration concludes, consider how intimacy might become not merely something we do but something we become: a way of approaching all existence with presence, courage, and curiosity that transforms not just physical connection but our fundamental experience of being alive. The most valuable gift of pleasure lies not in momentary satisfaction but in how it awakens us to the extraordinary nature of ordinary existence, how completely we might inhabit each precious moment before it dissolves into memory.

The Power of Sound

There exists a moment just before sound becomes touch. A threshold where vibration hovers between air and skin, not quite one or the other. I have spent years studying the geography of pleasure, mapping its contours with fingers and lips, yet somehow overlooked this invisible terrain where sound transmutes into sensation. Until him.

He arrived as Monaco transitioned from dusk to darkness, that liminal hour when the city's soundscape shifts: when champagne flutes replace coffee cups, when conversation drops to intimate registers, when the Mediterranean alters its rhythm against the harbor walls. I had prepared carefully, not with the usual visual seductions, but with acoustics in mind: windows cracked to invite the city's nocturnal voice, speakers positioned to create subtle ambient layers, lighting arranged to encourage focus on what would be heard rather than merely seen.

"You've created an auditory sanctuary," he observed immediately upon entering, his composer's ears cataloging the apartment's sonic architecture. He moved through my space with unusual awareness, registering the subtle percussion of my heels against marble, the soft whisper of my silk dress, the barely perceptible ambient composition I'd selected, ocean waves slowed to an almost subliminal rhythm.

I took his hands without speaking, watching his focus shift from the visual world to the acoustic one. His eyes closed briefly, head tilting as if to better capture the subtle soundscape around us. When they opened again, something had altered in his gaze. A different quality of attention now directed toward me.

"Most people think intimacy is visual first," I said, my voice deliberately lower than usual, feeling how the vibrations formed in my throat and traveled through the air between us. "But sound penetrates boundaries that light cannot."

His smile contained recognition, a shared understanding of the overlooked dimension we were about to explore together. "The ear never closes," he replied, his voice dropping to a register that seemed to resonate directly in my sternum rather than reaching me through air. "Even in sleep, it stands guard while all other senses surrender."

The first kiss came with its own acoustic signature: the subtle catch of breath, the whisper of lips meeting, the almost imperceptible hum that formed deep in his throat. I cataloged these sounds with the same attentiveness I typically reserve for tactile information, discovering how they formed a narrative more honest than words, more nuanced than images. There was a tremor in the silence between contact and deepening pressure, a kind of emotional resonance that spoke not only of desire but of permission, of vulnerability offered and cautiously accepted. That moment contained music only the body could compose, an unrepeatable symphony of nervous anticipation, memory, and instinct. It told me everything: what he feared, what he craved, and what he didn't yet know how to ask for. Long before his hands moved, his breath confessed him.

"Let me hear you remove my dress," I whispered against his ear, feeling how the words themselves created tiny shivers along his skin. He understood instantly, slowing his movements to accentuate each sound: the whisper of fabric against skin, the subtle click of a zipper descending tooth by tooth, the rush of silk surrendering to gravity as it pooled at my feet.

His fingers mapped the newly exposed landscape of my body while his lips found my ear. "Sound isn't just heard," he murmured, his voice creating vibrations that traveled from my ear canal directly to my core, "it's felt. Everywhere."

To demonstrate, he produced a low, sustained hum against my throat, not loud, but pitched precisely to create resonance that seemed to activate nerve pathways I hadn't known existed. The vibration traveled beneath my skin like an electric current, diffusing through tissue and bone to awaken sensations entirely different from touch. My response, an involuntary arch of the spine, a sharp inhalation, confirmed his theory with my body's evidence.

"The voice is an instrument few learn to play properly," he continued, each word deliberate, his breath warm against my neck. "Especially in bed."

I guided him toward the bedroom, where I had arranged the acoustic environment with particular care: sound-absorbing fabrics to eliminate harsh reflections, the subtle background of waves through distant speakers, the bed positioned to allow the night air to carry its Mediterranean whispers across our skin.

As articles of clothing disappeared, I focused on the sounds typically relegated to background: the leather whisper of his belt sliding through loops, the distinctive timbre of buttons released from fabric, the rustle of cotton against skin, the subtle symphony of disrobing that usually goes unnoticed beneath visual attention.

When he stood naked before me, I circled him slowly, allowing my breath to become audible, letting him hear the subtle changes in my respiration as I absorbed his presence. His response was immediate, a visible rippling of skin, a tension in muscle, his body responding to sound before touch had even occurred.

I positioned my lips near his ear, not yet touching, but close enough that he could feel the warmth of my breath. "The most honest reactions," I whispered, "are the involuntary ones." With that, I exhaled a soft, warm current directly into his ear canal, watching as the sound-sensation triggered an instantaneous cascade: his pupils dilating, a tremor running visibly from his shoulders down his spine, his erection responding as though I had touched him directly.

"Your turn," he responded, guiding me to the bed with gentle pressure. As I reclined against the sheets, he positioned himself beside me, his lips near my ear. "Close your eyes," he instructed, his voice dropping to that chest-resonating register that seemed to bypass my ears entirely and vibrate directly through my body.

What followed was unlike anything I had experienced in decades of intimate encounters. He began to construct an architecture of sound around and within me. His voice moving from whispered intensity at my ear that created localized shivers, to deeper tones against my sternum that resonated through my ribcage, to barely audible hums against the sensitive skin of my inner thighs that seemed to awaken nerve endings typically dormant.

"Sound creates pathways," he explained between these acoustic explorations, his fingers now joining his voice, inscribing patterns that complemented the vibrations he was generating. "Neural highways that sensation can follow."

I found myself responding not just physically but vocally. Sounds emerging from my throat without conscious formation, authentic expressions that surprised even me with their raw honesty. When his mouth finally found the center of my desire, he paused, looking up the landscape of my body to capture my gaze.

"Let me hear exactly what this feels like," he said, before his tongue began its deliberate exploration. "Don't translate or filter. Just sound."

The instruction, this explicit request for vocal authenticity rather than performance, unlocked something primal. As pleasure built under his skillful attention, the sounds that escaped me formed their own vocabulary of sensation: from sharp inhalations that marked sudden peaks of pleasure, to longer, lower tones that traced building waves of arousal, to broken syllables that signaled moments where conscious thought fragmented under sensory assault.

He responded to this acoustic feedback with precise adjustments: altering pressure, rhythm, focus based on the changing timbre of my vocalizations. This created an unprecedented feedback loop: my sounds guiding his techniques, his techniques provoking new sounds, each cycle building toward intensities I rarely accessed with new clients.

When my hunger for him could no longer be satisfied by his mouth alone, I grasped his shoulders and pulled him upward. His body, lean and strong from years of controlled breath work, slid against mine with delicious friction, skin catching on skin, the slight dampness between us creating a sound like silk tearing in slow motion. His cock pressed against my inner thigh, radiating heat that seemed to throb with his heartbeat. I reached between us, wrapping my fingers around the magnificent thickness of him, feeling the velvet-smooth skin stretched taut over rigid hardness.

"I need to feel you inside me," I whispered, my voice uncharacteristically raw with urgent desire. "I need to hear what sounds we make together."

I guided him to my entrance, already slick and swollen from his earlier attentions. He paused there, the sensitive head of his cock resting just at the threshold, and lowered his mouth to my ear.

"Synchronize with me," he whispered, his breath hot against my ear canal, creating shivers that cascaded down my neck and blossomed across my chest.

He entered me slowly, just the first inch, then withdrew, then slightly deeper, each movement deliberate. The wet sound of our joining was startlingly loud in the quiet, a primal percussion that echoed my thundering pulse. When he seated himself fully within me, the fullness was exquisite, a delicious stretch that made me gasp.

"Feel how sound travels through connected bodies," he murmured, his chest pressed against my breasts, his pubic bone applying perfect pressure against my clitoris. He began a slow, rhythmic movement, establishing a cadence with both his hips and breath. "Breathe with me."

Our exhalations aligned, creating a harmonic resonance. The vibration of his muscled chest against my sensitive nipples, the sound of our synchronized breathing, and the physical connection where he filled me completely formed a triad of sensation I'd never experienced before.

As our movements intensified, his hands explored me with musician's precision: fingers finding the exact curve of my waist, palming the roundness of my hip, gripping the soft flesh of my thigh to adjust our angle. The position allowed him to stroke against the most sensitive spot inside me, a place that made stars explode behind my eyelids each time he brushed against it.

He demonstrated extraordinary control over his vocalizations, using them not merely as expressions of his own pleasure but as instruments to heighten mine. When I wrapped my legs around his narrow waist, changing the depth of penetration, he delivered a deep moan directly against my neck. The sound traveled through my carotid artery with a vibration that seemed to pulse directly into my brain, intensifying the electricity gathering low in my pelvis.

His movements became more forceful, his magnificent length withdrawing almost completely before driving back into me with precision that left me gasping. A sharp, controlled exhalation timed precisely with a particularly deep thrust created a sensory counterpoint that made my toes curl involuntarily and my inner muscles clench around him, drawing him even deeper.

We rolled together in a fluid motion, and I found myself astride him, my thighs bracketing his narrow hips, my body taking him even deeper from this new angle. His hands cupped my breasts, thumbs circling the hardened peaks of my nipples, sending shockwaves of pleasure directly to my core. I began to move upon him, rising and falling with increasing urgency, my head falling back as sensation built like gathering storm clouds.

"Higher," he instructed when my sounds began to retreat into my throat due to long-established habits of restraint. His hand slid from my breast, down the sweat-dampened plane of my stomach, to press gently against my sternum. "Let it come from here," he added, encouraging sound to emanate from deeper in my body.

I could feel him pulsing inside me, his magnificent hardness hitting exactly the right spot with each roll of my hips. His other hand slipped between our bodies, finding the swollen bud of my clitoris with unerring accuracy. He circled it with slick fingertips, matching the rhythm of my movements perfectly, creating a counterpoint of sensations that made coherent thought impossible.

The permission, this explicit invitation to transcend social conditioning, unleashed something unexpected. As I allowed my voice to emerge from depths usually controlled, the physical sensations themselves intensified dramatically. My inner muscles began to flutter around his thickness, gripping him more tightly with each downward motion. Each vocalization seemed to open channels through which pleasure flowed more freely, as if sound itself was clearing blockages in sensation.

His body was a study in controlled power beneath me: the defined muscles of his abdomen contracting with each thrust, the tendons in his neck standing out as he lifted his hips to meet mine. Sweat glistened on his chest, catching the dim light as it trickled down the channel between his pectoral muscles. The sight of him, eyes dark with desire, lips parted with quickening breath, combined with the exquisite fullness where our bodies joined pushed me toward a precipice I could no longer resist.

When orgasm approached, he sensed it not through the conventional signs but through the changing harmonics of my breath. His hands gripped my hips, fingers pressing into the soft flesh with delicious urgency, guiding my movements to a rhythm that made stars explode behind my eyelids.

"Don't close your mouth," he instructed, his own voice roughened with desire, his cock throbbing noticeably inside me. "Let me hear you completely unravel."

What followed transcended conventional categories of pleasure. As climax overtook me, my inner walls clamped down on him with such force that I heard his breath catch. The sound that emerged from my lips contained no restraint, no social masking, a primal vocalization that seemed to come from evolutionary depths. My body arched, every muscle drawn taut like a bow, waves of ecstasy radiating outward from where we were joined. The release was so complete that boundaries between physical and acoustic sensation dissolved entirely. The vibrations of my own voice seemed to feed back into my body, intensifying and extending the ripples of pleasure beyond what muscle contractions alone could produce.

My climax triggered his own. His hands gripped my thighs with bruising intensity as his hips bucked upward, driving himself impossibly deeper. His composer's discipline shattered completely as his release overtook him: his head thrown back against the pillows, the elegant column of his throat exposed, a series of deep, guttural sounds emerging from somewhere primal within him. I felt the hot pulse of his orgasm deep inside me, each spasm of his cock triggering aftershocks in my still-sensitive flesh.

The sounds he made in that moment of complete surrender, raw, unfiltered, almost animalistic, revealed more of his essential self than any words could have conveyed. His face, usually so controlled and attentive, was transformed by pleasure into something beautiful in its complete abandon. In that moment of dual surrender, my body still joined with his in the most intimate embrace, I understood something fundamental: that authentic sound reveals what we most wish to hide and most need to express.

In the exquisite sensitivity that followed, we lay without speaking, the subtle symphony of our breathing gradually slowing in tandem. The sounds of Monaco filtered through the window: distant laughter from a harborside restaurant, the distinctive purr of a Ferrari navigating the tight streets, the eternal whisper of the Mediterranean against stone. These acoustic textures, normally background to visual dominance, now occupied the foreground of perception, each carrying information as rich as any image.

His fingers sketched invisible patterns on my still-trembling abdomen, occasionally pausing to feel the vibrations of my gradually steadying breath. "Most people," he observed softly, "never discover how sound shapes sensation, how the voice can unlock pathways of pleasure that remain closed in silence."

"We're conditioned to perform rather than express," I replied, noticing how even these words created subtle vibrations that traveled between us where our bodies touched.

"The difference," he said, turning to look directly into my eyes, "is like the difference between hearing recorded music and feeling an orchestra play while sitting in the front row. The vibrations move through you differently."

This observation, this perfect distillation of our exploration, captured something I had somehow overlooked in years of professional intimacy. Sound doesn't merely accompany pleasure; it fundamentally alters how sensation is received, processed, and experienced. The acoustic dimension of sexuality isn't supplementary but essential: a vibratory channel through which pleasure travels by entirely different neural pathways than touch alone.

As my fingers glided along the contours of his chest, feeling the subtle vibration of his heartbeat against my palm, I considered how many dimensions of experience remain unexplored even after thousands of encounters. How extraordinary that after decades of mapping pleasure's landscape, I could still discover entirely new territories, hidden continents of sensation waiting beneath the threshold of awareness, accessible through gateways as simple as surrendering to the authentic music of desire.

"Next time," he murmured as the night deepened around us, "I want to compose specifically for your body, frequencies and rhythms designed to resonate with particular parts of you." His hand moved to cover mine where it rested over his heart. "A symphony written in vibration, performed through flesh."

The promise lingered in the quiet darkness, a reminder that in the realm of sensuality, as in music, the most profound experiences often emerge not from what is explicitly sounded, but from the exquisite tension between sound and silence, between expression and anticipation, between what is voiced and what remains beautifully unspoken.

•

I have lived half a century in my body, yet only now do I understand what ancient cultures have known for millennia: that sound and body exist not as separate entities but as interwoven realities, whispering secrets to each other through pathways invisible to the eye. He awakened this truth in me not through erudite explanations but through a deeper language: the perfect attunement of voice to flesh.

I watched my composer dissolve the boundaries between sound and sensation, much as certain mystics dissolve the boundaries between body and soul. His mouth against my skin created not merely touch but vibration, a subtle architecture of tremors that resonated through chambers I hadn't known existed within me. Perhaps this is what the temple priestesses understood, what the tantric masters preserved: that the voice carries power beyond word and meaning, that it can transform the very substance of pleasure.

Haven't you noticed, in those rare moments of authentic abandon, how your voice seems to emerge from someplace beyond your conscious command? This primal voice, this sonic truth that rises from below thought, is not merely expressing pleasure but actively creating it. The Japanese understood this when they developed their concept of shikin-tai-shō, mind and body as inseparable entities. When we silence ourselves, lips pressed tight, throats constricted, we unknowingly create tension in the very muscles that need to release for ecstasy to flower within us.

Our cultural obsession with visual aspects of sexuality has left this sonic dimension largely unexplored, like a vast continent on ancient maps marked only with "here be dragons." Yet those who inhabit this territory, those who give full voice to their pleasure, consistently describe more profound, more transformative experiences than those who journey through intimacy in silence. The correlation isn't coincidental but causal: the liberation of voice creates physiological conditions where pleasure expands beyond conventional boundaries.

I remember watching him from beneath heavy eyelids as he moved within me, his composer's discipline momentarily abandoned as sounds emerged from him that no audience would ever hear: raw, unfiltered expressions that revealed more of his essential self than any symphony ever could. In that moment, I understood that authentic sound strips away the persona we present to the world, leaving only the unvarnished truth of who we are in our most vulnerable moments.

This sonic dimension explains, perhaps, why music has been associated with sexuality across all cultures throughout human history. Why rhythm and melody have always accompanied rituals of fertility and union. We intuitively recognize that sound creates bridges between separate beings, connecting through vibration what touch alone cannot reach. The voice, in its unrestrained expression, becomes both the most intimate confession and the most profound invitation, a momentary dissolution of boundaries that allows us to experience connection in its purest form.

When we remain silent during our most intimate moments, we deny ourselves not just expression but expansion: the opportunity to transform pleasure from a solitary experience into a resonant communication that encompasses both bodies in a single acoustic embrace. In finding your voice, you may discover not just greater pleasure, but a deeper capacity for authentic connection, a language more honest than words could ever provide, a communion more profound than silence could ever contain.

The Lesson:

Sound transforms pleasure through pathways both ancient and immediate. When we allow our voices complete freedom during intimate moments, we don't merely describe our experience, we fundamentally alter it.

Think of how a cathedral's architecture shapes the music played within it: how stone and space transform vibration into something more profound than the original notes. Our bodies operate by similar principles. The sounds we make resonate through tissue and bone, creating internal symphonies that intensify pleasure in ways touch alone cannot achieve.

If self-consciousness keeps your voice locked in your throat, begin your explorations in solitude. Notice how different sounds feel within your body: how a deep, sustained moan resonates differently than sharp, staccato cries. Feel how vocalization changes your breathing, sending oxygen rushing to awakened nerves, releasing tension from muscles long held rigid by silence.

For those who've never given voice to their pleasure, the journey begins with permission. A simple phrase like "I want to hear you" can unlock doors long closed by convention or shame. What matters isn't vocal performance but authentic expression, the unfiltered sounds that emerge when sensation overwhelms control.

The most profound expressions rarely match what we hear in cinema or imagine we should sound like. They may be surprising, unusual, even initially embarrassing, but they carry vibrational information that transforms connection in ways silence could never achieve. Remember that the most beautiful music often contains dissonance, unexpected notes that create tension before resolution.

The Art of Surrender

Mastery resides not merely in what we command, but in what we willingly relinquish. This contradiction has revealed itself to me repeatedly over the years, watching rigidity dissolve into rapture as clenched hands soften, as tightened shoulders ease, as bodies fortified against vulnerability yield to pleasures they never anticipated. The most remarkable surrenders invariably come from those who've spent decades building their fortifications.

Twilight had begun its russet seduction of my Monaco sanctuary when he arrived. Mediterranean dusk flooded through my windows, bathing walls in burnished copper. His knock, three calculated strikes, mirrored everything I'd heard: meticulous, commanding, permitting no indecision. When I opened the door, I faced precisely what I'd expected: immaculate in custom-tailored British worsted, platinum-dusted obsidian hair betraying just enough age to signal wisdom without weakness. His eyes, that peculiar blue that shifts between steel and ocean depending on the light, dissected me with that same intensity rumored to have unraveled numerous executive strategies.

"Bourbon, neat," he said after minimal greetings, a man accustomed to having preferences instantly recognized, not to mention fulfilled. Not a question, not a request, a statement of what would happen next.

As I poured the amber liquid, its bouquet releasing hints of vanilla and cherrywood between us, I studied his reflection in the vintage Venetian mirror behind my bar. His frame remained militarily erect even seated, his bearing preserving alertness despite his superficial relaxation. A body that had forgotten how to speak the language of abandon.

"Tell me," I said, placing the crystal tumbler within his reach rather than into his hand, "when was the last time you weren't in control?"

The question visibly startled him, as I had intended. His hand froze mid-reach, hovering over the glass like a predator momentarily confused by its prey.

"I'm not sure I follow." His voice carried that particular resonance of someone unaccustomed to clarifying himself.

"I think you do." I settled across from him, arranging my silk dress with deliberate attention. "Control demands constant vigilance. An endless series of calculations, predictions, adjustments. Exhausting, when sustained indefinitely."

Something flickered behind his eyes: recognition, perhaps, or wariness. He recovered quickly, lifting the bourbon in a small toast that acknowledged the direct hit without verbally conceding it.

"Vigilance has served me well. I oversee seventeen billion in assets. People rely on my decisions."

"And yet," I observed softly, "you've sought out the one environment where those decisions hold no currency."

The bourbon's journey to his lips paused almost imperceptibly. For a heartbeat, uncertainty displaced confidence in his gaze. Such a brief hesitation would have gone unnoticed by most, but in my profession, these microscopic surrenders reveal everything, small harbingers of greater yielding to come.

"Perhaps," he allowed, the word itself a minor concession.

I rose without hurry, positioning myself before him. Not near enough for contact, yet close enough that he would catch my fragrance, jasmine and vetiver with those subtle undercurrents of cardamom I prefer. His gaze lifted to meet mine, pupils already beginning their telling dilation despite his carefully preserved equanimity.

"Tonight," I suggested, voice dropping half an octave, "you make no decisions at all."

His chest expanded slightly with a deeper breath, the only visible response to my proposition. Yet in that subtle expansion lay all the answer I needed: his body's wisdom speaking before his mind could catch up, acknowledging what he wasn't yet ready to verbalize. It was a breath filled with hesitation, yes, but also surrender; not the kind that signals defeat, but the softer kind that precedes revelation. In that moment, I understood him more clearly than any words might have allowed. The body, when listened to closely, rarely lies. It offers its own consent, its own truth, often before the conscious self is willing to name it.

"Stand up," I instructed, the gentle command hanging between us like something tangible.

A moment's hesitation, that ingrained resistance to external direction, before he complied, rising to his full height, several inches above my own even in my heels. This close, I caught the subtle acceleration in his breathing, the faint spice of his cologne mingling with bourbon on his breath.

"Close your eyes."

This request presented greater challenge. Vision represents our primary control mechanism, the data-gathering that precedes management. His eyelids lowered halfway before resistance asserted itself.

"I prefer to—"

"I know exactly what you prefer," I interrupted, my voice soft yet implacable. "That's precisely what we're setting aside tonight."

Something in my certainty reached him. His eyes closed completely, immediately transforming his presence. Without his penetrating gaze projecting authority, his body told a different story: muscles maintaining unnecessary tension, hands slightly clenched at his sides, weight shifted forward as if prepared for sudden movement. A man experiencing weightlessness while still bracing against gravity.

I circled him slowly, my heels marking deliberate rhythm against hardwood, a sound allowing him to track my movement while denying the control of vision. When I paused directly behind him, I didn't immediately touch, instead allowing anticipation to build in the charged space between us. Our bodies' warmth mingled in this narrow territory, creating currents of air that carried my scent to him, his to me. I breathed him in – sandalwood, cedar, and beneath it that unmistakable musk of maleness that wakens something primitive in me, a scent that calls forth hunger from places I sometimes forget exist.

"Most people," I murmured, close enough that my breath warmed the exposed skin above his collar, "experience touch most profoundly when they cannot predict where it will land."

When my fingers finally connected with the precise knot of his tie, I felt the infinitesimal shudder that passed through him, that first surrender of his nervous system to unexpected pleasure. I didn't immediately loosen the silk, but traced its pattern against his throat, applying just enough pressure to remind him of the restriction while promising its eventual release. The expensive fabric warmed beneath my touch, absorbing heat from my fingertips.

"The mind," I continued, finally beginning to loosen the knot with ceremonial slowness, "constantly builds barriers against complete sensation. Analyzing, categorizing, preparing responses rather than fully receiving information."

The silk whispered free from his collar, slipping away like water between my fingers. I moved to stand before him again, close enough now that my breasts nearly brushed his chest with each breath. My nipples, already hardening beneath silk, ached for that momentary contact. His eyelids flickered but remained closed, honoring our unspoken contract despite evident temptation.

I addressed each button of his shirt with deliberate attention, my fingers occasionally grazing the skin beneath, each contact brief enough to create hunger rather than satisfaction. The gradual unveiling of his body: tanned skin stretched over muscle maintained through disciplined dawn workouts, revealed a form as controlled as his mind, cultivated with the same exacting standards as his portfolio.

When I pushed the fine cotton from his shoulders, I let my palms follow the contours of his arms as the fabric descended, mapping territories his bespoke suits usually concealed from touch. The light dusting of hair on his forearms raised beneath my touch, his skin responding with a honesty his expression still fought to contain.

"Keep your eyes closed," I reminded him as my fingers found his belt. "Trust occurs first in darkness."

This deliberate disrobing, this methodical dismantling of exterior protection, continued until he stood completely naked before me, my own clothing still intact. This intentional imbalance shifted power into perfect asymmetry, his vulnerability heightened by my continued coverage. Yet despite his nakedness, his body maintained its vigilance: abdomen tight, shoulders squared, even his breathing controlled. A man physically bare yet still fully armored in habitual restraint.

His cock stood half-aroused between his thighs, already substantial but not yet fully awakened. I refrained from touching it, though my fingers ached to trace the thick vein running along its underside. That deliberate denial created a tension more potent than immediate gratification ever could.

"You've trained your body never to reveal what it wants," I observed, my fingertips grazing his chest with butterfly lightness. "So thoroughly that you may no longer recognize its desires yourself."

His throat constricted around an unspoken response, the movement revealing more than any words could have. I guided him backward until his legs met the edge of my bed, the point of decision between standing and surrender. When gentle pressure against his chest suggested reclining, another moment of resistance preceded his acceptance, that constant negotiation between control and release playing visibly beneath his skin.

The linens, Nepalese silk chosen specifically for their tactile properties, welcomed him with a whispering caress. I directed his arms skyward, stretching them toward my headboard in a configuration that simultaneously exposed and neutralized him. His form against my bedclothes, all ridges and contours softened by coppery illumination, crafted its own wordless verse, a visual summons to contact that kindled something elemental within me. This formidable figure arranged in consensual defenselessness stirred me more profoundly than any choreographed enticement could have. Between his thighs, his cock continued its gradual awakening, thickening and lengthening as if drinking in the atmosphere of surrender through pores in its sensitive skin.

"Your only task," I murmured, retrieving the silk tie I had removed earlier, "is to feel everything, exactly as it comes to you." I wrapped the black silk around his wrists with deliberate gentleness, binding them together above his head. The restraint was symbolic rather than restricting; he could have freed himself with minimal effort. Its purpose lay not in physical constraint but in psychological permission, creating context where surrender became conscious choice rather than capitulation.

"Now," I said, voice descending to the register I reserve for moments of genuine desire, "you have no responsibilities. No decisions to make. Nothing to manage or direct."

I began removing my attire, each garment shed with deliberate ceremony. Though his vision remained veiled, his other senses monitored my undressing: the rustle of chiffon against flesh, the faint symphony of hooks unfastening, the altered acoustics as fabric rarified the atmosphere between us. His imagination, I recognized, would create scenarios more provocative than vision could deliver: that remarkable facility for conjuring longing from inference rather than disclosure.

As I released the final clasp, allowing my black lace bra to fall away, my nipples contracted in the cool evening air – dusky rose peaks eager for attention. Between my thighs, a delicious heaviness gathered, moisture already collecting behind the thin barrier of silk still covering me. I slipped my thumbs beneath the elastic at my hips and pushed downward, the whisper of fabric against skin creating its own secretive melody.

When I finally joined him on the bed, the first contact between our naked skin sent visible current through his body, a tremor beginning where my thigh pressed against his and traveling upward like summer lightning beneath the surface. His breath caught, held, then released in a slow exhalation that communicated everything his words had not: anticipation, apprehension, arousal intertwined in that single breath.

I positioned myself above him, knees bracketing his hips without fully lowering my weight, close enough that the heat between us created its own atmosphere, that the electricity of nearly-touching intensified each nerve ending to painful awareness. His erection had now reached its full magnificence, rising thick and urgent between us, the swollen head flushed deep crimson, a single glistening drop collecting at its tip like dew on velvet. My sex hovered inches above his rigid shaft, my labia already slick and swollen with anticipation, the scent of my arousal mingling with his in the heated air between our bodies.

"In your world," I whispered, lowering until my breasts barely grazed his chest, creating points of exquisite connection that appeared and disappeared with each breath, "you orchestrate according to strategy. In mine, we orchestrate according to sensation."

My mouth found his with deliberate precision, the kiss beginning with such delicate contact that it existed more as promise than fulfillment. Without his hands to direct the pressure or angle, without vision to anticipate movement, he had no choice but to receive, to experience the kiss as pure sensation outside his direction. I felt the moment when something yielded within him, when analysis surrendered to experience, when the mind that calculated billions relinquished calculation entirely.

His lips softened beneath mine, his tongue meeting my explorations with responsive heat rather than directive pressure. The subtle shift transformed our connection instantly, from transaction to genuine exchange, from performance to authentic presence. The taste of bourbon lingered on his tongue, mingling with the undeniable flavor of his arousal – a heady masculine essence that wakened something primal within me.

With this initial fortification breached, I commenced my exploration of his physique, a measured reconnaissance designed to rouse rather than simply excite. My lips journeyed past the predictable domains of torso and midriff to geographies frequently disregarded: the responsive depression alongside his sternum, the delicate skin behind his knee, the commonly-ignored frontier where waist curves into hipbone. Each discovered sensitivity became its own domain, cultivated with exacting devotion before I proceeded onward.

Without sight to categorize these sensations, without hands to direct their application, he experienced each touch with extraordinary immediacy, his nervous system registering pleasure without the filtering lens of analysis or control. His responses grew increasingly vocal, increasingly honest, sounds emerging from somewhere far beneath his cultivated exterior.

His cock responded with similar authenticity, hardening further against his abdomen with an insistence that contradicted his professional restraint. The impressive length of him strained upward, now fully engorged and throbbing visibly with each heartbeat. The head had swelled beyond the confines of its foreskin, exposing the sensitive glans – glistening, purple-red, and exquisitely vulnerable. Clear evidence of his desire continued to seep from its tiny opening, creating a slick trail that caught the amber light. Yet even here, I deliberately avoided direct contact, instead attending to adjacent territories with maddening precision. This carefully orchestrated delay, this stimulation of peripheral desire rather than its direct focus, intensified his sensitivity beyond ordinary boundaries.

When I finally took him into my mouth, the sound that escaped him contained nothing of boardroom composure, a raw, unfiltered response drawn from primitive brain regions that recognized no corporate hierarchies. The silken heat of my mouth enveloped him completely, my tongue tracing patterns along his length as I took him deeper, tasting the salt-sweet essence of his mounting desire. His cock pulsed against my palate, the velvety smoothness of its skin contrasting with the rigid steel beneath. I drew him deeper still, relaxing my throat to accommodate his considerable girth, my nose brushing against the taut muscles of his lower abdomen.

His hips lifted involuntarily, seeking deeper contact, but I withdrew slightly, maintaining orchestration of our connection.

"Patience," I murmured against his inner thigh, my breath hot against his wet skin. "Surrender comes in stages, not all at once."

I continued this deliberate oscillation between granting and withholding, between direct stimulation and tangential attention, watching his responses with rapt focus. His breathing established new patterns: deeper, less measured, occasionally catching on small sounds that revealed the dissolution of his careful self-management. The flush that had begun at his chest now spread across his throat, rising toward his face, physical evidence of barriers falling.

Between my own thighs, swollen tissues throbbed with increasing urgency. My sex had opened like a night-blooming flower, petals unfurling, nectar flowing with unrestrained abundance. Each time I took him into my mouth, each moan that escaped his throat, intensified the ache spreading through my pelvis – a delicious emptiness demanding to be filled.

When I finally straddled him, guiding his hardness inside me with exquisite slowness, his entire body responded with seismic intensity. The hot, thick length of him stretched me deliciously as I lowered myself inch by measured inch, my own wetness easing his entry while heightening every sensation. My labia parted around his substantial girth, the sensitive tissues clinging to him as if reluctant to release even momentarily. I felt the tension in his bound wrists above his head, not fighting the restraint but anchoring against sensation that threatened to overwhelm his remaining control. The penetration itself became ceremony: each millimeter of connection creating waves of pleasure that radiated outward through both our bodies.

I placed my palms flat against his chest, feeling his heartbeat accelerate beneath my touch. "Don't move," I instructed softly, my voice carrying the texture of my own mounting desire. "Let me create this for both of us."

I began to move above him with deliberate rhythm, controlling every aspect of our connection: the depth, angle, and tempo of each movement orchestrated to build pleasure in gradual waves rather than direct surges. My inner muscles gripped him with deliberate contractions, drawing gasps from his throat as I squeezed him with purposeful intensity, then released. Without ability to thrust upward, to establish his own cadence, he had no choice but to receive the sensation as I crafted it, to surrender to pleasure outside his direction.

Our joining created its own liquid symphony – the wet, succulent sounds of flesh meeting flesh, the subtle suction as I lifted, the soft impact as I descended. My clitoris, swollen and exquisitely sensitive, brushed against his pubic bone with each downward motion, sending electric currents shooting through my core.

The conflict manifested visibly across his countenance, that struggle between ingrained restraint and urgent liberation. His eyelids remained lowered as directed, yet his face disclosed everything: yearning, exasperation, euphoria, defenselessness rotating with unvarnished clarity across expressions typically preserved in calculated impassivity. I wondered if his business challengers ever glimpsed such unedited authenticity from him, if anyone in his realm ever gained access beneath his tactical veneer.

I continued our rhythm with precise attention, each adjustment guided by his responses: the hitching of breath when I shifted forward, the tension in his thighs when I slowed beyond expectation, the subtle lifting of his hips when I found exactly the right angle. My own pleasure built alongside his, my body responding to the beautiful contradiction of his strength held in voluntary constraint. My wetness increased as I moved above him, the slick sounds of our joining filling the room with the unmistakable melody of mutual hunger. My breasts swayed with each movement, nipples drawn into tight peaks that ached for contact.

"I can't—" he gasped, words fragmented by mounting sensation. "I need to—"

"You don't need to do anything," I reminded him, deliberately slowing my movements to extend his exquisite liminality. "Only feel. Only receive."

A sound escaped him then, something between frustration and revelation, a vocalization that belonged to no language yet communicated everything. His head pressed backward into the pillow, throat exposed, tendons standing in sharp relief against skin flushed with blood drawn to the surface by unstoppable response.

"Please," he whispered, the single syllable constituting the most profound surrender, a man accustomed to instruction now reduced to supplication.

I reached forward and released his wrists from their silken binding. "Touch me," I invited, "but don't try to control."

The distinction, subtle yet essential, registered instantly. His hands met my skin with reverent heat, exploring the landscape of my body with appreciative rather than directive intent. Something had shifted in him, an understanding that went beyond intellect. His touch followed the rhythms I had set, enhancing rather than commanding our connection. His fingers found my breasts, cupping them with perfect pressure, thumbs circling my hardened nipples with devotional care that sent lightning between my thighs. One hand drifted lower, to where we were joined, his thumb finding my clitoris: swollen, glistening, fully emerged from its hood and thrumming with arousal.

This perfect middle path between complete passivity and attempted dominance, this attentive participation without management, represented surrender in its most mature form. Not the submission of weakness but the yielding of strength, the conscious decision to experience without directing.

As pleasure mounted toward inevitable resolution, his face revealed complete transformation. The careful mask of competence, the strategic neutrality that surely served him in negotiation, had dissolved entirely. In its place emerged raw authenticity: a man experiencing sensation without mediation, without calculation, without the constant self-monitoring that had likely accompanied his every waking moment for decades.

When culmination eventually seized him, it materialized not as the linear carnal gratification that most accept, but as comprehensive corporeal capitulation: every sinew, every sensory terminus, every fiber engaging in delight that conspicuously surpassed mere physical consummation. His cock pulsed violently inside me, his hot release flooding my depths in powerful jets as his entire body arched in abandoned ecstasy. The utterance that heralded this release harbored no theatricality, no calibration, a vocalization divested of all pretense. My own crescendo ensued nearly instantaneously, catalyzed as much by the splendor of his relinquishment as by tangible provocation. My inner walls clenched rhythmically around his thickness, milking every drop of his pleasure as wave after wave of my own orgasm crashed through me. My clitoris throbbed beneath his touch, each pulse sending new contractions rippling through my pelvis – an endless feedback loop of sensation that seemed to transcend my physical form and dissolve the boundaries of selfhood itself.

In the quiet aftermath, I allowed silence to blanket us both, creating space for integration rather than immediate analysis. His breathing gradually slowed, his consciousness visibly expanding beyond the narrow focus of sensation, awareness returning to context, to circumstance, to the vulnerability he had permitted himself.

When he finally opened his eyes, they held momentary disorientation, that curious liminal space between complete immersion and returning cognition. His gaze found mine, holding a question that answered itself in the asking.

"That was..." he began, then paused, seemingly beyond language, unusual for a man whose fortune had been built on precise verbal articulation.

"Beyond category," I suggested, my fingers tracing idle constellations across his chest, still flushed with exertion.

"Yes." A smile touched his mouth, softening features normally maintained in authoritative neutrality. "I had no idea it could feel like that — to simply experience without managing the outcome."

"Most don't," I acknowledged, watching how the evening light transformed his skin to burnished gold, how vulnerability had somehow enhanced rather than diminished his inherent power. "We're conditioned to believe that pleasure, like profit, must be actively pursued, captured, maximized."

His hand found mine, fingers interlacing with natural symmetry. "In finance, we perform constant calculations: risk against reward, input against output, investment against return. This felt like... surrender without the spreadsheet. Vulnerability without the risk assessment."

The metaphor, so perfectly aligned with his worldview, made me smile. "The most profound pleasure often requires precisely that, trust without prospectus, surrender without projected outcomes."

We spoke then of the exhaustion that accompanies perpetual vigilance, of the weight of decisions that affect thousands, of the peculiar liberation found in temporary abdication of control. As darkness gathered outside my windows, Monaco's lights emerging like earthbound stars, his revelations flowed with increasing ease, professional armor yielding to human disclosure with each passing moment.

"I should go," he said eventually, though his body remained relaxed against my sheets, contradicting his stated intention.

"You could stay," I offered simply.

The suggestion presented its own challenge, extending vulnerability beyond the sanctioned parameters of our arrangement into undefined territory. I watched him consider this proposition with the same careful assessment he likely applied to investment opportunities, weighing variables, calculating potential outcomes.

"Yes," he said finally. A single syllable that somehow contained more surrender than our entire physical encounter. "I'd like that."

The night enfolded us like velvet, darkness softening the boundaries between professional arrangement and human connection. I listened to his breathing gradually deepen into sleep, that final surrender of consciousness itself, the relinquishment of the vigilance we maintain even in solitude. This man who controlled billions, who shaped industries with decisions, who maintained perpetual calculation, had surrendered to the most vulnerable state we can share with another, unguarded unconsciousness.

Dawn emerged with quintessential Riviera grandeur, radiance cascading through my casements to suffuse my chambers with molten bronze. I observed his awakening, that captivating instant when consciousness reconstructs itself following slumber's temporary oblivion, when personhood reconstitutes from shapeless vulnerability. His gaze, encountering mine, possessed a lucidity I hadn't discerned during our nocturnal exchange.

"I've been thinking," he said, voice carrying the particular texture that only sleep can impart.

"A dangerous activity," I teased gently, my fingers finding the silver threads at his temple that seemed to catch morning light with particular brilliance.

His smile transformed his features with unexpected boyishness. "Perhaps what makes surrender so powerful is precisely its temporary nature. If one remained permanently in that state—"

"It would no longer be surrender," I completed his thought, understanding immediately. "It would simply be submission."

"Exactly." He propped himself on one elbow, studying my face with new attention. "It's the conscious choice, the deliberate relinquishment of control, that creates its value."

This insight, this understanding of surrender as dynamic choice rather than static condition, revealed how completely he had assimilated the experience. Not merely as physical pleasure but as conceptual framework, as potential wisdom to carry beyond our encounter.

As he dressed with methodical care, resuming his exterior armor piece by precisely adjusted piece, I observed subtle differences in how he inhabited his body, a fluidity beneath the structure, a suppleness within the strength. The night's lessons had not diminished his natural authority but somehow enhanced it, as if in experiencing his capacity for yielding, he had discovered new dimensions of his power.

At my door, he turned back with uncharacteristic spontaneity, his hand finding mine in a gesture more intimate than our physical connection had been.

"Thank you," he said simply, the words carrying none of the transaction's acknowledgment but something more profound, gratitude not for services rendered but for transformation facilitated.

After he had gone, I stood at my window watching Monaco awakening to morning possibility, considering the alchemy I had witnessed. This man who commanded global finance had discovered treasure not in acquisition but in relinquishment, not in mastery but in its momentary suspension. The paradox contained perfect symmetry: that one must possess complete control before its surrender offers liberation, that strength finds its ultimate expression not in constant assertion but in knowing when to yield.

I contemplated the miracle of his metamorphosis, from tactical orchestrator to incarnate presence, from executive statistician to genuine entity. Throughout my vocation, I've witnessed innumerable variations of gratification, yet few rival the profundity of that juncture when a meticulously regulated individual discovers the magnificent liberation waiting just beyond the perimeter of their fastidious governance.

Perhaps this encapsulates the most precious revelation from my decades of intimate scrutiny: that capitulation constitutes not strength's antithesis but its culmination, not authority's desertion but its refinement into something more pliant, more attuned, more vibrant. Like mercury conforming to whatever vessel contains it while gradually transmuting the hardest metals, like the reed that submits to tempests yet endures when granite fractures, we discover our quintessential potential not through unyielding opposition but through calculated acquiescence, not via ceaseless declaration but through recognizing precisely when to concede.

•

In the secret theaters of intimacy, surrender and control perform their eternal ballet, each drawing luminescence from the other's shadow. What continues to enchant me after decades of observation is the transformative alchemy that occurs in this delicate exchange – how bodies long encased in armor suddenly flow like quicksilver, how spirits confined to calculation discover flight in momentary abandon.

The dance between surrender and power moves through us like an ancient tide, rising and receding in patterns as old as desire itself. I've witnessed this metamorphosis most dramatically in those who wear authority like a second skin – these commanders of industry and finance who have forgotten the sweet liberation of momentary release. For them, surrender isn't merely pleasurable but essential – the necessary counterweight to lives spent in constant vigilance and decision.

What fascinates me is how this surrender transcends mere submission, creating instead a living current of exchange. Where submission flows in one direction only, true surrender establishes a reciprocal current – giving and receiving intertwined like lovers' bodies, each finding completion in the other's presence. This sacred reciprocity transforms what might be mere physical coupling into a form of temporary transcendence – a dissolution of boundaries that paradoxically strengthens rather than diminishes.

The body, in its profound wisdom, understands what the mind often forgets – that strength requires flexibility to endure, that power discovers its truest expression not in constant assertion but in knowing precisely when to yield. Like the martial artist who redirects force rather than resisting it directly, those who master surrender discover capacities beyond what rigid control allows. I've watched countless powerful figures discover this truth on my silk sheets, their carefully constructed identities momentarily dissolving to reveal the raw, extraordinary humanity beneath professional armor.

My venture capitalist's journey reflects a universal truth I've observed across thousands of encounters – that our capacity for pleasure expands in direct proportion to our willingness to release control. When we momentarily set aside the exhausting vigil of constant analysis, different channels open within our bodies and spirits, allowing sensation to flow without the filtering screens of judgment and anticipation. Our pleasure becomes oceanic rather than channeled, expansive rather than directed, encompassing rather than pursued.

What moves me most deeply is how this transformation rarely remains confined to our nocturnal discoveries. I've received countless confidences from former clients who found this lesson permeating other domains – executives who became more flexible in negotiations, strategists more receptive to unexpected perspectives, controllers who discovered the strange power that comes from occasionally surrendering certainty. Like water finding hidden passages through seemingly impenetrable stone, the wisdom of surrender inevitably flows beyond the bedroom into the wider territories of life.

The beautiful paradox at surrender's heart is that what appears externally as vulnerability requires profound inner strength – the courage to exist, even momentarily, without our carefully engineered defenses, to experience life directly rather than through the mediating lens of analysis, to trust another being not just with our bodies but with our unguarded essence. This nakedness demands greater bravery than any assertion, more confidence than any command.

Perhaps this explains why genuine surrender remains uncommon despite its extraordinary gifts. Our culture celebrates dominance and control while viewing surrender with suspicion, never recognizing that the most profound mastery exists not in perfect command but in perfect balance – knowing when to grasp and when to release, when to direct and when to yield, when to speak and when to listen.

I've come to believe, watching the miracle of transformation unfold countless times within these walls, that true wisdom lives in this dynamic equilibrium – in understanding that sometimes letting go carries us to territories unreachable through determination alone, to realms of pleasure existing beyond the mapped borders of our planning, to experiences that transform us precisely because we allowed them to unfold rather than attempting to orchestrate their every moment.

The Lesson:

True surrender begins in the mind, not the body. Before physical release can happen, we must first let go of our addiction to constant evaluation: that relentless inner voice that labels, judges, and calculates each moment before we've truly experienced it. This mental surrender creates the foundation for pleasure that transcends ordinary sensation.

Start with simple moments of presence. During intimate encounters, bring your full attention to just one sensation: the warmth of skin beneath your palms, the cadence of your lover's breathing, the precise point where your bodies connect. When thoughts inevitably arise, simply notice them without attachment before returning to pure sensation.

Try small surrenders that ease the transition from control to release. Let your partner guide your shared journey without intervention, not to please them at your expense, but to discover pleasures beyond your familiar patterns. Close your eyes to heighten your sense of touch. Experience gentle restraint not as limitation but as freedom from the burden of always deciding what comes next.

For those who find surrender difficult, especially those accustomed to command in other areas of life, begin with clearly defined explorations beyond control. Like learning to swim starting in shallow water, create conditions where surrender feels safe before venturing into deeper vulnerability. Remember that true surrender paradoxically requires strength rather than weakness, the confidence to temporarily set aside competence.

Most importantly, understand that surrender exists not as a permanent state but as a choice we make and remake in each moment. Its power lives precisely in its voluntary nature, in the conscious decision to temporarily release control, to experience life's current without constantly trying to direct its flow.

The Enduring Connection

Rain streams down my windows tonight, transforming Monaco's lights into liquid gold. Each droplet catches and fractures the illumination from the harbor below, creating a constellation of trembling stars that mirror the ache I feel beneath my ribs. The warmth of my apartment contrasts with the cool glass beneath my fingertips as I trace the path of a single raindrop, its journey both inevitable and unpredictable, much like desire itself.

Tonight, like many nights, I find myself alone with my reflections. The confession feels strange coming from someone whose body has been a harbor for countless men, whose flesh has been the parchment upon which others have written their temporary ecstasies. Yet perhaps this is precisely what qualifies me to speak of connection. I understand its absence intimately: the way it hollows spaces between ribs, the particular weight it adds to limbs, the way it changes the taste of wine on the tongue.

My body remembers every touch it has received, each sensation preserved like pressed flowers between pages of memory. I recall the banker whose fingertips trembled when they first encountered the soft underside of my breast, as if touching something sacred. I remember the violinist whose hands, so precise with strings, became gloriously clumsy with desire when they explored the curve where my waist becomes hip. I can still feel the architect whose mouth would form perfect circles against my skin, each kiss a sealed promise, each breath a whispered secret. My nerves have cataloged these moments with meticulous precision, yet memory is a poor substitute for present skin.

As I press my palm against the cool window, I feel the phantom impression of countless hands that have traveled my body with varying degrees of attention. Some touched merely to take, fingers urgent and demanding against my flesh, their need consuming rather than acknowledging. Others touched to give, palms warm and generous as they awakened nerve endings I hadn't known existed, their pleasure emerging from mine like echo from original sound. But the rarest, the ones that haunt me most, touched to truly know, their contact a form of recognition that transcended the merely physical, their fingertips reading my body like Braille, deciphering the language written beneath my skin.

Those are the touches I contemplate tonight as I consider the enduring connection that has eluded me but whose absence has taught me to recognize its essential qualities, like a cartographer mapping territories she has never personally explored but understands through negative space.

For twenty-four years, I have served as temporary harbor for those whose intimate ships have lost their bearings. My body has become the shore where they briefly rest before returning to the deeper waters of their established lives. This unique vantage point has allowed me to observe the topography of connection through its absence, to understand wholeness through fragments, to recognize sustenance through hunger.

"I love my wife," they tell me, their voices catching in their throats as my fingers trace the tension accumulated in their shoulders. I feel the truth of this statement in their bodies: how they simultaneously tense and yield at the confession, the way their pulse quickens almost imperceptibly beneath my touch. "But something has disappeared between us."

Their bodies speak more honestly than their words, revealing the precise nature of what has been lost. In the way they startle at genuine eye contact, I see years of being looked at without being seen. In their surprised gasp when touched with full attention: when my hand slides deliberately down the plane of their abdomen, when my mouth claims theirs with unhurried intensity, I feel the gradual erosion of presence in their marriage. In the tears that sometimes come unexpectedly, not during climax but in quiet moments afterward when defenses have been temporarily dissolved by pleasure, I witness grief for connection once vital that has faded through mutual neglect.

I remember one man in particular, a diplomat accustomed to perfect composure. After we had made love with unexpected intensity, his sex still pulsing inside me as the final tremors of his release subsided, he buried his face against my neck, his body shaking with silent sobs he couldn't explain. His skin remained flushed with pleasure even as his shoulders heaved with emotion, the physical manifestation of joy and grief intertwined. When he finally spoke, his warm breath against my damp skin carried the bewildered pain of someone suddenly confronting a loss they hadn't fully acknowledged: "I'd forgotten what it felt like—to be touched as if I mattered."

The tragedy wasn't in his seeking pleasure outside his marriage but in the gulf between what he once had and had gradually lost, not through any sudden rupture but through the slow erosion of attention, the silent attrition of presence, the subtle substitution of habit for discovery.

I learn more from these bodily confessions than from hours of conversation. The sudden vulnerability of a man who maintains rigid control in all other aspects of his life, revealed in the moment he surrenders to pleasure: spine arching, control fracturing, a sound escaping his throat that belongs to no language but is understood by all bodies. The startled pleasure when an overlooked erogenous zone receives dedicated attention: the soft skin behind the ear where pulse becomes visible through thin skin, the tender hollow at the base of the throat where breath begins its journey, the exquisitely sensitive crease where thigh meets torso, that private valley known only to intimate cartographers. The way a body remembers what the mind has forgotten: how to surrender, how to receive, how to connect beyond the merely physical.

The irony doesn't escape me, that many who enter long-term partnerships seeking connection often find themselves, years later, paying for temporary intimacy with a stranger. Their bodies arrive bearing the evidence of their disconnection: shoulders perpetually tensed against vulnerability, jaws clenched against authentic expression, breathing shallow and restricted as if fearing to take up too much space in the world. Some wear their wedding bands during our encounters, the gold catching light as their hands move across my skin, fingers parting my slick folds with careful precision. Others remove this symbol, creating a tan line that speaks more honestly than their carefully edited explanations.

"We function perfectly as partners," they tell me, the tension in their lower backs belying the apparent contentment in their words. "But as lovers, we've become strangers." Their bodies yield to my touch with a hunger that reveals the depth of their starvation for genuine contact: sex hardening against my palm with urgent need, hips lifting instinctively toward my mouth, fingers tangling in my hair with desperate intensity.

Perhaps the most common misconception I've observed is the belief that love should maintain itself without deliberate tending, that genuine connection, once established, will naturally sustain itself like a perpetual motion machine, requiring no further energy or attention. Yet the body knows better. It cannot maintain its health without regular nourishment, movement, and care. Why should intimacy be different? Why should the most complex human achievement be the only one expected to flourish without attention?

"When we first met," a client once told me, his voice softening with memory as his fingers traced the curve of my hip, "I noticed everything about her: the particular scent of her hair after rain, the constellation of freckles across her shoulders, the different colors in her eyes depending on what she wore. Now I can be in the same room with her for hours and realize I haven't really looked at her once."

His confession made me shiver despite the warmth of his body pressed against mine, his half-hard sex nestled against my thigh, his hand absent-mindedly cupping my breast as if drawing comfort from its weight. This man didn't lack love for his wife. I could feel genuine affection in the tender way his hands moved over my skin, a tenderness intended for another woman entirely. What he had lost was presence. That quality of focused attention that transforms proximity into connection.

Another client, a brilliant architect whose buildings grace skylines across three continents, described his situation with painful clarity as we lay tangled in sheets still damp from our exertions, the lingering scent of pleasure tangled with designer fragrance: "At home, we've mastered efficiency. We coordinate schedules, divide responsibilities, resolve problems, and plan for the future with admirable precision. But we've become so skilled at managing life together that we've forgotten how to actually live it."

His words crystallized what I believe may be the first essential truth about sustaining connection: intimate relationships require inefficiency. They demand time that could be "better spent," conversations that don't advance practical objectives, touch that serves no purpose beyond itself. The architect's body told the same story. How he initially approached pleasure as a goal to achieve rather than an experience to inhabit, how he had to be taught to slow down, to savor, to allow sensation to build without rushing toward completion. His initial lovemaking had the same efficient lines as his buildings, impressive but somehow missing the organic imperfection that makes a space feel truly inhabited.

The lesson was one I learned long before I entered my profession, through childhood observation that shaped my understanding of what genuine connection looks like. When I was ten, shortly after my father had left, I began spending time at my friend Marie's house in La Trinité. Initially, I went simply because I didn't want to return to the hollow silence of my own home, a space defined by absence rather than presence.

But gradually, I found myself drawn to Marie's house for a different reason entirely: the remarkable connection between her parents. What fascinated me wasn't grand romantic gestures or dramatic declarations of love. It was the quality of their everyday interactions, the way they seemed perpetually engaged in a dance of subtle connection that never fully ceased, as if an invisible thread remained stretched between them regardless of physical distance.

When her father entered a room where her mother worked, his hand would find the small of her back, lingering just long enough to communicate something beyond mere greeting. Their bodies recognized each other before their minds did: a subtle relaxing of shoulders, a slight inclination toward the other's presence, an almost imperceptible deepening of breath. This physical awareness created a current between them that remained active even when they occupied opposite ends of a room.

Most striking to me were their greetings and farewells. When either returned home or prepared to leave, they enacted a ritual that I came to anticipate with a child's fascination. They would put down whatever occupied their hands, grocery bags, newspapers, garden tools, and turn fully toward one another. Their bodies would connect completely, hands gliding across backs, around waists, up to cradle faces. Their kiss wasn't the perfunctory peck I'd observed in other adults, emptied of meaning through repetition. They kissed with genuine presence, with a depth that suggested each time contained its own singular importance.

These moments might last only seconds, yet something in both of them remained transformed afterward. Their faces appeared more relaxed, more beautiful somehow, as if the brief connection had replenished something essential they hadn't known was missing. Lines softened, eyes brightened. Even their silence felt fuller, more resonant. The air in the room seemed to shift in response, as though intimacy had altered its molecular structure. It became thicker, more vibrant: charged with an invisible current that even I, a child observer tucked quietly nearby, could feel on my skin like the electric anticipation before a summer storm. I didn't have the words for it then, but I understood it viscerally: something unseen had passed between them, something real. And for a moment, the ordinary world around us felt like it was holding its breath.

I would return home afterward to our silent house, my chest tight with longing, with grief, with a child's inarticulate understanding that something essential had been stolen from my life. I became a student of intimacy long before I understood what I was studying, cataloging the visible evidence of invisible bonds.

Only years later did I realize what I had been witnessing in Marie's kitchen: an entire life constructed as extended foreplay. Every interaction contained an undercurrent of appreciation, of desire, of genuine seeing that culminated in moments of physical connection. They created countless moments throughout ordinary days that communicated to each other not just through words but through bodily presence: you are valued, you are desired, you are irreplaceable to me.

This memory stands in stark contrast to what I've come to think of as "lonely couples", those legally, financially, and logistically connected yet spiritually isolated from one another. I recognize them instantly at Monaco's restaurants and social events. Their bodies reveal what their social performance attempts to conceal: how they maintain careful distance despite physical proximity, how they've learned to touch without feeling, to talk without listening, to occupy the same space while existing in separate worlds.

Their disconnection often manifests physically as tension held in specific regions: the tight shoulders of someone perpetually braced for criticism, the rigid jaw of suppressed words, the shallow breathing of someone trying to minimize their presence. These bodily adaptations become so habitual that they persist even in private moments, creating physical barriers to sensation and pleasure that no technique, however sophisticated, can fully overcome. Their flesh has learned to construct walls that no casual touch can penetrate.

Presence alone, while necessary, isn't sufficient. In my experience, enduring connection also requires continued curiosity: a willingness to acknowledge that your partner remains, always, partially undiscovered territory, a landscape that shifts with time and requires perpetual re-exploration.

"After fifteen years," a client once told me, his fingers absently tracing the curve of my waist as we lay in post-coital quietude, "I realized I'd stopped exploring my wife's body. I touched the same places, in the same sequence, with the same pressure. I knew exactly which buttons to push for the most efficient result. Then one night, I accidentally discovered an entirely new sensitive spot along her spine, a place I'd touched a thousand times but never with full attention. Her response was so unexpected, so genuine, that I felt as if I were with a stranger."

His voice carried bewilderment, as if he'd discovered an unmapped room in a house he thought he knew completely. This sense of having fully mapped another human being, of having exhausted their mystery, may be intimacy's most subtle poison.

The phenomenon repeats across countless professional encounters: men who approach new sexual partners with meticulous attention to response yet touch long-term partners with thoughtless habit. The same fingers that note every shiver, every catch of breath, every subtle arching of my back become, by their own admission, mechanical in their marital beds. The tragedy lies not in declining desire but in diminished attention, the failure to recognize that familiar bodies contain infinite potential for discovery, that the same landscape viewed at different times of day reveals entirely new territories.

For this discovery requires the courage to remain vulnerable, perhaps the most challenging aspect of sustained connection. With me, clients can be temporarily vulnerable because I pose no real threat: I don't share their daily lives, their social circles, their ongoing narratives. The stakes are comfortably low. I am a safe harbor in which to drop the anchor of truth because they will sail away on the morning tide.

"I can tell you things I've never told my wife," clients often admit, sometimes with pride, sometimes with shame. When I ask why, the answers reveal intimacy's fundamental challenge: "Because you won't use it against me later." "Because you don't need anything from me." "Because disappointing you doesn't have lasting consequences."

Their bodies reveal the same story, how they gradually surrender armor with me that they maintain with those closest to them. The way muscles release tension beneath my touch that they hold rigid at home. The way their sex stands proudly erect when I first unveil it, revealing a vulnerability their words would never confess. The vulnerability they find temporarily in my bed requires continuous courage in long-term relationships, the willingness to remain open to someone who matters tremendously, who could hurt you deeply, who knows your past failures and future fears.

A cardiac surgeon once shared a revelation that had transformed his marriage. "I realized I was treating emotional safety like a destination, somewhere we'd arrive after enough time together. But it's actually a practice, something we create anew each day through how we respond to each other's vulnerability."

His medical background had given him a perfect metaphor: "The heart doesn't beat once and sustain life. It must continue beating, each contraction vital, each moment requiring renewed effort. Intimacy works the same way."

A truth about intimacy that applies to both professional encounters and lifelong partnerships is this: genuine connection often emerges not in carefully choreographed moments but in unexpected ruptures, when we are too exhausted, too vulnerable, too overwhelmed to maintain our usual armor. These moments of authentic vulnerability, properly received, create bonds that endure through subsequent challenges.

Perhaps this explains why certain aspects of long-term relationships generate such anxiety, resignation, and misunderstanding, particularly the evolution of sexual connection. Many clients express this concern with numerical precision: "We used to make love three times a week. Now it's once a month, if that."

The implicit assumption in such statements is that frequency equals vitality, that more is necessarily better. Yet in my experience, this quantitative approach fundamentally misunderstands erotic connection. The couples who sustain sexual vitality across decades aren't necessarily those who maintain the same frequency, but those who preserve the essential qualities that make physical intimacy meaningful: presence, playfulness, vulnerability, and what we might call "productive uncertainty."

One particularly insightful client observed: "The greatest enemy of desire isn't time or familiarity. It's certainty. When intimacy becomes entirely predictable, when we know exactly what will happen, how it will feel, when it will end, something essential dies."

This observation aligns with what psychologists call "optimal arousal theory": the principle that human beings are most engaged by experiences that balance familiarity with novelty, safety with risk. The sweet spot lies between these extremes, creating the conditions where pleasure remains discovering rather than merely confirming. We want enough certainty to feel safe, enough uncertainty to feel alive.

In long-term relationships, maintaining this balance requires deliberate attention to what bodies inherently understand: that repetition without variation eventually dulls sensitivity, that new neural pathways form only when familiar patterns are disrupted. This doesn't require elaborate scenarios or performances, often it's as simple as altering small elements of familiar interactions: changed pressure, unexpected timing, reversed initiation, shifted focus.

"I realized we always touched in the same rhythm, with the same pressure, in the same positions," a client shared during what would be our final meeting, seated across from me in my living room rather than my bed. "So I decided to slow down, to explore her body as if I was discovering it for the first time. I simply let my hands linger in places I usually passed over quickly. The shift in her response was immediate and profound, as if I had awakened nerve endings long dormant."

His eyes held a quiet wonder as he described the transformation in his marriage, his hands gesturing in the space between us, tracing invisible patterns in the air. "I learned to create these gentle circles that spiral inward, the pressure increasing by infinitesimal degrees. My wife's response was unlike anything I'd seen in years." His voice softened with gratitude as he met my gaze. "What you taught me about attention, about truly listening to another body's responses... it saved us. It's like a conversation where each touch is a question and each reaction an answer."

This willingness to disrupt patterns extends beyond physical intimacy to all aspects of connection. The couples who maintain vitality find ways to break routine: to see each other in fresh contexts, to engage in unfamiliar activities together, to continue revealing new aspects of themselves to one another. They understand instinctively that the familiar can become invisible, that we must sometimes alter perspective to see what remains in front of us.

Such deliberate cultivation of novelty creates what neuropsychologists call "encoding opportunities": chances for the brain to form new memories rather than simply strengthening existing patterns. These fresh experiences become part of the relationship's evolving story, preventing the sense that everything significant lies in the past rather than in the present or future.

I've begun to cultivate my own small garden on my apartment terrace: roses and lavender, rosemary and thyme. The rosemary is particularly stubborn, insisting on growing sideways rather than upward no matter how I try to train it. It respects my efforts but ultimately follows its own nature, a lesson in acceptance I'm still learning to embrace. In tending these living things, I've discovered truths that apply to human connection as well. A garden's beauty emerges not despite but because of its continuous change. The same rose that unfurls blood-red petals in summer retracts into protective dormancy during winter, only to emerge again transformed yet recognizable. There is wisdom in this cycle, in knowing when to flourish and when to conserve, when to display magnificence and when to focus on invisible strength-building beneath the surface.

The healthiest long-term connections resemble gardens more than monuments. They embrace evolution rather than resisting it, finding strength in adaptability rather than rigidity. They allow for seasons of dormancy without assuming death, for periods of wild growth without fearing chaos.

This brings me to perhaps the most vital factor in sustaining connection: the willingness to continue choosing one another, not once but daily, not despite changes but because of them. Many clients refer to their initial commitment, marriage vows, promises made years ago, as if it were the definitive moment of choice. Yet genuine commitment isn't a single decision but an ongoing practice of choosing the same person under continuously changing circumstances.

"I've been married to at least five different versions of my wife," a client once observed, his voice carrying a tenderness that contradicted the casual intimacy of our professional arrangement. "The ambitious young professional I first fell for. The gradually softening woman in our thirties. The fierce mother protecting our children. The caregiver when I was ill. And now, the contemplative empty-nester discovering new passions. I've had to fall in love all over again each time, and remarkably, I have."

His words stayed with me long after he left, his body's impression still warm on my sheets, his scent lingering on my skin, a mixture of earthen richness, clean sweat, and the indefinable essence that was uniquely his. There was something profound in this perspective, this recognition that we don't love static entities but evolving beings, that genuine connection requires continuous adaptation rather than fixed expectation.

This willingness to continually rediscover and rechoose one's partner stands in stark contrast to what I often witness in my profession, the pursuit of novelty through continuously changing partners rather than finding renewal within a sustained connection. My body has hosted countless men seeking the temporary thrill of the unknown, the momentary escape from familiarity. Yet what many fail to recognize is how shallow this novelty remains compared to the depths possible within long-term connection that combines security with continued discovery.

I recall vividly a conversation with a client who had sought my services regularly for years. Between his frequent international trips and his wife's demanding career, they had gradually constructed lives that functioned efficiently in parallel rather than in genuine connection. He justified his extramarital activities with the familiar refrain: "We've grown apart. The spark is gone."

During one visit, something shifted in his perspective. "I realized recently," he said, his voice uncharacteristically reflective, fingers tracing abstract patterns on my bare shoulder, "that I've spent more money and energy pursuing excitement with beautiful strangers than trying to rediscover it with the woman I claim to love. What would happen if I invested that attention in my marriage instead?"

Six months later, he contacted me, not to schedule an appointment but to thank me for our conversations. "We're seeing a therapist together," he explained. "It's the hardest work I've ever done, but also the most rewarding. I'm discovering aspects of my wife I never knew existed, or perhaps never bothered to see."

This willingness to redirect attention, to invest in renewal rather than replacement, represents perhaps the most courageous choice in long-term intimacy. It requires acknowledging that connection doesn't maintain itself but must be continuously recreated through deliberate attention.

Reflecting on the countless bodies I've known over more than two decades, I've noticed striking patterns. The relationships that remain vital, regardless of personality, background, or circumstance, share certain core practices. They value presence over efficiency. They stay curious instead of assuming they fully know one another. They create space for ongoing vulnerability. They balance safety with a touch of productive uncertainty. They view the relationship as a living narrative, not a finished accomplishment. And perhaps most importantly, they keep choosing each other—again and again—not despite change, but because of it.

None of these practices requires extraordinary talent or inexhaustible energy. What they demand instead is attention, the willingness to direct our finite awareness toward what we value most. In a culture designed to fragment and commodify our attention, this choice becomes increasingly radical.

•

My body has become a vessel for other people's desires, yet also an instrument for recording the subtle music of human connection. Through the landscape of my skin, I have observed with clinical precision how the mind creates maps that filter bodily experience: how thoughts about pleasure often prevent its direct experience, how preconceptions about intimacy create the very disconnections they fear. This curious duality, being simultaneously inside and outside the experience, has afforded me a perspective few others possess. Like a sensitive instrument recording tremors too subtle for ordinary detection, my professional encounters have allowed me to catalog the invisible currents that flow beneath the surface of human connection.

What emerges from this embodied research surprises me still. The power dynamics we imagine governing sexuality dissolve into something more complex when observed closely. The physically strong man who surrenders completely at the moment of climax, tears streaming unbidden down his face. The controlling executive who begs to be dominated, to surrender choice entirely. The intellectual who becomes wordless animal when pleasure overtakes analysis. These contradictions reveal something essential about desire itself. How it exists as counterpoint to our daylight identities, how it flows between polarity like electricity seeking completion.

I have witnessed through the intimate laboratory of my bedroom what psychology and neuroscience now confirm: that our bodies house wisdom older than thought, that the skin remembers what the mind forgets, that connection requires not perfect technique but perfect attention. When a lover truly sees us, not the projection of their desires, but our authentic, imperfect being, our nervous systems respond with a recognition that transcends social performance. The body knows truth from falsehood, presence from pretense. It registers the difference between touch that takes and touch that truly knows.

The Lesson:

Enduring connection requires devotion to practices rather than pursuit of ideals. To sustain intimate vitality over time, we must prioritize presence over efficiency, never assuming we've fully discovered another. Creating space for vulnerability, especially when it feels risky, builds the foundation for deeper connection. The balance between security and novelty, finding comfort without stagnation, keeps desire alive through decades.

Above all, recognize that meaningful connection isn't maintained through a single commitment but through thousands of small rechoosings: seeing your partner with fresh eyes despite familiarity, adapting to their evolution rather than clinging to who they once were. The most profound intimacy emerges not from perfect technique but from perfect attention: the willingness to truly witness another's authentic being, to consistently direct your awareness toward what you value most.

Final Reflection:

The rain has stopped now, leaving Monaco wrapped in the particular silence that follows precipitation, a hush that seems to invite confession. From my window, I can see lights gradually appearing in apartments across the harbor, each illuminated window representing lives intertwined in ways I can only imagine. I wonder how many contain the quiet miracle of sustained connection, that rarest and most precious of human achievements.

I have spent my professional life providing moments of intimacy to those who seek them outside their established relationships. I have created temporary spaces of attention, of presence, of focused care. I have listened to thousands of variations on the same essential story: the gradual fading of connection through neglect rather than rejection.

What most clients don't realize is how their stories have affected me, how each confession, each moment of vulnerability, each glimpse of genuine longing has shaped my understanding not just of connection but of myself. The weight of all these borrowed intimacies has sometimes felt like a wave gathering strength, preparing to break against the shore of my own solitude.

The truth I rarely admit, even to myself, emerges now in the darkness: there are nights when professional fulfillment feels hollow against the absence of the connection I've helped others understand. There are mornings when I wake reaching for someone who isn't there, has never been there, my skin hungry for touch that carries recognition rather than transaction. There are moments when being the vessel for others' intimacy while remaining fundamentally alone feels like a wound that refuses to heal, a persistent ache beneath my ribs, a heaviness that no amount of professional satisfaction can fully lighten.

Yet in charting connection's landscape from my position as observer rather than participant, I have developed an appreciation for its value that might otherwise have eluded me. Sometimes I think my professional life has been a long preparation, an education in what matters most, in what I might someday be brave enough to seek for myself.

If there is wisdom in my experience, perhaps it lies not in specific techniques or strategies but in a simple truth: what we attend to flourishes; what we ignore diminishes. Sustained intimacy isn't a state to achieve but a practice to maintain: a daily choice to see, to listen, to touch, to remain curious, to continue discovering the ever-changing person with whom we share our lives.

Tonight, I send these words into the world like seeds cast on uncertain soil. May they take root where they're needed. May they help those who find them to nurture the connections they value most. And perhaps, in some future I cannot yet imagine, may they help me find my way home to the connection I've spent a lifetime studying but never fully known.

Epilogue:
The Continuing Education

The Mediterranean stretches before me, its surface transformed into liquid gold by the setting sun. From my terrace, Monaco presents itself as a glittering amphitheater, witness to twenty-four years of my unconventional education. As I look out over this principality that has housed my intimate explorations, I find myself contemplating not endings but continuations, not conclusions but ongoing revelations.

When I began this manuscript, I wondered what wisdom might emerge from documenting these encounters across my career. What patterns would reveal themselves? What universal truths might crystallize from such diverse experiences? The answer, I've discovered, is both simpler and more profound than I anticipated.

Human connection, in all its messy, glorious complexity, defies absolute categorization. Each person who crossed my threshold brought their unique constellation of desires, inhibitions, and potential. What worked beautifully for one might prove entirely wrong for another. The banker whose life was transformed by learning to breathe properly would find little value in the filmmaker's mastery of anticipatory pauses. The marine biologist's revelation about female anatomy might seem elementary to the quantum physicist seeking connection beyond the physical.

And yet, certain truths emerged with such persistence that I cannot help but recognize them as essential:

The most profound intimacy begins with presence. Not performance, not technical mastery, but the revolutionary act of being fully present with another human being. In a world increasingly fractured by distraction, this simple quality has become our rarest gift.

Bodies speak languages the mind often forgets. Beneath our sophisticated reasoning, beneath cultural conditioning and social performance, our physical forms retain wisdom we've spent centuries trying to silence. The hand that instinctively reaches, the pulse that quickens unbidden, the breath that catches at unexpected beauty, these honest responses contain truths our words often obscure.

Pleasure exists not just in sensation but in meaning. The most satisfying encounters I've witnessed were those where physical connection became the medium through which something deeper was exchanged: understanding, recognition, temporary relief from our fundamental aloneness.

Vulnerability and power are not opposing forces but complementary aspects of the same experience. Those moments when a client revealed their unguarded self, whether through surrender or through claiming their desires without apology, often created the most transformative connections.

The greatest barrier to profound pleasure isn't lack of technique but fear: fear of being truly seen, fear of losing control, fear of discovering desires that contradict our carefully constructed identities. Those clients who found the courage to move beyond these fears, even temporarily, accessed depths of experience that technique alone could never provide.

To you, dear reader, who has journeyed through these pages seeking your own transformation, I offer this: Your fears about intimacy are universal, no matter how unique they may feel. The worry that you're somehow inadequate, that your body isn't beautiful enough, that your desires are too much or too little, I have heard these concerns from people of extraordinary beauty, of remarkable intelligence, of substantial power. These anxieties are not evidence of your failings but simply of your humanity.

What separates those who discover profound pleasure from those who merely endure intimacy is not physical perfection or innate talent but a single, courageous decision: the decision to feel. To be present in your body despite its imperfections. To allow yourself vulnerability despite the risks. To acknowledge desire without shame.

I have witnessed this transformation hundreds of times. The businessman whose carefully constructed façade crumbled at the simple touch of a hand against his face, revealing a capacity for tenderness he'd never acknowledged. The perfectionistic woman who finally surrendered control, discovering that her pleasure expanded exponentially when she stopped managing it.

The couple who learned that true intimacy requires not the performance of passion but the courage to reveal what they truly need.

You hold within you the same potential. The techniques described in these pages: the rhythms, the positions, the points of physical pleasure, are merely tools. The real transformation begins with three simple statements of intention that I invite you to consider:

"I want to be excited." Not just aroused in body, but awakened in spirit. Excitement transcends mere physical response; it engages imagination, emotion, and intellect alongside sensation. It requires openness to discovery rather than adherence to routine.

"I want to be aroused." Not as performance or obligation, but as authentic bodily response. True arousal emerges when we stop forcing our bodies to conform to expected reactions and instead allow them to reveal what genuinely stimulates us, which may surprise us, challenge us, even occasionally confuse us.

"I want to feel." Perhaps the most revolutionary statement in a culture that often prioritizes thinking about pleasure over experiencing it. Feeling requires presence, vulnerability, and the willingness to temporarily surrender our carefully constructed identities. It means allowing sensation to move through you without constantly analyzing, evaluating, or directing it.

The obstacles you face are real but surmountable. Cultural conditioning that separates physical pleasure from emotional connection. The vulnerability hangover that follows genuine intimacy. The fear that your authentic desires may alienate rather than attract your partner. I have seen these barriers dissolve not through elaborate techniques but through authentic communication, through treating intimacy as collaborative exploration rather than performance or transaction.

Begin with curiosity rather than expectation. Ask questions, of your own body, of your partner's experience, without presuming you know the answers. Touch with the intention to discover rather than to impress. Breathe fully, allowing your nervous system to register sensation without immediately attempting to categorize or control it. Speak your desires not as demands but as invitations to shared territory.

The most common regret I've heard isn't about trying something and failing, but about never having had the courage to express what was truly wanted. The widow who never told her husband how much she loved feeling his weight against her. The executive who never admitted his desire to temporarily surrender control. The young woman who performed what she thought was expected rather than asking for what would bring her pleasure.

As I bring this manuscript to its conclusion, I realize that my most valuable offering isn't a comprehensive manual of sexual techniques or a definitive map of erogenous zones. It's an invitation to approach intimacy with curiosity rather than certainty, with presence rather than performance, with the understanding that our most profound connections emerge when we allow ourselves to be both student and teacher in the classroom of desire.

I've often been asked if I plan to retire, to leave behind this unconventional career for something more conventional. The question assumes that what I do is separate from who I am, that my profession could be neatly excised from my identity like a benign growth. But after twenty-four years of witnessing humanity in its most vulnerable moments, I've come to understand that this work has never been merely occupation but vocation, not just what I do but who I've become.

The education I've received through these encounters has transformed me as surely as I hope it has transformed those who sought my guidance. Each client has left their imprint, some as delicate as a fingerprint on glass, others as profound as geological shifts that alter one's internal landscape permanently. Together, they've helped create the woman who now writes these words, neither saint nor sinner, neither mere body nor disembodied intellect, but a complete human being who has learned to inhabit the glorious complexity of existence without apology.

Perhaps someday I will step away from active practice, but I will never cease being the woman who learned to see beyond surfaces, who discovered how to read the subtle languages of desire, who developed the patience to wait for authentic connection rather than settling for its convenient counterfeit. These qualities have become as much a part of me as my heartbeat.

•

When examined through the lens of psychology, what emerges most clearly from my years of observation is how profoundly our physical connections reflect our psychological landscape. The anxieties, the defenses, the yearnings that shape our daily interactions manifest with startling clarity in intimate settings. Those who maintain rigid control in professional lives often seek surrender in private; those who habitually please others frequently struggle to articulate their own desires; those who present confidence externally may harbor the deepest fears of inadequacy in intimate contexts.

From an anthropological perspective, I've observed how cultural norms create invisible boundaries around pleasure that few dare to question. Western societies, despite their apparent sexual liberation, often maintain surprisingly rigid expectations about what constitutes "normal" desire. These unspoken limitations constrain authentic expression more effectively than explicit prohibitions ever could. The clients who experienced the most profound transformations were frequently those who recognized and challenged these internalized boundaries.

Most fascinating to me has been witnessing the neurobiological reality of intimacy: how touch, rhythm, breath, and presence physically alter our neurochemistry, creating states of consciousness inaccessible through other means. The integration of mindfulness practices with physical pleasure isn't merely philosophical preference but neurological reality; attention literally changes how sensation is processed, intensifying experience beyond what technique alone could produce.

The Lesson:

The ultimate lesson these and hundreds of other encounters have taught me transcends specific techniques or positions. It is simply this: Extraordinary intimacy emerges not from extraordinary skill but from extraordinary presence. The ability to be fully in your body, fully in the moment, fully with another human being, this quality transforms even the simplest touch into profound connection.

This presence requires practice. Begin by noticing when your mind drifts during intimate moments: planning tomorrow's meetings, wondering how you appear, comparing this experience to previous ones. Gently return your attention to physical sensation, to your breath, to the points of contact between bodies. This mental returning, this refusal to abandon the present moment for past or future, becomes easier with deliberate practice.

Communicate not just preferences but presence. Beyond telling your partner what you enjoy physically, share what helps you remain present: certain kinds of touch, particular environments, specific words. Ask what helps them stay present as well. This conversation itself often creates immediate deepening of connection.

Remember that vulnerability and power exist in dynamic relationship, not opposition. The willingness to be seen in desire, to express needs without guarantee of fulfillment, to reveal your authentic response rather than performing expected reactions, these acts require courage but create possibilities for connection that performance never can.

Above all, approach intimacy as ongoing exploration rather than destination. The moment we believe we've "mastered" physical connection is precisely when we stop discovering its endless variations. Maintain beginner's mind even in long-term relationships, approaching each encounter with curiosity about what might be discovered today, what new territory might be revealed between familiar landscapes.

Final Reflections:

The sun has nearly disappeared now, leaving behind a sky painted in impossible purples and crimsons. Lights begin to illuminate Monaco's elegant façades, each window containing its own universe of human connection and disconnection. Tomorrow, someone new will cross my threshold seeking guidance. They will bring their particular history, their unique constellation of desires and fears, their singular body with its own wisdom and wounds.

I will welcome them not as an expert with definitive answers but as a fellow explorer who has mapped certain territories they've yet to visit. I will offer what I've learned while remaining open to what they might teach me. And in that exchange, that mutual recognition of our imperfect, yearning humanity, we might momentarily transcend the boundaries that separate us, touching something that exists beyond words, beyond technique, beyond the temporary alignment of bodies in space.

This, I believe, is the ultimate wisdom these encounters have taught me: that intimacy, at its most profound, isn't something we perform but something we become: not a destination to reach but a continuous process of revealing and being revealed, a lifelong education in the art of being fully human.

My hope for you, dear reader, is not that you master every technique described in these pages, but that you find the courage to be fully present in your desires, to communicate them without apology, and to receive your partner's vulnerability as the precious gift it is. That you discover pleasure not as achievement but as ongoing exploration, not as performance but as authentic expression of your deepest self.

I am well aware that many find my profession morally objectionable. There are those who believe that what I do is fundamentally wrong, an affront to traditional values, a commodification of what should be sacred, a betrayal of feminine dignity. I understand this perspective, even if I do not share it. The judgment does not surprise me, nor does it diminish the value of what I have learned.

To those readers who may feel uncomfortable with the source of these insights, I offer this thought: The wisdom gained through experience remains valuable regardless of the context in which it was acquired. A doctor learns about healing by witnessing disease. A therapist understands mental health by confronting disorder. I have come to understand intimacy by experiencing its many expressions, some beautiful, some broken, all profoundly human.

Knowledge itself is neutral. What matters is how we apply it, the intentions behind our actions, the care with which we treat those who trust us with their vulnerability. You need not approve of my choices to benefit from the patterns I've observed over thousands of hours of intimate human connection.

The journey continues. The education never ends. And the capacity for profound connection exists within you already, waiting only for your decision to feel.

Isabelle M.

The Shadow Aspects: Acknowledging Reality

Several early readers of this manuscript expressed concern that I was presenting an overly romanticized portrayal of my profession. "You've written eloquently about connection and pleasure," one noted, "but what about the darker aspects? What about difficult or dangerous clients? What about the psychological toll of compartmentalizing intimacy?"

These questions are entirely valid. In focusing primarily on the meaningful encounters and lessons learned throughout my career, I may have inadvertently created an impression that my professional life consists exclusively of enlightening exchanges with respectful, self-aware clients. Reality, as always, contains more nuance.

I would be disingenuous if I didn't acknowledge the darker elements one encounters in my profession. My psychology training equipped me to recognize certain personality patterns that occasionally manifest in men seeking paid intimacy: patterns mirroring what researchers call the "Dark Triad" of narcissism, Machiavellianism, and in rare cases, psychopathic traits.

While psychological research has never established definitive percentages, studies have found moderate correlations between these traits and preferences for certain types of sex work. This isn't to suggest that most clients possess these characteristics, far from it. The research merely indicates tendencies, not causation, and prevalence varies significantly based on individual motivations for seeking intimate services. A man approaching paid companionship seeking genuine connection presents an entirely different psychological profile than one motivated primarily by desire for control.

These individuals approach intimacy as conquest rather than connection. Their lack of empathy reveals itself not through overt cruelty but in subtle dismissals of boundaries, in calculating attempts to negotiate beyond established limits, in a fundamental inability to recognize the humanity behind the service they've purchased.

My anthropology studies provided valuable perspective on these encounters. What I observed in challenging clients often reflected larger cultural narratives about masculinity, power, and entitlement. These men weren't simply expressing individual pathology but embodying specific cultural scripts about what constitutes desirable male behavior. I came to view these interactions as microcosms of larger cultural negotiations around intimacy, power, and exchange.

Early in my career, before developing refined screening methods, I occasionally found myself with such men. There's a distinctive quality to their gaze, a cold assessment that reduces the person before them to components rather than wholeness. Their questions focus exclusively on what they can receive rather than what might be created between us. Their touch betrays an essential disconnect, technically precise perhaps, but devoid of the reciprocity that characterizes genuine human contact.

My approach evolved with experience. Initially, I simply endured these encounters, completing our arrangement with professional detachment while protecting my essential self behind carefully constructed walls. Later, as my confidence and financial stability grew, I developed subtle tests during initial communications, questions designed to reveal capacity for empathy, respect for boundaries, and recognition of mutual humanity.

Through thousands of interactions, I've identified reliable indicators that warrant caution. These subtle red flags rarely announce themselves dramatically, yet they consistently predict problematic encounters:

Excessive negotiation over established boundaries. Those who persistently attempt to redefine my clearly stated limits during initial communications invariably continue this pattern in person. This behavior reflects not misunderstanding but fundamental disregard for consent.

Dismissive language about previous companions. Men who speak derogatively about other women they've hired, criticizing their bodies, performance, or personality, invariably bring that same judgmental energy to our encounter. This pattern reveals how they fundamentally view women in service roles.

Reluctance to provide basic verification information. While discretion is understandable, categorical refusal to participate in basic security protocols often indicates someone accustomed to operating without accountability.

Communication focused exclusively on physical acts. Initial messages that contain detailed physical requests without any interest in establishing rapport typically indicate someone seeking a receptacle rather than a person.

Resistance to direct questions about expectations. Those unable to articulate what they hope to experience beyond generic responses often view me as interchangeable rather than specific, a replaceable object rather than a chosen individual.

Unusually intense focus on discretion beyond professional norms. While privacy concerns are natural, excessive, repeated emphasis on secrecy often indicates problematic double lives or compartmentalization that extends beyond typical married clients.

The "bargain hunter" approach. Those who immediately focus on negotiating rates down or extracting maximum "value" typically bring this same transactional mindset to the intimate encounter itself.

Lack of basic courtesy in communications. Absence of pleasantries, demanding tone, or issuing commands rather than requests reveals how they conceptualize the power dynamic between us.

None of these indicators alone definitively identifies concerning personality traits, but their combination forms patterns that have proven remarkably consistent. My screening process evolved to detect these subtle signals long before physical meeting, creating a first-line defense that serves both my safety and the quality of my professional life.

What surprised me most was discovering how these challenging experiences enhanced my appreciation for the clients who approached our encounters with respect and genuine curiosity. Behind the transactional facade, I recognized patterns of genuine human need: for touch without judgment, for acceptance of desires long suppressed, for momentary escape from lives compartmentalized by expectation. The banker carrying the weight of decisions affecting thousands; the executive starved for genuine connection in his algorithm-driven world.

My observations eventually aligned with broader psychological research suggesting that while Dark Triad traits exist among a subset of clients, many fall into what some researchers call the "Light Triad" category. These individuals display empathy, respect for autonomy, and capacity for genuine human connection despite the commercial context of our engagement.

Two complementary developments transformed my practice. First, my increasingly sophisticated vetting process progressively filtered out individuals likely to view our encounters as conquest rather than exchange. Simultaneously, my perspective evolved. I began approaching each carefully screened client with genuine curiosity rather than defensive assumptions.

This dual transformation, better screening combined with a more open perspective, created a virtuous cycle. As problematic individuals were filtered out, I could engage more authentically with those who remained. And as I engaged more authentically, those clients responded in kind. The mirror I offered reflected not just physical desire but emotional and intellectual complexity. Our encounters increasingly transformed from transaction to genuine exchange, however brief.

Gradually, word spread. Those seeking my company increasingly arrived having been referred by previous clients who understood my particular approach. These new clients came prepared for an experience that offered more than conventional expectations. My questions about desires, fantasies, and boundaries were met not with surprise but appreciation. The financial arrangement remained, but its significance often receded beneath the more meaningful exchange of human recognition.

Security Measures as Professional Wisdom

Understanding these dynamics doesn't negate the need for practical security measures. For those I invite into my home, my sanctuary and workplace both, I've developed a multilayered system of protection that remains largely invisible to clients.

My choice to establish my practice in Monaco wasn't arbitrary. The principality's legal framework allows me to operate without the stress of criminalization. The Monaco police maintain professional awareness of the higher-end companion ecosystem, occasionally sharing information about potentially problematic individuals. This discreet communication represents a pragmatic approach. A recognition that forewarning helps prevent incidents.

Every potential client undergoes thorough verification through a specialized security service that manages my appointments. This arrangement provides an essential buffer, allowing comprehensive background checks and verification of personal details far beyond what I could accomplish alone. The service, staffed by former security professionals, has developed sophisticated methods for screening while maintaining the discretion my clients require. This intermediary not only enhances my safety but adds a layer of professional distance that elevates the entire experience.

My apartment building's security staff knows me well, though they remain discreet. I've cultivated these relationships over years, ensuring that unfamiliar visitors are always noted. Within my apartment, careful design choices serve dual purposes. The graceful layout creates an atmosphere of intimacy while ensuring certain areas remain private, with my bedroom positioned to allow easy exit if necessary.

I've invested in advanced locks, strategically placed security cameras, and cultivated relationships with neighbors who would respond quickly to any unusual disturbance. Over the years, I've developed an acute sensitivity to behavioral cues—those subtle shifts that signal escalating aggression or the early signs of boundary-testing. The appointment service I use is similarly attuned; they've been trained to recognize concerning patterns in tone, timing, or phrasing that may indicate someone unwilling to respect limits. Safety, for me, is not just a matter of precaution—it's a practiced discipline, a quietly vigilant part of the work I do every day.

There are, of course, additional security measures I choose not to detail. Some protections are effective precisely because they remain invisible. This calculated opacity is not born of paranoia but of prudent foresight, another aspect of professional wisdom.

I've also learned to be selective about Monaco's social calendar. I deliberately avoid periods like the Monaco Yacht Show and Formula 1 weekend, with their influx of visitors viewing women primarily as decorative accessories. These environments create an atmosphere of objectification antithetical to my approach.

These security measures serve a purpose far beyond mere protection. They create the essential foundation enabling me to do work I genuinely love. For intimacy to flourish, for true connection to develop, I must first feel completely secure. When confident in my physical safety, my mental and emotional resources remain fully available for the nuanced work of intimate education.

This is perhaps the most important insight about my profession: the most meaningful work happens only when foundational needs are thoroughly met. The apparent paradox is that measures which might seem to create barriers actually enable deeper connections. Like the secure attachment that developmental psychologists identify as necessary for healthy exploration, my carefully constructed security framework allows me to engage in vulnerable, beautiful work with an open heart.

The Transformative Majority

What truly transformed my perspective was recognizing that beneath financial transaction, most who sought my company were ordinary people with extraordinary needs. Needs they often couldn't articulate even to themselves. While my early years included challenging situations, approaching each person with genuine curiosity revealed dimensions of human desire far more complex than conventional narratives suggest.

This observation aligns with psychological research suggesting that the prevalence of Dark Triad traits in the general population hovers around 7%, while nearly half could be considered part of the "Light Triad", those displaying empathy, respect for autonomy, and capacity for genuine connection. My professional experience suggests a similar distribution among clients, though the self-selecting nature of my particular practice likely skews toward those capable of meaningful exchange.

Today, those who find their way to my door generally arrive having heard about my particular approach. They come seeking not just physical expertise but the experience of being fully seen without judgment, of exploring desires in an environment where curiosity replaces shame. The financial exchange remains, but has transformed into something more akin to compensation for expertise than payment for service.

These challenging encounters, rather than diminishing my view of human sexuality, actually refined it. They taught me to value authentic connection more deeply, to recognize its absence more readily, and to create conditions where it might flourish against considerable odds. They strengthened my conviction that intimacy at its best isn't about performance or power but about creating momentary sanctuaries where we recognize each other's fundamental humanity.

The journey from those early experiences to my current practice mirrors the journey I hope to guide you through in these pages, from potentially limiting conceptions of pleasure toward a more expansive understanding of what intimacy might offer when approached with genuine curiosity and mutual respect.

Perhaps the most profound insight emerging from these shadow aspects of my profession is this: to be truly open with another human being, we must first feel protected. No security measure, however sophisticated, can eliminate all risk from human interaction. But we can create conditions where we feel secure enough to shift from a defensive stance to a receptive one. Where genuine vulnerability becomes possible precisely because we've established boundaries that allow it to flourish.

This principle extends far beyond the specific challenges of my profession into the universal dynamics of human intimacy. The paradox is beautiful: by acknowledging potential dangers and addressing them consciously, we create the very safety that allows us to lower our guards, to reveal ourselves authentically, and to approach others with the compassion and curiosity essential for meaningful connection. Security, in its essence, isn't about creating barriers but about establishing the foundation that makes their occasional dissolution possible.

Made in United States
Troutdale, OR
05/06/2025